WITH FRIENDS LIKE THESE . . .

"One thing," said Franz Streseman. He didn't look young any more. "You are all brave, and no doubt you have weapons training. *I* am the soldier here, however."

He surveyed his four older companions. "Shoot first, shoot to kill," he said coldly. "Don't threaten and don't hesitate. It may be that Oanh will be mistaken for an opponent. I myself may mistake her for an opponent."

Ran hadn't seen anything as bleak as the young Grantholmer's expression since he faced the Cold Crew in Taskerville.

"I say to you," Franz continued, "it is better that Oanh die than that she remain alive in the hands of these folk. I know them, I *know* their type. She is not human to them. We must not hesitate."

Wanda Holly licked her lip~~~ "~~~ on that cheerful ~~~ ~~~ time to go."

She gla~~~ ~~~dded, "Good luc~~~ ~~~y, but I'm damne~~~ ~~~u."

STARLINER

DAVID DRAKE

STARLINER

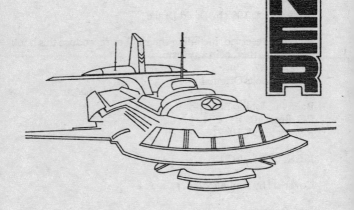

STARLINER

This is a work of fiction. All the characters and events portrayed in this book are fictional, and any resemblance to real people or incidents is purely coincidental.

Copyright © 1992 by David Drake

All rights reserved, including the right to reproduce this book or portions thereof in any form.

A Baen Books Original

Baen Publishing Enterprises
P.O. Box 1403
Riverdale, NY 10471

ISBN: 0-671-72121-6

Cover art by Paul Alexander

First Printing, June 1992

Printed in the United States of America

Distributed by Simon & Schuster
1230 Avenue of the Americas
New York, NY 10020

● EARTH: DOCKING

The starship shimmered yellow in the midst of three spikes of blue flux, the magnetic motors of the tugs which added their thrust to that of the larger vessel. Ribbons of aurora borealis filled the rest of the sunless sky with faint pastels.

Lieutenant Randall Colville didn't need to squint as he stared upward, because the limousine's sunroof grayed automatically to dim the dangerous brilliance of the tugs' discharges. The low-frequency rumble of the starship's passage through the stratosphere shook the car.

"Is that . . . ?" asked Lady Hilda Bernsdorf. She was in the driver's seat, but the limousine edged forward under external control in the line waiting for access to Port Northern's VIP parking.

Ran smiled at her, though there wasn't a great deal behind the expression at the moment. Hilda was a good lady, appreciative and quite appreciable. And the timing couldn't have worked out better. . . .

"The *Empress*?" he said. "No, probably a Planet-Class packet from Solar Traders."

Ran combed the fingers of his left hand through his short auburn hair as he considered the descending vessel. "The *Jupiter*'s on a Wednesday shuttle from K'Chitka. It's probably her. But she's not a third the size of the *Empress of Earth*, milady."

The limousine jerked forward again as the car at the head of the line cleared the final security check. The autopilot of Lady Bernsdorf's vehicle was capable of micrometric precision, but the Port Northern control worked in much coarser increments.

Ran made a mental note. The spaceport authorities should do something about that. Those with access to Port Northern's VIP lot understood the need for security as well as anyone on Earth, but they wouldn't put up with needless discomfort.

That wasn't a matter of concern to a junior officer of Trident Starlines . . . but thirty standard years in the past, Ran Colville had been born on Bifrost, the son of a hide-hunting ex-mercenary. Someday in the future, there might be a Ran Colville who was administrator of the greatest spaceport in the known universe.

"They're all ships," Hilda said. "They all take people places they don't want to be. . . . "

Her right hand tightened on the limousine's collective, a wheel with a 10-cm diameter. Forward and back motion controlled speed. Rotating the wheel turned the vehicle without need for the driver to consider the car's attitude or fan pitch. The control was disabled in the secure lane, so it didn't matter that the knuckles of Lady Bernsdorf's fine-boned hand were mottled with the force of their grip.

Ran laid his big left hand over Hilda's, squeezing just enough to remind her that he was present. Her features were as sharp and beautiful as those of a well-struck medallion. "Some people like to travel," he said gently.

He thought of Bifrost. *Some people know that wherever they go will be better than where they started out, even if that means working their passage in the Cold Crew, outside a starship in sponge space.*

Aloud, controlling his voice to prevent it from trembling, he said, "Is that why you didn't go with your husband to Nevasa? You don't like star travel?"

Hilda's hand twisted on the collective to grip his. She leaned toward him, reaching up with her free hand to draw him into a fierce kiss. Ran slipped his hand behind the woman and kneaded the flesh over her shoulderblades. The garment she wore was silk from a Waserli royal nursery chamber. The fabric was opaque despite its natural pale dun color, but it was so fine that he could feel the texture of Lady Bernsdorf's skin through it.

The line of cars advanced again. The stuttering motion was masked by shockwaves reflected as the starship and its tugs neared the ground.

Hilda turned her head, breaking the kiss but continuing to hold Ran cheek to cheek with her. "That and other things," she said. "Sven isn't pleasant to be around when he's on a mission. If things aren't going well, he takes it out on whoever's closest. After a while, I decided that that wouldn't be me anymore."

"Well, ambassadors have a lot on their minds," Ran said. He twisted slightly to watch the sunroof through the blond halo of Lady Bernsdorf's hair.

A spot on the clear panel darkened. The limousine's sensors had noted potentially dangerous actinics and polarized against them before human retinas could have reacted. "This may be it," Ran murmured.

"Umm?"

"My ship. The *Empress of Earth*."

Hilda stiffened, then relaxed and very deliberately released Colville. She straightened on her side of the car and touched a control. The limousine's windows were opaque to outside eyes; now the inner face of the windshield mirrored as well. She adjusted the angle of reflection and began fussing with her hair.

"I, ah . . . " Ran said awkwardly.

He wasn't sure what the woman wanted, but he knew he'd screwed up that time. She was a nice lady. She shouldn't feel that he didn't care about her when they parted, and he *did* care. But it had been a long road from Bifrost to Third Officer, Staff Side, of the *Empress of Earth*. . . .

"If your . . . if Count Bernsdorf is coming home early," Ran continued, "does that mean he's brokered peace and the emergency is over? Or, ah, that it's war for sure between Nevasa and Grantholm?"

"You're asking the wrong Bernsdorf," Hilda said curtly. She cleared the windshield as spaceport control jogged the limousine forward again. They were nearing the head of the queue. "Not that Sven would tell you anything. Or tell *me* anything. He's very professional. In five years, he'll be heading the Ministry of External Affairs."

The limousine shuddered from the hammering roar of the incoming starship. The eye-saving filter in the sunroof had expanded to the size of a gravy boat. It was almost black, indicating a near-uniform intensity of flux between the starship's own motors and those of the eight tugs aiding its descent. The vessel's mass was such that her own motors were being run at high capacity despite the large number of tugs adding their thrust.

"This is a — "

Ran Colville looked at Hilda in sudden confusion. Until she spoke, he'd forgotten she was present.

" — considerable promotion for you, isn't it, Ran?" the woman continued smoothly, as though her clear blue eyes had failed to notice her ex-lover's abstraction. "This ship is bigger than any of the others you've served on."

Ran gave a wry chuckle. "A Planet-Class liner is bigger than anything *I've* served on," he admitted. "And the *Empress of Earth*, well, she's the biggest there is, my love. . . . Except maybe for the *Brasil*, and that's a matter of how you measure the two of them. Yeah, this is a promotion."

Without changing her neutral expression, Hilda said, "Since Sven is coming home from Nevasa, that means he's failed. If there'd been a realistic chance of

Nevasa agreeing to peace talks, he'd have gone on to Grantholm. Federated Earth doesn't want an interstellar war to break out, but since both the principals do — they'll fight, won't they? Because they're fools."

"I don't figure it either," Ran said, staring upward toward the *Empress of Earth*. "Nevasa and Grantholm have everything they could want already. It's not like B-B . . . It's not like some of the fringe worlds, where people don't have anything to lose from a war."

Not like Bifrost.

The *Empress of Earth*'s descent had been braked to a near hover by thrust at high altitude. Now she was dropping again, supported primarily by the tugs. The limousine's filters paled, permitting details of the huge vessel to show through a gray haze. Landing outriggers extended from the cylindrical hull, and the panels concealing the lifeboat bays were withdrawn.

The podded reaction engines were snugged into hollows while the *Empress* maneuvered in a gravity well. They drove the vessel in sponge space, fed and maintained by the Cold Crew while everyone else was safe in the starship's insulated interior.

The limousine grated to a halt at the guard kiosk. A canopy clamped over the vehicle, sealing it from the North Polar elements. The driver's-side window withdrew before Hilda touched the control. An attendant in civilian clothes with an identibox on her left shoulder leaned into the opening.

"Lady Hilda Bernsdorf," Hilda said coolly. She stared directly at the identibox. "Meeting Count Bernsdorf, a passenger on the *Empress of Earth*."

"Randall Park Colville," Ran said. He blinked involuntarily, though he knew the tiny burst of laser light which painted his retinas was of too low an intensity for him to notice. "Reporting for duty as junior staff lieutenant aboard the *Empress of Earth*."

There was a brief *zeep* from the attendant's shoulder.

"Milady, sir," she said as she straightened. "Thank y—"

The closing window cut off the last of the perfunctory phrase. If Port Northern's data bank had not cleared the occupants' identifications, or if sensors had indicated anything doubtful within the vehicle, the limousine would have been shunted into a holding facility hardened against nuclear weapons before the check proceeded.

"Ran," Lady Bernsdorf said. She was facing the windshield as the limousine staged through the double airlocks which protected Port Northern against the elements. Hoarfrost formed despite the static charge of the dome covering the port facilities. It zigged like frozen lightning against the auroral pastels.

Ran looked down at his companion. "Milady?"

"We agreed that this was only for a few days," Hilda went on in a controlled voice. "That we'd never try to see each other again. Because it was too dangerous."

Ran thought he understood at last why Hilda had been so tense ever since they got up in the morning to make the drive. "Oh, milady," he said gently. She still wouldn't look at him.

He leaned over the console and kissed her rigid cheek. "Did you think I was going to wreck your life? Oh, love, I'm not that sort. You've honored me greatly with your company. I wouldn't do anything to hurt you. Least of all cause you problems with your husband."

The limousine halted in its assigned space — less than ten meters from the VIP entrance to the passenger terminal. Ran pressed the door release. The panel shrank from an impervious sheet to a centimeter-thick block resting on the lower coaming.

He got out. He thought Hilda had started to say something, but when he looked back she was still seated, and her eyes were straight ahead.

Ran stretched. Passengers and the uniformed but unarmed doorman glanced at him — a young man of middle height, in the white uniform of a Staff Side officer of Trident Starlines. Men on Bifrost were rangy rather than solid, but no one who had ever seen a Bifrost Cold Crew riot doubted the strength — or the ruthlessness — of those who came from that bitter world on the fringe of civilization.

The atmosphere of the parking area was slightly warmer than that set by the limousine's climate control. It contained vague tinges of lubricant and ozone from the vehicular traffic. At the distant rear of the lot, a monorail hissed to a halt and began transferring the normal mass of passengers and visitors to the slideways that would take them within the building.

Ran looked up through the clear dome of Port Northern. For a moment, all he could see was steam roiling in patterns of compression and rarefaction from the thrust that balanced the starliner's huge mass.

The view cleared abruptly. The motors of the tugs and starship had blasted away all the condensate on the landing field.

The *Empress of Earth* hung poised a few meters from touching the ground: 800 meters long, 150 meters across the diameter of her cylindrical hull; built to the precision of an astronomical clock despite her enormous mass.

The highest expression of technology within the known universe . . . and Ran Colville was an officer aboard her.

He straightened his cap. He considered throwing it in the air, but he'd gotten this far by not putting a foot wrong professionally. He wasn't going to jeopardize his chances of getting much farther.

Shouting with laughter hidden by the thunder of the starliner landing, Ran Colville marched toward the entrance and his future. He didn't look back at the limousine, which still sat with the right-hand door open.

Franz Streseman's monorail compartment was a

party of Grantholm citizens: two couples and six single men. All of them were middle-aged, all of them were buzzed if not drunk; and they were very loud. Franz sat stiffly, staring toward his hands crossed in his lap and thinking about the engineering degree he was leaving behind.

Perhaps forever; but "forever" was a concept beyond the experience of an eighteen-year-old, while the utter disruption of his life was a present reality.

"Damn, damn, damn the Mindanesians," sang the party from Grantholm, all the men and three of the women joining in on the choruses.

Franz knew the lyrics, from a camp song of the Mindanao campaign twenty years before. Mindanao had been settled from Earth, mostly by Filipinos and other East Asians, but with funding and control from Grantholm. The colony fell behind on its repayment schedule, because a significant proportion of its wireweed production was being diverted to interloping traders at free-market prices rather than going to Grantholm on fixed-rate contracts.

Grantholm's determination to have its rights sparked a full-scale rebellion.

"Cross-eyed, dirty-faced ladrones," the party sang.
"Underneath the triple suns, civilize them with our guns,
"And return us to our own beloved homes!"

The men in the Grantholm party were of an age to have served on Mindanao, but it was unlikely that all of them had done so. Grantholm had developed a network of dependant worlds through a combination of entrepreneurial drive and governmental action. Most of the armed forces which put down the Mindanese Rebellion — and they *did* put it down, though wireweed production was only now beginning to equal what it had been before the war — came from those subject planets.

Five years after the Mindanese Rebellion drowned

in blood, Mindanese battalions were serving Grantholm on Cartegena during the "emergency" there.

"Social customs there are few," boomed the Grantholm men.

"All the ladies smoke and chew ..."

The monorail swayed gently as its gyroscopic stabilizer matched the polar winds without difficulty. Ultra-high-frequency sound predicted the force and direction of gusts, feeding data to the stabilizer, so that the monorail actively met disturbances instead of reacting to them. Magnetic bearings supported the cars which slipped along above the rail without direct contact, and the podded drive motors vibrated only at the molecular level.

The cars' physical environment was as smooth as human endeavors could be in the real world. The social environment within Franz Streseman's compartment, however —

"And the men do things the padres say are wrong ..."

The compartment was designed to hold thirty people in comfort. Besides the Grantholm party, there were only five others, huddled, like Franz, at the further end, though the monorail was packed on this run.

A family of six — father, mother, and children, none of whom was older than ten standard years — shuffled into the compartment from the next car down. The adults hesitated for a moment, blinking as if fearful that the apparent emptiness was a trick.

A Grantholm man noticed the newcomers. "Hey!" he shouted. "This compartment isn't for slant-eyes!"

"Yeah," cried one of the women. "Ride out there!" She pointed to the white expanse beyond the car's full-length side windows. Violent winds lifted dry snow from the ground and whipped it into ghastly patterns. "There's plenty of room for your sort."

The newcomers were in origin Tamils, from low on

the Indian subcontinent. Their eyelids had no sign of an epicanthal fold —

And more particularly, they were as unlikely to be citizens of Nevasa as were those folk in the front of the compartment.

"Pardon?" said the man. His smile was broad and as humorless as that of a man dying in convulsions. "I am Parvashtisinga Sadek and — "

"Go back where you came from, slant-eye!"

"Hey, you can leave the wife. I might have a use for her!"

"Save the oldest girl, too!"

Very deliberately, Franz Streseman got up from his seat. He stood in the aisle, facing the Grantholm party with his legs spread and his hands crossed behind his back in a formal at-ease posture. He said nothing, but he met the eyes of any who looked his way.

He heard the Tamils slip into seats behind him. The children began to chatter, but their parents shushed them. When Franz was sure that the last of them was settled, he walked forward two places and sat down again himself.

"Hey, we're coming into the station," noted one of the Grantholm women who was looking out a side window to avoid having to note Franz Streseman's presence. As she spoke, the car shuddered with the *thump, thump,* of airlocks. The monorail had passed into the vast protected doughnut of Port Northern, encircling the open area where the starships landed. In the sudden stillness of the atmosphere, Franz felt the faint whine of drive pods braking the train.

Shapes and bright light fluttered past the compartment's windows. The images slowed to become platforms — empty to the right, packed with passengers for the return trip on the left of the train — as the monorail decelerated to a crawl. Thrust pulled Franz forward against his grip on the handrail. The

Sadek children squealed again, and the infant began to cry.

The car shifted with a loud *clack* as the superconducting magnets shut down and the monorail touched its support rail for the first time. The right-hand wall slid up and recessed into the car's roof. Warm, dry air bathed the passengers. The monorail's quiver had been too slight to notice during the high-speed run, but Franz noticed the absence now that they had come to a halt.

Baggage consoles were spaced a meter apart along the back wall of the platform, with a uniformed attendant waiting near each trio of machines. Franz didn't run, but he was young and alone. He made it to a console a half-step ahead of one of the Grantholm couples. The woman muttered to her husband as other members of their party spread across the consoles to either side.

Franz placed the ID chip he wore as a signet on his left little finger in the slot of the routing machine. The holographic display fluoresced in a random pattern, then reformed with the images of eight sealed, cubic-meter crates and four ordinary suitcases. The crates sat beneath a red mask; the suitcases were outlined in blue.

Franz nodded and pressed the pad of his thumb to the cursor pulsing on the immaterial screen. An attendant, a woman with a dark complexion and indeterminate features, stepped over to him and slipped her own chip into the paired slot of the console.

She smiled professionally. "So, Mr. Streseman," she said. "You identify this luggage as yours and request that it be loaded aboard the *Empress of Earth?*"

"That is correct," Franz said in the formal response to authority which had been ingrained in him since birth.

"Eight pieces of hold baggage, four pieces to accompany you in your cabin. Would you like to make any

changes now? You won't be able to do so once the vessel
is under way."

"No," Franz said. "That is correct. I am returning to
Grantholm for military service. I will not have need of
the items in my hold baggage until, until I resume my
education."

The luggage itself was in the lower compartment
of one of the cars of the monorail. Robot systems
would transfer it to the starliner, but there were
practical as well as legal reasons for requiring passengers to identify their own property immediately
before boarding.

"Say, *you're* from Grantholm?" asked the woman
behind Franz.

"And you authorize Port Northern and Trident Starlines to examine these cases in any fashion they choose,
Mr. Streseman?"

"That is correct."

The attendant placed her own thumbprint on the
cursor, clearing the display. She removed her ID chip.
"The *Empress of Earth* is at Berth 8, Mr. Streseman," she
said in a slightly warmer tone. "Follow the blue arrows
around the concourse if you don't know the way . . .
but I don't think you'll have any difficulty seeing the
Empress."

Franz turned from the console. The Grantholm
woman pushed past him but her husband said, " 'Scuse
me, buddy, but I heard you say you're one of the boys
going home to teach Nevasa a lesson. I'm Hans
Dickbinder."

He stuck out his hand. He was a black-haired man, a
centimeter or two shorter than Franz but thick and
soft-looking.

Franz clicked his heels and dipped his head in crisp
acknowledgement. He did not appear to notice the
man's outstretched hand. "And I am Franz
Streseman," he said.

He strode off to the head of the monorail platform, from which slidewalks led around the concourse.

"Welcome to Trident Village," murmured a disembodied voice speaking Universal as Lieutenant Wanda Holly walked through the authorized personnel only doorway. The badges Trident Starlines issued to emigrants when they paid their fares responded to UHF interrogation with the wearer's birth language. The greeting could have been in any of a thousand tongues.

If Holly's ID chip had not identified her as a Trident Starlines official, the voice would have added, "Please wait here until someone arrives to serve you." The intruder *would* wait, because both blast-proof anteroom doors sealed at the moment of unauthorized entry.

The door to the operations room collapsed open as Wanda stepped toward it. Danalesco, wearing coveralls with emigrant staff on the cuffs and supervisor in a red field on his shoulders, was alone in the room. He looked up from his console and called, "Yo, Wanda! Good to see you again. I thought you were done with us peons since you got your second stripe."

Wanda Holly wore a gray, one-piece fatigue uniform with the double stripes of a senior lieutenant on the cuffs. The upper stripe was twice the width of the lower, indicating that she was on the Staff Side, passenger matters, rather than Ship Side, navigation and control. On public occasions, Staff officers wore gleaming white, while the Ship officers were in dark blue which was less likely to focus the attention of a passenger.

Around the Trident Starlines badge on her shoulder was the name of Wanda's vessel in script: *Empress of Earth*.

"How's it going, Danny?" she said. Her voice was pleasant, but she was checking the systems board as she spoke. A dozen segments were in the amber, about par for the course; but three were redlined, and she couldn't have hidden her frown if she'd wanted to.

"Cholera," Danalesco said apologetically. "Stage One passed them. We've sealed the affected dorm and the one on each side."

"Blacklisted the labor supplier?" Wanda said. Only detachment prevented her voice from showing disapproval.

"About three seconds after I sealed the dorms," the emigrant specialist replied. "Why don't you teach your grandmother to suck eggs, girl?"

She smiled. "Sorry, Danny," she said. "I don't want a cholera outbreak ... and I *particularly* don't want the client-side supervisor to refuse a shipment and leave me with four thousand runny assholes in Third Class till we get back to Earth."

Wanda walked behind the console, shifting her viewpoint so that she could cover the panorama of Trident Village without interfering with the controls. It was Danalesco's unit, after all, though the decision as to whether or not to load a passenger or any number of passengers was made by the vessel's officers rather than members of the ground staff.

"Forty-two hundred and five," said Danalesco. "No, I'm a liar — seven. Three births and a death."

Wanda looked over sharply again. Danalesco spread his hands. "Hey, healthy twenty-three-year-old male, blew out an embolism. *Not* contagious, girl. Ease off."

She shrugged and forced another smile. "This is the part that scares me, Danny. It's like loading sardines. If there's one bad fish here, four thousand are bad at the far end."

"So send Kropatchek," the supervisor said with a chuckle. "This is the Third Officer's work, after all. And don't worry about the cholera. Your full load had processed through to the output side before that lot was admitted."

"Kropatchek quit us this voyage," Wanda said as she eyed the screens. "He got an offer from Consolidated Voyagers and left us on Nevasa. He's to be First Officer on one of their combination packets on the Earth-Wellspring-Nevasa Triangle."

Trident Village was a huge operation; more accurately, two large operations. Would-be emigrants arrived at the input side, either individually or in batches of up to a thousand delivered by a labor contractor. They were housed in barrack blocks one stage better than prison accommodations while they were bathed and examined, and the strictly-limited volume of their baggage was checked and sterilized.

When the emigrants were cleared, they were marched by blocks — now called Loading Units on internal documentation — to the output side of Trident Village. Output side was the finest living and social environment that most of the emigrants had ever seen in their lives. It was vanishingly improbable that any of them would see its like again.

On the output side, shops provided cheap, high-quality clothing, information on various destinations, and social events which integrated frightened individuals into groups with their own pride and ethic. Group identity would help the emigrants on their long voyage and ease their life on the world which received them.

"Tsk, he'll be staging out of Port Southern," Danalesco said. "I could never do that. The facilities are all right, I suppose, but I'd have to root up my family and move from Metro Chicago. Is Kropatchek married?"

"Yeah, but I don't think that's very high on his list of priorities," Wanda said drily. "Red thinks he's god's gift to women."

The shops around the Trident Village concourse were closed. Fairy lights drifted from lamp standards, providing a friendly, private illumination for the group dance going on. Traditional patterns formed and rotated, while the aurora borealis rippled the sky overhead.

"Chinese this time?" she asked. She was a pretty woman without being a stunner: of average height and a little too conscious of her weight to be comfortable about it. At the moment she was wearing her hair short and a color close to orange, but she would change back to her natural light brown before boarding the *Empress* on the outbound voyage.

"That's right," agreed the supervisor. "Thirty-five hundred for Biscay, the rest to Hobilo." He cleared his throat. "*You* don't think Kropatchek is god's gift to women?"

"Depends on the woman, I suppose," Wanda said. "I didn't notice that Red ever lacked for company."

Trident Village was not solely a humanitarian gesture, though there might have been some of that also. Even the largest corporations are run by humans, and humans not infrequently have humane whims.

There were business reasons for the solicitude as well. Most of the Third Class emigrants didn't pay their own fare: that was arranged by the recipient world, working through labor contractors. But, while the emigrants themselves were unlikely ever to make another interstellar journey, they *did* send letters back to family members and compatriots about the way they had been treated en route to their new life.

Urban slums and back-country villages accounted for virtually the whole of labor emigration, splitting the total down the middle in an average year. Word-of-mouth was the only form of advertising which worked in either environment.

Trident Starlines was willing to spend a little effort to encourage contractors to use its hulls because, though the fare per head was relatively low, four thousand

Third Class passengers together paid the round-trip running costs of the *Empress of Earth*. Figures for smaller Trident Starlines vessels were in proportion. The First and Second Class fares became pure profit when steerage was full.

"We're breaking in a new Third Officer this run," Wanda said. She opened an unoccupied console with her ID chip and began to run the medical profiles of the emigrants slated to embark on the *Empress of Earth*. She kept her finger on the scroll button, pausing the display only when someone spiked above the normal parameters. In each case that she checked, Wanda found that the individual was a member of a family group of four or more.

The recipient worlds could afford to take a few grandparents. Besides, old folks were useful to watch the infants while all the younger adults in the community were working.

"Well, I'm glad to have you back for one load, Wanda," Danalesco said in a mild, serious tone. "You're tough, but you ought to be. Some of the officers coming through, they act like Third was mud and me and my people were just janitors. That's not right."

He nodded toward the village dance. From the edges of the concourse, Emigrant Staff officials watched helpfully. Danalesco's personnel wore light cotton garments like those of the emigrants, with only saucer hats and Trident Starlines badges to set them apart from those they directed.

"They're people," Danalesco went on. "They oughta be treated like people, at least by us. When they get to Biscay or wherever, well, that's out of our hands."

"Yeah, well, this lot looks pretty good," the woman said. "The way it always does when it's on your shift, Danny."

"My pleasure," the supervisor replied, his tone underlining the truth of the words. "Know anything about the new guy? Somebody I've worked with in the past on other ships?"

Wanda removed her chip to shut the console down. "I don't think so, Danny," she said. "His name's Colville, Randall Colville. He's been with Trident for twelve years, which is something, but this is his first run from an Earth homeport."

Danalesco raised an eyebrow. "And they're putting him on the *Empress*?" he said.

Wanda laughed. "There's planets out there besides Earth, Danny," she said. "He spent a year and a half as First Officer on the *Princess Trader* out of Learoyd and Mithgarth, so he's got experience."

As Wanda opened her mouth to continue, her ear clip dinged a pure bell note. "Umph," she muttered, and attached the coil of hair-fine flex from the commo pod on her belt to a jack on the console. An artificial intelligence in Trident Starlines' central office clicked out orders in an emotionless female voice.

Wanda released the flex and stepped back. "Duty calls," she told Danalesco. "Colville's arrived in the terminal, and I'm to check him aboard the *Empress*."

"Good luck with him," the supervisor said.

Wanda crooked a grin at Danalesco. "Whatever that means," she said.

A passenger liner was taking off into the midnight sky. Its motors and those of the coupled tugs threw harsh shadows across the emigrants dancing on the concourse.

The terminal's top level was for crews and ground operations personnel alone. The floor was of a resilient, sound-deadening synthetic; practical but plain, save for the paths worn pale across it by decades of feet. There were elevators, slidewalks and communications booths, but Top Level had none of the frills and retail shops that packed the lower, passenger, concourses.

There was a great deal of open space, and there was an unmatched view of the *Empress of Earth* through the clear wall fronting the inner docks. Ran Colville walked along slowly, staring greedily at the vast bulk. He knew that he was attracting amused attention from the handful of uniformed personnel on the slidewalks, but he didn't particularly care.

The *Empress of Earth* wasn't beautiful, exactly, but she was magnificent. This was Ran's first look at her, and he was more concerned with that than with the image he projected to strangers he'd never see again.

Bulk freight was sometimes carried between the stars in nickel-iron asteroids, ballooned to colossal size by controlled fusion jets, but interstellar passenger liners were far and away the most massive constructions humans had ever designed to fly within an atmosphere. The *Empress of Earth* and the *Brasil* of Consolidated Voyagers, operating from Port Southern in Antarctica, were the largest of the starliners.

Though Trident and Consolidated were fiercely competitive across a wide variety of routes, there was a tacit agreement at the top of the commercial pyramid: the *Empress of Earth* and the *Brasil* sailed the same nine-planet route from Earth to Tblisi, but on inverted schedules. When one of the superships left Earth, the other was lifting off from Tblisi on her return voyage.

The *Empress of Earth* was a commercial venture, but she and her giant rival were also ships of state. The government of Federated Earth preferred not to interfere in the operations of private companies, but the greatest starliners in the known universe *were* representatives of Earth, like it or no. When the giant vessels were nearing completion three years before, quiet representations to the directors of Trident and Consolidated made it clear that the interests of humanity and civilization required that the ships be operated in tandem rather than in cut-throat competition. The government would see to those interests if the companies did not.

The companies quickly announced complementary schedules for their flagships. The decision benefited all concerned. Neither line had a vessel that could comfortably pair with their giant to create a balanced flow of trade instead of a series of indigestible pulses. Few members of the public even considered that there might have been another possibility. . . .

Wherever possible, the bureaucracy of Federated Earth worked on the principles of indirection and deniability. Nonetheless, the bureaucracy worked very well.

The *Empress of Earth* was a huge cylinder lying on its side. She was supported by the full-length outriggers she deployed when counter-thrust and air resistance had scrubbed off enough velocity in the upper atmosphere. On a solid surface, the lower curve of the hull didn't touch the ground. The thin soil of Biscay left yellow streaks meters high on the metal. These were steamed off during each landing on Calicheman, where a lake absorbed the raw power of starliners landing without tugs.

Teams pairing ground personnel with members of the ship's crew examined the docking bitts, the great hooks to which the tugs attached their cables. The motors of the *Empress of Earth* were powerful enough to lift the vessel at full load from a gravity well deeper than Earth's, but at that level of operation, the magnetic flux would be concentrated enough to sever the molecular bonds of bedrock. Normally, and always on Earth, tugs balanced a majority of the vessel's weight during lift-off and descent. The bitts which took that strain were tested by sonics and electrofluxing after each use — but they were also eyeballed by trained personnel who might notice corrosion or pitting before the hardware did.

The starliner's outer hull was not smooth. Apart from the podded fusion engines for deep space operation, their stores of reaction mass, and the hatches for passengers, crew, maintenance, and equipment routing, there were staples in rows running the circuit of the hull at twenty meter intervals. They were the handholds and safety-line supports for the Cold Crew, the men — and the handful of women — who maintained the *Empress of Earth*'s drive engines, riding the hull even in sponge space.

In theory, the Cold Crews worked with double safety lines. To move, a crewman was to set a new line before he freed the other one. In practice, and especially when the crews were shorthanded (as they were generally shorthanded, even on the vessels of top-of-the-line firms like Trident Starlines), the men did what they had to do to make the speed and bring the vessel in on any schedule that the captain set.

And every few voyages, somebody missed a step or was caught clearing a jet with his long-hafted adjustment tool when the engine sputtered and threw him—

Out. Into space, or into sponge space, without even stars for final companions. Into the Cold.

The Cold Crews worked four hours on the hull, followed by eight hours inside for sleep or rest or at least warmth (if their souls could accept it) before they had to return to their duties. The Cold Crews were clannish. They couldn't communicate at all in sponge space, and they spoke very little under other circumstances.

When they fought, which was often, they did so with the fury of men who knew Death and Hell too intimately to fear either.

Ran Colville stared, through the clear wall and deep into his past. After an uncertain time he shuddered to alertness again and resumed his saunter along the *Empress of Earth*'s vast hull. He forced a smile, both as camouflage and because he'd learned that a pretense of mild calm helped to drag his soul back from an emptiness deeper than vacuum in the sidereal universe.

"Lieutenant Colville?" called the woman who stepped from the lift shaft twenty meters ahead of Ran. She wore a fatigue uniform with two stripes; a senior lieutenant, and almost certainly Staff Side Second Officer of the *Empress*.

"Yes, ma'am," Ran said. "You're . . . ?" He nodded in the direction of starliner filling the view through the clear wall.

"Lieutenant Holly," she said, taking the hand Ran extended cautiously in case the SOP aboard the *Empress of Earth* was different. He'd served on some vessels in which officers saluted one another. It was a matter of the captain's whim, like much else aboard a vessel operating scores of light years from home — and much of the time outside the sidereal universe.

"Let's get aboard," Holly continued, striding back to the structural pillar from which she'd appeared. At Top Level, it included a crew car as well as the paired lift and drop shafts. "I landed immediately to make sure that the Third Class loading would be under control, but there's always dozens of passengers having hissy fits during disembarking. It's almost as bad as the hour before we undock."

Ran wasn't sure whether Holly spoke sharply because she felt pressured by the immediate circumstances, or whether she was simply curt in all dealings with her fellow crewmen. There were plenty of Staff Side officers who saved all their social skills for their duties toward the passengers.

She wasn't a bad-looking woman, not that Ran cared much about looks — or the fact that she was probably a few years older than he was. Personality might not be everything with him, but it accounted for a good ninety percent of his interest.

Anyway, he didn't mix business and pleasure. Women were always cheap, once you figured out what coin a particular lady wanted to be paid in. He liked women as well as any man in the universe did, but he wasn't about to let his pecker get in the way of his duty.

The crew car was reeling back from an open hatch on top of the *Empress of Earth*. The transparent vehicles weren't intended for use by large numbers; the twenty or so personnel aboard this one put it well beyond its listed capacity. The supporting girder of basket-woven monocrystal fibers swayed dangerously. It was unlikely to shear, but it might well jam, unable to extend or retract. If that happened, the car would bob in the polar winds until a maintenance crew reached it from a cherrypicker.

Lieutenant Holly glanced at the slowly-retracting car and stepped away from the access door. "We'd better keep out of the way," she muttered. "It looks like the whole Cold Crew's in the basket."

The car grunched against the building before locking home. Because of the extra weight, it hit the support step and had to bounce to clear it. The access hatch opened. Men, heavyset and dark-haired, with enough features in common to have all been members of the same family, burst from the car like buckshot from a gun barrel. They crowded into the drop shaft without a word or a glance around the concourse.

Holly waited till the last of them were clear, then stepped into the car they had vacated. "Kephalonians," she said. "Most of Trident's Cold Crews come from there or Pyramus."

"And Bifrost," Ran said without expression as he followed her into the car.

"Right, and Bifrost," Holly agreed. She smiled for the first time and stuck out her hand again. "My name's Wanda, by the way."

"Ran," Ran said, glad for the change in atmosphere.

"They say that if you look into a Cold Crewman's eyes, you can see all the way to Hell," Wanda prattled on. There was nothing hostile in the comment. It was as if she were discussing schools of fish in the Great Central Trench of Tblisi.

"I've heard that," Ran said. There wasn't enough emotion in his voice to make the words agreement.

Under the Second Officer's control, the crew car began to travel toward the *Empress of Earth* again. "Me, even the Starlight Bar — the observation dome in our nose — is too close to being nowhere," she continued. "I keep out of it except when I've just *got* to be there."

"Yeah, I can understand that," Ran said.

Normally, a sheet of First Class passengers would have been marching across the broad gangway extending from the terminal to the vessel. Today, the usual procedures were disrupted. A party of ten aides and bodyguards disembarked in a cluster around a tall man with a mane of preternaturally pale hair. A dozen other guards and officials, wearing clothes so formal that they might as well have been uniforms, advanced to meet him.

A slight woman in a tailored dress that flowed like beige fire stood at the terminal end of the gangplank.

Wanda Holly pointed down at the gathering. "That's Minister Sven Bernsdorf," she commented. "The Terran government sent him on a peace mission to Nevasa. He traveled out by the *Brasil* and then straight back with us. I hope that means good news."

"It's out of our hands, at any rate," Ran said. He stared for a moment at the slight, blond woman waiting for the ambassador. A good lady. He hoped she'd be well, but that was out of his hands too.

Then the car locked itself onto the hatch coaming, and Third Officer Ran Colville prepared to go aboard the *Empress of Earth* for the first time.

* * *

The initial Staff Side meeting was held in the officers' lounge of the *Empress of Earth*.

The room was decorated in the style of an 18th-century English coffee house. It had a central table with benches of coarse-grained wood, seats built into the sidewalls, and the autobar was hidden in a paneled kiosk whose pillars supported a wooden canopy.

The fireplace opposite the door was of marble, but the realistic flames were switched off for the moment. Instead, holographic birds flitted across the spring-blue sky beyond windows of small, square panes.

There was no reason that the room shouldn't have been of simple, utilitarian pattern, but the decorators who designed the public areas of the *Empress of Earth* hadn't quit when *that* series of jobs was done.

Something that to Ran Colville was merely a little gray bird sat on the "outside ledge" of a window and chirruped in a tiny voice. Despite his tension, Ran grinned at the hologram.

His initial reaction to the period decoration had been negative. *This sort of nonsense was for passengers, not for the professionals.* Thirty seconds later, he found the ambiance growing on him. He didn't especially like the dark, heavy wood and the clumsy furniture, but the lounge had character. *A* character, instead of feature-less homogeneity that could have been interchanged with similar spaces in a thousand other ships.

Character was what made the *Empress of Earth* special. Passengers were attracted to her for her size, for the quality of her table and the service provided by her human and automated staff . . . but repeat customers and the word-of-mouth they provided came because passengers felt comfortable aboard the vessel.

Interstellar travel was a nerve-wracking business even for a ship's personnel. Vessels still vanished for reasons that could only be conjectured. Perhaps catastrophic engine failure, perhaps collision with debris in the sidereal universe; perhaps a sponge-space navigational disaster that left the vessel wandering without hope of recovery or even of making a planet-fall within the limitless volumes of space.

A lifeless box, however prettily decorated, was no more reassuring than the surface pleasantry of a robot whose thought processes were both hidden and utterly inhuman. The officers' lounge of the *Empress of Earth* wasn't simply an exercise in period imitation. It had an eccentric spirit of its own.

A ship with character at all levels was likely to breed a crew whose competence protruded at the corners through their smooth veneer. Between them, they would get more custom than mere schedule-keeping and safety statistics alone would explain.

"Where's Babanguida?" asked Commander Hiram Kneale, head of the *Empress*'s Staff Side. He stood in front of the kiosk, clearly ready to start the meeting.

Ran hadn't met Kneale before. The commander was a broad man of middle height, with strong features and hair that swept back across his temples like a flow of gray cast iron. He had a resonant voice which civilized but did not conceal his irritation at the missing member of his team.

"He's on the way, sir," offered a senior rating with the name MOHACKS over the left breast pocket of his white uniform. "Had to make a comfort stop, is all."

For the purpose of the meeting, the vessel's entire Staff Side — three officers and five ratings who should have been six — was gathered in the officers' lounge. Mohacks had a superficially open face, but Ran hadn't missed the look of cold appraisal in the enlisted man's eyes when he looked at the new Third Officer.

"If he's late again," Kneale said without bluster, "he can see how comfortable he finds the galley for however long he remains in the crew of the *Empress*."

The door opened and closed again so swiftly that it

was hard to imagine how the tall man with skin the color of African Blackwood had been able to slip through it during the interval. "*Very* sorry, Mr. Kneale," the newcomer said. "I found a little boy in the head off the Embarkation Hall, crying his eyes out. He was trying to get into the supply closet 'cause he'd mistook it for the outside door, and his mother, she was some strict religious order and wouldn't go into the Men's to fetch him."

Babanguida met Kneale's glare with warm, brown eyes as innocent as those of a puppy wagging its tail from the middle of a puddle of urine. After a moment, the commander said in a neutral tone, "Good to have you with us again, Babanguida." Kneale hadn't forgotten anything, wasn't promising anything. He was just holding the matter in abeyance.

He cleared his throat. "Very well," he began. "Most of us know one another already, but there are two new faces. Crewman Second Class Blavatsky — stand up, Blavatsky."

A plump woman in her mid-20s obeyed, smiling nervously, and sat back down again on one of the seats along the bulkhead.

"Blavatsky has transferred to us from Ship Side, so perhaps some of you know her already," Kneale continued. "She'll be on my watch. And we have a new Third Officer, Lieutenant Randall Colville. Yes, that's right, stand up."

Ran rose, meeting the eyes of his fellows with a swift deliberation that acknowledged everyone but didn't delay the proceedings. He nodded to the commander and seated himself again on the bench across the central table from Wanda Holly.

"I understand you've been running Colville through his paces already, Ms. Holly?" Kneale said.

"He was in his whites, so I let him field calls while I changed from fatigues," Wanda said with a smile.

"There weren't any problems. He can do my work any time."

"Passengers are pretty much passengers, whichever side of the galaxy," Ran said easily. "The only tricky one was the family of K'Chitkans who wanted to disembark on the crew car — "

"How did you handle that?" Kneale said, responding with the quick certainty of an autoloader returning to battery after a shot.

"The birds?" Ran said. K'Chitkans were thick-bodied and had large heads, but their distant ancestors had once flown. They didn't look particularly birdlike in Earth terms, but males had a crest of tall feathers and vestigial beaks were common among both sexes. "Well, frankly, I loaded them into a crew car, went over with them, and made sure they got on the drop shaft to the passenger level. They'd booked the Asoka Suite. I decided that was enough of an outlay for Trident Star-lines to live with a kink in the rules."

Kneale smiled crisply. "A good decision," he said. There was no emotional loading in his voice. The message was in the words themselves. That sort of man was dangerous, because it was easy to believe that he didn't mean what he said . . .

"Very good . . ." the commander repeated. "Mr. Col-ville, the ratings on your watch are Crewmen First Class Mohacks and Babanguida. They're experienced men. You'll find them capable of dealing with most situations without calling for help . . . but the responsibility is of course yours."

"Yessir," Ran said. He didn't look toward the crew-men, but he knew the type well enough to imagine the air of bland appraisal with which they stared at his back.

Mohacks and Babanguida were clever, intelligent career enlisted men. They'd have their scams and fiddles which earned them several times the salary Trident

Starlines paid them, and they'd think they were smarter than the officers who were their titular superiors.

What Mohacks and Babanguida *weren't* were officers. They would never understand why some folk gave orders and *they* obeyed, for all their intelligence and experience. They thought it was education or class or pull . . . and all of those things had an effect; but the difference in mindset between those who led and those who didn't was more basic than background.

Mohacks and Babanguida were going to survive, because they were smart and skilled and kept a low profile by avoiding responsibility. They didn't want rank, because they didn't think it was real the way what *they* had was real: wealth and comfort and freedom in their terms.

Most of the folk who worked their way off Bifrost on starships died in the Cold Crews, or died on shore as flotsam washed up on the shores of sponge space. A Bifrost boy who cheated his way from the Cold Crew of an unscheduled freighter to Trident Starlines' Officers Academy couldn't imagine how someone else could stop because he felt comfortable. Comfort wasn't an option on Bifrost, only survival.

Commander Kneale's face set. There was no particular emotion in his expression, only assurance. "Most of you have heard this before. Listen anyway. We are the Staff Side of the finest starship in existence today, the *Empress of Earth*. Ship Side navigates us to our destinations. The Purser's section provides the passengers with the services they require, as they would require them in a dirtside hotel. Engineering makes sure that the fusion drive propels us in deep space and the magnetic motors land us and lift us off safely. All of these things are important.

"But *we* are important as well," Kneale continued. The level of his voice had been rising by imperceptible degrees as he spoke. "Staff Side is the lubricant that makes our *Empress* the success she is. You'll hear

Ship's officers mutter that all the Staff is for is to keep passengers from pestering the *real* officers . . . but without those passengers, there wouldn't be a need to navigate the *Empress* anywhere."

Kneale's voice boomed. This wasn't a lecture or even a pep talk, Ran realized. It was a sermon by a fire-breathing preacher so committed to his beliefs that he would willingly die for them.

"You'll hear stewards say that they do the real work," the commander said, "while Staff Side just swanks . . . but if the unexpected occurs, if Third Class riots, or a couple starts fighting with steak knives in the First Class dining room, *we're* the ones who'll deal with it. If all the engineering officers collapse from food poisoning, *we'll* nurse the *Empress* home. I *did* that on the *Capital de Buch* between Lusignan and Arcwell, and any officer who serves under me is qualified to do the same!"

Kneale stood splay-legged and set his massive fists against the points of his hips. "The *Empress of Earth* succeeds, and she will succeed, because we of Staff Side will make her succeed, whatever it may cost us personally. If there's anybody here who doesn't think he or she is capable of giving one hundred percent to Trident Starlines if the necessity arises — tell me now, because that'll be easier than having me learn the truth the hard way."

He glared around the lounge. Nobody spoke.

Ran met the commander's eyes without expression. His lips were in a state of repose, neither tense nor smiling.

Commander Kneale broke into a grin. "So long as you know I mean it, children," he said mildly.

"We know you do, sir," said Mohacks.

Kneale unclenched his fists and tented his fingers in front of his chest. "Very good," he said. "Mr. Colville, do you have any questions before we break up?"

Ran cleared his throat. "I intend to be worthy of the *Empress of Earth* and of the trust Trident Starlines has put on me, sir," he said. The truth was more complex than that, but that was true.

He turned and looked at Mohacks and Babanguida. The faces of both ratings froze. "I intend to be a good officer to the men under me, but I understand that I *am* their officer. It's part of my duty to see to it that they do theirs."

"Yes *sir*!" Mohacks said. Babanguida's face could have been cast in concrete.

"For the rest," Ran said, facing around to Kneale again, "it's like I said before. Passengers are passengers, ships are ships. I have a lot to learn about the *Empress*, but there's nothing in my duties aboard her that I haven't accomplished on lesser vessels."

Kneale smiled vaguely. "Are there any questions for Mr. Colville, then?" he said.

"Ah, sir?" asked Crewman Blavatsky. Her voice was hesitant from doubt that enlisted personnel were included in the offer.

Ran nodded. "Yes?"

"Is your family from Earth, then?" Blavatsky said.

"It's a full ten years since I've set foot on the planet, Blavatsky," Ran said. He chuckled in the well-tested belief that good humor would deflect attention from the way he avoided answering the question. "I left Earth at the end of Officers' Academy, and I haven't been back since."

"If there are no further questions," Kneale said calmly, "you're all dismissed in accordance with the duty roster. Have a safe leave, people."

The enlisted personnel were all on their feet before the last syllable was out of the commander's mouth.

"Where *is* your family, Ran?" Wanda Holly asked in a firm, clear voice.

"Ma'am, I don't have one," Ran answered flatly. He smiled. There was no humor in the expression.

The pause among the ratings dissolved into a rush out the door. Ran started to follow them.

"If you wouldn't mind, Colville," Commander Kneale said, "I'd like a word in private with you in my office."

"Certainly, sir," Ran said. His face was as bland as Mohacks' a moment earlier —

And he felt the pressure of Wanda Holly's eyes on his back.

The file on Randall Colville came aboard from the mail gig which met the *Empress of Earth* when she dropped from sponge space into the solar system. The gig, making one or two more sponge space transits than the starliner dared and by braking her slight mass hard, would arrive on Earth twelve hours ahead of the larger vessel — a half day that could be crucial with some information that couldn't be entrusted to electro-optical transmission no matter *how* scrambled.

Commander Hiram Kneale read the file as soon as the gig was under way. The new man's, Colville's, record with Trident was exemplary. His background before taking service with the line was sketchy and somewhat unusual, but there wasn't anything remarkable in it. Colville had been born on Earth, in the Aberdeen Prefecture, and had emigrated to Satucia with his parents as an infant.

There were no file entries after that until Colville reappeared as supercargo — purser's assistant — on the *Prester John*, whose captain had enthusiastically nominated Colville for a place in the Trident Officers' Academy in Greenwich Prefecture. Colville had started slow in the academy, but he'd proceeded at an accelerating pace and had been rewarded with a Third Officer's slot on a mixed-load packet that traded between Wallaby, Grantholm, and Munch. From there on out, Colville went from successful tour to success — as was to be expected in an officer assigned to the *Empress*.

Only . . . unscheduled freighters like the *Prester John* didn't carry supercargos, and one glance at Ran Colville in the flesh told Kneale what the holographic portrait in the files had led him to suspect: Colville didn't come from Satucia, and he probably hadn't been born on Earth. He was a Bifrost man, as sure as Hiram Kneale had been raised in the lemon groves of Sulimaniya, where each tree had its own drystone wall as protection from the summer winds.

"So, Mr. Colville," Kneale said from behind the desk in his office. "I hope you'll be comfortable aboard our *Empress*. She's a fine ship. The finest."

Holographic projections curtained the walls of the commander's office. Many officers used that luxury fitment to display scenes of their homeworlds or their families. Kneale's walls were four views of the *Empress of Earth*, docking on Earth and Tblisi, Grantholm and Nevasa — the major worlds of her run.

On the ceiling was a fragment of the *Empress*'s bow, framed by the twisted light of sponge space. The hull metal shimmered with the rime of gases which had migrated from the vessel's interior when she dipped back into the sidereal universe. Ran Colville's eyes kept flicking up toward that view. His expression was unreadable.

The hologram had been taken from one of the *Empress*'s lifeboats. The photographer, a Szgranian hexabranch, displayed her genius in the shot, because relationships in sponge space were not what they appeared to the eyes of the body. To correctly judge the direction and distance that a camera — or ship, or gun — would travel on its path to another object in sponge space was a calculation at which the most powerful artificial intelligences failed a dozen times for every success.

Military forces throughout known space continued to experiment. Sponge space was the perfect cover for an attack — if one could calculate where one's target was.

"I'm very honored to be assigned to the *Empress*, sir," Colville said. "I hope I'll be worthy of her. I'll do my best to be worthy of her."

He met Kneale's eyes firmly, perhaps fiercely. Well, there was no falsehood in those statements. Colville was willing to die trying. That was how he probably *would* die one day, always pushing harder to be the best at whatever he saw as the next step up, until it turned out that what had seemed to be a step was really a long drop....

"The *Empress* is special, Mr. Colville," Kneale continued. "And I don't mean that she — she and the *Brasil* — are valuable artifacts, though they're that as well. We can be quite sure there are men on Grantholm and Nevasa today calculating how many troops they could pack aboard either superliner for a lightning invasion of the other planet."

Kneale didn't know how to explain to the stiff-necked young officer across the desk from him that Colville had already succeeded. The very falseness of Colville's beginnings made the man Colville's will created more real — and therefore more useful to Trident Starlines — than a fellow who'd simply walked up the path of success which his birth laid out for him.

"But she's more than that, our *Empress*," Kneale continued softly. "She's a symbol of all that's best of civilization. She mustn't be perverted from that course."

Kneale read poetry in the silence of his suite during placid moments, Millay and Donne and Vergil. He had never found in verse quite the solemn beauty which the *Empress of Earth* represented to him.

"I don't entirely follow you, sir," Colville said cautiously. He was as obviously tense as a cocked trigger spring — afraid that his new superior was mad, and afraid that this was some lengthy charade to inform him that he'd been found out at last ... which of course he had. He would never believe that it didn't *matter* that Kneale knew or suspected the truth.

"Were you ever a soldier, Colville?" Kneale asked abruptly.

"I . . . " the younger man said, "haven't been, no. My—"

The pause was to find the right words, because it was already too late to burke the statement. "My father was a, a soldier, sir. He didn't talk about it much, but when he died I found a batch of chips from his helmet recorder. I . . . watched them when I found a playback machine."

Kneale's smile was as grim as a granite carving. "From Svent Istvan?" he asked. Thirty-five years ago, Grantholm had intervened on behalf of its nationals trading on Svent Istvan. Several of the battalions had come from Bifrost, one of the worlds already under Grantholm hegemony.

"No sir," Colville said in a colorless voice. The question told him that Kneale suspected — or *knew* — the truth about his new Third Officer's background. "From Hobilo. During the Long Troubles."

"Right," said the commander, a place-holder while he considered his next words. "Then you have a notion of what I mean when I say that war is the greatest evil that man has had to face since before he was human. Because it's a perversion of skill and creativity; because it focuses all his abilities on destruction."

Colville licked his lips. "Yes sir," he said in the same flat voice.

"Starships are the means of bringing help and communication between worlds, Colville," Kneale went on. "In a war, it's troops and weapons and violence instead. Those of us who understand that evil have to prevent it from happening here on the *Empress*."

"But Earth isn't going to take sides in a war between Grantholm and Nevasa, is it?" Colville said, shocked into more openness than he'd permitted himself since entering his superior's suite. "Surely not!"

"No," Kneale agreed, "not that. But we have passengers from both planets, going home ahead of the crisis, and we'll be touching down on both planets unless war actually breaks out. It was tense on the run back from Tblisi, but it's going to be a great deal worse on the outbound leg. We — you and I and Lieutenant Holly — are primarily responsible for keeping the cancer from affecting the *Empress*."

"I wonder . . . " said Colville, turning his keyed-up brain to a problem that involved him professionally rather than personally. "— If it wouldn't be a good idea to take both Nevasa and Grantholm off the route now, before the shooting starts?"

He looked up at the ceiling again and continued, "Because as you said, sir, there are a lot of people looking at the military use they could make of the *Empress*. Both planets have national-flag fleets, but none of their ships has a quarter of our capacity, and — ships can't keep formation in sponge space. Having a large force on one vessel rather than spreading it out in packets on four hulls or more . . . that might be the difference between a beachhead and a disaster."

Kneale nodded appreciatively. "You're quite right, Randall — do you go by Randall?"

"Huh? Ah, Ran, sir. Actually. Though — " Colville smiled in a not-quite-calculating manner. " — I've answered to shithead a time or two. Anything you please. But Ran for choice."

"Staff Side officers traditionally don't stand on ceremony when we're alone," Kneale said, smiling also. "I'm Hiram — unless you screw up royally. Just don't make the mistake of calling Captain Kanawa 'Sam' — or anything else but 'Sir!' "

Kneale paused again, eyeing the younger man. Without really intending to do so, he'd thrown Colville badly off-balance. The threat of exposure, unstated and un*meant*, still hung over the man, but going to a first name basis was a positive sign. You drove laboratory animals mad more quickly with random punishments and rewards than you could with a regimen of brutal punishment alone.

"Neither side is going to do anything as crude as an open seizure of the *Empress of Earth*," Kneale resumed. "Every planet but Earth is still a frontier, though some pretend they're not. The outworlds, particularly Grantholm, sneer at Federated Earth because she has so much power and doesn't use it the way they would — but they respect the power. They know that Earth could swat them, any one or all together, as easily as a whale could swamp a dinghy. Whatever else they do, they won't *force* the whale to take action against them; and commandeering Terran shipping would do just that."

Colville cleared his throat and said, "If the *Empress* were just to vanish, though, the Legislative Council would dither. The Federation bureaucracy wouldn't be able to act without authorization. And maybe if the ship was handed back after Grantholm won the war — with an indemnity for Trident Starlines and any passengers who were in the wrong place when the shooting started — they might get away with it. Grantholm might."

The left corner of Kneale's mouth lifted. "That would be risky too, don't you think?"

Colville shrugged. "War's a risk."

"And you think Grantholm will win this war?"

"I think everybody on Grantholm thinks they'll win it," Colville stated flatly. "Personally, I think if it comes to open war, they'll both lose, but they'll wreck fifty planets and kill millions of people to prove it. But that's not my business. The *Empress of Earth* is my business."

Kneale stared at the younger man for long moments, deciding whether or not to say more. At last he went on, "Trident Starlines has a very rigid set of rules. For

instance, the safety of passengers is paramount. I'm sure
that Captain Kanawa would unhesitatingly surrender
his ship, this ship, if he felt that by doing otherwise he was
risking the lives of his passengers."

Colville nodded, wary again, certain that the conversation was about to veer from normal channels.

"But some officers, even in an organization as *controlled* as Trident," the commander went on, "have bent
the rules when they had to. And they're willing to do it
again. For Trident, for civilization."

"Sir?" Colville said softly.

"I knew a fellow from Sulimaniya," Kneale said. His
eyes were focused in the direction of the holographic
mural behind Colville, the *Empress* undocking from
Grantholm. The blue glare of the starliner's magnetic
motors reflected between the low overcast and the soft,
fresh snow covering the hills around the spaceport.
"He killed a man — his business partner."

Kneale smiled. His expression was terrible to see. "Actually, he'd killed quite a lot of people a few years before,
but they told him that made him a hero because he'd
been guarding the Parliament House during the En-
lightenment Riots. But this was different. He had to run.

"He got off planet — that was easy. What planet he ran
to doesn't matter; it could have been almost anywhere.
And he got a job as ground staff for Trident Starlines.
That wasn't terribly hard either, because he was only a
janitor, hitting the spots that it wasn't cost-effective to
program the cleaning robots to get. And that put him
around the data base at night, when nobody else was in
the terminal building."

Ran Colville was looking at Kneale with the expression of a man facing a snake he *knows* is poisonous, but
which may or may not be hostile to him. Colville said
nothing.

"Nobody expects janitors to be able to use central
computers," Kneale said. "People are sloppy. They

leave mechanical lock-outs open and they write passwords down on memo pads. So my friend built himself up an identity, confirmed it, and cut himself orders for Trident Officers' Academy. He didn't have a lot of problem after that. He really *had* the background, you see. Only he couldn't use the real one since he'd murdered the son of a bitch who'd been robbing him blind because he knew my friend trusted him."

"What are you telling me?" Colville said in a voice like shingles creaking in the night.

"I'm telling you that Trident Starlines needs resourceful officers," Kneale replied. "I'm telling you that people will believe a man is what he seems to be. I'm telling you that a man *is* what he seems to be. So it's very important that you and I and our friends all act like dedicated officers to whom Trident Starlines is more than our lives."

And to whom civilization is more even than Trident Starlines, but Commander Hiram Kneale didn't say that aloud.

His smile softened. "That's all, Ran. But particularly now, I thought it was important that you hear it. Go on about your business. I'm sure you have personal business to take care of before undocking."

"Thank you, sir," Colville said. He stood and saluted crisply.

He turned, then paused and looked back over his shoulder. "I — expect to make myself worthy of your trust, Commander."

"Hiram," corrected Kneale. "I expect you will too, Ran."

And that was god's truth. Because otherwise, Kneale would have seen to it that this hard-faced imposter was *under* the jail.

• EARTH: UNDOCKING

"Excuse me, Captain," said the beaming passenger *just* as Ran Colville's ear clip buzzed him. "I wonder if I might trouble you to stand by my wife for a picture? To show people back home that we were really here, you know."

The clip rattled again. Somebody sure thought it was an emergency.

The center of the Social Hall — the *Empress*'s First Class lounge — was a huge expanse, almost the worst room in the ship for Ran to find a place in which to flex his communicator to part of the structure. The walls sported holographic images of the buildings surrounding the Roman Forum in the time of Augustus, and the designers hadn't needed to modify the scale greatly to fit the available space.

Ordinary radio communications didn't work within the mass of metal and electronics that was the *Empress of Earth*. On so large a ship, a public address blaring audio requests from tannoys in every compartment was, for both practical and esthetic reasons, possible only in general emergencies. For most purposes, messages were pulsed in recipient-coded packets from infra-red lenses in the vessel's moldings. These were picked up and converted to audio alarms by the clip each crewman wore behind one ear.

For actual communication, the crewman switched on the commo unit on his waistbelt and turned so that the unit had a line of sight to a ceiling transceiver. When the commo unit was on and properly positioned, the system provided full two-way communication between all portions of the vessel's interior.

About a hundred passengers sat in the lounge or stood, viewing the holographic murals with awkward nonchalance. They had arrived early and, with their luggage stowed in their cabins, had nothing very obvious to do. Most of them were new to interstellar travel — old hands at the business tended to arrive hours or less before undocking, perhaps having first called "their" steward to see that "their" cabin (or often suite) would be ready for them to slip into with the ease of putting on a favorite pair of shoes.

The furniture in the Social Hall mimicked the curves and color of the ivory stools of Roman senators, but common sense (or Trident officials) had prevented the designer from more than suggesting that thoroughly uncomfortable fashion. The chairs and couches had backs — which adjusted to users' posture. They were upholstered in red-purple silk, the true color of "imperial purple," though few of the *Empress*'s passengers were going to make that connection.

Silk was neither more comfortable nor more lustrous than many of the synthetics that might have been used in its place, but First Class clients of the *Empress of Earth* could be expected to tell the difference. Thin silk cover cloths were laid over a synthetic base, edge-bonded, and replaced as soon as they showed signs of wear.

The used covers were a perk of the stewards. They were in demand among dockside whores in each of the *Empress*'s ports of call.

"Of course . . . " Ran said professionally while his eyes searched his immediate surroundings and his brain dealt with three problems:

What was the emergency?

Where was the IR head serving this huge room?

How could he get shut of these lonesome passengers without offending them?

Some minds lock up when faced with simultaneous tasks. Others deal stolidly with one problem at a time, even though everything's going to hell in a handbasket outside their immediate narrow focus. Ran Colville treated batches synergistically. His responses weren't deep and they didn't even attempt to be "best"; but he was very fast, and fast got you a long way in a crisis.

"Right over here, madam," he said.

The IR head would be central, so he needed to move the passengers if his commo unit was to face the correct direction. He took the female passenger by the arm and swept her a short distance to the side where a cleaning robot industriously polished the floor.

In keeping with the decor, the robot was disguised as a meter-high column base, covered with contorted acanthus vines. Ran toggled off the mechanical switch and dropped the unit firmly to the deck. With the woman in the crook of his left arm, he said, "Lieutenant Colville. Go ahead."

The passengers beamed, and Bridge — in this case the central control AI buried somewhere deep in the *Empress* — spewed information through the ship's structure and up the flex to the commo pod, which broadcast it to Ran's ear clip microphone.

Like her husband, the woman was well into middle age, overweight, and as desperately good-natured as a puppy. She was dressed in high style, a pleated dress of natural linen and a great deal of gold and faience jewelry, both mimicking Egyptian taste of the Amarna Period. She was obviously uncomfortable in such garb, but she was determined to be In on the voyage of a lifetime.

"Stateroom eight-two-four-one," said the artificial intelligence. "There has been a double booking. The Purser has requested aid."

The man's camera was a skeletonized handgrip supporting a body the size of a walnut. The triple lenses were of optical fibers as fine as spidersilk, with a 150-mm spread to create a three-dimensional image. The unit whirred as Ran turned to the woman and kissed the tips of her fingers. "Madam, sir," he said with a broad smile. "Enjoy your voyage on the finest vessel in the galaxy!"

Ran spun on his heel and strode from the Social Hall with a set expression that dissuaded other passengers from accosting him. Three steps along, he realized that he'd forgotten to turn the cleaning robot back on.

The hell with it. *That* was a problem the stewards could handle.

The prefix 8 indicated a First Class cabin. 241 was a location: Deck B, starboard rank. Deck A cabins were often thought to be the premium units because entrances to the main public rooms were off that lower deck, but a number of sophisticated travelers preferred the higher level for just that reason. Traffic in Deck B corridors was only a small fraction of that on A.

Passengers, stewards, and luggage on static-repulsion floats littered the halls in sluggish movement, like cells in human blood vessels. Cabin doors stood open as stewards fed cases inside one at a time while occupants discussed shrilly where the items should be stowed. It would all get where it was going, eventually; but Ran Colville at the moment regarded the bustle as a moving obstacle course.

A party of Rialvans stood with their backs to the stretch of balcony overlooking the Dining Salon. They waited stolidly while, across the corridor, the dominant Rialvan female looked over their two-cabin suite with the steward. The process might take more than an hour, but it wasn't a problem. The heavy-bodied Rialvans were painstaking to a degree that would be considered insane in any human culture, but they tipped well and they never made *active* problems for the staff.

No, the trouble was down toward the end of the corridor. Two stewards, dark-skinned men from New Sarawak like most of the Trident cabin staff, snapped to attention when Ran appeared — not because of his rank, but because they were so glad to pass the problem on to someone else.

A pair of male passengers, Caucasians who looked to be about 70 years old, waited in the corridor as well. One of them was a trim, tall man who stood with military stiffness. His fellow was short, soft, bald, and seated on a cabin trunk. The plump man leaned against the corridor wall — a mural of a prairie in late summer, with the milkweed pods beginning to open — with his right ankle crossed over his left knee.

"Ah," said the tall passenger as he noticed Ran. "Lieutenant, I believe? *Very* good to see you. I'm Richard Wade, this is my friend Tom Belgeddes —"

The shorter man grunted to his feet. "Charmed," he said in a friendly tone. He sounded rather as if he meant something more than conventional pleasantry.

" — and there seems to be a bit of a problem with our cabin," Wade continued without having paused for his friend to speak.

The cabin door was open. Another man popped his head out, then disappeared back inside.

"You'll take it from here, sir?" a steward asked Ran.

"Stick around," Ran replied. "There's going to be some luggage to move in a little bit."

He stood in the doorway. Wade and Belgeddes closed in to either side, making it look as though the Third Officer was the shock troop for their point of view — which was the last thing the situation called for. Ran stepped into the cabin and switched the door down behind him, closing the passengers out in the corridor.

Luggage, much of it in the form of bales and packets instead of purpose-built cases, filled the center of the bed-sitting room. A family of six was positioned around the gear like the Huns at Chalons prepared to defend their leader on a pile of saddles.

"I am Parvashtisinga Sadek," announced the man who'd looked into the corridor. "This is my cabin. See!"

He offered Ran his ticket, a data crystal etched on the outside with the company's trident. The crystal was a wafer, 1-cm by 2. Its information could have been contained on a microscopic speck: the additional size was necessary for handling by life-forms rather than by computers.

Ran put the ticket in the palm-sized reader on his belt and projected the data in the form of a hologram that hung forty centimeters in front of his eyes. It was an Earth to Tellichery ticket, via the *Empress of Earth* in Cabin 8241, with everything in order. Five-person occupancy, which might be arguable, but a babe in arms would normally travel free. Date of issue was the twelfth of last month, three weeks before. The only unusual circumstance was that the ticket had been cut on Ain al-Mahdi rather than either of the terminus worlds.

"Thank you, sir," Ran said as he returned the wafer. "I'll check the other gentlemen's tickets, now."

"This is our room!" Sadek said in a shrill, forceful voice. "We will not move."

He, his wife, and three of the children stared at Ran as if they expected the white-uniformed ship's officer to draw a long knife at any moment and begin to butcher them. The infant on the mother's breast looked up, hid his/her face with a happy gurgle, and peeked out again.

Ran winked, drawing another gurgle.

Ran left the door in the up, open, position as he stepped back into the corridor. "Mr. Wade, Mr. Belgeddes," he said, "might I — "

He paused, because Wade was already extending his hand with the two ticket chips in it.

"Of course, of course, my boy," Wade said. "By the book, just as it should be. I've been an officer myself, you know — at least a dozen times, if you count all the penny-ante rebellions that somebody decided to make me a general."

"That's right," said Belgeddes as Ran fed a ticket into the reader. "Dickie here, he never could keep out of trouble."

The ticket was Belgeddes' own, and it was perfectly in order: Cabin 8241, round-trip, Port Northern at both termini. Issued *through* Trident's home office in Halifax *on* the first of the previous month. Eleven days earlier than the Sadek family's ticket.

Before he spoke, because it was a lot easier to check now than clean up the mess later, Ran switched Belgeddes' ticket for Wade's in the reader. The ticket data were identical save for the name and retinal print of the passenger.

Pity. It'd have been a hair easier if the proper cabin-holders were the people holding the cabin at present . . . but if they were all easy, Trident Star-lines wouldn't need people like Ran Colville to back up the *Empress*'s stewards.

Ran aimed his transceiver link toward the IR head above the doorjamb. The Sadek family stared at him: the husband stiff, as though he faced a firing squad; the wife fierce, the children obviously frightened . . . and the infant gurgled again.

"Colville to Bridge," Ran said. "Project a First Class occupancy plan through my reader."

"Do you remember on Matson's Home, how the government made me a colonel after the rebels ambushed the sight-seeing train and I potted a few of them just to keep *us* from being shot?" Wade said. "Heaven knows, *I* didn't care anything about their politics."

The *Empress*'s controlling artificial intelligence obediently shunted data through deck-conduction radio to Ran's hologram projector. The lens system couldn't handle a double spread, so it switched rapidly between the A and B levels.

All the cabins in both arrays were coded red, occupied.

"Oh, for pity's sake!" Ran snapped. "Bridge, give me a list of empty cabins. The whole *ship* isn't full."

"Be fair, Dickie," Belgeddes was saying. The two men were clearly playing out a well-practiced skit. "The general was going to make you a captain until he threw his arms around you and you knocked him down because you weren't sure of just what he had in mind. *Then* he made you a colonel."

"The whole ship is not full," the AI replied tartly. "All the First Class cabins are occupied, however — as the plan I projected at your request clearly shows."

"Why on earth are — " Ran began; and stopped himself, because it was the wrong thing to worry about when he had a real problem to solve.

The artificial intelligence answered the half-spoken question anyway. "A Szgranian noblewoman has taken a block of sixty-four cabins and the Wu-Ti Suite, for herself and her entourage," it said. A long row on A Deck, starboard outboard — the rank of cabins directly beneath 8241, in fact — glowed yellow, then returned to red highlighting.

"All right," Ran said, "tell me what *is* open."

Cabin Class was a ring of accommodations amidships. They were designed for multiple occupancy by strangers, with two pairs of bunk beds in each room and relatively spartan facilities otherwise. There were only 204 places in Cabin. The real purpose of the class was to provide a physical separation of First Class and the packed mass of Third Class passengers further aft. Some people who could afford First preferred Cabin, however, because the very small number of passengers traveling together fostered friendliness and camaraderie.

There were about a dozen empty bunks, scattered throughout the Cabin Class area.

"Right," Ran said. "Bridge, clear me compartments four-thirty-two and four-thirty-four. Assign them to the Sadek party, six persons, in place of the eight-two-four-one assignment made in error."

"Passengers already assigned aren't going to like moving," one of the stewards said, ostensibly to his fellow.

"Berths in Cabin Class are assigned in accordance with the company's pleasure," Ran responded sharply. "If you mean that some stewards have already pocketed bribes for arranging lower bunks for people who'll have to move to top ones — that sounds like a personal problem to me."

"We will not move!" Mr. Sadek cried. "Our ticket is correct!"

"Sir," Ran said, "you have a valid ticket, and responsibility for the error rests with Trident Starlines. But there *was* an error, and — "

"You *say* our ticket is correct and you *say* that the fault is yours!" Sadek said. His eldest daughter edged closer to her mother, and the two-year-old boy began to cry. "Racism is the only reason that you move us and not them!"

Ran looked at the smaller man, considered his next words and their possible side effects — and spoke the flat truth anyway. "No sir," he said. "I said your ticket is valid, but it's not correct."

He took a deep breath. "And I said Trident is responsible for the error . . . but as for what actually happened, I'd guess you knew the *Empress* was fully booked, but you got a friend at Golconda Travel Agency — " the issuing agency on the Sadeks' ticket " — to cut you a ticket through their Ain al-Mahdi office where the data base hadn't been updated. If necessary, I'll see to it that the company reviews its arrangements with Golconda — "

Mrs. Sadek gasped and tugged her husband's sleeve. It was long odds that Golconda Travel Agency would turn out to be a relative from her side of the family.

" — but for the moment, what's important is that they were authorized to ticket for the *Empress* at the time they did so, even though the space had been assigned some *weeks* earlier. Therefore, on behalf of the company, I'm arranging a double cabin for you with a little more than twice the space — full First Class entertainment in both cabins — "

The hologram feeds were run to all living spaces as part of the emergency information net. Entertainment programming required only a software change.

" — and of course, use of all the First Class public spaces. What I *can't* offer you — " Ran smiled tightly to underline the irony " — are programmable murals. Yours will be one scene apiece."

"Cabin four-three-two is a Kalahari display," Bridge volunteered. "Cabin four-three-four is a coral reef."

"You'll have a desert and an underwater scene," Ran said. "Or you can turn them off."

Mrs Sadek tugged her husband's attention again and whispered furiously into his ear while he continued to watch Ran. The cadence of her voice was audible, though her words were not.

Sadek suddenly and unexpectedly smiled. "Twice as large?" he said. "And a separate room for the children?"

"You bet," Ran said. "It'll take a moment to configure the beds the way you decide you want them, but it'll be more comfortable than this."

8241 was set up with two twin beds. The Sadek's steward had brought a crib and an inflatable which now rested in the corridor on the opposite side of the door from the Wade/Belgeddes luggage.

Mrs. Sadek whispered again.

"And there will be no difficulty for my brother-in-law?"

"Not on this one," Ran agreed. "But you might pass on the word that if I personally have a situation like this arise on a Golconda ticket again . . . then I personally will see to it that the next time's the last time."

Sadek giggled. "Yes," he said, "yes, of course." He straightened. "Let us go, then!"

Ran glanced at the stewards. "Your move, gentlemen. Four-three-two and four. Oh — and make sure full holo is enabled."

He nodded to Wade and Belgeddes as he backed away from the cabin.

Wade stepped close and murmured, "Fine job, my boy. Good to see that the sons of Earth haven't forgotten how to handle these fringe-worlders. Why, I remember when I was supervising a prospecting team on Hobilo before the Long Troubles — "

"Thank you, sir," Ran said firmly. "I very much regret the delay, but I trust you'll enjoy your trip with us nonetheless."

He strode off down the corridor, heading toward the bow to permit him to turn his back on Wade. He didn't like having Sadek call him a racist. He liked much less to have Wade approving of him as a racist.

And while the Sadeks' home planet, Tellichery, had a highly developed industry and culture, Ran Colville's own Bifrost was a fringe world in every disparaging sense of the term.

"Whoopie ti-yi-yo," Mohacks sang in a low voice, *"git along, little dogie. . . ."*

"Don't you let Commander Kneale hear you saying that sorta crap," Babanguida warned. "He'd have your guts for garters."

"It's your misfortune and none of my own. . . ." Mohacks continued.

Third Class loaded along a single meter-wide walkway instead of a broad ramp like that which accommodated First and Cabin Class. The passengers were segregated by sex rather than family, with the only exceptions being children less than ten years old who were permitted to stay with their mothers upon request.

"Where's this lot going?" Mohacks asked.

"Biscay, the most of them," said his partner. "A few of them's for Hobilo, for the mines."

Ground personnel conducted the mass movement — Trident's Emigrant Staff here, officials from the labor contractor or other receiving agency on the destination world. All aspects of the *Empress of Earth*'s loading were ultimately the responsibility of the ship's crew, however. Mohacks and Babanguida stood at the head of the gangway where they could see both the interior of the hold and the long column shuffling forward.

The emigrants were nervous but hopeful. Each wore company-issue coveralls and carried the company-issued 20-liter pack which contained absolutely all the personal effects an emigrant was permitted to bring aboard. A few mothers staggered under two or three packs, their offspring's allotment as well as their own.

"Poor *stupid* bastards," Mohacks said. "Don't they know what they're getting into — for the rest of their life?"

"You don't know what they're leaving behind," Babanguida replied.

"I don't need to," Mohacks said with a snort. "I've seen Biscay mebbe fifty times since I've been working this route. Each trip is one more time too many."

The emigrants moved in units of forty-eight, each led by a member of the Emigrant Staff with a blazing red holographic arrow. Unoccupied segments of the Third Class section were open and lighted in bright pastel colors. The single bunks, laid with plaid or pais-ley bedding, were in four-high stacks.

The guides took their groups left or right alternatively at the head of the walkway. Individual barracks areas were set out by lines glowing on the deck. Only when a group had been marshaled within the proper position did bulkheads drop smoothly from the ceiling.

The guides remained inside the barracks rectangle until the emigrants' first trapped panic had subsided. This was where the Emigrant Staff earned its pay. The guides spoke calmly, either through the translators on their shoulders or directly if they knew the dialect of the emigrants. Only when a section was calm did a guide back out through the door keyed to staff ID chips.

If necessary, ceiling nozzles could spray contact anes-thetic. With a full manifest of four thousand plus, it would normally come to that at least once during loading.

"You think Colville's got a bleeding heart for the Thirds, the way Ms. Holly does?" Mohacks asked idly.

"That one?" Babanguida sneered. "*His* heart don't bleed for nobody, starting with himself. But I don't think he likes us, Howie boy. Saying something about the cattle sheds — "

Babanguida waggled an elbow toward the interior of Third Class.

" — where he can hear us would be *just* the kind of excuse he'd like to bust us back to Ship Side and get a couple newbies he could snow."

The black rating snorted. "He's got games of his own, you bet. He knows we'd see through him and he'd have to cut us in."

The barracks sections were being filled in a checker-board pattern rather than solidly from the ends to the middle. When the bulkheads were down, they outlined a narrow corridor in woven shades of gray and pastels. Once the ship was under way, the corridor bulkheads would become transparent though those between sections remained opaque.

"Like a prison in there," Mohacks said as his eyes followed the spaced column of emigrants. "Get out for two hours exercise in twenty-four, and that with a thousand others. Never see a woman — or a man, if you are one, 'cepting the crew."

"Bloody little of that this run," Babanguida muttered. "Not till we suss out Colville, and I'm *not* real hopeful."

He chuckled, then went on, "Still, so far as these Chinks go... It's clean in there and it's safe. The food's not fancy but it's good enough. *I* ate worse when I signed on with Union Traders out of Grantholm. You don't need to feel sorry for them."

When a staff guide had delivered a group, he or she returned quickly along the even narrower passage mounted on one side of the emigrant's walkway. Occasionally an emigrant would be startled to see someone in uniform going in the opposite direction. The guides patted the passengers' shoulders and murmured reassurance before they moved on.

"Sorry for them?" Mohacks said. "Not me, buddy. My brother Buck was on a tramp carrying a Mahgrabi labor battalion around the Rutskoy Cluster — harvesters, you know."

"Your brother Buck?" Babanguida interjected. "*You* were on the *Ildis* in the Rutskoy, and I know it because I saw your experience record on your ID."

"That may have been," Mohacks said in an aloof voice, "but this happened to Buck. Like I was saying, they got to Marignano for the vintage and it was *just* good luck that there was a squad of hardcase Grantholm labor supervisors aboard because they could catch a scheduled run home from Marignano. You know that sort — they didn't trust anybody with a dark complexion."

"Happens I do know them, you bet," Babanguida agreed grimly.

"So there's Buck on watch, half asleep and nothing but a pistol by him. The *Ildis*, the tramp, she comes out of sponge space, and bingo! up come four hundred Mahgrabis and tear down the bulkheads. *He* shouts and drops the first five — "

"He just started shooting?" Babanguida said. "At passengers?"

"At Thirds," Mohacks replied, "except on the *Ildis* they called them cargo. Anyway, one of Buck's rules is 'When in doubt, empty the magazine.' It wouldn't have done much good, though, only about the time Buck got to the hatch with the other three hundred and some screaming Mahgrabis behind him, down come the Grantholm crew. *They* carried shotguns and sub-machine guns in their cabin baggage, and I don't mind telling you the next thirty seconds was pretty busy."

"I don't believe you've got a brother," Babanguida said.

"Sure I do," his companion said. "Well, when the smoke cleared, damned if the captain didn't sober up enough to see there was an intra-system packet bearing down on a converging course. It blew two magnetics, trying to brake when it saw the *Ildis* wasn't stopping. Buck hopes they went sailing on out till they all froze, 'cause a hundred to one they were going to crew the ship once the labor battalion took it over. It was all planned."

Babanguida sniffed.

"It happened just like I said," Mohacks protested. "Any starship, even a tramp, is worth a fortune. What the *Empress*'s worth, well . . . if you ask me, they could mount flamethrowers down here in Third and I wouldn't mind."

"*That* I might believe," Babanguida said. "But if you've got a brother, then I'm President of Trident Starlines."

Gray-clad emigrants moved along. A child began to sing in a loud voice. His mother shushed him, then flashed a nervous smile at Mohacks and Babanguida as she passed.

Her expression glowed with inner hope.

The male Szgranian facing Kneale in the VIP Lounge was twenty centimeters shorter than the commander and, though relatively broad in proportion to the human, had a flattened look. He wore a parcel-gilt silver breastplate covered with jagged symbols which Kneale supposed were writing, and his harness was hung with six holstered weapons.

One for each hand.

A generation or so ago, Trident Starlines had accepted the argument that the weapons of a Szgranian warrior were cultural artifacts which the warrior had to be allowed on shipboard. Even then, the company had forbidden projectile weapons, but the swords which Szgranians wielded with their upper pair of arms and the broad-bladed push daggers for the middle pair were permitted.

That ended with an unfortunate incident on the old *Princess Royal*. An aide to the female head of a Szgranian clan decided his mistress had been defiled by the offer of a birthday cake. It was the chef's unfortunate notion to mold the cake in the lady's own likeness, but the table steward paid the price. He was lopped into several pieces before four of the vessel's officers piled onto the aide and overpowered him.

Since then, Szgranians wore cultural artifacts of demonstrably non-functional plastic, for so long as they were in spaces controlled by Trident Starlines. Nevertheless, the aide had a set of teeth developed to pulp hard-shelled grain — Szgranians were vegetarians, not omnivores — and which could go through major human bones like a hammermill.

"You are the captain?" the aide squeaked forcefully. He was accompanied by five other Szgranians. They were presumably of lower rank, because their rig-outs were less glittering in precisely regulated stages. Despite the strong jaws, most Szgranians could be mistaken for Terrans from the neck up.

"I'm Commander Hiram Kneale," Kneale boomed back. No one familiar with Terran hippos expected a species to be placid because it was vegetarian. "If you want a starship navigated, Captain Kanawa is your man. If you want honor done to a passenger, *I* am the highest ranking officer for the purpose in Trident Starlines. *I* represent the *Empress of Earth*!"

The aide snorted and stepped back to the group of his subordinates. They chittered at one another, waving their arms like a storm in a pine thicket, while Kneale waited stolidly.

Szgranians *per capita* traveled about as frequently as any other non-human race with which mankind had come in contact. The handiworks of the Szgranian craftsman class, particularly carvings in the round accomplished on a jig with double mirrors, were exquisite and in demand at high prices throughout the civilized universe. The foreign exchange they earned permitted the upper level of Szgranian society to travel at will.

Despite that, relatively few starship officers had experience with Szgranians. The mistress of a clan traveled with a huge entourage — several hundred in the present case of Lady Scour — but no individual ever left the planet. Either you had scores of Szgranians on your plate, or none. Given that most of the travelers were nobles, warriors by birth and breeding and extremely punctilious of their clan's honor, learning to deal with Szgranians was much like learning to swim by being thrown into the deep end of the pool.

This was Kneale's third experience with a party of Szgranians, but it would be the first for Holly and Colville. They were both solid officers, though; and they had to learn some time.

The aide returned. Szgranians moved with the grace of gazelles. They seemed stiff until you realized how fast and precisely they accomplished every physical task.

"Commander Hiram Kneale," the aide trilled. He curtsied to indicate Kneale's high rank — a prerequisite if the clan mistress was to be entrusted to him. "Lady Scour will honor you with her presence. Please await her."

He took a spherical gong of chiseled iron from his belt and struck it with the fingertips of the middle hand on the opposite side. An angelically clear note filled the lounge.

The aides crouched like a party of Hindu gods preparing for a footrace, their culture's attention posture. In the bottom pairs of their holsters, above the "quaint" swords and knives, were non-functioning copies of pistols every bit as modern as those in the *Empress of Earth*'s small armory.

The same wealth on which Szgranians traveled the galaxy allowed them to import the advanced weapons which guaranteed planetary independence. Szgrane's nearest neighbor through sponge space was Grantholm. The degree of Grantholm influence was limited sharply by knowledge that a planet with a suicidally brave warrior class *and* energy weapons could be destroyed but not ruled by outsiders.

Commander Kneale braced his back and clicked his heels together. In theory, every First Class passenger boarding the *Empress of Earth* was a VIP. Certainly most thought of themselves in that fashion. Realistically, though, a foreign potentate who took a block of sixty-four cabins and an imperial suite expected bowing and scraping beyond the general norm. Thus the VIP lounge, though it was officially called the Special Needs Room of the Trident terminal.

A double line of Szgranian attendants entered the room and flared to either side. Lady Scour stepped between them like shot from the muzzle of a blunder-buss. Commander Kneale bowed low, thinking, *Good lord, she's beautiful!*

Szgranian females of the upper class were larger than the males — a common occurrence in polyandrous species. Lady Scour was Kneale's height though of a willowy build. She moved with a suppleness so strikingly different from that of her male attendants that the commander wondered whether their metal breastplates made them awkward. Again, it was possible that the clan mistress was simply unique of her species. Kneale was willing to believe that.

Lady Scour's garment was a one-piece trouser-suit of purple silk matched perfectly to the color of the irises of her large eyes. Instead of sleeves, her arms extended through a fringed slit on either side. Her skin was covered with a light down like the belly fur of a cat, and the thin fabric left no doubt that Szgranians were mammals — albeit four-dugged mammals.

"You may rise, Commander Kneale, and lead me to my quarters," Lady Scour announced, speaking Standard in a well-modulated voice. Szgranians of all classes were notable linguists. Those who traveled beyond their planet rarely needed AI translators. Even so, Lady Scour's accent and enunciation were exceptionally good.

"Thank you, milady," Kneale replied. He touched his commo transceiver to the inner doorway of the lounge and said, "Kneale here. Is our path clear? Over."

Bridge replied to the prepared question by throwing a holographic chart up from the commander's reader.

Kneale had arranged a route to the Szgranian wing which, though not the most direct, was fully controllable. It went through the Cabin Class areas in which Bridge could lock passengers in their compartments while stewards cleared the corridors. That sort of high-handedness in First Class would cause problems.

Fewer problems, though, than running a party of hot-tempered Szgranians — not human, and *not* civilized by human standards — through a mass of people, some of whom were certainly arrogant enough to gawp and laugh. During most of the voyage, Lady Scour's party could be expected to stay within the wing blocked off for their use. Commander Kneale was determined to avoid insults — and retribution — during boarding and disembarking. If he'd had to clear a First Class corridor, he'd have done so.

Lady Scour offered her lower right arm. Szgranians used their various pairs of arms for socially distinct purposes. No doubt she was making a statement regarding their relative rank, but that was her affair. Kneale had only to keep her happy. He crooked the arm in his and stepped through the automatically opened inner doorway.

Kneale's two ratings, Bechtel and Blavatsky, had manually draped the portion of the gangway beyond into a red velvet tunnel. Kneale strode up it with Lady Scour beside him. Her entourage, except for the aide with the gong who marched alone, followed the leaders in double column.

"How did you get along with Rawsl?" Lady Scour asked. "My chief aide?"

"Hmm?" said Kneale. Szgranian hearing was within human parameters, though biased toward slightly higher pitches. Rawsl could certainly listen to them. "Quite well, madam. He appeared very — " *Professional? Alert?* " — gallant."

"I rather fancied him at one time," the clan mistress

said coolly. "Indeed, he's quite well born, and I was
thinking of adding him to my lovers — until one of my
maids mentioned that she thought Rawsl was handsome. Don't you find that things are terribly defiled by
the appreciation of the lower orders, Commander?"

"Umm," said Kneale. "That's a — an under-
standable attitude, madam."

Maybe somebody understood it. Kneale wasn't sure
he wanted to meet that person, though.

Their feet touched the firm resilience of the *Empress
of Earth*'s deck. Lady Scour's fine legs flexed like a cat's.

"Welcome to the finest ship in the galaxy, Lady
Scour," Kneale said, glad to be able to change the
subject.

The bulkhead at the head of the gangway was mirrored. In its reflection, Commander Kneale saw that
Rawsl's fists were clenched, all six of them.

Abraham Chekoumian looked at the Social Hall's
bandstand — a copy of the Rostra, complete with
projecting bronze rams like those the Romans had
taken from captured Carthaginian ships. Holographic
temples cloaked the wall beyond. Chekoumian thrust
his hands in his pockets, flaring the skirt of his magenta
jacket, and laughed loudly.

"Pardon, sir?" asked a female crewman passing at
that moment. She was attractively short and plump,
with shingled black hair that contrasted nicely with her
brilliantly white uniform.

"Oh, I — " Chekoumian said. He grinned broadly.
"I'm very happy, you see. I'm here in this — " he took
out one hand and pointed, waggling the index finger
in a circle " — this luxury, I who worked my passage
from Tblisi five years ago in the hold of a tramp
freighter as a baggage handler. And — "

He reached into his breast pocket and withdrew a
pack of letters in durable spacemail envelopes.

Chekoumian's garments were cut and styled to the moment. His trousers were pale pink, while his shirt and shoes were identical shades of teal — the Now Neutral, according the arbiters of Terran fashion. The slight shimmer at the seams came from threads of metallic gold used in the stitching.

" — I'm going to be married!" he cried. "Do you know what these are, ah — Blavatsky! But what is your real name?" He waved at her nametag. It rested at a slant on the rating's breast because of the swell of the bosom beneath it. "Your given name?"

"Well, Marie, sir," Blavatsky admitted, "but I think Commander Kneale would prefer that with passengers —"

"Poof, Commander Kneale!" Chekoumian said with a theatrical flourish of his letters. "When you have the same name as *my* beloved Marie, I should call you 'Blavatsky' as if you were some cargo pusher in my warehouse? And I am Abraham Chekoumian, but you must call me Abraham."

"Well, I certainly wish you and your fiancee every happiness, Mr. Chekoumian," Blavatsky replied. She'd come to the conclusion that the passenger was simply very happy, as he'd said, rather than a madman about to erupt; but it was her job to check dining table assignments with the Chief Steward in three minutes, and *she* couldn't dismiss Commander Kneale with the aplomb of a First Class passenger.

"I came to Earth to make my fortune," Chekoumian said, looking around the Social Hall with satisfaction. "And so I have done!"

There were already several hundred passengers present, many of them with their seat backs reclined so that they could look upward. On the morning and afternoon before undocking, it was traditional for First Class passengers to gather in the lounge. A bird's-eye holographic projection on the ceiling showed the

Empress of Earth in her berth as ground crews and their machinery swarmed about with the final preparations.

Blavatsky realized that Chekoumian wasn't bragging about his wealth, precisely. He knew that no matter how successful he had been, a substantial part of the *Empress*'s passenger list could buy him a dozen times over. His was the self-made man's pride in his *success* — a matter worthy of the emotion, in Blavatsky's terms.

"Well, sir," she said, "you've picked the right ship to go home on, then. The *Empress* means success!"

Unless you rode her in Third Class, in the spaces that would double as cattle byres when the *Empress of Earth* lifted from Calicheman.

The passenger beamed at Blavatsky. He wasn't listening, but he was glad of her presence because he needed an audience to burble his joy aloud. "Marie doesn't know I'm coming back," he explained, waving the sealed letters again. "I'd return when I'd made my fortune, we agreed, and every two weeks of those five years she's sent me a letter. By the *Brasil* or by the *Empress*, voyage and voyage. And what I've done — "

Chekoumian looked around to see who else might be listening. No one was. He added in a confidential voice anyway, " — you see, these past three months, when I knew I was going home to marry Marie, I've saved her letters. I'm going to read one at each planet-fall, and then when we reach Tblisi — I'll have my Marie herself!"

Blavatsky looked at the passenger. He was a sophisticated man as well as being rich and successful. Unlike many of those in the Social Hall, Chekoumian wore his stylish clothes with practiced ease. He wasn't dressing up for the voyage; he looked as he did to his business associates, at what must be a very high level of his field of endeavor.

But he was also childishly enthusiastic, especially when he was talking about his Marie. Blavatsky smiled,

genuinely pleased by Chekoumian's good fortune —
and his fiancee's. Her expression couldn't be pure
laughter, though, because she remembered how
recently she'd thought she was that happy also.

"Five years ago, I had nothing but the clothes I stand
in," reminisced Chekoumian. He looked around at the
ivoroid and silk, at successful passengers and the images of a supernal empire on the walls. "Ship's clothes
they were, too, bought from the bosun's slop chest.
And now, only five years — the Beakersdorff chain
decides they must have *my* connections on Szgrane and
K'Chitka. They pay me a million three — so much
from *nothing*, in five years!"

Chekoumian had spoken of his warehouse. It
sounded as though he was an import-export
specialist — had been one, and would certainly be *something*, maybe the same thing, again soon. His kind of
man didn't sit on his hands just because he'd found
himself rich.

"I'm glad of your good fortune, Mr Chekoumian,"
Blavatsky said aloud. She knew she needed to get on,
but she no longer felt the pressure of a moment before.
Quiet longing eased over her as smoothly as the sea
across tidal flats. Commander Kneale's anger was as
remote a possibility as the threat of lightning; and in
any case, it didn't rule Blavatsky's soul.

"The best of my fortune," Chekoumian said, "is my
Marie. She can't realize how well I've done. I tell her,
but a letter is a letter, you know . . . and *I* didn't realize
until Beakersdorff made their offer three months ago!
Many women wouldn't wait five years, you know."

And some men wouldn't wait four weeks, Blavatsky
thought. *The length of a round-trip voyage, Earth to Tblisi
and back, with the wedding planned for the day the* Empress
docked on her return. . . .

"That's quite true, sir," Blavatsky murmured. "I
hope you continue to be so happy."

The uniformed rating walked toward the real exit framed by the pillared facade of Rome's Temple of Concord. Chekoumian's Marie was a very lucky woman. Blavatsky hoped—and doubted—that she knew it.

Chekoumian settled himself into a chair. He was too absorbed in his own affairs to notice that Blavatsky had gone without leave or ceremony. That wasn't the sort of thing that mattered to him, anyway.

He touched the edge fold of the earliest letter with his chip-encoded signet ring. The envelope peeled back neatly, like tensed skin drawing the flesh open along a cut. If the seal was broken in any other fashion, the envelope would have melted with enough violence to ignite the paper within.

Chekoumian extracted the letter and began to read:

My Dearest Abraham,

Today Mother and I went shopping for Nita's baby shower. You know Nita. Oh, don't put yourselves out, she says, but if we didn't you can be sure she'll be telling everybody what cheapskates our side of the family is until she's a gray old woman! Well, we. . .

The five passengers in the Starlight Bar, all of them male, watched the clear, curving wall as tugs on ground transporters crawled toward the *Empress of Earth.*

Wade wore his credit chip on a bracelet of untarnished metallic chain, an alloy from the heavy platinum triad. "I'll take this round, then," he said, and inserted the chip in the autobar's pay slot.

Other men began punching selections into the pads on their chair arms. "Many thanks, ah, Wade," Dewhurst said. "The next one's—"

The autobar chirped in irritation. "I'm sorry, sir," said the machine in an apologetic male voice. "I believe there's a problem with this chip. If you'd try another one, please?"

Wade withdrew the chip with a look of amazement and outrage on his aristocratic features. "Oh, good lord," he said. "I haven't recharged this from my Terran account! Look, fellows, I'll just pop down to the Purser's Office — "

"Pretty busy just now, don't you think, Dickie?" Belgeddes warned with a lifted eyebrow.

"Never mind," said Dewhurst. "I'll pay for the round."

"Much obliged, old fellow," Wade muttered. "Very embarrassing."

"Dickie's always doing that sort of thing," Belgeddes said indulgently.

"I dare say," agreed Dewhurst as he summoned a whiskey and water. The autobar chuckled happily over Dewhurst's credit chip.

Da Silva looked up into the auroral sky. "The first time I traveled," he said, "I thought that — " he gestured toward the whispering light with a rum drink " — was what the stars would look like when we were . . . "

He paused and cleared his throat. "In sponge space, you know. But it was nothing like that."

"Even though the bulkhead shows exactly what an optically clear panel would show," Wade said, "in here we're still completely cut off from the insertion bubble. If you've only seen sponge space from the insulated interior of a vessel, you haven't a hint of what it's like to be out in the cold, twisted radiance with nothing but a suit to protect you."

Dewhurst snorted. "I suppose you've been a Cold Crewman, then, Wade?" he said.

"Oh, good lord no!" Wade chuckled. "But back long before you were born, I volunteered when Carlsbad decided to raise a sponge space commando during their unpleasantness with Jaffa Hill. Wasn't my quarrel in the least, but I thought it might be interesting."

He shook his head and looked deep into his drink. "It was that, all right," he said. "Bloody interesting."

"Dickie was the only member of the unit to survive," Belgeddes explained to the others. "They found that practice isn't the same as the real thing."

"Practice was bad enough, though," Wade murmured.

Reed stared at the crystalline mural over the autobar. The *Empress of Earth*'s ports of call were sculpted as icons. They ranged from Earth — bands of rose quartz and topaz to suggest the aurora borealis — to three onion-domed towers representing Tblisi. The bead of red light now on Earth would follow the *Empress*'s progress across the arc, while the blue indicator for the *Brasil* moved in the opposite direction until they merged briefly on the oil derricks of Hobilo.

"I don't like this talk about wars," Reed said morosely. "It's going to cause trouble, I feel it. I just hope that we make Ain al-Mahdi. After that, well, I wish all you other fellows the best, but it's not *my* problem once I've gotten where I'm going."

"We won't land on Nevasa or Grantholm if the war breaks out," Dewhurst said. "They'll pick nearby neutrals and offload passengers there."

He sounded calm enough, but what started as a sip drained most of the whiskey from his glass. "Anyway," he added forcefully, "I think it's all overblown. They'll back off, you'll see. Both sides."

"I *said*," Reed snapped, "that I didn't want to talk about it!"

"I wonder," Wade said, "if you gentlemen are familiar with the beach walkers of Ain al-Mahdi?"

The others looked at him. "The legend, you mean?" said Da Silva. "Beautiful women who, shall we say, make friends with men at night on the beach, but they drink them down to a hollow skin?"

"Ah, well," Wade said. "I thought it was a legend too. Still, it's a big universe, isn't it? We shouldn't be surprised when we learn that it's a little stranger than we'd expected."

"On Ain al-Mahdi?" Reed said. "Look, buddy, my company's based me on Ain going on fifteen years now. Beach walkers and flats, they're the sort of thing you hear about in sailors' bars — period."

"I should have thought that was where you'd expect to hear about them," Belgeddes commented. "From transients. If there were such a thing as a beach walker, it wouldn't prey on locals, surely?"

Wade pursed his lips in consideration. "Flats," he said. "They look like a pool of shadow, but when you step on them — "

He brought his hands together with a clop of sound.

" — like that?"

"That's the story, all right," Reed said over his gin. "But it's always the friend of a friend of a sailor who's seen it, not anybody *you* meet."

"Unless Mr. Wade has met one — as I rather think he may have done," said Dewhurst.

"Hmm," said Belgeddes. "You never mentioned that to me, Dickie."

"That's because I've never seen such a creature," Wade said stiffly. He pursed his lips. "Unlike the beach walker, which I met — well, I can't tell you how long ago it was." He glanced at Reed. "Certainly before your time, dear fellow. They've probably gone the way of the dodo by now."

"Of the unicorn, I would have said," Dewhurst murmured into his drink, but he spoke in a low enough voice that Wade could pretend not to hear.

"Well, tell us about it, Wade," said Da Silva. "Or — would you care for a refill?"

Wade clinked the ice in his glass. Scotch whiskey was only a hint of amber in the meltwater. "Thank you, friend," he said as he slid the glass toward Da Silva. "Embarrassing situation, as you can imagine."

"Could have happened to any of us, Dickie," said Belgeddes.

"Tarek's Bay wasn't but a few fishing shacks and the warehouses, back then," Wade said. "Ain orbited its primary, and the storage bladders from the gas-mining dipper ships orbited Ain, like moons of the moon. That was before the place became primarily a trans-shipment point. I don't suppose any of the dipper ships still operate, eh?"

He cocked an eyebrow at Reed.

"There's still gas mining," the younger man said, "but now it's geosynchronous siphons and the storage is in primary orbit, not Ain's." He looked uneasily aware that by validating the background of Wade's story, he would seem to lend weight to the story itself— even in his own mind.

"Ah, that's a pity," Wade said. "On nights when the primary was illuminated, the gas bladders drifted across the face of her like soap bubbles, each of them reflecting a view of Ain itself down to the surface. I used to lie out on the beach at night, looking upward and imagining . . . well, I was young then. You know how young men are: romantics."

"Not a lot of romance about Tarek's Bay in the early days," Dewhurst interjected. "Not from the old-timers *I've* talked to."

"Also," said Reed, "the beach is gravel."

"No, not much romance at all," Wade agreed without dropping a stitch. "That's why I went out alone with nothing but an air mattress for company."

He took a sip from the refilled glass Da Silva brought him from the autobar. "And you can imagine how surprised I was when one night a young lady spoke to me."

"*I'm* not surprised," Dewhurst said into his drink, but he was listening too.

"Well, we talked," Wade continued. "You know how

it is. I was young, and there was no doubt what I had in mind ... but remember I'd been looking for romance.

"And there was something odd about the girl. I mean, there couldn't be much doubt what *she* wanted either, or she wouldn't have come up to me that way ... but she didn't seem like a professional. She was quite young and quite beautiful, and, it seemed to me, quite innocent."

"How young?" Da Silva asked with a hard underlayer to his voice.

Wade met the other man's eyes. "Old enough," he said. "Not twenty standard years, though. You'll remember that I wasn't much older than that myself."

Da Silva dipped his head in curt approval.

Reed grimaced, interested despite himself. "What was she wearing?" he asked. He faced slightly away from the storyteller to keep from seeming *too* eager.

"Cast offs," Wade said crisply. "The light was poor—"

"I thought you said the primary was full?" Dewhurst said in a verbal pounce.

Belgeddes raised an eyebrow. "I don't recall you saying that, Dickie," he said.

"No?" said Wade. "No, I don't believe I did—"

He smiled at Dewhurst. "But it's true nonetheless. I don't suppose you've been on Ain, my friend? Reed—"

Wade clicked his gaze sideways, like a turret lathe moving from one setting to the next.

" — how would you describe the way Ain's lighted under the primary?"

Reed shrugged and said apologetically to Dewhurst, "There's quite a lot of light, actually, but Wade's right — it's blotchy, multicolored pastels from the gas bands in the primary's atmosphere. It conceals as much as it hides, to tell the truth."

"Quite," Wade said primly. "So while it *appeared* to me that the girl was dressed in little better than wiping rags, I couldn't be sure. And fashions differ, you know."

Dewhurst snorted.

"I had a miniflood clipped to my sleeve," Wade said. "But it didn't seem the time to switch it on."

"You *have* been out in the evening with young ladies, haven't you, Dewhurst?" Belgeddes asked.

"Yes," said Dewhurst, admitting defeat. "Yes, I can see that."

"So we chatted —"

"Sitting on your air mattress, I suppose," Reed said.

"Sitting on my air mattress," Wade agreed with an appreciative nod. "She said she was local but from another island. A fisherman's daughter, I assumed. *Not* professional, I was sure of that now, but not disinterested either. I put a hand on her shoulder, and she slid open the front closure of my shirt."

Wade leaned back in his chair, savoring perhaps the memory and certainly the focused interest of the others in the lounge. Belgeddes smiled like a father watching his youngest perform in a church pageant.

"Well," the storyteller continued, "I thought I knew where matters were proceeding. Now, of course, I think they were intended to proceed in a very different fashion. But her fingers touched the garnet locket that my mother had given me on her deathbed. I always carry it, you know. Mother said it would protect me from harm. Silly superstition, I suppose, but there you are."

"And I suppose you're wearing it now?" Da Silva asked, more precise than hostile in his tone. "The locket?"

"At this very moment?" Wade replied. He patted the breast of his tailored gray-and-black shirt. "I believe it's in my cabin. I can go get it, of course."

"Shouldn't say he was in much risk at the moment, would you?" Belgeddes said. He chuckled. "Unless you fellows are a syndicate of starship gamblers preying on poor innocents like Dickie and me?"

"Huh! Catch *me* playing cards with you two!" Dewhurst muttered.

"Well, she touched the locket and she pulled back like she'd been burned. 'Why, that's nothing!' I said, pretty hasty as you can imagine. Not wanting anything to spoil the moment, so to speak. So I flipped the locket out, and I turned my light — I mentioned having a light, didn't I?"

"A miniflood," Belgeddes agreed approvingly.

"I switched on the light — aimed at the locket, mind, but there was scatter *from* it and *through* it, though the garnets. And when that red light flickered across the girl, as I thought she was, she simply melted."

"Melted to nothing?" Da Silva demanded.

"Not at all," said Wade. "Into a pool of what I suppose was protoplasm, but it seeped at once down into the soil."

He nodded toward Reed. "The coarse gravel, as Mr. Reed noted."

"I suppose the clothes melted with her?" Dewhurst said.

"No," Wade answered equably, "they were there when I came back the next morning. As was my mattress. I didn't stand on the order of my going, as you can imagine."

"Cast offs," Belgeddes said. "Saw them myself when I came back with him. Sort of trash you could pick from the town midden in Tarek Bay back then."

"What I believe," Wade said, "is that the beach walkers are — or were — " he nodded toward Reed again " — if Mr. Reed is correct in believing them extinct — "

Reed opened his mouth to protest at being misquoted, but he swallowed the words before speaking.

"At any rate, the beach walkers were a life form indigenous to Ain al-Mahdi that mimicked other species," Wade continued. "When men colonized the planet, they mimicked men — or women, at any rate, for the same purposes."

"Which we can guess, easily enough," Belgeddes interjected. "Dinner, not to put too fine a point on it."

"Food or reproduction," Wade said. "Survival of the individual or survival of the species. The basic drives of all forms of life. But its mimicry broke down under intense red light."

He looked at Reed and raised his eyebrow for confirmation. "You've heard that only a ruby laser can kill a beach walker, I suppose? Well, that's not true. It's the angstrom range, not simply destructive energy. And it's not fatal, only — disconcerting to the creature."

Dewhurst's mind riffled the guidebook through whose images he'd browsed in his cabin's bathroom. "There aren't any large animals on Ain," he said. "Except men. There never were."

"Not in the seas, old boy?" Belgeddes responded. "That's not what I recall. I seem to remember some of those arthrodires weighing tonnes, with jawplates spreading wide enough to swallow a catcher boat on a bad day."

"Well, yes, I suppose. . . ." Dewhurst mumbled. "But a — a sea creature doesn't just come up on land!"

Wade got to his feet and smiled at Dewhurst. "Fish don't, that's true," he said in gentle mockery. "At least they usually didn't on Earth."

Belgeddes stood up also. "Time we got back to the cabin, Dickie," he said. "We've still got some unpacking to do before we lift off."

He gave the other men a finger-to-brow salute. "Be seeing you later, I'm sure, chaps."

"One lies and the other swears to it," Dewhurst said when Wade and his companion had left the bar.

"Yes. . . ." agreed Da Silva judiciously. "But I think that story was worth the price of a few drinks, do you not?"

"The funny thing is . . ." Reed said.

The others waited for him to pick up where his voice had trailed off.

"Yes?" Dewhurst prodded.

Reed shook himself and punched in a refill for his gin. "I've lived on Ain for fifteen years," he said. "But you know, he had me believing that for a moment?"

Ran Colville had programmed the three walls of his office alcove to show a Terran country scene. A road of yellow gravel, crushed chalk from the Cretaceous Sea of North America, wound over a hill. The side ditches were bright with Black-eyed Susans and the rich blue of chicory flowers.

Ran didn't talk about his background so that he wouldn't have to lie. He didn't mind easing others into their own false assumptions, however.

He'd attached his transceiver to the alcove terminal while he took a hypnotic crash course on Szgranian language and customs. Shards of light coalesced behind his eyes, then fanned outward into an external reality which was disconcertingly flatter than the roil of images still churning within his mind.

The terminal chirped again.

"Go ahead," Ran muttered. The effort of speaking brought vertigo. He was supposed to be off duty. . . .

"Sir," said a voice. In Ran's present state, it took him a moment to recognize it as Babanguida's. "There's something funny going on. I passed six guys in Corridor Twelve with a float full of equipment — electronics. Not our people or the company's either. They unlocked the hatch into officers' country — "

"Unlocked it?" Ran said. He shook his head to clear it and found right away that had been a *bad* idea.

Because of the disorientation it caused, many people refused to use a hypnogogue. Virtually all the knowledge that fitted Ran for his present position came out of one, though. His father had brought home a teaching unit and a university data base of software . . . from Hobilo, loot gathered when Chick Colville served there as a mercenary.

The elder Colville had never touched the hypnogogue, except to demonstrate it to his son. But on the long nights of Bifrost's winter, the unit had hammered Ran Colville through a template of civilized knowledge.

"That's right," Babanguida replied. "I know I'm off duty, but I asked them what they were doing and they told me to stuff it. I, ah, couldn't follow them through the hatch."

Balls. Babanguida had chips to every door in the *Empress of Earth* or Ran was badly mistaken. The rating had quite reasonably figured this was a good problem to pass off.

It was nice to know that Babanguida hadn't simply ignored the oddity, though. Lots of people would have done just that.

"Right," Ran said aloud, wishing that he felt all right. "How'd they come aboard, do you know?"

"By the main gangway," Babanguida said. "Cooper was on duty. He says he checked their passes and they were fine, so what's the big deal. Cooper!"

"And didn't inform Ms. Holly?" Ran said. He was too fuzzy to have remembered whose shift this was, but Cooper was on Wanda's watch.

"That's a negative," Babanguida agreed. "You know Cooper. He figures any day he doesn't put his pants on back to front, it's a win."

"Roger, I'll handle it from here," Ran said. "Over. Bridge, give me a time plan of hatches opening from Corridor Twelve into officers' country and doors *in* officers' country. Starting ten minutes back."

He closed and rubbed his eyes for a moment. That helped a little, but he continued to have flashbacks of still-faced Szgranians dancing while their arms swayed together like the limbs of mating spiders. Ran sighed and got to work again.

The *Empress of Earth* had visual monitors only in the Third Class spaces. There were times that a full-ship system would have been useful — this was one of them — but neither passengers nor the vessel's officers would have stood for it. For that matter, records of who went to which cabin with whom were an incitement to blackmail by entrepreneurial crewmen, which wasn't the sort of thing Trident Starlines needed either.

Ran's terminal now displayed an alternative. Corridor Twelve was one of those running the full length of the vessel. Going forward from the Embarkation Hall, it passed through First Class and then, through separate locked hatches, gave access to the crew and officer accommodations.

A pair of engineering officers had entered or left their cabins recently, but that was several minutes before the most recent use of the Corridor Twelve hatch. The only cabin opened after that point was Commander Kneale's, two doors down from Ran's own.

"Bridge," Ran asked. "Where's the commander?"

"Commander Kneale left the ship three hours and seventeen minutes ago," the AI replied. "He has not as yet returned. I have no information on his present whereabouts."

"Right," said Ran. It sure didn't feel right. "Request Second Officer Holly to meet me in the commander's suite soonest. I'm headed that way now."

Ran stood up, wobbled in a flurry of false six-armed memories, and went out the door. He paused to put on his hat.

He *thought* of taking the pistol in the locked drawer beneath his terminal; but if that was the way the situation had to be solved, Ran Colville wasn't in any condition to solve it.

The corridor was empty as usual. Trident Starlines didn't stint their crews. Officers' cabins on the *Empress of Earth* were of First Class quality, and the corridor walls were programmed with a holographic reproduction of sea grasses moving beneath a Tblisi lagoon.

Ran would just as soon have had gray paint. He wasn't afraid of water, exactly, but he caught his breath every time he stepped out of his cabin.

He walked past Lieutenant Holly's door and stopped at Kneale's. Setting his ear to the panel didn't tell him anything, not that he'd have expected it to. Worth trying, though; and it took up a moment before he had to act.

Ran set his ID chip against the lock plate. An officer could open any door on the ship, even the one to the captain's suite. Of course, Ran could knock instead, but he figured he'd learn more this way.

The man who was leaning against the inside of the door staggered backward when the panel withdrew into the coaming. Ran stepped around him, moving fast so that he was past the entry and bathroom before the man he'd passed grabbed him from behind and another rammed a sub-machine gun into his chest. Together they slammed him up against the wall.

"Who the hell is he?" another man demanded.

All six of the strangers wore civilian clothes, but that was as far as "civilian" went. Both the men holding Ran had gun muzzles against his body. For all his strength, he couldn't have broken free if he'd tried, and he was pretty sure either of them could have handled him alone.

Bare-handed, at any rate. With a Cold Crewman's adjustment tool or even a shovel — maybe not.

Three of the others had shifted Commander Kneale's terminal into the center of the floor. They were wiring a panel into the bulkhead behind it. That was fast work, even with a modular system, but the technicians were obviously pros — as were the two holding Ran, in their own fashion.

The sixth man, the one asking the question, was in his late 40s, with iron-gray hair and a face to match. He hadn't drawn a gun when Ran burst in, but he certainly looked as though he'd seen his share of sight pictures over the years.

"I'm Third Officer Colville," Ran said. One of the men held Ran's face hard against the wall so that he couldn't look around at the work going on. "And who are *you*, gentlemen?"

"Let him go," the man in charge said abruptly.

The guns and gripping hands fell away. Ran turned slowly. He was going to have a stiff neck in a day or two. The panel the technicians had been working on was hidden behind a holographic screen. With the hologram projector working and the terminal slid back to where it belonged, the additional panel would be completely hidden.

"Mr. Colville," said the man in charge, "we're here on company business." He offered Ran an ID chip embossed with a gold trident. "Check this with your reader, please."

Ran obeyed because that was simpler than refusing. His commo link trilled in his ear, "John Brown, Central Office. Bearer is authorized to enter all Trident Starlines locations. Direct any questions to Department Five, Central Office."

Ran handed the chip back without comment.

"Colville," said the man whose name was as likely Brown as he was likely a Trident employee — not very, "you probably think you were doing your job. We *are* doing ours. Get out of here now and forget all about it. Otherwise, you won't have a job with this company or any other that lifts off of Earth."

Ran didn't doubt that the cold-voiced statement was a promise rather than a threat, nor that it was a real one. But why was the government of Federated Earth installing a —

"Freeze!" ordered Wanda Holly from the open doorway where she stood with her right hand in the pocket of her coat as though she was pointing a pistol. "Drop those guns *now*!"

"It's all right!" Ran shouted. He didn't step toward the Second Officer because the gunmen might use the cover of his body to swing their weapons up and —

"Lee, Damson!" snapped the man in charge. "*Don't* move." When he was certain that his subordinates had heard him, he added like the rustle of a bullwhip, "Since you left the *damned* door open."

"Wanda, it's all right," Ran said in a calmer tone as he stepped quickly toward the corridor before "Brown" decided to hold them. "These gentlemen are from Central Office. They've got a perfect right to be here."

"Colville," said Brown. He paused for a moment, got an unheard prompt and continued, "Ms. Holly. *Don't* talk about this, don't even remember it. Right?"

"Right," Ran said. He keyed the door shut behind him. For a moment he was afraid that the government gunmen were going to follow him out, but the door stayed closed. He guided Wanda quickly back to his own cabin.

"What was that all in aid of?" she asked, speaking more calmly than Ran could have done, but the guns hadn't been pointed at her.

"The government — the Federation — is installing an autopilot in the commander's cabin," Ran said. "I'll check that he knows about it, but I don't think it would be a great idea to say anything more about what happened."

"I'll check," Wanda said. "Since it happened on my watch."

"Look, Babanguida called me because Cooper didn't see anything to report, even when Babanguida brought it up," Ran muttered defensively. "And just as a suggestion, that sort of fellow doesn't bluff worth a damn with a hand in the pocket."

"I'll remember that the next time I bluff somebody," Wanda said. She lifted the flat pistol from her jacket pocket, put it on safe, and dropped it back where it came from. "And I'll take care of Cooper. He's got a great career back in Maintenance where he came from."

Ran swallowed. "Look," he said, "I'm shook. I was on a hypnogogue learning Szgranian when the call came, and getting slammed up against a bulkhead didn't help a lot. I screwed up and I'm sorry."

Wanda started to giggle. "You're shook?" she said. "Can't imagine why. Me, I'm going to go change my pants, because I'm afraid I had a little accident when I saw those sub-machine guns."

She sobered. "You saw a problem and you fixed it, Ran," she said. "It's a pleasure to serve with you."

The way Second Officer Holly said that, Ran thought as his door spread shut behind her, he'd have kissed her if she weren't a fellow crewman.

The bridge of the *Empress of Earth* was in the center of the vessel, to make the current path for the controls as nearly as possible the same for each bow and stern pairing. The internal walls were real-time holograms fed by sensors on the *Empress*'s skin. The members of the Ship Side command group could watch a panorama of Port Northern, marred only by seams between the holographic panels.

The officers were all familiar with the illusion, but even Captain Samuel Kanawa paused on occasion when he caught the scene out of the corner of his eye and the wonder of it struck him anew.

The *Empress of Earth* was moments from undocking. Kanawa looked around deliberately now, a tall, spare figure with the mahogany complexion of his Maori ancestors. His blue Ship Side uniform was tailored so perfectly that it might have been cast as a part of his body.

On even the finest ship, in the best-appointed port in the known universe, there was a possibility of disaster on lift-off and landing. Kanawa never forgot that. Before every undocking, he let his eyes feast on the world that he might be leaving in a metaphysical instead of the planned physical sense.

The sensors ignored the *Empress* herself, so the eight tugs lashed to the starliner's bitts stood like great stones in a neolithic astronomical temple. The tugs were squat and as ugly as toads. Backwash from their own motors had blackened and rippled their skins, and multiple lift-offs and landings every day inevitably torqued their frames.

Appearance mattered only to passengers watching from the terminal as the tugs crawled into position. That wasn't important enough for the port authorities to attempt the impossible job of maintaining cosmetic beauty in the brutal conditions under which the little ships worked. Function was another matter. To the extent that any human contrivance was trustworthy, Port Northern's tugs could be trusted not to fail at the moment their thrust was most needed.

The *Empress*'s autopilot had checked the tugs' location, then calculated the precise vector for their motor outputs based on the thrust each had developed during its most recent use. When the tugs lighted up for undocking, Bridge — the artificial intelligence, not the physical location — would make such corrections as it found necessary.

Seligly, the new First Officer, had checked all Bridge's calculations. She'd captained an Earth-Martinique shuttle, and before that served as First Officer of the moderate-sized starliner *Queen of Naples*. Though Bridge had never failed and Seligly's background was beyond cavil, Captain Kanawa rechecked the figures. All were in order.

"Three minutes, sir," murmured the Third Officer

from his console. The seventeen officers and ratings on the *Empress*'s bridge were all seated, with the exception of Kanawa himself. It was the captain's choice to remain standing while his ship entered or left a gravity well, despite company regulations to the contrary.

"Very good, Mr. Rigney," Kanawa said. "Stay alert, ladies and gentlemen. Remember Captain Stoltzer."

The *Empress of Earth*'s own magnetic motors had been a low-frequency rumble for several minutes. Now they were joined in pairs by those of the tugs — the quick shock of lighting, a rising pulse as Bridge ran them up to test their response to its control, and then back to idle as another pair came on line. Bright blue light glimmered through the holographic panels, mimicking what was reflected from the frozen soil.

All eight tugs were ready. The *Empress* quivered like a horse at the starting post. Kanawa glanced down at his terminal. Actual outputs were all within one percent of those calculated. He noted with approval that Seligly was checking also.

"Are you familiar with Captain Stoltzer, Ms. Seligly?" Kanawa asked.

His First Officer looked up at him from her console. "No sir, I'm not," she admitted.

"Then you should have asked," Kanawa chided. "Never be afraid to ask for clarification. It might mean all our lives some day."

"Two minutes, sir," the Third Officer said, speaking into his console so as not to seem to be interrupting his captain.

"Thank you, Mr. Rigney," Kanawa said. The rhythm of the motors was building. There was an occasional jolt and flash as an output antenna cleared its throat of debris.

"It happened seventy years ago, Ms. Seligly," Kanawa resumed. "The captain under whom I trained, Captain Kawanishi, was on the bridge of the

Ensign with Stoltzer when it happened. She told the story at every docking or undocking, and I've tried to keep it current in my time."

"I've heard of the *Ensign*, sir," Seligly said apologetically.

"Yes, of course," Kanawa agreed. "A record holder in her day, though *The City of New York* had just bettered her time on the Earth-Harkona run. That was the prime route of the day."

Seligly nodded. The deck had a queasy feel, and the tugs could be seen to bob as their thrust edged toward perfect dynamic balance with the *Empress*'s mass.

"One minute, sir."

Kanawa cleared his throat. "Yes, thank you, Mr. Rigney," he said. He glanced at the levels on his display, then the lambent fury of the tug motors in holographic image.

"The *Ensign* was in Earth orbit, maneuvering to attach her tugs," the captain continued, "when Captain Stoltzer disengaged the autopilot and engaged the backup system. The *Ensign* began to drop out of orbit on her own. The First Officer just gaped. Captain Kawanishi — Third Officer she was then, of course — tried to take manual control, but Stoltzer grabbed her."

Kanawa chuckled. "That was back in the days when some people didn't think women were tough enough to be Ship Side officers. Kawanishi had her captain's ear in her mouth before they hit the deck together, but that wouldn't have helped a lot if the Second Officer hadn't switched the main autopilot back in and brought the *Ensign* to orbit again."

"Had he gone out of mind?" Seligly said in amazement.

"Exactly!" Kanawa said, beaming. "He was mad as a hatter. He'd programmed the backup system to drop the *Ensign* squarely onto New York City with no more braking thrust than it took to drop them out of orbit."

"That would have killed a hundred thousand people!" Seligly said.

"That would have killed tens of *millions* of people," Kanawa corrected. "The *Ensign* massed some forty kilotonnes — only a fraction of our size, but still enough to turn the whole metropolitan area into a crater if it hit at orbital velocity. It turned out —"

Kanawa paused to smile brightly at the horror on the First Officer's face.

" — that Captain Stoltzer was so disturbed at *The City of New York* bettering his *Ensign*'s time by six hours that he'd determined to wipe them off the face of the Earth. Not the ship but the city itself."

Seligly shook her head.

"Lift-off," said Rigney. Bridge raised the tugs' motors to full thrust over a ten-second span, while the *Empress*'s own motors built up power at a cautiously greater rate. The huge vessel vibrated but did not seem to move.

"So watch me, ladies and gentlemen!" Captain Kanawa shouted over the bone-deep throb of the magnetic motors. "Because anyone on the bridge, myself included, may be every bit as crazy as Captain Stoltzer!"

With a roar like rising thunder, the *Empress of Earth* mounted toward the stars.

• IN TRANSIT: EARTH TO NEVASA

It was barely ship's midnight, but more than half the celebrants had melted away in pairs and larger gatherings from the whirl of First Night. Ran Colville had danced two numbers out of every three, chatted to a circle of passengers — mostly female — during every break; and turned down at least a dozen propositions, ranging from the subtle to the extremely direct, also mostly involving women.

This was the first chance he'd had to draw a deep breath. He did so, standing beside the holographic facade of the Aemillian Basilica, as he looked over the double ring of tables and out onto the center of the huge room cleared for dancing.

The gaiety in the Social Hall wasn't far removed from the orgies of delight at the end of a major war. In the course of a voyage, a starliner became a solid and permanent world by implication. At the first undocking, though — no matter how experienced the traveler — there was a pang as the planet vanished, leaving the passengers with only the work of human hands between themselves and the void.

First Night was an affirmation of life regained. Straitlaced passengers abandoned caution for one night, while those who looked for thrills of every persuasion found rich pickings.

"Sighting in on one for later?" Wanda Holly asked unexpectedly from beside Ran's shoulder.

"Nope," he answered with a slow smile that began before his head turned to meet the gaze of his fellow officer. "Just wondering how long I need to keep this up. After all, it's not my regular watch."

He cleared his throat. "And I don't know what you may have heard, but I don't mix business and pleasure. Right now, I'm an officer of the *Empress*."

Ran looked back at the dance floor. Commander Kneale was there, with a woman of twice his age and girth . . . and very possibly enough money to buy the *Empress*, had Trident Starlines been willing to sell. Several Rialvans watched stolidly from the fringes, and a pair of K'Chitkans danced with exaggerated sways of their bodies.

If Ran was correct about the K'Chitkans' crests, both dancers were male. He didn't even want to guess what that meant.

Many of the human passengers wore period garb or more exotic costumes. A Terran female was draped in leaves like a medieval Wild Woman, and three male mining engineers from Hobilo wore suits suggesting carnivorous bipedal reptiles from their homeworld. The reptiles, at least as reproduced by the costumes, had prominent genitals.

Brief masks were common. Passengers couldn't really hide their identities from one another, but the pretense of anonymity made it easier for some to get into the spirit of First Night.

"For afterwards, then," Wanda prodded. She sounded amused. "When we're off duty on the ground."

Ran sighed inwardly. A ship the size of the *Empress of Earth* was bound to have crewmen who'd served with Ran Colville in the past, and he supposed he did have something of a reputation. Still, it wasn't as though he'd ever made a set at a passenger. Not infrequently it worked the other way . . . and occasionally there'd been contact on the ground when he was off duty, that was true.

But he didn't see it was anybody's business save his and the lady's. Not Lieutenant Holly's business, at any rate. He'd never so much as patted her hand!

Aloud, Ran said, "You make it sound like a job that you have to work at, Wanda. If I felt that way about it, I'd ... watch foot-racing instead."

"Ah, Captain?" said a voice from behind the two officers. They both turned, uncertain whether the speaker was a throaty woman or a high-voiced man.

A man, dressed as a Roman soldier: quite young, and quite obviously nervous.

Wanda peeled off expertly to field him while Ran nodded and moved away. The Second Officer's cheerful "Welcome to First Night, sir," blended with the passenger's, "I was just wondering how often you've been shipwrecked?"

Hard to tell whether the poor guy was worried, or if he thought a shipwreck was romantic. It *wasn't* romantic, though if a starliner's systems failed in the sidereal universe, there was at least a chance the lifeboats would save the people aboard her. . . .

There was a stir from the entrance directly across the Social Hall where a party of Szgranians had appeared. The clan mistress, Lady Scour, was accompanied by four females of her entourage.

Commander Kneale was walking his dance partner back to the table where her husband waited. Ran saw the commander miss a step, then regain his composure when he realized that no Szgranian warriors were present. They had a right to use any of the First Class facilities as they chose, but the potential for trouble *that* posed in the loose atmosphere of First Night was terrifying to anybody who felt responsible for the consequences.

The orchestra was eleven pieces and live. Music synthesized by an artificial intelligence could be proven to be better by any number of objective criteria — but enjoyment was a subjective reaction, and the humans who made up the majority of the *Empress*'s First Class passengers overwhelmingly preferred live performers on authentic instruments.

The first violin acted as conductor. She glanced toward the doorway and called a direction to her fellows. The orchestra segued from a Franz Lehar waltz into a Szgranian tune in which the double bass rumbled the main melody while the other ten instruments, all strings, wailed in a complex and wholly separate pattern.

The Szgranians froze for a moment. Then Lady Scour strode into the center of the area cleared for dancing. One of her attendants protested by flinging herself to the floor in front of her mistress, but the lady stepped onto her and over with an extra twist of her heel.

It was a case of a little learning being a dangerous thing. The orchestra was playing Szgranian music, all right, but it was from a ritual which required both female and male participants . . . and there were no male Szgranians in the Social Hall. The load of hypnochunked information which Ran's mind had received but not fully assimilated told him that much. He hadn't any idea what the result was going to be. *He* wasn't a Szgranian expert either.

Lady Scour began to dance, waving her hands in a stylized pattern while her right leg beat time with the deliberation of a horse counting. She looked about the room, her gaze icy.

What the hell. Ran walked across the floor and joined her.

Lady Scour's eyes were the color of amethysts. The orbits were rounder than a human's, but the effect was exotic rather than freakish . . . to Ran Colville, at any rate.

Their bodies came into synchrony, two meters apart.

Ran had been following the music, while the Szgranian clan mistress led the notes. She adjusted her timing to match the human norm before he even realized the cause of the initial disjunction.

Ran didn't know the proper motions at a conscious level, but so long as he left matters to the instinctive where the hypnogogue had imprinted the knowledge, he was fine. At any rate, his arms *were* moving, and he supposed it was proper because Lady Scour looked a great deal more friendly than she had when she began dancing alone.

The piece ended. "Lord have mercy!" Ran muttered, louder than he'd intended to speak.

Spectators all around the room began to clap.

Lord have mercy!

"And you are Junior Lieutenant . . . ?" Lady Scour asked. The pale skin of her forehead was lightly frosted with perspiration. One of the attendants scampered up and used the tail of her sash to dry her mistress. Ran was shocked and amazed when another tiny Szgranian female wiped *his* forehead.

"Randall Colville, ma'am," he said. Szgranian clan mistresses were supposed to be sharp, but most human passengers wouldn't have been able to identify the rank markings on an officer's uniform. "Third Officer, Staff Side."

Lady Scour waved a hand before her face in a place-holding gesture, a sort of physical throat clearing. Close up, the six-armed torso was odd but not unpleasant to view. Her pale green tunic clung to her bosom. Bosoms.

Her eyes focused back on Ran. "*Oh promise me now Clerk Colville,*" she sang in a high, clear voice, "*or 'twill cost ye muckle strife —*"

How had she known *that* old Terran ballad? But Ran knew it, knew it well from the loot his father brought back from the Long Troubles on Hobilo.

"Ride never by the Wells of Slane, if you would live and brook your life."

"Now speak no more my lusty dame," Ran sang back to her, and nobody'd *ever* claimed he had a singing voice, but you did what you had to do. *"Now speak no more of that to me.*

"Did I never see a fair woman but I would sin with her body?"

Both of them began laughing with an enthusiasm that must have sounded mad to onlookers; but the onlookers hadn't been in the dance, and the bond from that short ritual — an interlude from the harvest festival — was surprising.

"You knew the song!" Lady Scour said. "I've found that your people never know your own songs."

Ran shrugged. "Well, there's a lot of history," he said, a diplomatic answer. "How did *you* happen to know it?"

Szgranian civilization had reached its present level long before humans began raising megaliths, much less pyramids. Szgrane hadn't changed since then, however, until contact with human starfarers forced the static society to adapt.

The clan mistress smiled. "The same way you know *The Dance of the Grubs Building Their Cocoon,*" she said. "When I learned one of the officers on the ship that would carry me was named Colville, I learned about Colvilles."

The smile brightened. "Are you like your ancestor, then?" Lady Scour added.

"I don't know about ancestor. . . ." Ran said. One of the Szgranian attendants offered him a tiny tumbler of carved glass, Szgranian workmanship and worth the price of First Class passage on the *Empress*. Lady Scour drank from another, making the contents last for three minuscule sips.

Ran carefully touched the liquid with his tongue. It was chilled water, poured from one of the muff-like portmanteaus all the attendants carried.

"As I say," Ran resumed, "I don't claim the relationship . . . but it's been suggested that I like, ah, fair women, yes."

For Clerk Colville had indeed gone to see the lady, mermaid rather, at the Wells of Slane; not the last man to go where his pecker led, nor the last to get in trouble for it.

The orchestra resumed playing. A circle of onlookers surrounded Ran and the Szgranians at a respectful distance. Lady Scour was a sight to be remarked on under any circumstances, and the bi-specific dance made that true in spades.

If Lady Scour had researched "Colville," with Ran only assigned to the *Empress of Earth* seventy-two hours before undocking, then she'd certainly done the same with the names of all the other officers aboard the starliner. There wasn't anything unusual about that performance. Szgranian nobility had virtually nothing to do except consider literature, genealogy, and honor. From what the hypnogogue had "told" Ran, a decision about the garments to be worn to a festival could absorb days of a court's discussion.

"I'm interested that you used only the upper-arms motions in the Cocoon Dance," Lady Scour said.

Her four attendants fluttered their multiple hands in front of their faces. Flowing sleeves made the attendants' gestures look like the display behavior of butterflies.

"Well, ma'am," Ran said. "I'm, ah, brachially challenged." He spread his two hands, emphasizing the obvious. "Frankly, the hypnogogue must have done the best it could with what was available. I didn't have a lot of conscious input."

Lady Scour trilled another long laugh. She reached out with her upper pair of arms and touched her index fingers to Ran's. "So you didn't understand the significance of upper-arm gestures alone?" she asked.

"No ma'am," Ran said.

That wasn't in the data he'd been chunked. Maybe the information didn't exist in the system, maybe the way he'd been pulled out of the sequence to deal with the government types had cost him a piece of Szgranian custom that would have been *really* useful to know. He thought he could guess what it was now, though.

"Come," said Lady Scour decisively. She put her left middle hand on the crook of Ran's right elbow, a human gesture which she had obviously learned for the purpose. "You will act as my escort tonight."

"Yes ma'am," Ran said. His screw-up — his turning the ritual into a mating dance — might have put paid to his career with Trident Starlines. Lady Scour could ask Ran to turn backflips across the Social Hall without getting an argument from him.

She walked toward the refreshment buffet. Ran kept pace, and the four attendants followed in pairs.

"Normally custom wouldn't permit a person of my status to appear in public without a male escort," Lady Scour said conversationally, "but as I told Rawsl, 'I *am* the clan mistress.' Still, it's better to obey custom whenever circumstances permit. You *will* protect me, won't you?"

She laughed.

"Yes, ma'am," Ran agreed. "From whatever threatens."

"Except from yourself," said the Szgranian, and she laughed again with overtones that Ran Colville had heard often in the flirting voices of human females.

● NEVASA

The magnetic motors began to throb as Ran entered the Starlight Bar. Bridge was preparing to drop the *Empress of Earth* out of her parking orbit above Nevasa.

The bar in the *Empress*'s prow was more crowded than Ran had ever imagined he would see it. There were chairs for fifty, chromed frameworks that slid above the deck without friction but locked safely into place when a passenger sat down. A few seats were empty, but there were standees around the autobar also.

Ran saw Wanda Holly near the center of the room, seated at a table with two drinks — clear, with lemon slices — waiting on it. He sat down in the seat the second drink saved and said, "Umm, what did you need, Wanda?"

He wasn't out of breath, but he'd moved pretty fast from the main lounge when he got the call, *Ms. Holly requests your presence in the Starlight Bar at your earliest convenience*. Not an emergency, maybe, but it wasn't standard operating procedure either.

"You've never been on Nevasa, have you, Ran?" Wanda asked. She raised her glass and offered him a silent toast. "Hope you like sparkling water," she added.

"If it's wet, I drink it," Ran said absently. He didn't drink like he had on the Cold Crew, but he wouldn't have turned down something stronger. All crewmen were on standby during docking maneuvers, but Ran had been officially off-watch for the past thirty minutes.

He considered the Second Officer's question. "No," he said, "I haven't been here before. Worried about the authorities because of the war scare, you mean?"

Wanda shrugged. She was looking out the holographic panel that mimicked the curve of the starliner's bow. "That'll be a problem, sure. But right now, I just wanted you to see what it's like to land on Nevasa."

She glanced around the bar. She wore her hair in a brilliant blond swirl today. Ran liked blondes, but he thought Wanda probably looked her best as the brunette her genes had made her. "That's what everybody's here for," she explained. "People who've landed on Nevasa before or talked to somebody who has."

"Oh . . . " murmured a dozen throats.

Ran looked through the clear forward bulkhead. The sky around the *Empress of Earth* was beginning to fluoresce.

Streaks of bubbling color rippled through the stratosphere, similar to Earth's auroras but momentary and a thousand times brighter. The *Empress* was dropping slowly, at a shallow angle, so she made about as much motion forward as down. The light bloomed from her magnetic motors and those of the eight tugs which coupled the starliner in orbit, streaming back over the ship and her wake through the disturbed air.

It was perhaps the most beautiful thing Ran had ever seen in his life.

"Nevasa's atmosphere has a high proportion of noble gases," Wanda explained. "A high-density magnetic flux excites them. It's the most beautiful thing I've ever seen in my life."

A cold, green flare bathed the vessel, covering the bulkhead like a lambent curtain. Passengers gasped in awe and delight.

Wanda looked at Ran. "The thing I don't under-stand," she said, "is . . . "

Her voice trailed off as three pulses of topaz yellow followed the green, drawing her eyes by reflex.

"Is . . . ?" Ran said softly.

"Is how they can live here and rush into a war, not that the war's all their fault," she said to complete the thought.

"I suppose," Ran said as he stared wide-eyed at a light show the size of a continent, "they don't see things the way outsiders do. . . . "

"This war," cried Miss Oanh from the center of the family room, paneled with painted screens, "is evil!"

"War with Grantholm," said her father gently, "is probably inevitable and certainly morally right."

Mr. Lin knew his long service in Nevasa's Ministry of External Affairs was the cause of many of his family problems. His daughter had spent half of her eighteen years on foreign worlds with him. The three years on Earth, where Mr. Lin had been ambassador before being brought back to the ministry, had been par-ticularly unfortunate in forming Oanh's attitudes regarding planetary honor — and filial piety.

Lin cleared his throat and went on, "I realize that you feel you have a right to your own opinion, but please keep it to yourself for the time being. I become a plenipotentiary when I arrive on Tellichery. So long as we remain on Nevasa, I do not have the prerogative of overruling the security services."

Mr. Lin's aides in the open, adjacent rooms which served as Lin's home office discretely avoided staring. The squad of gray-clad guards seemed equally focused on people other than the minister and his daughter. They watched the aides and the petitioners waiting in the outer office. Many of the latter were foreign nationals.

The three-meter area cleared around the perimeter of the family room's open doors was a result of the civilians' nervousness about the guards' openly carried weapons.

Almost certainly some of the guards were members of the Counterintelligence Bureau. The chances were good that one or more of the personnel from Lin's own ministry reported to the bureau as well.

"It's *never* morally right to kill other human beings!" his daughter snapped.

Lin sighed inwardly. Oanh hadn't wanted to leave Earth, where her friends were, and she was even angrier to be uprooted again in less than six months. He would have preferred to leave her on Nevasa, since in most senses she was capable of looking out for herself—

But Oanh's anger at the situation came out in the form of statements that were likely to be viewed as treasonous if war with Grantholm broke out.

When war broke out. Mr. Lin wouldn't have been sent on this mission were war not inevitable and alliance, military alliance, with Tellichery not a crucial factor in that war's outcome.

"There may be no war," he said aloud, in the calm voice that he knew grated on his daughter's nerves worse than a shriek would have done. Lin couldn't help it. In a tense argument he became preternaturally calm, which was a reason for his career success . . . but had driven his wife into the arms of a grain merchant on Skeuse and was looking as though it might drive his daughter away as well.

Oanh sniffed.

"And in any case," her father continued, "the behavior of the Grantholm military leaves it open to question whether they can be considered human."

Lin's spacious home overlooked the heart of Nevasa City to the east, and Con Ron Landing, the starport, to the west. An incoming vessel and its tugs formed a bright ring above the family room's clear ceiling. The panels of smoked polycarbonate were mounted in flexible troughs so that they did not rattle audibly, but the starliner's roar made them vibrate and caused the image to quiver.

"What a *fascist* pronouncement," Oanh said without looking at him. "And I suppose only the military is going to die in this moral crusade?"

"Oanh," Mr. Lin said. "Please."

He knew it was his fault. She'd never had a proper home, even before her mother fled. Lin's duties required that he work eighteen hours on those days he didn't work twenty-four. Servants could care for Oanh and teach her — but they couldn't give orders that the strong-willed daughter of an increasingly high official had to accept.

For all that, she hadn't become wild. Just opinionated; and under present conditions, voicing the wrong opinions could be more dangerous than drunken sprees.

"Father," Oanh replied — but at least she did lower her voice so that it might not be heard over the pulse of the starship, "you know as well as I do that this war isn't necessary. It isn't even over things, it's just perceptions. There's no excuse for it!"

"There may be no war," Lin repeated softly.

To an extent, his daughter was right. A nation can always avoid war, almost always, by rolling over on its back and baring its belly. Whether that could ever be considered a valid alternative, however, was another matter entirely.

Private firms on Grantholm and Nevasa had together begun to develop Apogee, a world with a climate that was moderate and also unusually stable because the planet had no axial tilt. Nevasa saw Apogee as a rice basket, while the Grantholm entrepreneurs developed resorts on their sections.

Both plans had been set out publicly before any colonization took place. The problem arose when the Grantholm government — not the private developers — noticed that the population in the Nevasan sections was a hundred times greater than that in those under Grantholm control. Rice is a labor-intensive crop. Nevasa was importing a labor force from disadvantaged regions of Earth — from the Orient of Earth.

Grantholm claimed that the pattern of development was a plot to bring the entire planet under Nevasan suzerainty . . . and Mr. Lin knew that in the secret councils of the Nevasan government, that possibility had indeed been floated. All Nevasan activities on Apogee to date had been perfectly in line with the original agreements, however.

The arrogance of the Grantholm delegation which *ordered* Nevasa to cease shipping colonists to Apogee would have been quite unacceptable to any sovereign government. Certainly to the government of Nevasa, which had the military potential to teach Grantholm the lesson for which that world had been begging for so long.

Probably. And certainly with the support of Tellichery. Almost certainly with the full support of Tellichery.

"Oanh," he said, "I understand your feelings."

Lin didn't know whether or not that was true. As with so many of the statements he had to make, truth or falsity did not matter as much as appropriateness did.

"But you must understand," he continued over his daughter's attempt to reply, "that honor is not merely a word."

"Neither is life, father!" Oanh said.

Any further discussion was lost in the resonating boom of the *Empress of Earth* landing.

* * *

Transient Block, the ground facility on Nevasa for Trident's Third Class passengers, was neither a slave pen nor a prison. It wasn't a palace, either, and Ran didn't like the sound of the door banging behind him to shut out the soft night.

The block consisted of three levels of rooms built around a central court. It housed Third Class passengers while the *Empress* was on the ground. That way the on-board accommodations could be thoroughly cleaned, and the human cargo got a degree of variety when that was possible.

Residents now crowded the court, the stairs, and the interior walkways serving the rooms on the higher levels. The speaker addressing them through a hand-held amplifier spoke in an unfamiliar language, but the translator on Ran's shoulder chirped, "Join us, then, brothers and sisters, so that you *personally* can live better lives — "

Mohacks was close to the door with a woman wearing a green Trident ground staff uniform and a set expression. From the look of her, she was a local or at least of oriental descent.

"Sir!" said Mohacks. "These *indigs* — " starship crewmen rarely had much use for ground-based personnel, but Mohacks made "indigenous staff" sound like "dog shit" " — let in unauthorized people and — "

"They're not unauthorized!" the woman, a supervisor, snapped. "They're Nevasan government officials, and this *is* Nevasa, *sailor*."

"Sailor" had the intonations of "cat vomit."

"Your enlistment will be on the same terms as that of Nevasan citizens," said the translator through Ran's right earpiece, "and after the war you will be granted citizenship of — "

The speaker wore civilian dress, a smooth-fitting business suit of rusty color with white accents. The four men with him were in gray uniforms. The leader carried a small pistol in a ludicrous little holster dangling from a broad Sam Browne belt, but the sub-machine guns of his subordinates weren't just for show. Babanguida stood in the midst of the group with a set look on his face. Two Trident ground staffers were nearby also, smiling in calm approval.

Ran unspooled a transceiver disk from his commo unit and set it against the doorframe. Thousands of eyes were turned on the man speaking; the building breathed with the crowd's anticipation.

"I warn you!" the ground-staff supervisor cried. "I've disabled the gas dischargers! Using force on a high official of the — "

" — free the universe from racist Grantholm tyranny!" the translator said.

"Block," Ran ordered the building's artificial intelligence, a modular unit common to most large-scale Trident facilities throughout the operating area, "give me a feedback loop from the government gentleman's amp through your own PA sys — "

The screech preceded Ran's final syllable.

" — tem!"

The crowd bellowed in pain and fear. Ran hadn't said anything about amplitude, but the AI made the right decision: more is better. Ran winced at the impact, and the Nevasan guards whipped around with their weapons raised.

The squeal stopped. The Nevasan official had dropped his amplifier. He picked it up again, looking around in angry question.

"You can't do — " the supervisor said to Ran.

"Block," Ran said. "Keep it up until I countermand the order."

He grinned at the local woman. Not bad looking at all, though ground-staff uniforms didn't flatter females. Not that it mattered, of course.

"Sure he can, girlie," Mohacks said. "This is Mr. Colville!"

Ran realized that he'd just been promoted, in a manner of speaking.

The official must have spoken again with the amp still keyed to his voice, because the PA system shrieked like a horse being disemboweled. Babanguida bent close to the man and spoke into his ear. A Nevasan guard prodded the rating with the muzzle of his submachine gun. Babanguida ignored him.

Babanguida and the official moved toward Ran. The local man protested. Babanguida grinned, and the armed guards fluttered like birds around a blacksnake.

"Block," Ran said, "give me the PA for a moment. Ladies and gentlemen — " his voice slapped with phase-timed clarity from all the speakers in the Transient Block " — we apologize for this problem. Please return to your sleeping quarters while we sort it out."

The speech ended with another painful squeal. It might have been a fault in the system, but Ran had noticed that with some AIs, "intelligence" was the operative word rather than "artificial." In any case, the jagged blade of sound got the keyed-up crowd moving obediently.

"Whose idea was it, I wonder," Ran said mildly, "to lower the barriers between male and female sections?"

He was looking at the supervisor. There was nothing mild about his eyes.

She grimaced and turned away.

"This man — " snarled the Nevasan official as he waved his amplifier in Ran's face. Feedback howling through the PA system drove a mass cry from the crowd.

Babanguida took the amp from the stunned local and switched it off. He handed the unit back. His smile could have lighted the building.

The Nevasan swallowed. "This man says you're

responsible for . . . ?" he said. The sonic clawing had cowed him.

Ran saluted. "Yessir," he said. "Lieutenant Randall Colville, Third Officer of the *Empress of Earth* — and in charge here unless one of my superiors arrives. And you are . . . ?"

"I'm Level Six Minister Thach," the official said, regaining some his poise. "I demand that you stop this interference with my duties!"

"Sir," Ran said, "Trident Starlines is contracted to deliver these passengers to certain destinations. Nobody on board the *Empress* has the authority to change that. I — "

"The Government of Nevasa, which I represent, has the right to recruit troops on its own soil," Thach said. "Stop this nonsense!"

"Sir," Ran repeated, "I don't question your right, it's not my business to even discuss your rights. My duties require — "

The Nevasan officer muttered something to his subordinates. Two of them thrust their sub-machine guns into Ran's ribs.

Ran began to laugh. "Blow me away and your superiors'll throw you to the sharks so fast your head'll spin!"

"Stop that!" Thach snarled to his uniformed contingent. "Stop that now!"

The guns jerked away from Ran's side.

Passengers had paused to watch. The PA system gave a low-frequency growl that moved them on again. Trident ought to give this AI a medal. . . .

"You, ma'am," Ran said to the ground-staff supervisor. He hadn't caught her name tape. "Your folks had better help with getting passengers back where they belong. *Now*."

He didn't raise his voice, but the last syllable had teeth.

The supervisor looked from the ship's officer to Thach, looked down, and began to sidle away.

"You have no right to do this!" Thach said.

"Sir, *please*," Ran said. "I can't make policy. I don't doubt you've got the right to do whatever you're doing, but I've got to do my duty until one of my superiors changes that duty. Take it up with them, sir. Please."

"You're on Nevasan soil," said the uniformed officer. "The ship may be extraterritorial, but this building isn't. I could arrest you for insult to an official in the performance of his duties."

Thach hadn't made the threat, but he waited intently for the result of it.

Ran nodded. "Yessir," he said. "And then your diplomats and Earth's diplomats would discuss it, and it wouldn't do anything about the question of Nevasa recruiting transients shipped on labor contracts — which is the only thing that matters to us standing here. But I expect you to do your duty, as I'm doing mine."

Ran's face wore an expression of sad calm. Mr. Thach glared at him.

Thach gave the amplifier to the uniformed officer with almost the crispness of a blow. "Come along," he snapped as he stepped to the door.

Ran opened it quickly. Thach turned and added over his shoulder, "We'll be back!"

"Yessir," said Ran. He didn't doubt it in the least.

Ran closed the door. His ratings grinned at him in delight. The ground-staff personnel had disappeared, helping chivvy passengers back into their dormitories.

Ran could understand how the locals had felt, trapped in the gray area between patriotism and loyalty to their employer. They'd made the best decision they could. In the larger scheme of things, it didn't matter a hoot that their decision had made life for a few of the *Empress of Earth*'s crew harder.

But if they thought Ran Colville wasn't going to see that every one of the bastards on duty tonight at the Transient Block was fired, they were dreaming.

"What do we do when they come back, sir?" Mohacks asked. It was a real question, not a nice way of saying, "We're shit outa luck when they come back."

Ran touched his transceiver to the doorjamb again. "Block," he said, "get ground transport for the full Third Class list here at once. I'm authorizing overtime for the drivers and support people."

He looked at his ratings and shivered with sudden relaxation. "What we do," he said, "is make sure that all contract passengers are back aboard Earth territory *before* that gentleman can organize a better try. It's after office hours, after all. We ought to be able to manage it."

He took a deep breath and added, "Anyhow, we'll give it a good try."

Without a pause, Ran went on, "Block, patch me through to the *Empress*. The Purser had better have Third Class ready, because the passengers are going to be back, ready or not!"

It was three hours before Ran got back to the *Empress*.

The trouble with a white uniform, Ran thought as he strode into the Embarkation Hall, *is that it really shows grime*. Fatigues were the proper garb for directing trucks loaded with Third Class passengers around a detour, but the first part of the job that called him to the Transient Block had required all the swank he could muster.

As it turned out, he should have stopped to change instead of coming straight to Commander Kneale to report. Kneale was in the Embarkation Hall, where nearly a hundred passengers were processing already, even though it was a full twelve standard hours before the *Empress* undocked. Ran was a lot dirtier than he'd realized until he reached the hall's bright lights. Passengers gave him nervous, hunted glances, and the commander looked concerned instead of furious.

"Trouble?" Kneale murmured when he was close enough to Ran that they wouldn't be overheard. The two officers stood by a pilaster, looking out the broad gangway toward the terminal's lighted concourse. Nevasa wasn't Earth — all the human colonies together weren't Earth — but Con Ron Landing passed a tremendous quantity of commerce in its own right.

"Not really," said Ran. "Traffic's really screwed up, is all. There's a rally or something in the middle of the boulevard, so we had to take back streets to the terminal. The trucks don't have commo, so I played traffic cop at the second corner."

He glanced ruefully at what had been a white sleeve. "It just *looks* like I got dragged all the way from Transient Block. Sorry. I'll go change."

The clothing and features of the incoming passengers suggested a variety of ethnic backgrounds. Most of them were foreigners leaving Nevasa as the planet teetered above the chasm of war . . . though there were clumps of Nevasan women and children as well.

"Umm," said Kneale. "Well, I think you've earned yourself some sleep. Why — "

The terminal slidewalk brought a party of well-dressed Nevasans toward the *Empress of Earth*. They were escorted by gray-uniformed guards who jogged beside the slidewalk with weapons in their hands.

"Thach was quicker off the mark than I'd have guessed," Ran said mildly while his mind raced. If they raised the gangplank —

Useless; the machinery wouldn't respond fast enough, and half the crew was on leave in Nevasa City besides. Anyway, Commander Kneale was in charge. . . .

Kneale strode to meet the problem at the lower end of the gangway. Ran fell into step at his superior's heel.

"Good evening, gentlemen," Kneale said in with loud cheerfulness. "Welcome to the *Empress of Earth*."

There were nine Nevasan civilians. Eight of them were virtually indistinguishable, though the group included two females and the age spread was about thirty standard years. They all wore rigidly proper clothing — "proper" in higher official circles on any human planet — and they cultivated blank, vaguely disapproving expressions.

The ninth member of the party was odd girl out: probably not as young as her fine bone structure suggested to Ran, but certainly still in her teens. She was dressed in London chic, a black and yellow frock which spiked over the right shoulder and fell off the other. Tights of translucent matching fabric encased the right leg, while the left was bare to her ankle boots.

A nice face, though angry now, and not a bad pair of legs at all. . . .

But the important thing was that if that girl was in the party, it wasn't an official demand to enroll contract passengers into the armed forces of Nevasa.

"I am Minister Lin," the eldest of the civilians said to Commander Kneale. "You have a suite booked for me and my staff, I believe?"

"Yes indeed, Minister," Kneale replied. Only an expert would have caught the relief in his voice. "The Asoka Suite. You're boarding early?"

He made a gesture behind his back. Several senior stewards stepped toward the cabin luggage arriving on floating carts.

"Father has to arrive early," the girl said in an overly audible voice. She glared at Kneale. "So that he can be sure that it's safe for military secrets!"

Mr. Lin coughed. "You're connected to all ground media while we're docked, of course?" he said.

"Of course," Kneale agreed. "Ah — your attendants will have to surrender their weapons before boarding, you know, sir. They'll be returned — "

"That's impossible!" snapped one of the civilian

aides. "They're responsible for the minister's security."

"Trident Starlines is responsible for the security of all its passengers," the commander replied calmly.

Ran looked toward the girl. His face was expressionless to hide his anger at this latest problem.

The Nevasans were being deliberately obtuse. Trident Starlines made no attempt to restrict what passengers had in their hold baggage. On Calicheman, pistols were as standard an item of dress as hats against the fierce sunlight, and many of the fringe worlds were harsher places yet.

The Nevasan security men could have their submachine guns as soon as they left the ship at any landfall. Nobody but Trident officers had guns aboard the vessel. As for the minister's safety against a mob of other passengers — given the facilities of the *Empress*'s imperial suites, there was no need at all for him to leave his quarters during the voyage.

The girl saw Ran looking, she thought, at her. She turned her head in embarrassment. Obviously, she was more inhibited than she wanted her father to think.

"That's impossible!" the aide repeated.

"Then it's impossible for Minister Lin to board the *Empress*," Kneale replied. "I'm truly very sorry."

Lin looked at his aide. "Oh, don't be a fool, Tran," he said. "I haven't got all day to stand here and argue about trivia."

He nodded to Kneale. "If you'll direct me to my suite, then?"

The commander bowed and gestured a steward forward. Ran sighed and stepped back. A shower would feel good, and he'd have to see what Housekeeping could do with this uniform. . . .

A company of infantry, helmeted and wearing mottled battledress, double-timed toward the *Empress* in a column of fours that filled the slidewalk. At a shouted command, they jumped from the moving walk with a crash of bootheels and clattering equipment. Two of the men upended when their boots hit the fixed flooring.

"Minister Lin," said Kneale in a hard voice. "What is this?"

A non-com sorted the troops into formation while their commissioned officer trotted up the gangplank. Ordinary passengers fled the Embarkation Hall with glances over their shoulders.

Lin looked at the soldiers disdainfully. "Not my department, Commander," he said.

"Are you the captain?" the military officer demanded.

"I'm Commander Hiram Kneale and I'm in charge here, sir," Kneale said. "On behalf of Trident Starlines, that is. Minister Lin of course represents your government."

The soldier did a violent double-take. Ran smiled internally. Kneale had played his cards perfectly — though nobody was really sure what was trump in a situation this confused.

"I'm Major Dung," the soldier resumed after a moment's deliberation. "My men are here to search your vessel and detain enemy aliens."

"Has war been declared, then?" Ran said, knowing that the *Empress*'s AI would have informed him if there *had* been a declaration.

"War has *not* been declared," Lin said sharply — to the major, not Ran. "Whose orders do you claim to be executing, sir?"

"I — " blurted Dung. "I — my orders came directly from the Ministry of Defense."

"Vessels retain the nationality of their flags by international compact," Commander Kneale noted, looking at his fingernails. "Armed invasion of the *Empress of Earth* would be an act of war directed against Federated Earth."

"Precisely *who* gave you these orders, Major?" Lin demanded. "And don't tell me the building did!"

"Ah, Minh — " Dung said.

"Field Marshal Minh?" Lin cried. "I can't believe he would have done anything so clearly *ultra vires!*"

"No sir," the major mumbled. He didn't know *ultra vires* meant "beyond his authority," but he *did* know he was in way over his head. "No, it was General Minh in Operations Planning. . . . "

Mr. Lin glared at Dung as though the soldier had just urinated on the carpet. "Please take your comic opera company out of here, Major," he said. "You can have no conception of the trouble you almost caused by your illegal and ill-advised actions."

Dung swallowed, saluted, and scurried back to his troops. They looked like recent inductees, clumsy and nervous. Which didn't make Ran feel better about what had nearly happened. At least with veterans, you could be pretty sure they weren't going to shoot you unless they meant to.

"Thank you, Minister," Commander Kneale said quietly as the troops straggled aboard an out-bound slidewalk.

"It was nothing," said the girl. "Father enjoys bullying people."

Ran winced.

"To my suite then, please," said Mr. Lin as though he hadn't heard his daughter's comment.

The Nevasan delegation moved off, guided by the Chief Steward. Two of the uniformed guards collected the weapons of the whole detachment and disappeared with them toward the VIP lounge. The guns would return in a few minutes, discreetly cased in a piece of luggage stamped "not wanted on voyage."

"Nice job, sir," Ran murmured to his superior.

Commander Kneale looked very tired. "Sometimes you get lucky, my boy," he said. He sighed. "I was going to give you the rest of the night off. Instead — can you find the Terran embassy?"

Ran shrugged. "Sure," he said. "Bridge can

download me a map. It may be a little tricky getting there tonight, what with everything."

"I want a detachment of Earth troops here at the gangway," Kneale said. "There don't have to be many, just enough for a tripwire. Terran troops are a — more believable warning than me spouting international law may be. And the embassy doesn't want an incident any better than I do."

Ran saluted half-seriously. "I'll see what I can do," he said.

He thought of changing his uniform but decided not to. Chances were, he was going to look a lot worse by the time he made it to where he was going.

The lobby of the Terran embassy was three stories high. It was supported by fluted pillars of polished black stone on conglomerate bases. Glass light-fountains springing from the foreheads of stylized alabaster horses accented the decor.

Ran found it a haven of peace after the outer court full of shouting, crying people, many of them clutching children and bundles of personal belongings.

"Tough time, sir?" asked the sergeant commanding the six Terran soldiers who'd passed Ran into the building.

"Tough enough," Ran murmured. He straightened his uniform jacket. When the door opened for the Trident officer, at least a dozen other people had tried to force their way past him. "Are all those folks out there Earth citizens?"

"Not a one of them," the guard said. "They're fringe-worlders and they're scared, that's all. They figure Earth can protect them. West Bumfuck or wherever they come from sure-hell can't."

"Mr. Colville?" called a plump civilian from the second balcony. He looked about Ran's age or a few years younger. "I'm very sorry you've had this useless trip. I told your Commander Kneale — "

"I'm coming up!" Ran interrupted in an artificially cheerful voice as he headed for the stairs.

Kneale had called ahead to announce him — without that, Ran would never have gotten through the embassy doors at this hour and set of circumstances — but the whole reason for his presence was to make a face-to-face request. It's harder to turn down a person than it is a voice.

The stairs were of the same black stone as the columns, but inset grip pads prevented the treads from being lethal to someone in a hurry, as Ran was now. As he passed the second-floor landing, three people whispering in the open hallway turned and stared at him. Their faces were as frightened and uncertain as those of the crowd outside the building.

The man who'd called to Ran shifted his weight from one foot to the other as though he had a desperate need to run for the bathroom. "Really, Mr. Colville," he said, "there's nothing more to —"

The third-floor hallway had doors on the outer perimeter and overlooked the lobby on the inside. Paintings of women wearing 17th-century dresses covered the ceiling in broad, filigreed-silver frames. Your taxes at work . . .

Money spent on expensive buildings wasn't going to get anybody killed. Hiring dithering fools to make decisions in a crisis just might do that.

Ran stuck out his hand. "And you are, sir?" he said.

The embassy official shook hands in a practiced reflex. "Emrys-Dunne," he muttered. "Assistant Political Officer. As you can imagine, we're quite busy just now. I should be in a meeting right —"

He nodded toward the door standing ajar across the hall beside them. Ran could see half of those around the table within. The striking blond woman would have been worth comment in other circumstances, but none of the conferees were senior people. An older man near the foot of table was clearly a Nevasan national, locally employed embassy staff.

" — now."

You bet. There's a crisis, so call a meeting and cluck. With luck, the ambassador and other ranking personnel were doing something useful, but Ran wasn't willing to bet on that.

"Sir, I know this is a crisis, but the *Empress of Earth* is more than just a hugely valuable vessel," Ran said as persuasively as he knew how. He was so tired and hungry that he was getting light-headed. "She's a symbol of Earth itself, just as the embassy here is. A few Terran soldiers may be the only thing between normal lift-off and an ill-judged attempt to seize her. That sort of mistake could bring Federated Earth into the *war*, as you know."

"That's out of the question!" said Emrys-Dunne, more forcefully than Ran would have guessed the plump man could be. "Deploying members of the guard detachment off embassy property would be a clear violation of the treaty — "

The meeting in the conference room broke up. The people spilling out the door looked drawn and gray. Ran suspected that Emrys-Dunne had kept the gathering together longer than would otherwise have been the case, and that his absence gave the others an excuse to leave.

"Sir," Ran said, "There's already been one — "

"No!" snapped the official. "No, absolutely not. What you're suggesting could be construed as an act of war on our part."

That was probably true, but — there wasn't a snowball's chance in Hell that the government of Nevasa would try to make anything out of it. Whereas a Nevasan misstep here, in the middle of the crisis, might arouse the sort of public outcry at home that forced Earth to take public action. The government of Federated Earth collectively hated to act as much as Emrys-Dunne seemed to dislike the idea as an individual.

"Sir, just as a symbol," Ran pleaded. "To make it clear that the *Empress* is Earth territory and —"

"No!"

The blond woman stopped nearby, looking intently from Emrys-Dunne to Ran. "We could send a few watchmen," she said unexpectedly. "He's right, you know. The department won't thank us if we let Earth be dragged into this because the Nevasans — or *some* Nevasans — miscalculated."

"Uh?" said Ran.

"This is Ms. Hatton," Emrys-Dunne said through a grimace. "She's our General Services Officer. And I remind you, Susan, that this is a political matter."

"On the contrary, Clovis," Hatton replied, "the private watchmen are a GSO matter, just like the maintenance staff and all other aspects of personnel billeting. And it seems to me that this is a proper use for them."

"Wait a minute," Ran said. He was too tired to be sure of what he was hearing. "These are Nevasan citizens hired to guard embassy housing?"

"Not Nevasans," the blonde corrected. "We hire third-planet nationals for the job. And they guard our supply warehouses as well, of course."

She pursed her lips. "The important thing from your standpoint is that the guards wear uniforms with Terran Embassy shoulder patches," she went on. "But they also have Nevasan approval to carry lethal arms."

"You have no right to authorize personnel paid with embassy funds to guard private property!" Emrys-Dunne objected.

"Trident Starlines will pick up the tab, no problem," Ran said. "Just get me to a line that can access Bridge — ah, the *Empress of Earth*, I mean."

"Yes, come with me," Hatton directed as she turned

and led the way down a short corridor to an office. She looked just as good going away as she did from the front. Ran was partial to blondes, not that it really mattered.

The office was a small one adapted for two people, presumably the GSO and a local assistant. Hatton used one line while Ran, at the opposite desk, clipped his transceiver to the other phone and patched through to the *Empress*'s AI.

"Six be enough?" Hatton asked.

"Yes," said Ran. If six weren't plenty, then a battalion wouldn't be.

Hatton talked for a moment, her voice muted by the interference field of her phone, and looked up at Ran with satisfaction. "They'll be there in half an hour," she said.

"Time and a half to everyone who makes it," Ran said. "Double-time to any of them who're at the *Empress* in fifteen minutes."

"*Accepted*," said Bridge through the Third Officer's earpiece.

Hatton raised an eyebrow and spoke again into her phone. She switched off the line and said to Ran, "I don't know if any of them will make it, but they're certainly going to try. I hope it works."

"We all hope it works," Ran said. He stood and stretched. "Including everybody with good sense in the Nevasan government. Anyway, you and I did what we could to avoid trouble."

He looked down at Hatton. She was wearing something clingy and gauze-fine, but as opaque as a brick wall. The fabric was a soft blue that shimmered metallically when the light hit it from the right angle.

"I really appreciate your help," Ran said. "I know it's safer to sit on your hands than to help. That's anywhere, I mean, I'm not down on the foreign service."

Hatton sighed. "Spend four hours in a meeting with

Emrys-Dunne and you *would* be down on the foreign service," she said. "Well, if there's nothing else I can do for you, Mr. — "

"Ran Colville," he said with a smile. "And if you can tell me — is there a hotel around here? I don't look forward to getting back to the ship tonight, and if I did I'd get rousted before my head hit the pillow. Also I could use a meal."

Hatton looked at him sharply. "Yes, there are hotels," she said. "And restaurants, though I don't know what'll be open with things — the way they are. I can take you past one on my way home, since I'm leaving now myself."

"Ah . . . ?" said Ran. "Could I offer you dinner too?"

Hatton sniffed. "And have it look as though Trident bribed me to provide guards? Not likely, sailor."

"Trident isn't picking up the tab," Ran said. The comment didn't bother him, but he injected a touch of acid in his voice to make the blond woman feel guilty. "I'm off duty, I'm in a strange city, and all hell's breaking loose. I was just hoping for the company of somebody who's acted like a friend."

Hatton grinned ruefully. "Sorry," she said, "it's been a long day. Sure, let's have a meal — but Dutch treat. And — "

Her face hardened.

" — I want it very clear: we're having dinner together. We're not going to bed."

Ran chuckled. "Milady, I don't doubt you've had a hell of a day, but believe me, it's not a patch on mine." He crooked his arm for her to take it. "There's some things that're just beyond human limits."

Which was perfectly true. Though in that one particular category, Ran Colville hadn't found his limits yet.

The parking lot beneath the embassy building

smelled of oil and damp concrete. The cars were an odd mix of Terran, Nevasan, and a scattering of models built on various other planets where embassy personnel had been stationed previously.

"Be careful out there, Ms. Hatton," warned the attendant. He was slim and dark, a Nevasan native. "Mostly they're acting happy — but people are scared, and you can't tell what's going to happen."

"Thank you, Lee," Susan said. "I'm leaving my car here. From what I see out the window, it wouldn't be possible to drive out anyway."

"As you wish, Ms. Hatton," Lee said. He looked Ran over. "And good luck to you too, sir," he added.

"Thank you," Ran said formally. "I and my employers are very appreciative of the embassy's help in this crisis."

Of course Lee's comment had a double meaning. *Of course* Ran Colville knew better than to embarrass a lady in front of her staff.

Lee stepped into his kiosk at the head of the exit ramp and threw a lever. Motors winched up the armored door.

"Come!" Susan directed, tapping the back of Ran's hand, and they darted through together. The door crashed shut, leaving them with the glowing Nevasan night.

A crowd filled the street — not solidly but by small groups and individuals, the way jellyfish swarm to the surface of a calm sea. No one spoke loudly, but the air hissed with conversation and the miniature radios that more than half of the people carried. Occasionally a cheer would rumble from far away, like angry surf.

"All the government ministries are within a few blocks of here," Susan explained. "People want to know what's going on."

"They could learn more by staying home and watching the news," Ran said. He was keyed up, though the day had wrung him out too thoroughly for his jitters to be obvious. "They're like kids before they run a race, too nervous to sit still."

Susan nodded them to the right at the intersection with the boulevard fronting the embassy. The park across the way was full of people. Buildings facing the park were brilliantly floodlit, and someone was speaking through an amplifier. Ran couldn't make out the words, but the crowd responded with waves of sullen enthusiasm.

"Parliament and the presidential palace," Susan said. Then she added, "If they understood what was going to happen, they wouldn't be cheering."

Ran shrugged. "It's going to happen anyway," he said. "Whatever ordinary people think, whatever they do. They might as well be happy while they can."

On one of the helmet recordings Ran found after his father died:

The broken buildings were gray and jagged. Three bodies lay in the gutter. A machine gun spat over them from a cellar window.

The stone transom puffed and sparkled with bullet impacts, but the rebel machine gun continued to fire. A grenade wobbled toward the gun and burst into waves of violet smoke.

The viewpoint shifted as Chick Colville stood up. *A rod of brilliantly-white flame, napalm enriched with powdered aluminum, stabbed toward the concealed gun position. Smoke sucked and swirled, but it continued to screen the cellar window even after secondary explosions shook the rubble.*

Three rebels ran into the street. Their clothes were burning. Bullets killed them and covered the bodies with dust knocked from the stone of the ruined building. The oldest of the rebels might have been fourteen. . . .

There wouldn't be street fighting here in Nevasa City . . . but a nuclear weapon might get through despite the rings of defenses, and certainly many dinner tables would have empty places that the dead would never return to fill. Sure, cheer now.

Either Ran shivered or something showed on his face. When he glanced around at his companion, she was staring at him. "No problem," he said with a smile that admitted maybe there had been one.

Instead of responding, Susan said, "We'll go to the Parisienne." She had to raise her voice to be heard over the murmur of the crowd. "It's the hotel the embassy uses for delegations, and the grill room is famous."

Inconsequently, she added, "It's only a block from my apartment."

Ran looked toward her. She didn't meet his eyes.

The boulevard was divided by a central spine of trees with bushes planted to either side of it. Buildings in this district were set back from the street, behind walled courtyards like that of the Terran embassy. Awnings of plush and silk jutted over sidewalk at the courtyard gates. Sometimes the fabric bore a crest or a legend: MINISTRY OF CULTURE, for example, or TYDIDES CORPORATION, and some in scripts unfamiliar to Ran.

A taxi with square lines and a great deal of chrome brightwork was stopped against the central plantings. A large crowd was gathered around the vehicle. A man wearing Nevasan formal kit, embroidered robes suggesting those of Earth's Ming Dynasty, stood on the taxi's roof.

"We must not be backward in defending our civilization against arrogance and barbarism!" the man cried. Drink slurred and hoarsened his voice. "The tree of liberty grows in the soil of martyrs' bones!"

Listeners at the back of the circle looked over their shoulders at Ran and the woman. Nevasans tended to be short and slightly-built by general human standards. The two foreigners stood out, even without Ran's white uniform and the glitter of Susan's dress.

Ran stepped to the outside and put his arm around

the woman. He didn't look aside at the crowd, nor did he quicken his pace.

An emergency vehicle drove slowly down the boulevard. A blue strobe light pulsed above the cab, though its siren was silent. The driver was a policeman, but two soldiers in battledress sat in the open back of the vehicle, dangling their feet over the bumper.

"There's the Parisienne," Susan said quietly. She had a make-up mirror in her hand. She used it to glance at the street behind them. She didn't pull away from Ran, though they were past the group gathered around the taxi.

She closed the mirror. "They aren't following," she added. "I — didn't think it would feel like this. It frightens me." Her voice was calm.

"It's a bad time to be an outsider," said Ran, who'd been an outsider all his life. He quickened his pace slightly. A broad marquee labeled PARISIENNE jutted out in the middle of the next block, guarded by a uniformed concessionaire.

They crossed an alley between two extensive courtyards. A stone bollard at the mouth blocked the passage for any but pedestrian traffic. Signs dangled from either side of the alley, but the expensive boutiques were locked and shuttered.

Ran slowed. "Is there a back entrance to the hotel?" he asked. "I . . . don't like the look of the folks across the street."

Susan leaned past Ran for a better view. The mob — this lot wasn't a crowd or a gathering — filled both opposite lanes of the boulevard and was trampling the bushes of the divider. Ran could hear metal ring under heavy blows.

"The Grantholm embassy," Susan said. "The staff left yesterday, all but a caretaker or two."

"Come on," Ran said harshly. He turned and strode back toward the pedestrian way, half dragging the woman with him when she hesitated.

"The authorities shouldn't let that happen," Susan muttered. "The host country is responsible for the safety of *all* embassy — "

Someone at the rear of the mob saw the woman's blond hair and shouted, "*There* go a couple of Grantholm dog-fuckers!"

"Go!" said Ran at the alley mouth. He gave Susan a push in the right direction and released her.

The shop nearest the corner specialized in carved jade. Chromed steel rods two and a half meters long slanted from the wall to support the plush marquee. Ran grabbed one of the rods and wrenched it free. He backed a few steps down the alley, out of the pool of the streetlight at its mouth. His hands were set a meter apart at the center of the rod.

Well-dressed Nevasans, their faces contorted with fury, foamed around the bollard like the tide racing past a bridge pier. One of the leaders brandished a pistol. Ran stepped toward the mob, swinging the rod with all the strength of his torso behind the motion.

The man with the gun screamed as his skull cracked. He jerked a shot into the ornamental brick pavement at his feet.

Ran backed, stabbed with the tip of the rod, and swung in another broad arc. This time he used the opposite end of his weapon. A Nevasan gripped the rod. Ran judged his angle, smiled like the angel of death, and thrust forward with all his weight. The glittering tube slid through the Nevasan's hands and punched his front teeth into his palate.

Ran backed another step. The shot had spooked some of the mob, and those still thrusting forward stumbled over the ruin of their front rank. Ran scanned his target. Both ends of his rod were black with blood.

"Don't breathe!" Susan Hatton said sharply. She hadn't run when he told her to. She reached past Ran, bracing her left hand on his shoulder.

The canister in her right hand went *poom!* and belched a cloud of gas toward the mob. The recoil lifted her arm. Nevasans sprawled.

"*Now* run!" she shouted. They fled together. No one followed. Stun gas lay as a bitter haze at the alley mouth.

Under the light at the end of the block, Ran threw down the steel tube. It was kinked at both points his grip had formed the fulcrum for his blows.

Susan led him across the street, dodging the light vehicular traffic. "The hotel?" he said.

She stopped at a grillwork gate. The building beyond the courtyard was of four stories, with balconies shielded by carved screens at each level. "Where did you learn to fight like that?" she asked as she touched the thumbprint lock.

"On a Cold Crew. In sponge space," said Ran. His eyes were dilated. "Only we used cutting bars and adjustment tools, and sometimes a man's line broke and he went sailing off forever."

There was no expression in Ran's voice. His eyes stared all the way to Hell.

"Ran?" the woman said. She brushed his cheek wonderingly. Her fingers came away smeared with the blood that had spattered him.

He shuddered. "I'm all right," he said. It was a prayer, not a statement. "I'm fine." He hugged her fiercely.

"Not here," she said, but she kissed him anyway. "Come on, inside my apartment."

"I'm all right," Ran Colville whispered as she thumbed the lock to the entrance elevator. "I'm fine...."

The phone rang. It had a pleasant-sounding mechanical bell. Ran didn't associate the chime with the cause until Susan Hatton lurched over him to lift the handset. "Four-two-four-one," she said crisply.

A voice squeaked from the unit. Susan looked puzzled and gave the phone to Ran. "It's for you," she said.

"Colville," Ran said as he straightened up in bed. Who knew that he was —

"Ran," Wanda Holly said in a tone that melded humor with the grating seriousness of the words, "you need to get back aboard the *Empress* ASAP. We'll be making an early departure from Nevasa. Parliament has just declared war on Grantholm."

"Right, I'm on my way," said Ran. His mouth was open to say more, but Wanda broke the connection at the other end.

He put the handset on its cradle and looked at Susan. She had tossed the bedclothes back. Her body was supple and flawless. "It's war, so we're undocking early," he said. "I've got to get to the ship soonest."

He swung his legs out of bed. Pain slashed through his shoulders and the sheets of muscle over his ribs. He gasped involuntarily and tucked his elbows in close for a moment.

Susan touched his back. Her fingers were warm.

"It's okay," Ran explained. "I — haven't had that particular sort of exercise in about ten years, God be praised."

She looked startled. Ran laughed. "Oh, not *that* exercise," he said. "I meant earlier last night, the . . . the trouble."

The spasm passed and he stood up.

"I . . ." Susan said. Her tongue touched her lips. Her nipples were small and very pale. "I hadn't been with anyone in three months. Since Tom was transferred to the consulate at Bu Dop on the other side of the planet. But you seemed to need me as much as I . . . ?"

Ran leaned over and kissed her. He reached gently between her thighs. Her labiae were swollen. "Umm," he said. "You're going to be bruised, m'dear."

They hadn't slept much. Every time he started to doze off, Susan had hugged him to her again; and he'd responded. He didn't know that was really what she'd wanted, but it was what he had to give, and give again.

"And he laughs, the brute!" she said chuckling. Then, in a neutral tone, she voiced the first question to cross his mind when he heard Wanda speak. "How did she know where you were? The woman who called?"

"I should've clipped my commo unit to a phone when I took it off," Ran said. He'd pulled on his trousers and shirt, but he waited a moment before he dealt with his boots. "I didn't, but they could still locate it from the *Empress*. Bridge, that's the AI, must have dug the telephone address of the location out of the local system's records."

The marquee support had trailed a line of bloodspots across the sleeves and front of his tunic. The white fabric filtered the blood as it wicked through. Each spot had dried as a black center in a reddish ring, with a pale brown margin surrounding the lot. Ran put the garment on anyway.

"I'll be leaving Nevasa City in two days," Susan said from the bed. "There was a commercial attache slot open in Bu Dop. I put in for a transfer to be with my husband."

Ran finished sealing his boots. Momentary twinges suggested that he'd broken a rib, but he was sure it was just muscle strain. He didn't say anything.

"I — don't suppose," Susan said, "that your ship will be returning to Nevasa anyway, because of the war?"

Ran put on his commo unit. He knelt on the bed to kiss the blond woman again. "Not during the war, no," he said as he held her. "Trident probably should have chosen an alternative port even for this run, but nobody really expects a crisis to get worse yet."

He stood up again. He didn't remember ever having seen a more perfect body than hers, and he'd seen a few....

"After the war, whenever that is," he said, "you'll know when the *Empress* docks. And what you do then is your business."

He made his way out of the apartment alone. Susan lay on the bed, her eyes empty.

*   *   *

The sky-stabbing departure horn of the *Empress of Earth* sounded its three notes for the second time as the taxi dropped Ran Colville at the gangplank. It had been a quiet drive. Debris from the vast assemblages of the previous night lay over many of the streets, but the mobs themselves had dispersed.

Second Officer Wanda Holly waited at dockside. Men in bright blue uniforms stood protectively before the gangplank. Their shoulder patches and cap tallies read Terran Mission. Ran nodded at them in approval. One of the guards saluted, though they couldn't have the least awareness of who the man in the dirty uniform was.

"You're the last, except for a few of the Cold Crew," Wanda said crisply as she swung into step with Ran. "Did you have a pleasant time last night?"

Ran looked at her. "I went," he said without emotion, "to arrange for the embassy to send guards. The embassy did do that, and we're able to leave Nevasa without a major problem. So yes, Wanda. Success in a difficult mission is always pleasant."

"Glad you made it back," she said. She turned and walked away at the top of the ramp.

Ran headed for his room and a change of uniform. He was whistling absently.

When he thought about the tune, he realized it was the old ballad, *Clerk Colville*.

Tables in the Dining Room were set for groupings of two, four, and six. It seemed natural enough, when places were adjusted after the exodus and influx of passengers on Nevasa, for Reed, Da Silva, and the Dewhursts to share one of the larger tables with Wade and Belgeddes.

The huge room was illuminated by surface emission from ceiling coffers and the tall vertical columns separating panels of mythological bas reliefs. The lights had been dimmed when serving robots brought out the dessert, *Glace Empress*, flickering with blue brandy flames. Now sated diners were beginning to leave, and the walls brightened to accommodate them.

The grand staircase from Deck B, down which the splendid made their entrances, was a less romantic feature as folk climbed it again at the close of the meal. Most people chose to leave by the side doors onto Deck A.

Wade looked at the panel beside him, a scene of Roman fishermen with nets and rakes gathering in the riches of a sea packed with life. The stone was a bluish marble gilded to pick out details of the figures. Men, sea creatures, and the choppy waves were executed in realistic style, but none of the people seemed aware of the fish-tailed Tritons and Nereids sporting among them.

"Reminds one of sponge space, doesn't it?" Wade said, gesturing toward the relief with his coffee cup. "Where what you see generally isn't anywhere near you."

"But we're in sponge space now, aren't we, Mr. Wade?" said Ms. Dewhurst, a slightly shorter, slightly more rounded version of her husband. She wore a choker of diamonds and pearls, the latter with a mauve iridescence that marked them as coming from Tellichery.

"What he means, Esther," Dewhurst said, "is when you're out on the hull of the ship in sponge space, not inside the envelope like we are."

"You've been outside the ship, Mr. Wade?" Ms. Dewhurst asked in amazement.

A human steward began to clear the table, handing items into the open maw of the robot which trailed behind him. Flatware and dishes with remnants of the ice vanished without so much as a clink to mark their passing.

"Wade's been everywhere, didn't you know?" Reed muttered.

"Ah, lots of people have traveled," said Belgeddes. "Dickie's *done* things wherever he was. Just one of those lucky fellows that things happen to, you know."

"Oh, yes, back in the old days — long, *long* before you were born, Mistress Dewhurst," Wade said. Ms. Dewhurst beamed, an expression that made her broad face unexpectedly attractive. "We used to go out with the Cold Crews and throw targets for each other to shoot at."

"That's impossible!" Dewhurst said.

"Well . . ." said Reed through a grimace, "I do recall old-timers on Ain talking about that sort of thing. It was something they'd heard of, not done, though. That must have been in the *really* early days of star travel, though."

"There's ships and ships, you know," Belgeddes commented. "You mustn't think that the standards of Trident Starlines are quite the same as what you'll find on some of the tramps Dickie and I knocked around on in our salad days."

"Not impossible, Dewhurst," Wade said easily, "but damned difficult, I'll grant you. It wasn't a matter of accuracy, you see. I've sailed with some crack shots — lizard-hunters on Hobilo, chaps who could knock the eye out of a squirrel at a hundred paces, even wearing spacesuits. Out on the hull, they couldn't hit a thing."

"That," said Da Silva, "I believe."

"I suppose you didn't have any problem, though?" Reed asked.

"No problem?" Wade replied. "I certainly can't claim that. I needed several shots, sometimes half a dozen, before I got a feel for where to aim. The spatial relationships in another universe — that's what each cell of the sponge is, you know — are utterly different from those of our own. And they changed after each insertion, of course."

"A quick study, Dickie is," Belgeddes said approvingly.

The main room was emptying out. The *Empress of Earth* had six smaller dining rooms as well. Large parties could book them, but normally the separate rooms were used to accommodate groups of non-humans traveling on the vessel. The door of one opened and disgorged a herd of Rialvans, their jaws working in a sidewise rotary motion as they continued to masticate their meal.

Dewhurst sighed. "Anyone for a drink?"

Da Silva shrugged. "Fine by me. Starlight Bar all right?"

"Ugh, not me," said Ms. Dewhurst. "I'm going back to the room, dear. And I believe there's a dance in the lounge tonight."

"It gives me the creeps, looking out at all that — light," Reed said.

"That's good," replied Da Silva. "You can get a meal and a drink in any hotel in the universe. Up there — sponge space — is what makes this different."

"Ah . . ." said Wade, shooting both cuffs of his loose velour shirt. Neither wrist bore a credit bracelet. "I don't seem to be wearing my — "

"No problem," said Da Silva. "I'm buying."

They all got up. A steward and robot poised to make a final sweep.

"As usual," murmured Dewhurst. "Except when Reed's buying, or I am."

Nobody appeared to hear him.

"You know . . ." Reed said softly as he followed Da Silva out of the dining room. "The *Empress* is supposed to have an impressive shooting gallery. . . ."

● BISCAY

"But I just want to get off and stretch my legs!" the woman cried to Commander Kneale. Her voice rose into a shrill blade of sound that sliced the muttering of the Embarkation Hall where three hundred First Class passengers waited.

These were the folk — all of them human — who hadn't heard the announcement that First and Cabin Class unloading would be delayed, or who had ignored the announcement or who simply thought that the delay would be much shorter than the two hours which had already passed. Commander Kneale himself had thought the delay would be much shorter. . . .

"I'm sorry, madam," Kneale said calmly, "but we can't permit passengers to disembark at the moment, for their own safety. I assure you that when the gangplank can be lowered, we'll announce it in all the lounges."

"But I want to get out *now!*" There was an edge of hysteria in her tone. There were people who could keep the feeling of being trapped in a metal coffin at bay — until landfall. Then they had to get out . . . and the trouble was, Kneale didn't dare lower the gangway until he got the all-clear signal from Third Class.

Another white uniform cut through the crowd: Crewman Blavatsky, carrying a tall glass of varicolored fluids on which bits of fruit floated. "Ms. Fessermark?" the rating said. "Would you sit with me for a moment? I'm not feeling well. . . . "

Startled, the passenger turned from Commander

Kneale and allowed herself to be guided out through a corridor. The leather banquettes in the Embarkation Hall were filled by passengers waiting with slightly more patience than Ms. Fessermark had shown.

Blavatsky and her charge paused for a moment. Ms. Fessermark took the drink and downed a good three ounces of it before she lowered the glass. *That* ought to calm her down, if it didn't simply knock her legless when the full effect of layered rums and liqueurs set in.

Kneale's transceiver was attached to a pilaster that would recess into the gangplank when it finally opened. "Holly, what's your estimated completion point?" he demanded.

"Another twenty minutes and we'll have it, sir," answered Colville, not Holly. "The contractor's short, real short."

"You'd better have it!" Kneale snarled in a whisper.

He raised and smoothed his voice to say, "Ladies and gentlemen? I've just been in touch with the authorities here on Biscay. They hope to have the problem squared away in twenty minutes, but it certainly won't be sooner than that. If any of you would like to wait in your rooms or the lounges, I'll be making a general announcement just as soon as we're allowed to open the ship."

There were groans and sighs from the crowd. A few people actually turned and left the hall.

Kneale took a deep breath. The trouble was that almost none of the First and Cabin Class passengers had Biscay as a final destination. These folk simply wanted to get off and view the sights. They didn't have to worry about luggage and all the other normal delays of disembarking.

On the other hand, more than eighty percent of the *Empress of Earth*'s forty-two hundred Third Class passengers were on Biscay at least until they'd served out their labor contracts. Many years before, there'd been a nasty incident when emigrants from the *King Wiglaf* saw their new home for the first time — and the main gangplank was lowered, with only a few surprised crewmen to try to halt the stampede back aboard the starliner.

Mind, the wealthy, privileged folk here in the Embarkation Hall weren't going to spend long on sightseeing themselves. Thirty seconds of Biscay was a bellyful for most people. . . .

"Another truck's arrived," Mohacks announced over the radio. He was somewhere in the loading area, invisible behind a curtain of dust.

"Release Section Thirty-three," Ran called from the head of the Third Class gangplank.

Babanguida, scowling over the respirator which concealed his lower face, trotted up the outside of the walkway. The Staff Side ratings weren't pleased to be doing the job of ground personnel, but there didn't seem to be a lot of options on this run.

A gust of wind rocked Ran against the hatch coaming. Emigrants on the walkway staggered. They looked like dim ghosts in the yellow dust. During a momentary lull, Ran heard the wails of children . . . and of some adults.

The *Empress*'s ventilation system ran at redline to provide positive pressure within the huge bay, but occasionally gusts overpowered the fans. Fine dust covered the last five meters of the corridor like a blond carpet, and drifting motes made the emigrants sneeze almost as soon as their sleeping quarters were unsealed.

The sky was a saffron haze, brighter toward zenith. It must be close to noon, but Ran wasn't sure how many standard hours a day was on Biscay. Section 33 — females and children — processed past him, led by one of Wanda Holly's ratings. Each of the emigrants stumbled at the hatchway when she saw the choking waste beyond.

Ran waved them onward stolidly. "It'll be better in the trucks," he said. His voice was thickened by his respirator. "The air in the trucks is filtered."

A woman clutched him with both hands, jabbering in a dismal, high-pitched voice. The translator on Ran's shoulder caught a few words, but most of the complaint was as inarticulate as the wails of a trapped coyote.

The line halted. Babanguida and Wanda appeared to either side of the woman. The rating loosened her hands from Ran's utility uniform while Wanda touched the emigrant's cheeks and murmured consolingly. The two of them, officer and emigrant, walked a few steps down the gangway before Wanda patted her and returned to the hatch.

"They're the last," Wanda said to Ran. "Poor bastards."

Babanguida began edging away from the officers.

"Babanguida!" Ran snapped before the rating could manage to disappear. Technically, Third Watch was off-duty, but Babanguida knew better than that. "Change your uniform fast and report to Commander Kneale. Don't go off on your own till he releases you or I do."

"Sir," the big crewman muttered. He didn't sound angry, just regretful that he'd been caught.

Wanda hadn't been wearing her respirator as she opened sections down the corridor. She put it on now.

"Is it always like this?" Ran asked, gesturing into the haze.

"No, but often enough," she replied. Then she added, "It isn't right to bring people here. It isn't moral."

Ran looked at her. "How so?" he asked. "I thought there was an ocean of ice bigger than the Pacific under this loess. In twenty years, Biscay's supposed to be supplying food for the whole Ain al-Mahdi system. Isn't that so?"

"In twenty years, maybe," Holly said. "Look at these people now."

The last of the emigrants were out of sight in the yellow blur. Several figures staggered up the gangway toward the ship.

"They come from western China," Ran said. "Do you think this is the first time they've seen a dust storm, Wanda?"

"I don't think they knew — " she began.

"They signed up because they thought it was a better life," Ran said. He was shocked at his own fierceness. "And it *will* be a better life, if they work at it and *because* somebody worked at it."

"They thought it would be better now!" Wanda said. Their respirator-muffled faces were close together in the hatchway.

"Did you ever survey the *Empress*'s Cold Crew?" Ran demanded. "Did you ever ask them if they knew what sponge space was like? Because sure as God, Wanda, they *didn't* know when they signed on. And we're here because they keep the engines fed and trimmed while we ride inside the envelope. That's worse than a dust storm, lady. That's worse than Hell, if there is a Hell besides sponge space."

Mohacks and a stranger in unmarked coveralls stopped at the hatchway. Wanda's two ratings followed them up the gangway at a slight distance.

"They're all on the trucks, sir," Mohacks said. The Second Officer aimed her transceiver toward the receiving lens and relayed the message to Commander Kneale. Dust in the air fuzzed the IR signal.

The stranger stuck out his hand. "Tom Urdener," he said. "Latimer Trading. We're the contractors on this lot."

"Why the hell didn't you have your people in place?" Ran demanded. "You barely provided enough to drive the trucks! By the contract, our personnel aren't responsible for the emigrants once we've opened the berth sections on the ground!"

"I know that," Urdener said, "I know that. What happened is that I lost over a hundred of my staff when you radioed news that war had broken out. They're boarding your ship right now."

"Huh?" said Ran.

"Grantholm nationals," Urdener explained. "Reservists, most of them. They're going home to join their military."

He sighed and shook his head. "We shouldn't have hired so much of our staff from one planet, I suppose," he went on. "But — you know, there's nobody like a Grantholmer to keep a labor crew's noses to the grindstone. Nobody like them at all."

Urdener touched his forehead in a half-serious salute. "Can't stand here gabbing," he said. "Just wanted to apologize to you, is all."

He headed back down the gangplank.

Ran looked at Wanda. "I'm sorry," he said. He thought of adding something, but he couldn't decide what to say — especially with the two ratings on Wanda's shift staring at the officers. Mohacks had disappeared down the corridor.

"You're right," Wanda said. She touched the switch that shut the compartment to the outside. The hatch began to swing closed from top and bottom simultaneously.

"And Federated Earth is right," she continued, staring out as the rectangle of yellow haze narrowed. "At home, they're surplus population. Here they're doing something for themselves and for mankind. Eventually."

"I don't like it either," Ran said softly. He might have touched her hand if it weren't for the enlisted personnel.

The hatch ground closed, then coughed several times to clear its seal of dust. Pressure in the compartment increased momentarily; then the ventilation fans cut to idle.

"I've had a pretty comfortable life," Wanda said. She met Ran's eyes. "I guess I don't like having my nose rubbed in the fact that a lot of people don't, even on Earth."

She smiled, shifted to put her body between herself and her subordinates, and squeezed Ran's hand.

"Let's get cleaned up and help the commander," Ran said. "If he's got a hundred Grantholm slave drivers coming aboard, he's going to want us around."

• IN TRANSIT:
BISCAY TO AIN AL-MAHDI

Miss Oanh found the Quiet Room tucked at the end of a blank corridor. The bulkheads whispered. They enclosed the starliner's service mains, not living spaces.

The *Empress* provided a generally acceptable ambiance for her Third Class passengers and expected them to adapt to it. For those who could pay, however, the huge ship had nooks and crannies molded to every foible.

Most passengers would visit the Starlight Bar only once in a voyage, if that often; but the "experience of sponge space," or the possibility of that experience, might affect their choice of a starliner and the enthusiasm with which they recommended the *Empress of Earth* to their friends.

The wrought iron gateway of the Quiet Room passed even less traffic than entered the Starlight Bar; but those who wanted solemn silence in a setting apart from that of their suite often wanted it very much.

Lanterns hung to either side of the arch, softly illuminating through the grillwork an interior paneled in dark pine. A Kurdish runner, woven from deep reds and browns, carpeted the center of the small retreat. The exposed flooring was of boards thirty centimeters wide, pinned to the joists beneath by dowels. The four high-backed chairs were of black oak, with leather cushions fastened to the frames by tarnished brass brads.

At the end of the room was what could have been an altarpiece, richly carven but without specific religious content. A pair of electronic "candles" stood on the wood, programmed to sense the slightest breeze and to flicker in response.

Miss Oanh stepped into the empty room. Two of the chairs faced the altarpiece. She started to sit down in one of them.

It gave a startled gasp. She screamed.

The young man who'd been sitting in the chair jumped to his feet. "I'm terribly sorry!" he blurted. "I didn't hear you come — "

Oanh put a hand to her chest. "Oh my goodness!" she said. "I'm so sorry, I thought the room was empty."

As Oanh spoke, she looked around quickly to be sure that there weren't people scowling from the chairs facing one another from the sides of the room.

"No, no, it's just us," the young man said. "Ah — I'm Franz Streseman. Though if you want to be alone, miss, I should be going anyway. I'm just. . . "

"Oh, please, no," Oanh said. Franz was a slim man of average height — for most cultures, the delicate builds of Nevasa being an exception. He had strong, regular features with a small moustache which to Oanh gave an exotic tinge to his good looks. "I wasn't. . . That is — "

She looked at her hands. "It isn't that I wanted to be alone, but if — "

" — you were going to be alone anyway, you didn't want to do it in a lounge with a thousand people watching you," Franz said, completing her sentence and her thought perfectly.

"Yes," she said, meeting the young man's eyes. "That's how I felt."

"Ah — " Franz said. He looked away, then back. "Ah — I was planning to get something to drink. Ah — coffee, perhaps, or . . . ?"

"I've thought of seeing the Aviary Lounge," Oanh said, smiling shyly. "If you'd like that, I . . . ?"

Franz offered his arm. "Let's do it now," he said. His face wore a lithe, active expression, a complete change from the cold gloom with which he'd been staring at the altarpiece.

"You know how to find it, then?" Oanh asked. "The ship is so big, I'm afraid I'll get lost every time I leave father's suite."

The woolen carpet was only a meter wide, so their outside heels clicked on the boards until they passed through the archway. The corridor floors of the *Empress of Earth* were of varied appearance, but all were of a synthetic which deadened noise as well as cushioning footsteps.

Franz laughed cheerfully. "We'll find it," he said. "We'll have an adventure, just the two of us."

Oanh joined his laughter. It occurred to her that this was the first time in ... weeks, certainly — and probably longer — that she'd felt cheerful.

"You," called a passenger in one of the alcoves of the gallery connecting the Embarkation Hall with the Social Hall. "Boy!"

Babanguida turned with a neutral smile and walked toward the alcove. Four men sat around a small table, three of them on chairs and the fourth, the obvious leader, alone in splendor on the curved banquette. They'd come aboard on Biscay, but they were Grantholm nationals.

The hologram covering the wall behind them showed a mountain valley on Grantholm, overlooked from a crag by a strikingly handsome couple. The passengers themselves were windcut in a pattern that outlined the respirators and goggles they normally wore. Their knuckles were scarred, and in all they looked harder than the idealized rocks in the hologram.

They had drinks. The steward who fetched them

from the service bar at the end of the gallery stood several meters away from the alcove, watching from the corners of his eyes. His attitude toward the Grantholmers was that of a cat eying a large dog through a screen door.

"Yes sir?" said Babanguida to the man who faced him from the banquette. The passenger was as tall as Babanguida but much broader in proportion. He looked to be in his forties, with a flaring black beard and black hair except for the white flash where a knife scar trailed up his cheek into the temple.

He grinned at Babanguida and said, "Don't worry, boy, you're not in trouble yet. My name's von Pohlitz, Gerd von Pohlitz. Maybe you've heard of me?"

Babanguida had. Von Pohlitz was on the watch list Bridge generated when it ran the names of new passengers through the data banks Trident Starlines shared with other major shipping companies. Von Pohlitz had been involved in several incidents with dark-skinned or oriental members of starliners' service crews.

"Very glad to have you aboard the *Empress*, Captain von Pohlitz," Babanguida said smoothly. "Can I help you with something?"

The other three Grantholmers were physically of a piece with their leader, but they lacked the force of personality that glared from von Pohlitz like heat through the open door of a blast furnace. They looked at Babanguida with expressions mingled of disdain and distaste.

"You're Staff Side, aren't you, boy?" von Pohlitz demanded. "That's what the white uniform means, right?"

The Grantholmers were dressed in business suits they'd obviously bought in the *Empress*'s Mall when they boarded. There wasn't much call for First Class dress on Biscay. In place of the normal cummerbund, von Pohlitz wore a scarf of stained yellow silk across his belly.

Anything could have caused the three small perforations in the silk. Given the way the Grantholmer flaunted them, Babanguida assumed they were bullet holes.

"Yes sir," Babanguida said. "That's right."

"Don't think I look down on you for that," von Pohlitz chuckled. "That's what we all are here, aren't we, boys?"

His companions nodded and grunted assent. One of them noticed his glass was empty and whistled at the steward.

"The engineers lay out the job, that's fine," their leader continued. "But then it's up to me and the boys to see that the wogs get to work instead of sitting on their hands. Staff Side, see?"

"Yes sir, I can see that," Babanguida said calmly.

A few commands to Bridge would cause the entertainment center in von Pohlitz's cabin to put out a low-frequency hum, sensed though inaudible. Von Pohlitz and his roommate, another Grantholmer, would probably go berserk after a few hours of that. There'd be evidence in the data banks if anybody thought to check, though. . . .

"So you know things about the ship," von Pohlitz continued, "and you can go anywhere aboard her?"

Babanguida nodded very slightly.

The steward arrived with a fresh drink. He backed quickly away, without bothering to wait for a tip.

"I hear that there's a bigwig from Nevasa aboard," von Pohlitz said bluntly. "But he doesn't leave his suite."

"That might be the case," Babanguida said. His eyes were on the clean, triumphant-looking hologram behind the alcove.

Von Pohlitz nodded. One of his companions handed Babanguida a chip. "This *might* be fifty credits," the Grantholmer rumbled.

It was. Babanguida discharged the chip into his reader. All the Grantholmers beamed when they saw him accept the money.

"Minister Lin has embarked with eight members of his staff and family for Tellichery," Babanguida said quietly. "I don't believe he has left his suite, no. Certainly they're taking all their meals there."

"Now I'll bet," von Pohlitz said carefully, "that a boy in your position could copy a passkey to that suite."

Babanguida stood like an ebony statue.

"It would be worth another two hundred credits if you did," the Grantholmer pressed.

"It would be *worth* two thousand," Babanguida said softly.

"Balls!" von Pohlitz snarled. "Do you take me for a fool?"

"I'm not bargaining with you, Captain," Babanguida said. "I'm giving you free information. For two thousand credits, I would call my friend who's in the Housekeeping office right now and have him bring down a one-pass copy. For nineteen hundred and ninety-nine credits, I'll keep walking right on into the Social Hall, where I'm supposed to be now anyway."

"It won't be any — real trouble, hanging trouble," von Pohlitz said. "Just a little something for him to remember — and maybe some of his files get scrambled."

"Two thousand," Babanguida repeated without emphasis.

The Grantholmers looked at one another. Von Pohlitz grimaced and ostentatiously loaded a chip from his reader — two, zero, zero, zero, End. His blunt fingers stabbed like miniature battering rams.

Babanguida shifted his commo unit toward a point on the ceiling and said, "Mohacks? Three." Then he clipped a scrambler disk onto the transceiver and waited for a reply. Mohacks had a girlfriend in Housekeeping, which was frequently handy to the men's other business interests.

"Yeah?" Babanguida heard Mohacks normally, but the conversation recorded as only a ripple of static in the *Empress's* data banks.

Babanguida gave a series of brief directions. He didn't bother to explain anything to his partner. When he was finished, he removed the scrambler and looked at the Grantholm party with a complacent smile.

"Now what?" von Pohlitz demanded. The black crewman's new expression made him uncomfortable.

"Now we wait fifteen minutes," Babanguida said. "And then we exchange chips, hey?"

Mohacks appeared in just under nine minutes. He set the key, a chip with a hand-lettered legend, on the table but covered it with his palm until von Pohlitz slid the two thousand credits to Babanguida. Both ratings strode toward the Social Hall without looking back. The steward watched them go.

"What was that all about?" Mohacks asked when they stepped through the doorway into imperial Rome.

"A thousand apiece," his partner said. "*That's* what it's about."

"Why the hell did they want *that* room?" Mohacks demanded.

"They didn't," explained Babanguida. "They wanted the Nevasans. But I thought it'd be more interesting to have them bust in on Lady Scour's bodyguards in the middle of the night."

The Szgranian maids converged on Ran Colville from either end of the Bamboo Promenade, near the entrance to the Cochin Coffeehouse. Stiff "plumes" of pastel gauze sprang from their backs, giving each of the tiny females the volume requirements of an abnormally fat human.

Ran paused with a professional smile — wondering as he did so what the expression meant to a Szgranian. Well, they were in a human environment, so they had to adapt to human body language. . . .

Passengers walking in the promenade ranged from

sauntering couples, chatting and peering with vague attention at the bamboo growing along the sides and spine
of the walkway, to serious exercisers who pumped their
arms and kept track of time, kilometers, and calories
burned. The latter proceeded with their mindless
schedule, but those to whom the promenade was primarily a change of scene paused to view the Szgranians.

The Cochin had a roof of simulated thatch, supported
by poles set in a low stone foundation so that those within
the shaded interior had a broad view of the promenade.
The half dozen customers, drinking iced and sweetened
coffee, now watched Ran and the aliens.

The young man at the table nearest the entrance was
Franz Streseman. Ran recognized him because the Grantholmer had been spending time with Ambassador Lin's
daughter. All three Staff Side officers were nervous about
the situation, though thus far it seemed to be a young male
and female getting together on a voyage; which was as
common as breathing, if not quite as harmless.

"Our mistress requests that you accept the honor of
her presence," said the maid in a yellow outfit. The
Szgranians' six arms and gauzy dress made them look
rather like butterflies.

"You may take a reasonable time to prepare yourself
with ablutions and ceremonial garb," said the maid
wearing green as pale as a Luna moth's wings. "Does
your species wear ceremonial garb?"

"Or perhaps you can write a poem," added yellow.
"It is traditional for those honored by the clan mistress
to thank her with a poem."

Half of Ran's mind concerned itself with the question
of how the maids had found him. That was simple.
They — or Lady Scour — had asked the ship's AI to
locate Lt. Randall Colville; and the question was as point-
less as it was easy to answer. All it did was to keep Ran
from thinking about the real problems.

According to Ran's hypnogogue crash course in

Szgranian culture, "honor with her presence" meant exactly what Ran would have assumed it did had the summons come from a wealthy, bored human female. And, because Lady Scour was a passenger, his response was going to have to be the same also.

"I'm very sorry," he said aloud. "I am honored beyond words by your mistress's notice, but because of my duty to Trident Starlines, I am not able to respond appropriately."

The maids looked at one another in disbelief. One of them tittered in a high-pitched voice, covering her lips with four of her hands. The other thrust her arms straight out to the sides, the intervals as precise as those scribed around a circle by a compass set to the radius. Ran recognized that as a gesture of utter horror; suited, for example, to a high-caste female who learned that her lover had disgraced himself with a mere servant.

"We can't tell her that!" pale green cried.

"You must," said Ran. "Your mistress understands duty. She will understand that I have my duties, so long as I'm aboard the *Empress of Earth*, and that I will be faithful to my charge."

The Szgranian maids scampered off together, looking more like butterflies than ever with their plumes rising and falling as they ran.

"Bravo!" a passenger called, half-seriously.

Ran glanced around. He was unpleasantly aware that though he'd kept his voice low, the maids had spoken loud enough for everyone within several meters to hear. To a Szgranian, there was no need for privacy. It was literally an affair of state.

Ran smiled and gave an exaggerated shrug. As he started to walk away — he tried to chat with the Purser's Assistant on every watch, to get that officer's different perspective on the voyage — Franz Streseman called, "Excuse me, Lieutenant Colville? Might I speak with you for a moment?"

"Of course, Mr. Streseman," Ran said as he stepped into the Cochin. "Have you been having a good voyage?"

A potential human problem who wanted to talk became a first priority for Staff Side.

"Oh," said the youth as he sat down again. "You know my name?"

"We try to learn the passengers' names," Ran said, which only by implication was a lie. To the brown-jacketed steward who appeared at his side, he added, "A coffee for me, please."

Autoservers had their place. The unit in every First Class cabin could handle virtually any drink demand, as well as supply food better than that available in most groundside hotels. Some of the *Empress*'s public areas were served in the same coldly efficient fashion — but there were good commercial reasons for human stewards as well.

Many of those who could afford star travel felt that ordering humans around was a necessary way to display power. Also — and somewhat less demeaning of the species — many planets simply didn't have the technological base to build and maintain service robots. Passengers from such worlds were uncomfortable when faced with machinery they didn't understand. It was no business of Trident Starlines to make a large proportion of its wealthy passengers feel inferior.

"I, ah, have a problem," Streseman said as he peered intently into his glass. He swizzled the ice and dregs with his straw. "You — "

He looked at Ran in concern. "I don't mean to be personal."

"I can live with it," Ran said, smiling. "Tell me."

"You've had a lot of experience with women, haven't you, sir?" Streseman said. He held the straw precisely upright as if someone was about to drive it into the glass with a maul.

"Not on the *Empress* or any other ship I've served

on," Ran said calmly. "Apart from that, yes, some."

The steward brought his iced coffee. Ran raised the glass and sipped the rich, sweet fluid without taking his eyes away from Streseman. There was a touch of coconut milk in the drink.

"I . . ." the youth said into his glass again. "I haven't. Much, I mean. But I've met a really wonderful girl. Just by accident. Only her father is a government official from Nevasa and I, ah, I'm from Grantholm."

Ran set his glass down carefully. "I can see that might be difficult," he said with equal care.

"Oh, it's not, not really!" Streseman insisted. "I mean, we're both against the war. It's stupid and worse! Horrible, really. Only —"

He paused, staring at his drink while synthetic crickets chirped in the synthetic thatch above the table.

"Her father doesn't approve?" Ran suggested quietly.

"No, it's not that either," Streseman said. "Maybe — well, if he knew, I suppose he'd forbid Oanh to see me, but he doesn't pay her any attention. He's too busy with his staff, planning —"

He gestured broadly, angrily. "Planning whatever they're going to do on Tellichery. He doesn't care about his daughter at all."

If he didn't care, boy, Ran thought, *he'd have left her on Nevasa. But you're young.*

"If that's not the problem . . . ?" Ran said aloud.

Streseman prodded his ice with the straw. "She doesn't know I'm from Grantholm," he said miserably. "I told her I was an engineering student on Earth —"

He looked up sharply. "And that's true! But —"

Face and voice lost animation again. "You see, it just never came up that I was from Grantholm. And now I'm afraid to tell her."

Ran sipped his coffee. "Tell her," he said gently.

"She'll think I've been hiding it," Streseman said. "That I'm a spy or something. She won't see me again."

"That's possible," Ran agreed. "But what she does is her business. It's your business to tell her the truth."

"I don't know why I'm worried," the youth muttered. "I'll never see her after we reach Grantholm, anyway. I — "

He swallowed. "I'll be assigned to my father's old unit, the Seventeenth Commando. I — don't expect to survive the war."

"Ah . . ." said Ran. Now he was the one who was uncomfortable. "You don't approve of the war yourself?"

Streseman straightened. "I know my duty," he said stiffly. "Stresemans have always known their duty."

Ran finished his coffee and stood up. "Then *do* your duty, Mr. Streseman," he said. "If you can face death, then you can face one young girl."

The youth began to laugh. "Yes, that's so simple, isn't it?" he said. "Only hard to do."

He grimaced. "But I will do it, when we land. I don't — "

He shrugged and flared his elbows. "Your ship is confining, for all her size. I don't want that when I tell Oanh."

Streseman rose and shook Ran's hand. "Thank you, Lieutenant," he said. "I — you have helped me see my duty."

"Women don't always make a fuss over the same things that men do," Ran said. That was fair, after all, because women certainly did fuss over things that men could take or leave . . . and generally left. "Good luck, though."

As Ran walked away, he thought about Lady Scour. *Good luck to both of us, Streseman. Whatever that means.*

"Ah," said Wade, as Reed bowed and gestured him forward. "So this is your surprise."

The doorway was a high arch bordered by SHOOTING GALLERY in large letters. The sign's color metamorphosed slowly through the optical spectrum. At the moment, the letters were a green gradually being absorbed by its own blue component.

"We thought that with all your shooting experience," Da Silva said, "that you'd like to try the facilities here. We've booked the gallery for the next hour."

Dewhurst gave Wade a hard, humorless grin. "Yes," he said. "Lizard hunting on Hobilo, wasn't it?"

Without waiting for a reply, Dewhurst stepped forward. The "door" quivered about him. It was a hologram rather than a physical panel.

"You know," Wade said with a puzzled expression as he followed, "I don't recall mentioning that to you fellows. The lizard hunting, I mean."

"Don't believe you did, old man," said Belgeddes. "That was just before the Long Troubles broke out, when the Prophet's boys were trying to get you to run guns for them, wasn't it?"

"That was it, all right," Wade murmured from the other side of the shimmering curtain. "*Not* the sort of business a chap wants to dwell on."

Reed looked at Da Silva. They stepped through, into the gallery, themselves.

A party of K'Chitkans had taken the gallery ahead of Reed's party. They were still excited, bobbing their heads and chirping to one another in simultaneous cacophony as they waved their down-covered arms. When the humans appeared, the bird-folk bowed formally and exited through the hologram, still gabbling.

"Wouldn't think they could handle guns meant for men with those short arms," Da Silva said.

"Needs must when the Devil drives, friend," Wade said. "I recall firing a Zweilart cavalryman's gun once, with a curled stock and a bore I could stick my arm down. I was so keyed up under the circumstances that I didn't feel the recoil, even though it knocked me flat on my fundament. I jumped right up and let go with the other barrel."

"There's a story there, I shouldn't wonder," Reed said, glancing at the ceiling.

The interior of the shooting gallery was almost entirely a holographic construct. An autoserver by the door held a selection of rifles, shotguns, and energy weapons which it provided when a passenger presented his ticket for identification. The "weapons" weren't real, but they were full weight and the shooter could set them for any desired level of flash, bang and recoil.

"What's your choice, Wade?" Dewhurst said gleefully. "Don't believe they've got Zweilart hand-cannons here, but a black powder 8-bore ought to be pretty similar, don't you think?"

The gallery had scores of possible backgrounds. The scenery which the K'Chitkans had chosen was modeled on the veldt of southern Africa with a profusion of life unseen since the 19th-century. Elephants, zebras, and antelope of many varieties paced back and forth in the middle distance, but the score displayed in letters of light above the counter was entirely of lions: 117 of them.

Dewhurst handed the immense double rifle to Wade. "No, no — " Wade said with a gentle smile. A black-maned lion leaped from behind the thornbush an apparent hundred meters away and began bounding toward the men.

"I'm truly sorry," Wade said, his back to the target, "but I absolutely can't shoot under these — "

The holographic lion made a final spring and vanished in the air.

" — conditions."

"Jungle?" Reed offered. He touched the control panel on the counter. Lush foliage of green light replaced the holographic bush. A snake thirty meters long slithered through the air, gliding around treetrunks on its flattened ribcage.

"Or ice cap?" Jungle flashed into a wasteland in

which snow-covered blocks alternated with wedges of blue ice, shattered and overturned as the glacier that spawned it broke up in a bay just deep enough not to freeze to the sea floor. A creature humped toward the viewers across the irregular surface. Occasionally it bared yellow tusks.

" 'No' generally means 'no' when Dickie uses the word, fellows," Belgeddes said. There was enough of an edge in his voice that Reed cleared the display, leaving only a large, circular room with gray walls.

"That wasn't Earth, was it?" Dewhurst said, blinking toward where the last creature had been before the projectors shut off.

"Bifrost," Wade said. "A sea devil, though the real ones are usually shot from the air."

Belgeddes clucked his tongue against his palate. "You got yours on foot, Dickie," he said.

"I suppose this just isn't real enough for you, is that it, Wade?" said Da Silva.

"Oh, not that, friend," the tall old man protested. "Quite the contrary, in fact. It's far *too* real. A setting like this and a gun in my hands, well — too many memories, you see. I don't want to live them again."

"Kindly thought you fellows had, though," Belgeddes said.

"Doesn't bother you to talk about it though, I notice," Dewhurst said, looking up at a corner of the ceiling.

"Not the same thing, friend," Wade replied. He handed back the replica 8-bore. "Talk isn't the real thing, you know."

Reed snorted. "*That* the three of us know quite well."

Dewhurst offered the rifle to Belgeddes. "Here," he said. "Do you fancy a try?"

Belgeddes threw up both hands in mock horror and said, "Heavens, no! Palling around with Dickie, I've made an effort, but I was absolutely *hopeless*. Isn't that so, Dickie?"

Wade chuckled. "'Fraid it is, yes. When Tom's got a rifle in his hands, the safest place to be is in front of the target."

"Well, since we've got the gallery anyway . . ." Reed said. He touched a button on the control panel. The empty room became a reed-choked riverbank. A bipedal "lizard" the size of a cow darted past, glancing toward the humans.

"Hobilo," Reed said in satisfaction. He drew a modern rifle with a fat magazine of rocket-assisted projectiles from the counter's stores. "Unless this disturbs you, Wade?"

The older man chuckled and leaned against the back wall. "Not in the least, my boy," he said. "So long as it's you."

Another lizard trotted by. Reed turned and fired. The rifle lifted in his hands with a hiss*crack!* as the simulated projectile broke the sound barrier beyond the muzzle. The lizard continued running.

Dewhurst shouldered the antique elephant gun. A huge carnivore burst out of the swamp. Reed fired twice, missing each time, while Dewhurst tugged in vain at his triggers.

"This damned thing doesn't work!" he shouted as the holographic monster bore down on him.

Belgeddes leaned past Dewhurst and lifted back one of the 8-bore's exposed hammers. "Got to cock these old smoke-poles, laddie," he said.

Dewhurst yanked the front trigger again. The simulated recoil knocked him flat as the holographic carnivore vanished around him.

"Reminds me of a time on Kesterman Two . . ." began Wade, smiling indulgently at the other men.

● AIN AL-MAHDI

Clouds in the upper stratosphere of Ain al-Mahdi whipped in holographic clarity past the curved bulkhead of the Starlight Bar, as though the structure of the *Empress of Earth* was really transparent.

"Not much to see," Reed muttered. "We'd have a better view of the landing in the Social Hall."

"Everybody goes to the Social Hall to watch the takeoff and landing," objected Dewhurst.

Da Silva swirled his drink morosely and said nothing. Reed would be leaving the ship here. The five men had achieved a prickly sort of kinship which Da Silva, at least, would be sorry to lose.

"What they see on the ceiling of the Social Hall isn't real," said Wade. "It's a computer construction of what the view would be if we were above the *Empress* looking down."

"This isn't real either," Dewhurst said. He gestured to the curved image. "It's just interference patterns in light."

"Well, if it comes to that," said Belgeddes, "what you see here —"

He tapped the autobar with his knuckles. It made a flimsy sound.

" — is just reflected light, too. You know what Dickie means."

"Another round?" Reed offered.

To the general chorus of agreement, Wade said, "Really, shouldn't I pay for . . . ?"

"My treat, old boy," said Reed. "On the occasion of getting home safe. Despite the war."

He cleared his throat and added, "Hope the rest of you are as lucky."

"Going to look for a beach walker while you're here, Wade?" Dewhurst gibed.

"Didn't look for the first one, friend," Wade said as he took a glass of whiskey from Reed.

"I'll grant you're an expert on the difference between real and imagined, that's so," said Dewhurst.

"Reed was right about them probably being extinct by now anyway," Belgeddes said. "You've got to remember that we're dinosaurs, Dickie and I."

"There's dinosaurs on Hobilo," Reed said. "Near enough."

Ain al-Mahdi's vast primary swung into view, filling much of the holographic sky with its multihued luster. The men paused, staring at the sudden beauty.

"*That's* worth seeing," said Da Silva.

On the wall above the autobar, the bead of red light representing the *Empress of Earth* backlighted the turquoise and tourmaline sea monster indicating Ain al-Mahdi; and the *Brasil*'s blue glow settled over Calicheman, the agate head of a bull.

The building whose painted sign proclaimed it the Grand Hotel Universal faced the bubbling surf. It was constructed of cast concrete, three stories high, with full-length balconies for access to the rooms. The sunscreens with advertisements that shaded the balconies during the day had been rolled out of the way. Most of the shops on the ground floor had lighted signs of their own — WEXLER FINE TOBACCO PRODUCTS, THE SEAFRONT LOUNGE, and COURIER TORPEDOES TO ALL DESTINATIONS — ONE BLOCK DOWN.

The Grand Hotel al-Mahdi was across the street which led away from the water. It was exactly the same as the Universal, except that its third story was of thermoplastic and had been added after the original construction. The primary was barely on the horizon and the city had no streetlights; for the moment, the external floods that lit the *Empress of Earth* a kilometer distant were enough to see by.

Ran Colville sighed. *Welcome to Tarek's Bay, heart and soul of Ain al-Mahdi.*

Bare-breasted women hung from the balconies, while in the street shills promised cut-rate delights for those willing to walk a block, two blocks . . . a lifetime if you chose the wrong street and hadn't had sense enough to keep in a group with your shipmates. Mini-buses cruised the seafront, carrying sailors from the *Empress* and the freighters in port —

And passengers from the starliner as well. Mixed bus-loads were sightseeing. Their guides would take them to some of the tamer clubs, where they would be charged three times the going rate for drinks and a moderately raw floor show. That was value for money, because they would have stories to tell back home about wicked Ain and how they saw it; and they would survive to get home, to get back to the *Empress*, at any rate.

Other buses carried men only, or occasionally a load of hard-looking women. They too would get what they were asking for, and sometimes a great deal more. There was usually a missing passenger or two when a starliner lifted off from Ain, and the ship's medical facilities would be busy the following day.

For all that, Ain al-Mahdi wasn't the asshole of the universe. Her primary was a panorama of slowly changing beauty, a great jewel in the sky.

The human settlement of Tarek's Bay, however — *that* was the asshole of the universe.

Ran walked slowly, feeling the shingle beach scuff against his boots. He didn't have a destination. He'd never landed on Ain al-Mahdi before, but he'd known a hundred Tarek's Bays over the years and he didn't belong in any of them.

The New Port, originally a separate island but now joined to Tarekland by a causeway, was fenced and gated. The port and the neatly planned community within its boundaries were administered by a consortium of the major shipping companies. All but the rattiest tramp freighters landed there, because the amount of theft at Tarek's Bay was ten times the cost of docking fees in the New Port.

Hotels within the port complex were clean, and passengers could vary their stopover with sightseeing trips. The New Port was obviously the choice of the sensible traveler — except that it had no more soul than Ain (whose surface was a thousand gravel islets in a gray sea) had sights.

The transshipment trade made Ain al-Mahdi a center of commerce. She had begun as the collection point for miners in the vast sea of asteroids which shared the system with Ain's giant primary. Later, Ain's fortunate location through sponge space — "near" in terms of time and effort to many heavily populated worlds, Earth included — had expanded her transit trade across interstellar routes.

The New Port was necessary to the smooth functioning of interstellar commerce; but so is a warehouse necessary, and men do not choose to live in warehouses. Perhaps that explained Tarek's Bay, though Ran didn't care for the implied comment on the nature of Man if it did.

He'd reached the west end of the Strip. Where the buildings stopped, so did all semblance of lighting. Ran had a pistol in his pocket, but he wasn't looking for trouble and there was nothing he'd meet farther out along the shingle except trouble.

If he wanted to, he could hire a car to fly him to an uninhabited islet. There he could toss gravel into the waves and watch the primary rise in perfect safety.

He could hire a woman to go with him. Again, perfectly

safe, because escort services operating out of the New Port provided full medical histories of their employees. So far as Ran was concerned, that was as empty a proposition as trying to skip stones over live water.

He could cut out one of the *Empress*'s passengers, no problem at all for Ran Colville. And then spend the rest of however long she was booked for trying to dodge somebody who might very well make a scene no matter what she said beforehand about understanding the ground rules. It wasn't that women lied, they just had no more control over some things than a man with a stiff prick did. An evening's fun wasn't worth a week or a lifetime of trouble. . . .

Ran sighed. He might as well get back. There was always work. That was the only important thing, anyway. He had the engineering officers' course loaded in his hypnogogue. It felt strange to learn the theory behind the fusion drives he'd fueled and trimmed as a Cold Crewman in another existence.

An aircar in ground effect mode pulled up beside Ran and touched down. "Going somewhere?" asked the driver.

Female, mid-twenties at a guess, but the car's yellow-green dash lighting didn't tell much. Her face was heart-shaped and strikingly beautiful.

"Going nowhere," Ran replied, squatting to put his head on a level with hers. "Headed back to my ship, to tell the truth."

The car was a two-seater. The small luggage space behind the seats held a makeup case and something flat rolled into a tube. If there was a bruiser waiting to knock Ran over the head, he wasn't hiding in the vehicle.

"I'd offer to show you Tarek's Bay," said the driver. The fans hissed at idle, occasionally driving a pebble to click against its neighbor. "But if you've walked this far, you've seen it all."

She smiled. "And besides," she said, "if I thought there was anything in the place you'd be interested in, I wouldn't be talking to you. It's the armpit of the universe."

Ran laughed out loud. "You know," he said, "that's almost exactly the phrase that crossed *my* mind. But you've been more gently brought up than I was."

The driver's smile became wistful. "Don't you believe it," she said. "I've lived on Ain al-Mahdi all my life.

"But Ain isn't all like — *this!*" she added sharply, gesturing back toward the Strip. Her fingers were long and shapely. "There's parts of it that are beautiful, only it takes time to find them. The people who live here don't care, and the transients don't have the time."

"I've got fourteen hours," Ran said deliberately.

She touched a control. The passenger door swung open. "Hop in," she said, "and I'll show you the moonfish spawning in a lagoon."

Then she said, "And there's an air mattress in the back."

Tug motors hammered as they helped a tramp freighter down into the New Port. The blue glare was reflected from the office building opposite and through the glazed front of the Port Complex Towers.

Miss Oanh turned her face toward the empty lobby and watched her shadow lengthen across the tile floor. Disks behind the clear tube of the drop shaft paused, indicating that someone had gotten on at a higher level, then began to fall smoothly again. *When she called up to his room, Franz had said he would be only a moment.*

The starship dropped below the rooflines of the outer buildings in the complex. The cutting light vanished and the noise dulled to a rumble. Oanh looked out the front window again. *If she stared at the drop shaft, Franz wouldn't be the one to appear in it. . . .*

The hotel was fully automated. The only living things besides Oanh in the lobby were the local life forms swimming in an aquarium. Fish on Ain al-Mahdi tended to metallic colors and vertical rather than horizontal compression, but Oanh's only interest in the creatures was as possible food —

And food was the farthest thing from her mind, now.

Most First Class passengers took ground accommodations during the *Empress's* layovers. Minister Lin did not. He expected Oanh to remain in the suite with him and his staff. They spent the time digesting the information sent to meet them by courier torpedo: data from Nevasa, Tellichery, and very possibly from agents on Grantholm itself. His daughter was simply to wait, safe and silent until the *Empress of Earth* was starborne again.

Oanh didn't have credit in her own name . . . but Franz had booked a room here at the Towers. While they were aboard the starliner, there was a constraint that affected both of them though they had never mentioned it.

The safety door of the drop shaft rotated open. Oanh turned, her smile as bright as her dress of gold-shot natural silk, and faced the four big men who stepped off the platform.

She recognized them as passengers from Grantholm traveling aboard the *Empress of Earth*. They'd stared whenever they noticed her in the starliner's public rooms. Though the Grantholmers never said anything, they were the last people Oanh would have chosen to meet off the ship.

"Well, what have we here?" the leader of the group said in delight.

The men seemed to have been in a serious accident since Oanh last saw them. Two of them walked stiffly, one had a patch over his right eye, and half the leader's beard had been shaved away so that a ten-centimeter slash up his cheek could be covered with SpraySeal.

The Grantholmers looked even more like a gang of pirates than they had aboard the *Empress of Earth*. Oanh turned very quickly and walked out of the hotel. The filter field across the open doorway tugged momentarily at her hair and clothing.

The air outside was five degrees warmer than that in the lobby — closer to what Oanh personally preferred. Night-flying insects, whose ancestors were unintended immigrants aboard earlier starships, buzzed about her face. The filter kept them out of the hotel as it sorted air molecules by energy level, directing slow molecules inward while shunting the faster ones outside.

Bioliers on high curved standards flooded the street with their soft gleam, about forty percent of normal daylight illumination. They were balanced toward the green in a way that Oanh found unpleasant. A minibus and a large cargo hauler moaned past.

At the side of the Towers building was a barred rank of rental vehicles, two- to eight-place in size. Oanh stepped toward them before she remembered that her credit chip was valid only on Nevasa.

She turned. The four Grantholmers were already on top of her. They must have moved like cats, for all their bulk and injuries. "Looking for a ride, girlie?" one of them said. "We'll give you a ride."

"Rent one of those vans, Golschbauer," the leader ordered curtly. "The closed one."

Oanh tried to dart between two of the men. The leader caught her easily and gripped her from behind at the base of her skull. His thumb and forefinger clamped like ice-tongs. Oanh tried to scream, but she couldn't make any of her muscles obey. Her vision slipped through screens of orange and blue. The edges of things blurred.

"*Now*, Golschbauer!" the leader snarled from a great

distance. "Don't do anything to offend the spy cameras."

Holding Oanh with an ease that mimicked gentleness, he smiled and nodded in the direction of the recording unit on the nearest biolier. An artificial intelligence patrolled the streets of the New Port, fed by cameras mounted to view all of the community's open spaces.

Any event which departed from the accepted matrix — a fight, a vehicular accident, a drunk returned from Tarek's Bay waving a liquor bottle — brought a human emergency services team. The teams had medical support and enough firepower to splatter a determined problem over a city block.

The New Port was run not by democrats but by an oligarchy of shipping corporations. Municipal services were carried out with brutal efficiency.

Vehicles passed in the street. No one looked toward Oanh and her captors with even the vaguest interest.

"What's going on here?" someone demanded in a voice like gunshots. "You there — von Pohlitz! Let that woman go unless you plan to spend the rest of your life on a penal asteroid as soon as you next touch Grantholm soil!"

Oanh didn't recognize the voice. Her captor turned to face the question, carrying her with him.

She saw Franz, his face thinned into a hatchet by white fury.

The bar containing the rental vehicles dropped. A large van pulled from the rank.

"And just who are you to interfere with me and my girlfriend, little fellow?" the Grantholm leader asked in a harsh, contemptuous voice. He gripped Oanh even more firmly. Her knees buckled, but she remained standing like a skeleton clamped in a display stand.

The van swung around tightly in the street and pulled up where it blocked the nearest camera's view of

Franz. One of the Grantholmers stepped close to trap the smaller man against the vehicle.

"Who am I?" Franz snarled. "I'm the nephew of the Secretary of State for Foreign Affairs, you dogturds. *I'm* the grandson of the man who commanded the Grantholm Legion on Lusignan. I'm Franz Streseman, that's who I am!"

The Grantholm leader grunted as though he'd been gutshot. He released Oanh and stepped back. She started to fall. Franz caught her around the waist and shoulders and nestled her body against his. Her skin was flushed and she felt as though she was being dragged through a bed of nettles.

"Sir, we meant no — " one of the Grantholmers began.

"Get into that car and get out of New Port!" Franz snarled in the voice of a man Oanh hadn't met until this moment. "*Don't* come back until the *Empress* is ready to lift!"

There was a bustle of motion, big men scuttling into the van as though whips instead of words cracked against them.

"And if I see *any* of you feces during the rest of the voyage, it will be the worse for you when we reach Grantholm. I, Franz Streseman, promise it!"

The springs of the rental vehicle yelped as the last man leaped aboard. The engine wasn't powerful enough to chirp the tires as the driver stamped on the throttle, but the van continued to accelerate for as long as it remained in sight.

Oanh's vision was returning to normal. Her skin felt clammy. Franz kissed her.

"Darling," he murmured. "My love? Are you all right?"

"Franz, let's go inside," she said. Her voice was hoarse.

"Please!" he begged. He stepped back, holding

her by both shoulders. "Please — now that you
know. Is it . . . ?"

"I don't want to talk about it now," Oanh said. "Let's
go up to the room."

She threw herself into his arms again and kissed him
fiercely. She couldn't see for her tears. She knew that by
her statement, she *had* answered Franz's question and all
the questions behind it; all the questions he had been
afraid to raise and she was afraid to look at, even now.

"I don't want to talk about it ever!" she shouted in a
despairing voice as she clung to her lover.

The primary was at zenith, filling half the sky. The
water in the lagoon boiled with moonfish, ten-centimeter
disks of succulent flesh. They formed streamers of blue
and silver and magenta, rotating and coalescing as they
shifted. By now they covered most of the enclosed water,
mimicking the primary's opalescent atmosphere with
their own varihued skins.

She stretched over the air mattress, supporting herself on toes and fingertips with her pubic wedge the
highest point of a perfect arch. Ran looked down at
her. The primary mottled her pale skin with bands of
color more intricate than the finest tattooing.

"Do you like it?" she asked softly. Her eyes were
closed.

Ran knelt beside her on the mattress again. "It's
beautiful," he said.

"I told you my planet was beautiful," she said. "Not
just the moonfish, but the moonfish now. Of course,
everything becomes beautiful in breeding season."

She held her position like a painted ivory bow. It was
uncanny. He began to fondle her. Her vaginal muscles
accepted his finger greedily, but the rest of her body
remained frozen.

"Humans have the power here," she said. "That's
not wrong — it's like the storms on the face of the

primary. Nature can't be wrong. But they're the wrong kind of humans, don't you think?"

"Yes," said Ran. He continued to hold her, but his member had lost its renewing stiffness. There were stories about what you found on the beaches of Ain. . . . "I think so, yes."

She lifted her right hand from the mattress and combed her fingers through his hair while she balanced on only three points. "What would you do about it if it were your decision, starman?" she asked. Her eyes opened. They reflected the rich light of the planet above.

"I might try to kill them," Ran said, his finger stroking in and out. His clothes lay in a neat pile on the other side of the mattress. The pistol was with them.

"That's not a solution," she said, smiling up at him. "Humans *have* the power. Power to sterilize the planet if they became angry and frightened enough. And the problem isn't humans, it's the kind of humans. Much better to replace them. Over time."

Ran Colville was as still as ice, except for his right hand.

"Silly!" she said. "Not like that, not anything bad."

She seated herself and drew Ran's lips to hers with the same lithe motion. Leaning back from the kiss, she said, "I'm human, darling. *You* know that."

"Yes," Ran's lips agreed.

"There's a fishing community on the other side of the planet," she said. "It's been growing for fifty years. And it's been very successful commercially."

"That's where you come from?" asked Ran. Her flesh was warm and smooth. The contact reassured him.

"No," she said, "though I visit." Her slim, muscular fingers caressed Ran's bare shoulders.

"They're good people," she said. "Their fathers cared about more things than they could find in Tarek's Bay — or in the New Port either." Her mouth worked in a moue of distaste. "That place is almost worse. It's sterile."

"And their mothers?" Ran asked quietly.

She pulled him close again. Her erect nipples tickled his chest hair. "Their mother cares about the planet," she said. "Very much."

She made a soft purring noise in her throat before she continued. "There's an address in the pocket on the driver's side. It's a public garage. Leave the car there when you get back to Tarek's Bay."

"But . . . ?" Ran said.

"I'm going to stay here and swim for a while," she explained. She giggled. "But afterward."

She drew him down over her. Ran couldn't imagine that he'd be able to do either of them any good under the circumstances —

But the circumstances took over. As she'd said, she was human. Or as close as made no difference.

● HOBILO

"Stabilized," said the Second Officer in a tone of relief, as though he personally had been pushing upward to bring the *Empress of Earth* to a halt above the surface of Hobilo.

"Very good, Mr. Bruns," said Captain Kanawa. "Ms. Seligly, initiate docking sequence."

The First Officer engaged the autopilot. The star-liner shuddered as the artificial intelligence took command of the six tugs locked against the hull. Seligly's fingers fanned over the manual keyboard, touching nothing but ready to assert control at the first sign of a hiccough in the software.

The Third Officer's console displayed the Mainland Terminal, a sprawl of buildings on raw red soil. The terminal was in the central highlands of Hobilo's larger continent. A web of pipes and monorail tracking joined at the terminal, but the lines' further ends disappeared into the mist-shrouded lowlands where all other human development on the planet had occurred.

Seven ships were already on the ground at Mainland Terminal, besides the rusting hulks of a dozen more dragged to the edge of the plateau. Four of them were purpose-built tankers, comparable in size to the *Empress* herself. The others were combination vessels with large cargo holds and provision for a limited number of passengers.

"Sir, we've beaten the *Brasil* in," the Third Officer noted.

"We have?" said Kanawa. His voice was so empty of

emotion that the officers who had served with him for several voyages knew that he was concerned.

The *Empress* lurched, steadied, and began to drop at a smoothly constant rate of acceleration. Seligly tapped in a command to counteract a hint of rotation. One of the tugs was operating at well below optimum thrust, and the autopilot hadn't gotten the correction factor precisely right.

"Bridge, give me a ground link," said Captain Kanawa, continuing to stand beside his console. His left hand switched the display from figures to a visual of the terminal, but he didn't bother to look at it.

"*Empress* to Terminal Control," Kanawa continued after a pause.

"Terminal Control," said a colorless voice. Because Kanawa was using the general pickup, the response came through the bridge speakers unless he chose to switch it through a lockout channel to his ears only.

"Advise me as to the status of the starliner *Brasil*," Kanawa said. He stood rigidly upright, with his wrists crossed behind his back. "Over."

Mainland Terminal swelled on the visual displays. At higher magnification, patches of jungle could be glimpsed through the mist over the lowlands.

"The *Brasil* is seven hours and thirty-two minutes overdue," Terminal Control replied without emphasis.

"Control," Kanawa ordered. "Switch me to a human operator. Over."

The *Empress* trembled as the magnetic motors increased their braking thrust and the pulses reached a harmonic with the starliner's hull. The First Officer's fingers dipped, but this time the autopilot had erased the problem before Seligly could react to it.

The speakers crackled, then burped as though someone had tapped a microphone. "*Empress*, this is supervisor Vogt," said a voice with normal human intonations. "What can I help you with? Over."

"Ground, what's the situation with the *Brasil*?" Kanawa said. "You must have had some reports about her. Over."

"Not a word, *Empress*," the terminal supervisor said. "We thought you might know something yourself. Over."

"And why did you think such a bloody stupid thing as that?" shouted Captain Kanawa. "*Empress of Earth*, out!"

All those on the *Empress*'s bridge kept their eyes focused on their instruments. A rating swallowed a sneeze to keep from calling attention to herself. Her eyes bulged.

Kanawa switched his console back to an alphanumeric display of thrust, fuel, and force vectors. It was the first time any of his bridge crew had seen the captain openly lose his temper.

"Know where you're going, Ran?" Wanda Holly asked from behind him on the noisy platform.

"You bet," Ran said, turning. "But I haven't a clue to how I'm going to get there. I figured there'd be signs up in the station."

The remaining contingent of Third Class passengers were marching down the rear ramp of the *Empress* into a huge shed whose sidewalls stood only a meter and a half high to permit the sluggish breeze to flow through. The emigrants looked around curiously, nervously. Some of them fanned themselves with their shirtfronts.

"If it's this hot in the highlands," Ran added, "what's it like down where the settlements are?"

"Muggy," Wanda said. "Not really hotter, but you can get used to anything if you have to. *They'll* have to," she added, nodding toward the emigrants.

First Watch was responsible for off-loading this time. The task was deemed simple enough that Kneale hadn't drafted in personnel from other watches.

"They don't seem to mind when they get off the ship here," she mused, as much to herself as to Ran. "But in a lot of ways, Biscay might be an easier place to live, once you settle in."

Wanda shrugged, as though losing a weight. "Where is it you want to go, then?" she asked.

"Taskerville," Ran said. "I'm not sure the place even exists anymore."

"Oh, it exists, all right," Wanda said. She pursed her lips. "By way of Kilmarny," she said, "but it's on the Hunter's Hill line, and that's down at this — " she pointed and began walking " — end of the platform."

Diesel-electric monorails passed with a hiss and the rattling of valves. Most of them were only two or three cars together, garishly painted but scraped and battered in appearance. The roof of the lead car invariably mounted a machine gun on a Scarff ring.

Some of the rough-clothed men and women on the platform carried guns of their own, powerful rifles or even plasma weapons. Ran glanced at them and frowned.

"It's for the wildlife," Wanda commented. "The Long Troubles ended when the Prophet Elias was hanged."

Ran nodded. "I didn't know what . . ." he said.

Wanda stopped at a two-car train whose engines chittered at idle. A metal sign above on the platform's overhang said Hunter's Hill, though corrosion had eaten away all but the first letter of Hill. Six people were aboard the train already. They sat in sullen apathy. Each guarded a bale of goods purchased or picked up at the port.

Wanda thumbed toward the sign. "They figure on Hobilo that you either know where you're going or you don't. Either way, it's no concern to anybody else. Unless you're a load of oil."

The monorail tracks dipped over one another leaving the terminal, but there seemed to be no common lines. Ran's index finger caressed the reader on his belt.

A man detached himself from a refreshment kiosk

and walked toward the cab of the train. He glanced at the Trident officers but didn't speak.

"That'll be the driver," Wanda said. She cleared her throat. "Do you want some company, Ran?" she added.

"Yeah, I think maybe I would," Ran said. "But it must be out of your way?"

A train accelerated out of the station with a squeal and clatter that devoured all conversation. Wanda Holly stepped to the cab and thrust a credit chip into the reader there. The driver watched without expression as he revved his engines up to operating load.

"Taskerville," Wanda said. The AI in the device debited her chip by the amount of the fare. "There isn't much difference in where you are on Hobilo, except for Crater Creek, where the city's domed and environmentally controlled. I wouldn't mind seeing Taskerville."

Ran paid his fare and followed Wanda into the lead car. The driver didn't bother to let them settle on the hard plastic bench before he threw his shift lever into drive and the train lurched forward.

A small freighter screamed skyward on its own motors and those of a pair of tugs, making the monorail sway as it plunged off the plateau toward the misty forests below.

"Why Taskerville?" Wanda said. When Ran didn't answer, she went on, "If you don't mind my asking?"

Ran cleared his mind of an image of guns winking in a swamp, while muzzle blasts splashed the water beneath them. "Sorry Wanda," he said. "Because my Dad was here."

Forest closed in as a green shadow. The driver extended a cutter from the bow of the lead car. Almost at once the sharp-edged loop began to slap at tendrils which had grown toward the line since the train made its inward run.

"During the Troubles?" Wanda asked.

"The end of them," Ran agreed. "It was three more

months before they caught the Prophet, but Dad always said they'd broken the back of the Troubles at Taskerville."

He licked his lips. "He was one of the mercenaries hired by the corporations. I once asked him what he'd gotten out of — being a mercenary. And he said, 'A lot of things to think about, Ran.' Later, I found the chips his helmet had recorded during, during Taskerville. And I thought I'd . . . see the place myself."

"Your father's dead?" Wanda asked gently.

"Oh, yes," Ran said. "Nothing left of him but bones and maybe a few memories."

"No maybe there, friend," Wanda Holly murmured so softly that her lips scarcely seemed to move.

Something the size and shape of a dirty gray blanket hung from a tree just off the cleared line. It rotated as the monorail passed. One of the passengers on the rear car fired her rifle at the creature without evident effect.

Ran Colville's mind filled with bloody memories of sights his eyes had never seen.

"You can drive, you know," Oanh said as she pulled the aircar in a tight bank around a stand of conifers whose peaks reached many meters above the vehicle's present altitude. Oanh spoke harshly, and she showed a hard hand on the controls. They were traveling through the close vegetation at 40 kph.

"I've never driven one like this model myself," Franz said precisely. "You're doing better than I could."

He was half lying, but he didn't want a fight, and anyway, Oanh *was* in full control of the aircar. She was driving uncomfortably fast and cutting too close to obstacles, but those were deliberate ploys to get him to object — and thus put himself in the wrong.

They blasted down a boggy creek. Bands of denser mist flicked past the windscreen of the open car.

The danger was that in trying to make Franz react, Oanh would drive the vehicle into a tree or down the throat of a giant carnivore.

A dozen quadrupeds weighing between one and three tonnes apiece browsed among the reeds. They lurched up on their hind legs as the car overflew them. Each male had a coiled resonator on the end of his beaked snout. They hooted in mournful surprise.

Franz twisted in his seat to look back at the herbivores. "The guidechip said that you had to get much farther from the terminal to see herds like that," he said. "I guess it was wrong."

"Well, that's not surprising," Oanh said, her eyes straight ahead and her hands clamped like claws on the controls. "Everybody's wrong except you, aren't they?"

"Oanh, set her down and let's talk," Franz said.

"I don't want to set down!" Oanh shouted. She turned to glare at her passenger. "And there's nothing to talk about anyway, since you've made up your mind!"

"Love —"

An air plant lowered a trailer from a high branch, angling for an open space in which its fluorescent bloom would be visible to the nectar-drinkers that fertilized it. The car slammed into the flower with a jolt and a splotch of sticky pollen that looked like a bomb-burst on the bow and windscreen.

The tendril, freed of the flower whose weight it supported, sprang up. A coil of it snagged the barrel of the rifle Franz held upright beside his seat.

"Hey!" the youth bellowed. He managed to grab the weapon before the plant pulled it away.

Oanh gave a cry of despair and backed off the throttle. The aircar wobbled downward. They were headed toward a bed of spiky vegetation whose leaves slanted up at forty-five degrees to channel water to reservoirs in the stubby trunks.

Franz started to say something. He decided not to.

Oanh advanced the throttle again, adjusted the fan attitude to bring the car to a hover, and landed them ably in a patch of lace-leafed plants shaded by the branches of tall trees. The same tendril that grabbed the gun had snatched Oanh's cap off and raised a red welt across her forehead.

Franz nestled the rifle back into its butt-clamp. The weapon was part of the rental vehicle's equipment, like the radio beacon, flares, and emergency rations.

Oanh shut off the motors and slumped on her controls. Franz put his arm around the girl's shoulders and kissed her cheek because he couldn't reach her mouth. She twisted to return the kiss. Her lips were wet with tears, and she continued to sob.

A pair of small creatures fluttered and chased one another through the branches above the vehicle. Occasionally a flash of vivid yellow would show through the foliage. Bits of bark pattered down.

Oanh drew back. "You say you have to go," she said, enunciating carefully. "But you don't. We'll be diverting from Grantholm because of the war, so they can't take you off the ship. And you say you *hate* the war!"

"The war is stupid and it's unnecessary," Franz said. "I knew that before I even met you. But I'm a Streseman, love, and I — have to go."

"There's no *have* to," she pleaded. "Individuals have to make decisions for themselves. Otherwise there'll be more blood and more death and everybody loses!"

The contradiction between Oanh's words and her determination to decide for Franz raised a touch of rueful humor in the boy's mind, but the expression didn't reach his lips. She was right, he supposed. And he was right, saying that he had to do his duty, because Stresemans *did* their duty at whatever the cost.

The whole system was rotten, but Franz Streseman turning his back on ten generations of family tradition wasn't going to change it for the better.

"I'm sorry," he said. He leaned toward her. For a moment, Oanh drew further away before she met his kiss. She began to cry again.

An animal *whuff*ed close by. Franz sat bolt upright. He couldn't see the beast, but it was large enough that he could feel its footsteps on the thin soil. He freed the rifle from its boot and chambered a round.

Oanh wiped her face with her sleeve and switched the fan motors back on. The blades pinged through stems which had sprung into their circuit when the motors cut off. She swung the car steeply upward. A little forward angle would have smoothed the wobbly liftoff, but that would have taken them closer to the source of the noise while they were still at low altitude.

The creature walked into the clearing on four legs. It had a barrel-shaped body with a small head and a meter-long spike on either shoulder. One of its eyes rotated separately to follow the aircar without a great deal of interest. Ignoring the soft vegetation underfoot, the creature lifted up on its hind legs and began stripping tree branches of their bark and prickly foliage.

Franz laughed in relief. "Well, I guess it could've stepped on us," he said, "so I won't say it's harmless. The damned thing scared me out of a year's growth."

"Are there more of them?" Oanh asked. She held the aircar in a hover, even with the herbivore's raised head. "It must weigh five tonnes."

"At least," the boy agreed.

He held the rifle gingerly, now that he didn't need it anymore. The weapon was of an unfamiliar design. Franz wasn't sure how best to empty the chamber, and he was afraid to put it back in its clamp with only the safety catch to prevent it from firing in event of a shock.

They were both glad the creature had changed the subject, because they knew the discussion wasn't going anywhere.

"The guideb—" Franz said.

The creature that burst out of the shadowed undergrowth was bipedal and ten meters from nostrils to tailtip. It had the lithe ranginess of a bullwhip. As the herbivore tried to settle and turn, the attacker caught it with long, clawed forelimbs and slammed fanged jaws closed on the victim's throat.

"Back!" Franz screamed as he pointed his rifle over the side of the car and leaned into it. Oanh had already slammed her throttle against the stops, transforming the vehicle's hover into a staggering climb.

The animals below shrieked like steam whistles as they rolled together across the forest floor. The carnivore kept clear of its victim's defensive spikes, but the shock of hitting even soggy ground beneath the tonnes of scaly body should have been devastating. A sapling twenty centimeters in diameter shattered when the creatures slammed against it.

Franz took a deep breath and relaxed, swinging the rifle's muzzle upward again.

"You didn't shoot," Oanh said. They were hovering again, a hundred meters in the air. The battle went on below through wrappings of mist roiled by the aircar's fans.

Franz looked at his weapon. He still didn't know how to clear the chamber. "There wasn't any need," he said. "If I'd had to, I would have shot."

Oanh was staring at him. It made him uncomfortable, though she no longer seemed angry. "Well," Franz said, "we're getting our money's worth of sightseeing, aren't we?"

Oanh adjusted the fans forward and brought the car around in a sweeping turn. "Let's go back to the terminal," she said. "There'll be a hotel there, or we can use your cabin on the ship."

Franz nodded, his face neutral.

"We don't have very much time," Oanh explained. She swallowed. "I don't want to waste what we have."

*   *   *

The fringes of Taskerville were colorful prefabs of reinforced thermoplastic, one or two stories high. They had been erected in the past fifteen or twenty years, since Hobilo got its own industrial base to process the hydrocarbons which permeated all levels of the planet's rocks.

Old Taskerville was built of limestone and concrete. In surviving structures, plastic tile had replaced the original roofs of shakes laid over wooden trusses, but the walls were as solid as rock outcrops.

That was true even of the buildings which had been blasted beyond repair in the fighting that ended the Long Troubles. Two of them stood gaunt and blackened on the north side of the square: a cube and a tall pyramid of concrete struts which had once been joined by full-height stained glass windows.

Originally the structures had been the Municipal Building and the Roman Catholic cathedral for the Western See of Hobilo. At the start of the Long Troubles, they became the military headquarters for the Sword of the New Dispensation and the home of the Prophet Elias, late Father Elias, an itinerant priest whose congregation spanned scores of hunting camps and wellheads.

Twice during twenty-seven years of war, flying columns of troops of the government in Crater Creek had penetrated to Taskerville. Both units were cut off. They attempted fighting retreats which dissolved into routs with eighty percent casualties. Mercenaries from a dozen fringe worlds, officered by Grantholmers and paid by a consortium of multiplanetary corporations, finally achieved the total victory which had eluded the local government.

At a cost.

"There's a monument in front of the burned-out buildings," Wanda said. She frowned. "It's been defaced."

"I don't think it's been defaced," Ran said. He walked slowly across the square, avoiding shills and pedestrians without seeming to look at them. "I think it's just birdshit. Or the local equivalent."

Ran guessed the permanent population of Taskerville was in the order of a thousand, but there was a floating supplement of at least twice that. The streets were thronged with lizard hunters and oil drilling personnel — and sailors. He'd already noticed several bands of crewmen from the *Empress of Earth*. Because Taskerville was the center of a frontier region, it had the facilities to entertain the rougher sort of starfarers as well.

The square was an open-air market of kiosks and barrows, each covered with a bright sheet against the morning and afternoon rains. The permanent buildings were given over to businesses which required a degree of security: banking, high-stakes gambling, accommodations for wealthy transients, and — on the upper floors — prostitution, both high-volume knocking shops and a modicum of privacy for the independents working the square.

The monument was a Celtic cross, of stone rather than cast concrete and three meters high. Large letters on the crossbar read SACRED TO THE MEMORY OF THOSE WHO DIED THAT FREEDOM MIGHT LIVE, but the double column of names down the vertical post was obscured by years of white streaking.

The creatures that flapped away from Ran's deliberate approach were winged and seemed to have feathers, so perhaps they *were* birds.

Ran keyed the chip that had been recorded by his father's helmet during the final assault. He saw —

Three of the armored personnel carriers in the square

were burning. They bubbled with thick black smoke, from lubricants and plastics and the bodies of troops who died when rebel weapons destroyed the vehicles.

A dozen more of the APCs had survived. Their cupola guns fired ropes of pearl-white tracer point blank into the buildings the rebels still held on the north side. Other friendly troops — all of them from the Adjunct Regiments, the mercenaries; there were no Hobilo natives present except for those serving the Prophet Elias — shot from the cleared structures to the left and right, adding to the base of fire that prepared the assault.

The recording lens in Chick Colville's helmet lurched upward as he and five other mercenaries climbed through the top hatch of their vehicle. They jumped down to the pavement of cracked concrete and ran in a squat, as if forcing themselves against a fierce wind.

Colville was the last man. The troopers to either side of him fell, one like a sack of potatoes, the other twisted onto her back, a ragged tear in her thigh and a look of disbelief on her face when her visored helmet rolled free.

The muzzle flashes of the shots that felled them twinkled from twenty meters up the spire of the cathedral. Ricochets sparked away in puffs of powdered concrete.

Chick Colville was slower than his comrades because he carried the flamethrower. The fat nozzle rose into the field of view as he aimed. Recoil from the jet of metallized napalm shifted the viewpoint back a further step, but the flame rod arched between the concrete struts like a thread into the slot of a needle. An explosion cascaded sparks both inside and outside the cathedral.

Ran walked forward, seeing only the projected hologram. Vendors offered fruits at the edge of his awareness. He heard Wanda say harshly, "No, we don't want any!"

The cathedral's bronze doors had been blown into the sanctuary; cannonfire had cut completely through the stone post between the right and center portals. There was no one *alive in the circular nave. The floor was littered with rubble and bodies.*

"Careful, Ran," Wanda said. Her hand was on his arm, guiding him. "There's three steps."

The last snipers had used a scaffolding supported at mid-height by a wooden trellis. It was ablaze. A corpse hung from a crossbeam, and two bodies which had fallen to the floor also burned from Colville's flame.

The mercenaries preceding him stumbled over litter in their haste to reach the door behind the wrecked altar. An APC's automatic cannon fired into the nave. White flashes filled the air with shell fragments that, for a wonder, seemed to hit nobody.

A trooper from Colville's squad hurled a satchel charge through the doorway. Someone on the other side threw it back. Everybody flattened. There was a flash and a jolt. Everything jumped, and the rockdust lifted in a clinging pall. Colville scrambled to his feet.

In the hologram, a stone statue of the Virgin lay broken on the floor of the sanctuary. Wanda murmured a warning, but Ran's feet were already avoiding an obstacle which had not moved in thirty years.

The flamethrower was the weapon of choice for clearing the room beyond, but before Colville's nozzle steadied, two mercenaries jumped into the doorway firing their automatic rifles. Other troopers lobbed grenades past them. One of the men fell, but the other ducked clear just as the grenades slammed black pulses through the opening.

Wobbling like a drunk, Chick Colville reached the doorway with a woman from another APC carrying a magazine-fed grenade launcher.

Originally the space beyond had been a dressing room for the officiating priests. The followers of the Prophet had opened out the walls to create an inner sanctuary as large as the nave.

There were hundreds of people inside. Most of them were children, old folks, and the sick or wounded. They were chant-

*ing hymns, nodding to a dozen tempi. The eyes in their
upraised faces were blankly glazed.*

*A handful of adult men, naked except for the sheen of blood,
were cutting the throats of the others with butcher knives.*

*One of the healthy males, tonsured as a priest, turned
and faced the recording lens. He bayed something that
would have been madly unintelligible even if the helmet
had recorded sound. The priest thrust his knife into the neck
of an infant and jerked the blade forward through the
tough gristle of the child's windpipe. When he tossed the
spouting corpse aside, its head and torso were connected
only by the spinal column.*

*The flame rod struck the priest in the face, then swept right
and left across the big room. Ten seconds worth of fuel remained
in Colville's bottles. When he had expended it, the abattoir had
become a funeral pyre for dead and dying alike. The flames
leapt and shuddered as the grenadier emptied her weapon also,
and other mercenaries loosed into the charnel nightmare which
the fire erased.*

The recording ended.

Ran Colville sank to his knees. Wanda was holding him. "Are you all right?" she said. "Are you all
right?" When he finally heard her voice, she was
shouting.

Ran put his arms around the woman. He spat out
words like bursts of automatic gunfire. "My Dad said,
'When you're old enough, kid, I'll show you; but you won't
understand.' But he didn't show me. He died. And I found
his chips. I watched them. I didn't understand."

He drew in a shuddering breath. "Only now I think
I understand."

Wanda patted his back awkwardly, then eased him to
his feet. "I don't know about you," she said, "but I
could use a drink."

Ran forced a smile, hugged the woman close for a
moment, then turned her loose.

"You know," he said in a falsely cheerful voice as they

headed toward a kiosk selling home-brewed beer in plastic cups, "I thought Dad was a cold-hearted bastard. He never gave me a pat on the back when I did something right, and he never let it pass when I screwed up. And then he died."

Ran reached over without seeming to look and caught Wanda's hand, squeezing it. "He was a bastard, I guess. But I wish the poor bastard was around. So I could apologize for all the things I thought about him."

The single monorail car rocked around an outcrop almost concealed by the jungle. A trio of long-necked female herbivores cocked their heads at the vehicle. The male, forty meters long and twice the bulk of the members of his harem, hooted querulously and puffed out his bright red throat wattles. Ms. Dewhurst gasped in delighted amazement.

The car hummed back into its tunnel through the vegetation.

Wade chuckled contentedly. "There, old fellow," he said to Dewhurst. "I told you this is the way to sightsee on Hobilo. Basic passage on one of the local runs, none of this nonsense about renting an aircar."

"If we'd rented a car, we wouldn't have just whipped by them and gone," Dewhurst grumbled, fulfilling his end of the symbiotic relationship.

"I shouldn't have thought you'd be driving under the canopy, here," Belgeddes said. "I wouldn't, at any rate. I leave that sort of thing to people like Dickie, here. He never saw a risk without wanting to take it."

"Tsk!" said Wade. "If I'd been thinking, I'd have suggested that we bring a cooler like that vendor at the back of the car has. This would be a good time for a beer — if I'd only thought ahead."

"Vendor?" asked Da Silva, looking at the half dozen Hobilo natives sharing the vehicle with the tourists.

One of them was a woman of indeterminate age, seated on an insulated cooler that looked bigger than she herself was.

"So I surmise," agreed Wade. He looked tactfully away. Da Silva stood up, fumbled out a credit chip, and made his way down the swaying aisle toward the woman.

"Well then, Belgeddes," Dewhurst said. "We could all have rented one car and Wade here could have driven us himself. What were you here on Hobilo, Wade? A field marshal?"

Dewhurst turned to glance out at the landscape of fleshy, spike-edged leaves just as a pair of lizards banked away from the window. The creatures were only thirty centimeters long nose to tail, and they were cruising for arthropods stirred up by the monorail's passage. They glided on flaps of skin stretched by their hind legs while they used their webbed forepaws like canard fins to steer.

Dewhurst saw open jaws of needle teeth fringing scarlet palates. He shouted and jumped back while his wife, who'd watched the lizards' approach, oohed in delight.

"Actually, my friend . . ." Wade said as he looked toward the jungle. His mouth held only the slightest twist of satisfaction. "The last time I drove in this tangle, I hit a tree and had to hike the next twenty klicks. Nothing I'd choose to do again, either one of those things, I assure you."

Da Silva came back with five glass-bottled beers, jeweled with condensation.

Ms. Dewhurst looked at the local brew with an expression mingled of curiosity and horror, the way she might have viewed the *thing* her cat was playing with on the rug. She waved the offer away.

"All the more for the rest of us," Belgeddes said contentedly.

Dewhurst mopped his face with a kerchief and settled his expression behind the cloth. "Racing to rescue hostages during the Long Troubles, I dare say, Wade?"

he said in a slightly wheezy voice. "When you had the crash, I mean?"

"Coming back, actually, weren't you, Dickie?" Belgeddes said around the mouth of his beer.

"Yes, that's right," Wade agreed. "And they put a burst into the rear linkages — firing from the church dome." He shook his head sadly. "I was a young fellow then, idealistic. I didn't dream the rebels would put armed men in their churches, for pity's sake!"

"Dewhurst was wondering if you were a field marshal," Belgeddes said. "That's not how I remember it."

"Certainly not," Wade said. "Civilian, purely a civilian at the time. But the poor fellow's daughters — Varkezadhy, it was, planetary manager for Simourgh Corporation — had been kidnapped as hostages. Whatever you thought of the chap — "

"Simourgh gives a bad name to greed," Da Silva said through pursed lips.

" — or of Simourgh," Wade agreed, nodding, "I couldn't let that happen to a pair of sweet little children. Slipped in from behind on foot — "

"That can't have been easy, Dickie," Belgeddes said.

The monorail hummed over a slough of water black with tannin dissolved from the logs rotting in it. Animals stared at the car or dived away, but even Ms. Dewhurst was watching Wade now.

"Not so very hard," Wade said in self-deprecation. "They weren't expecting it, you see. One man, that is. And I stole an aircar when we escaped."

He sighed. "I often think," he continued, "that if I'd assassinated the Prophet instead of snatching the girls back, things might have been different."

"The Prophet Elias was there?" Da Silva blurted.

Wade nodded. "Oh, yes," he said. "It was at Taskerville, don't you know? But I was naive, as I say. Cold-blooded murder was just beyond me then."

"Wait a minute," said Dewhurst. "If the car crashed,

then what happened to the hostages? The little girls, you call them."

"Eight years standard," Belgeddes said. "I'd call that little." His hand wavered toward the full bottle. "I wonder, if no one else is interested. . . ?"

Wade's slim, aristocratic fingers closed on the bottle's neck. "A thirsty business, thinking about old times," he said. "If no one minds?"

He took a deep draft from the bottle. Something that looked like grass floated in the liquid.

"The girls?" Wade resumed. "Well, I brought them back with me, of course. They could walk, most of the way, and I was younger then and fit."

He sighed. "I don't mind telling you, though — "

Belgeddes pointed. As if on cue, a monster with high shoulders and hog-like jaws crushed through a flowering shrub and rasped a buzzsaw challenge to the monorail. The beast was very nearly as big as the vehicle. The car speeded up. The driver tracked the creature with the automatic cannon over his cab until they were safely past.

" — that there were times I was nervous about it," Wade concluded. He smiled and finished the beer, grass and all, with a rhythmic pumping of his throat.

"I think I could take the heat," Wanda said, "but not the humidity."

The mist-shrouded sky was a sheet of white metal in which the sun was only a brighter shimmering. Driven by warmth, moisture, and light diffused over sixty-two percent of the daily cycle by Hobilo's atmosphere, the jungle encroached not only from the fringes of Taskerville but also from above. Air plants draped themselves from most horizontal surfaces of the town, and saplings managed to root themselves wherever mud had splashed.

Ran smiled. "People can take whatever they have

to," he said. "It wouldn't be my choice for home either, though."

He finished his beer — which had a fruity taste. Not bad, exactly; wet, which his dry throat had needed, and from a refrigerated keg; but he was pretty sure he didn't want to know a lot about the conditions in which the stuff had been brewed. "I wonder if there's a place to get a decent meal around here?" he asked.

The counterman had one eye and a withered arm. From the look of the scars, they'd been made by a knife rather than a lizard's claws. He squirted more beer into Ran's cup, filling it halfway with a head that spilled down the sides.

"There ought to be something," Wanda said. "There's a good place back at the Terminal — "

"Hey buddy!" the counterman said. "You didn't pay for the second beer!"

Ran's eyes glazed. "You're right," he said in a frozen voice. "And I didn't see how far I could stuff the cup up your asshole. So I'd say we were quits."

The counterman jerked against the back of his kiosk. His hand groped for something under the counter, but he didn't look down and his hand clutched air. Wanda offered him a mocking salute, then took Ran's arm and guided him away. "He didn't expect that from a starchy Trident officer," she said in amusement.

Ran managed a chuckle. "He wasn't talking to any kind of officer," he said. "That — Dad's recording. Kicked me back, you know?"

"You've done it, so it's over now," Wanda said as she steered them through the ruck.

A woman selling jewelry made from lizard teeth and light metal clutched Ran's wrist, crying, "Buy a pretty for your — "

Wanda leaned across her companion to stiff-arm the woman away.

"We didn't talk much, Dad didn't," Ran said musingly.

He put his hand on Wanda's nearer shoulder as if he needed her support. "I knew he'd carried a flamethrower, though, and once I asked him what it weighed. He said — and I didn't think he was answering me — he said he didn't know any flamethrower man who'd survived Hobilo. I said, 'But you did, Dad.'"

Wanda reached up and squeezed Ran's hand against the epaulet of her uniform.

"And he said," Ran continued in the same wondering tone, "'No I didn't, boy.' And he told me to leave him alone, like he usually did. And he got even drunker that night than usual. And I didn't understand."

They were walking toward the south entrance to the square. The buildings to either side of the street had concrete walls on the ground floor but plastic for the upper three stories.

A bank had the corner location in one of the buildings. An outside staircase beside the bank served the upper floors. At its foot, six men in blue uniforms stood around a prostitute wearing a backless lime-green dress with fishnet stockings of the same hue. The color and pattern made her look like a reptile, an impression which her narrow face reinforced.

"They aren't wearing caps or nametags," Wanda said, recognizing trouble by the fact the group of men were prepared for it with anonymity.

"Look, not *all* of you," the whore said. "Two at a time, for another five *over* — "

"They're ours," Ran said, jolted back to the present and glad to return. "They're from the Cold Crew."

"Let's not have any trouble, gents," said the pimp walking up behind the group. He was tall and snake-thin. He kept his hands ostentatiously in his pockets. "Little Mary's going to give you — "

Two of the sailors spun as though they'd rehearsed the maneuver a hundred times — and maybe they had, in the docks and dives of that many planets. They grabbed the pimp by the elbows, bent his arms back, and hurled him against the window marked SECURITY FINANCE.

The protective grating saved the glass. The pimp bounced back. His hands flopped loose. There hadn't been time to use whatever weapon he carried. The whore screamed. A sailor grabbed her from behind, with one calloused hand across her mouth and the other gripping her throat.

Wanda reached under the front of her tunic. Ran caught her hand. "Mine," he said.

A proctor with a tall red hat and a brassard dangling on his chest turned toward the commotion. He carried a shock rod and a pair of stun-gas projectors.

A sailor pointed his index finger at the proctor. "You want some?" he cried. "There's plenty for you!"

Spectators spun as though the finger repelled them. The proctor stared up at the top floor of the building, then pivoted slowly and sauntered in the other direction.

The two men with the pimp hurled him again. This time they missed the window. The victim walloped soddenly against the concrete wall.

The prostitute wasn't struggling. Her eyes were alert but resigned.

Ran approached the group with his hands at his sides, fingers spread and empty. One of the Cold Crewmen grunted a warning to the others.

"Want to join him, buddy?" a sailor snarled.

"Not me," said Ran. "Kephalonians, aren't you?"

It wasn't what the Cold Crewmen expected to hear from an officer of the *Empress of Earth*. Orders in a tone of false comradeship; wheedling perhaps; threats if the fellow was a fool, and he was fool enough to get involved, that was clear from the start.

"You got a problem with that?" the same sailor responded.

"Nope," Ran said. "Niko Mazurkas was from Kephalonia. I saw him trim three engines himself on the *Askenazy* for nine hours, till we made Manfred's Reach."

"Bullshit!" a sailor said. "You're a fucking officer!"

"You bet I am," Ran said. "Now. But I worked one engine and Niko worked three, nine hours and no relief. I was just a kid and it almost killed me, but we did it."

"God himself couldn't keep three engines trimmed smooth," said the man holding the whore.

"Smooth?" Ran crowed. "It was rough as a cob! But we got the bitch there, and we got five more men to replace the six gone blind from the rotgut they bought on Wanslea."

"Bullshit!" a sailor repeated.

"No, he's telling the truth," said the apparent leader. "Look at his fucking eyes."

The man holding the whore let her go, then gave her a little push to convince her that it was really happening.

"Ever since then," Ran said in a flat voice, staring a million klicks through the lichen-scaled concrete of the building, "I like to buy drinks for Kephalonians. Can I buy you men a drink?"

The Cold Crewmen looked at one another. "Naw, that's okay," the leader said. "Last thing I want is to have pay in my pocket when I go back aboard."

He took his soft cap out of his pocket and settled it on his head, then adjusted it by feel so that the legend embroidered on the tally, *Empress of Earth*, could be read by anyone looking at him.

"C'mon, you bastards," he added in gruff embarrassment. "Let's find a proper cathouse."

As the sailors strode off, arms akimbo and kicking their toes out with each step, one of those who had grabbed the pimp turned. "Hey, Lieutenant?" he called. "See you round!"

The prostitute half knelt, half squatted beside her pimp. Her clothes, though brief, were constraining.

The pimp groaned softly, which meant his head was harder than anybody would've expected. Ran nodded toward the whore and started to walk away.

She moved fast and with birdlike grace, putting herself in his way. Wanda stepped forward but paused.

The whore looked tiny up close. What Ran had thought was a skullcap was her own hair. It was dyed in streaks of black and a color close to that of her garments, then lacquered down. The marks of the sailor's fingers were red against her pale throat.

"I suppose you expect a freebie for what you did, huh?" the whore demanded in a shrill voice.

"I don't expect anything," Ran said. He tried to step around her.

She blocked his way again. She wasn't as young as he'd first thought. "I guess you think you're too good for me!" she said. "Is that it?"

He looked at her and she glared back. Whatever she saw in Ran Colville's eyes didn't bother her the way it did others when he wasn't careful; when he forgot or remembered, however you wanted to say it.

"I'm not too good for anybody," he said aloud. "Quite the contrary."

"Then come on up," the whore said crisply as she took him by the hand. "It's just up on the third."

Ran looked over his shoulder at Wanda Holly. "I'll be a little while," he said without inflection.

She raised an eyebrow. "Take a long time," she said. "Take twenty minutes. I'll have another beer."

She turned and stepped toward a drink kiosk — a different one — before Ran could reply.

If he intended to.

• CALICHEMAN

Ran Colville drew in a breath whose cool humidity felt good in his lungs. On Calicheman Trident Starlines docked at Longleat, a broad canal served along both sides by railways. Starship landings generated huge quantities of steam, most of which recondensed into droplets before the gangplanks lowered.

From the *Empress*'s pilotry data, society on Calicheman was similar to that of Ohio in the 1820s. It was a less uniform culture than many. Not surprisingly, its worst — and most extreme — aspects were concentrated in the district surrounding the starport.

A train, aided by scores of cabs and hire cars, had carried off those of the *Empress*'s passengers who disembarked — for good or just to stretch their legs. Calicheman's main export, beef from the feral cattle which roamed all three of the main continents, was coming aboard by the carload from the broad — 2-meter — gauge trains drawn up alongside the dock.

The beef would fill what had been the Third Class spaces, now refrigerated. The cargoes were comparable from a commercial viewpoint; on a bad day, Ran might have said that the connection was closer than that.

But this was a very *good* day, as sunny as Ran's disposition, and so far as he could tell, he was off duty now. He'd already freed Mohacks and Babanguida. Now he touched his transceiver to the lower end of the First Class gangplank and said, "Colville to Holly. Want to see what's happening on Calicheman, Wanda? Over."

"A lot of cows are turning grass into methane, unless the place has changed in the past three weeks," replied Wanda's voice, thinned by the transmission channel. She didn't need to cue Bridge, because the AI routed the response by default to the initial caller. "I'd take you around, but I've got deck watch. Sorry. Over."

A train energized its bearings and clanked upward from the rails. It chuffed forward the length of one car. Then it settled with a similar clang and resumed off-loading its pallets.

"This is the Commander's watch," Ran said in puzzlement. "Over."

"He's got something hush-hush at the embassy," Wanda explained. After a pause, she added, "The *Brasil* didn't touch down here either, you know. It looks as though she, well. . . But go enjoy yourself. Calicheman's not a bad place, so long as you mind your own business. The locals get pretty touchy about individual rights, though. Over."

"I've got no problem with that," Ran said. "Well, maybe you can look me up when you get free. Colville out."

Wanda snorted. "I'm not into threesomes," she said. "Holly out."

Ran didn't have problems with much of anything, not since Hobilo. The shadow of his father's past had been lifted — burned away as though by the metal-charged flame of Chick Colville's weapon. Seeing the actual place didn't make the events less horrible, but it proved they were over . . . as they had never been over for Ran's father, or for Ran until that moment of catharsis.

The taxi rank was empty, but a cab returning from Tidal had turned into the approach road. The noise of machinery chuckling as it shifted beef aboard the *Empress of Earth* seemed thin in the breeze and open spaces, but it completely covered the sound of two late-leaving passengers until they fell into step with Ran.

He turned in startlement. "Good morning, Lieutenant Colville," said Franz Streseman. The young Grantholmer held two overnight cases in his left hand. "May I present my friend Miss Tranh van Oanh? Or have you met?"

"Formally only," Ran said, "and barely that. Very glad to make your acquaintance, ma'am."

He bowed to Oanh. The girl looked like a lute string tuned a key above normal, but the problem wasn't between her and Franz. They'd been holding hands until Ran turned.

"Would you care to share a cab into Tidal, sir?" Franz offered.

"If you'll call me 'Ran' instead of 'sir,'" Ran said, and he opened the taxi's door for the young couple.

The prairies of Calicheman were covered with grasses close enough to those of Earth that some botanists claimed to have cross-bred the strains. These claims were disputed by others. Now that panspermia was no longer a hypothesis but simple observation, nobody familiar with the vast adaptability of plant species denied that it was theoretically possible.

The road from Longleat to Tidal, the largest of the nearby towns, was undermaintained, and quite a lot of the planetary traffic was off-road entirely. Local vehicles were designed for the prevailing conditions.

This cab, driven by a dour woman who carried her pistol in a cross-draw holster, rode high over large wheels. The vehicle gave the three passengers in back a good look at the rolling terrain of grasses, flowering shrubs, and small trees — not stunted, but saplings whose lifespan was limited by frequent prairie fires. From a non-specialist's standpoint, the landscape could have been the next panel from the hologram of the North American Midwest in Ran's cabin. Only the profusion of animal life provided an obvious difference.

Tidal was five kilometers away from the port. The trip was a panorama of brindled cattle, mixed in approximately equal numbers with a score of native herbivores.

Halfway along the jolting, swaying journey, Oanh leaned forward to look past Franz toward the Trident officer. "Are there proper docking facilities on Szgrane, sir?" she asked.

"They haven't docked anything our size," Ran said, stifling a wince at being called "sir" as if he was the girl's grandfather. "But then, neither had Grantholm until the *Empress* touched down on her maiden voyage."

He mentally reviewed the pilotry data. "They've got four modern tugs," he went on. "That's enough if they don't mind us digging a bit of a hole with our own motors at three-quarters power, which Trident will pay to repair."

"A backwater," Franz said, "but the port averages three landings a day. I've been there."

"No doubt a very suitable place from which to ferry all the soldiers returning to Grantholm to kill my compatriots," Oanh said. Her tone was noticeably cooler by the end of the comment than it had been at the beginning.

"Szgrane has an established trade with Grantholm," Ran said carefully, staring out the window so that he wouldn't have to notice the expressions on the faces of the young couple beside him. "But there's absolutely no possibility that the authorities on Szgrane would permit any insult to our Nevasan passengers. They're very — punctillious about their honor, the Szgranians."

The highway, such as it was, paralleled the railroad tracks. A twelve-car train howled by in the opposite direction, carrying more beef toward the *Empress* at 150 kph. Ran's teeth grated, and portions of the taxi moaned.

Railways on Calicheman used ultrasonics to clear the way ahead of them. The speed at which the trains sailed over their tracks on magnetic runners meant that the pulses had to be of high enough amplitude to ring harmonics from any object in the same county.

On many planets there would be laws to prevent the railways from such an obvious hazard to public health. On Calicheman — at least near the starport — a cowboy being hammered by ultrasonics was likely to take a shot at the train — but then, the train driver might well shoot back. Other lands, other customs.

Franz leaned forward and said to the driver, "Ah, can you drop us at the best hotel in Tidal, please?"

"I'll drop you in the square," the driver replied, "and you can walk to any damn hotel you please."

Ran sighed. He was as interested in personal freedom as the next fellow, but he couldn't understand people who felt that it was demeaning to do what somebody else paid you to do. That attitude got in the way of doing the best job possible . . . and Ran Colville didn't have any use for people who did less than the best job possible.

It was possible that the taxi driver was some sort of aberration. More likely, she was a foretaste of the hotel staff, waiters, clerks, and everydamnbody else he'd have to deal with in Tidal.

It was still a beautiful day.

Tidal wasn't on any body of water, which was a pity. Even a lake would have been useful to flush the effluvium of the slaughterhouses at the edge of town. Earthmoving equipment dug trenches to replace those already filled with stinking blood and offal. Flies and the native equivalents formed clouds that looked thick enough to walk on. Layers of quicklime, and the dirt bulldozed onto the trenches when evaporation had shrunk and congealed their contents, did little to discourage the insects.

"This is — hideous!" Oanh said.

"Amazing," Franz echoed in scarcely less pejorative tones.

"This is certainly the home of the rugged individual," Ran said mildly. "Nobody's asking us to live here, of course."

Though Calicheman was a beautiful place in its own stark fashion. Only the human colonists gave Ran pause. Not the first time he'd thought that about one planet or another.

Tidal was built in a melange of styles, most of them garish. High walls concealed and protected the homes of the wealthy, and virtually everyone Ran noticed on the streets was armed. There were no sidewalks, though paved plazas fronted some businesses.

The taxi pulled up hard enough to make the chassis sway on its springs. "Forty-two dollars," the driver said, tapping the sign on her reader.

"I'll get it," Franz said, extending a credit chip.

"Double if it's drawn on an off-planet bank," the driver added. She'd unholstered her long-barreled pistol. It lay on her lap, not pointed anywhere in particular but a blunt warning.

"*I'll* get it," Ran said mildly. "My credit's through the local Trident office."

He fed his chip into the reader, his face without expression. Oanh got down from the car's high body. Franz tugged their overnight cases from under the seat.

Oanh screamed. Two big men wearing bright garments beneath rough-out leather vests and chaps had the girl by the elbows. They tossed her into the back of a closed car and leaped in behind her.

Ran grabbed the taxi driver's pistol. "Hey!" she bellowed as she caught the barrel before he could aim. The kidnap vehicle accelerated away with all four wheels squealing.

"I'll buy the damned thing!" Ran shouted.

"Like hell!" the driver shouted back. She tried to bite his hand.

Ran let go of the gun. It was too late for that. The other vehicle had vanished into the sparse traffic. He wasn't sure he'd have fired anyway. He'd never been much use with handguns, and Oanh has likely to be injured in the crash even if he'd managed to shoot out a tire.

Franz Streseman was shouting for the police. Ran didn't bother. The *Empress*'s pilotry information had made it clear that self-help was the only help there was on Calicheman. Locals were watching the event with various levels of amusement.

A public telephone, armored like a tank, stood a few meters away. Ran retrieved his credit chip from the taximeter, ran to the phone, and punched TRIDENT on the keypad. The response was strikingly fast.

"Bridge," announced the *Empress*'s AI through the flat-plate speaker.

"Emergency," Ran said. "Deck officer. Over."

The speaker rattled. "Holly, over," it said tensely.

"Wanda, a Trident passenger has got a problem," Ran explained, "and we're going to solve it."

Ran made a series of curt statements and requests. One thing he *didn't* say, because he didn't want it on record, and because he didn't know how Franz Streseman, distraught at his elbow now, would react.

Ran hadn't recognized the actual kidnappers. But he was quite certain that the face glaring from the back of the kidnap vehicle was that of Gerd von Pohlitz.

Wanda Holly was alone in the rental car. Ran waved her over to the front of Tidal's Municipal Building, a one-story structure with rammed-earth walls and a littered areaway. Twilight and neon from nearby establishments helped disguise the building's aura of filth.

"You got to understand," said the Town Marshal, a woman named Platt with gray hair in unattractive curls, "that just because a couple outsiders say there's a crime, that don't make it a crime."

"We understand you perfectly, madam," Franz Streseman said in a voice that could have struck sparks from steel. He started to get into the car.

"*Just* a minute, buddy," Platt snapped, thrusting her arm out in front of the young Grantholmer. If she'd done that to a local, she'd have been handed the limb back with the fingers missing, but she obviously figured it was safe to bully passengers from a luxury starship. They wouldn't make a scene.

Platt turned her attention to Wanda in the driver's seat. "What kind of weapons you got in there?" she demanded.

The deputy, a fat drunk named Boardman, with a billiard-ball scalp and dried vomit on his vest, watched the proceedings from behind an automatic shotgun. If he did start shooting, he was as likely to cut his superior in half as he was to do whatever passed for his intention, but that wouldn't help whoever else was around during the wild volley.

"Weapons?" Wanda said in open amazement. "Why, none. I'm just here to pick up a distressed passenger from my ship."

Platt bent to check the empty luggage spaces under the seats. Rental vehicles were built without frills like paneling and insulated bodies. This car obviously carried nothing but the Trident officer herself.

"Surely it's not illegal to be armed in Tidal, Marshal?" Ran asked.

Someone in a passing car jeered and threw a fruit skin at Platt. It slapped her pants leg. She didn't appear to notice. "Don't you be telling *me* what's against the law here, buddy!" she snarled. "We don't need Earthmen telling us what's what!"

She lowered her arm and backed away. Franz nodded curtly and climbed into the car. Ran followed, calling, "Our government will protest about this!"

"Fuck you outsiders!" Platt cried. "Just because some broad goes off for a good time with a couple local boys, you wanna make it a crime! Well, I'm not having you starting a shootout in *my* jurisdiction!"

Boardman, her deputy, belched. He'd been doing that regularly since Ran and Franz appeared to make their complaint. Tidal needed some sort of officialdom, however minor; the trouble was that in a society which prided itself so thoroughly on rugged individualism, the sort of folks willing to take municipal jobs were incapable of handling *any* job competently.

Wanda put the car in gear. It rode even more harshly than the taxi had. "What was that charade about?" she asked.

"Just that," Ran agreed. "A charade. If we didn't make a formal complaint like civilized people, they'd figure that we were going to behave like locals — and be ready for us when we did."

"They, in this case," Wanda said, "being a rancher named Humboldt who came here from Grantholm thirty years back. He's not in a big way of business, but he's got about a dozen hired hands at any given time."

Wanda looked like a nervous driver because her head and eyes were constantly in motion. Ran noticed that her hands and feet were steady on the controls, however, making only necessary corrections and those small ones. The car was headed back toward Longleat and the *Empress*.

"How do you know this?" Franz demanded. The front seat was wide enough for three slim people, but there was nothing for him to hold onto. The slick fabric cover had him sliding into one officer, then the other.

"She used Bridge to penetrate the municipal data banks," Ran explained. "It was long odds they'd cleared the business with their tame law, just to avoid accidents."

"Nope," said Wanda with a smile. "It was easier than that. The kidnappers called her father, the minister, and I back-traced the call to the Humboldt ranch. *Then* I checked the records office."

Ran grimaced. "How did Lin react?" he asked. "I suppose they want him to turn over all his data to get his daughter back."

"Probably," Wanda agreed, "but I didn't let the call through. Bridge'll keep noting a fault until somebody removes the block I put on."

She turned and leaned forward to be able to catch Ran's eyes. "This is going to be a real embarrassment if things don't work out," she added. "Though I don't suppose we'll have to worry about answering questions."

Ran nodded grimly.

Wanda pulled off the road as soon as she was beyond the slaughterhouses and their waste dumps, lethal pit-traps in the growing darkness. They continued cross-country at 30 kph, a moderate speed under any other circumstances.

The young Grantholmer's face was set in a hawklike expression in the instrument lights. "Where are we going?" he asked.

"Just out of the way," Ran explained. "We don't want too many people watching the rendezvous. Some of them might guess what was going on."

A great beast with wrinkled skin and tusks like shovels loomed up in the driving lights. Wanda wrenched the steering wheel hard, but the animal blatted and fled. The tuft of white hair on its tail wobbled like a flag in the beams' side-scatter.

"Ah — Franz?" Ran said. He barely avoided saying "boy" instead of using the youth's name. "You should maybe opt out of this one."

Streseman looked at him. "Of course not," he said crisply. "This is properly my affair, as a man, as a — as a lover, of course. You are the ones who are going beyond what could be expected of your duty."

"It's just possible Commander Kneale would feel that way," Wanda murmured. "He's not the sort to second-guess his people, though."

"What I mean, Franz . . ." Ran said. He rocked forward in his seat as Wanda braked to avoid a straggling line of cattle, their eyes flaring red in the headlights. "What I meant is, now that we know it's Grantholmers who've grabbed Oanh."

"You assumed that, surely?" the youth said coolly. "I've never claimed that all my fellow-countrymen are saints. We have thieves, have murderers; have kidnappers. All the more reason for me to wish to right this wrong."

"The people who did this," Ran continued deliberately, "are going to think of themselves as patriots. And so will a lot of people back on Grantholm if they learn about it."

Franz shrugged. "Stresemans have never been afraid to support the right," he said. "Even when it was unpopular." He was as matter-of-fact as if he'd been discussing the scarlet sunset.

Ran sighed. It must be nice to be so certain about right and wrong. "Were you able to find me a long gun?" he asked Wanda.

"Sorry," she said. "The armory only has pistols and submachine guns. But we'll be at close range, won't we?"

"Who knows?" Ran said. His palms were beginning to feel cold. Until now, he'd been too focused on each next step to worry. "Yeah, I suppose. Maybe a submachine gun, that'll be all right. But I'm no good with short guns."

"Your training was only with rifles?" Franz asked curiously. He seemed perfectly calm.

"There wasn't any training," Ran explained. "I'm

from Bifrost. I was a hide hunter before I ran off on a tramp freighter."

He grimaced. "I hated it," he said. He laced his fingers together. "But at the margin of profit on a shagskin or even a sleen, I couldn't afford to miss. And with a rifle, I don't."

"I see," said the youth. He frowned. "How much farther do we drive, then?" he asked.

The sky began to flicker blue. Wanda stuck her head out her side window and craned her neck upward. "I think . . ." she said, "that we've arrived."

She stopped the car and took it out of gear. Even as she did so, Lifeboat 23 from the *Empress of Earth* coasted to a roaring halt beside the ground vehicle. The boat was only thirty meters long, but as it settled through the dusk it looked as huge as the starliner itself.

The sidehatch was open. Crewman First Class Babanguida stood in the hatchway, lighted by the glare of the magnetic motors reflecting from the grasses. He held a submachine gun in his right hand and, in his left, a rifle as long as those used on Bifrost to hunt the twelve-tonne shagskins.

"Our chariot awaits, gentlemen," said Wanda Holly as she unlatched her door. Then she added, "*Boy*, is there going to be hell to pay if we blow this one."

"Here," Wanda said as she handed a long, loose shirt to Franz Streseman. Mohacks, at the controls of the grounded lifeboat, and Babanguida already wore similar overgarments of shimmering fabric. "Put this on. Ran—"

She lifted another from the locker and tossed it to him.

" — here's one for you."

Ran took the shirt absently and laid it beside him. He was checking the sights — holographic, with a bead-in-ghost-ring backup — and mechanism of the rifle

Babanguida had given him. It was semi-automatic, with a three-round magazine holding cartridges as long as his hand. The bore was about fifteen millimeters. There were no markings on the receiver and the cartridge headstamp, MN 93, didn't tell him a lot either.

"An insulating wrap?" Franz said doubtfully. "I'm not cold, and it's likely to tangle."

"That cost us a right good amount, sir," Babanguida said. "Thirty-two hundred creds for the gun, and fifty apiece for the shells. He only had twenty-three shells."

"It'll do," Ran muttered. "It isn't an army we're going up against."

"I told you not to buy arms locally," Wanda said sharply. "You're likely to have tipped off Humboldt and von Pohlitz."

Ran fumbled two chips from his pouch and set them on the deck beside him. "This ought to cover . . ." he said as he eased back the charging handle on the empty magazine.

The rifle was two meters long and weighed upwards of twenty kilograms. The complex muzzle brake would bring the recoil down to bearable levels, but the resulting backblast would rattle shingles for a block behind the shooter.

"Oh, I trust you for the money, sir," Babanguida said, though his black hand quickly covered the chips.

Ran snorted. "I don't *trust* I'll be alive come morning," he said.

The rifle felt good in Ran's hands. It felt just like the weapon he'd used for six years after his father died, to feed and clothe himself and his mother . . . until she died too, and the young hide hunter became a Cold Crewman on the unscheduled freighter *Prester John*.

"There's local and local, Ms. Holly," said Mohacks from the control chair. "We had some time — and the boat, since the Officer of the Deck had cleared us to take it out. So we looked up an old bastard in a lodge three hundred klicks up in the hills. When he feels like it, he guides folks as want to hunt land whales."

"He wouldn't give his mother the time of day," Babanguida added. "He's not gonna be calling around to see if anybody cares that a sailor bought a rifle."

"We figured," Mohacks said piously, "that if Mr. Colville felt comfortable with a cannon, then it was our job to get him a cannon."

"The reason we told my watch and left yours aboard the *Empress*," Ran said as he loaded the rifle's magazine, "is that Mohacks and Babanguida aren't going to check the regs before they make a move."

He grinned at his ratings. They grinned back.

"Of course," Ran added, "they probably think there's some money to be made out of this deal."

"I will of course see to it that those helping on this enterprise are properly compensated," Franz said stiffly.

Babanguida chuckled. "Don't you worry yourself, sir," he said. "We figure, when this is over, there's likely to be something laying around that the owners don't need."

"Mind," Mohacks added, "a suitable gratuity wouldn't be misplaced at the end of this — if you keep from getting your head blown off, sir."

"Streseman," Wanda said harshly, "get into your jacket. We'll be using passive infra-red goggles at the start. The insulating fabric will give us a lower thermal signature so that we'll be able to tell each other apart from the locals."

Ran quickly stood and pulled his own shirt over his white uniform. He didn't need the tic in Wanda's cheek or the unexpected sharpness of her tone to tell him that she was right on the edge. They all were, even the seemingly relaxed ratings.

"We don't have any information about the layout of the ranch," Ran said. "Calicheman doesn't have a government that keeps records like that. We've got the exact location the phone calls are coming from. With luck, that's spitting distance of where Oanh is being held. We don't know that."

He took a deep breath. The other four members of the team — not really his team, any more than the fingers belonged to the hand — watched him soberly. Each held a submachine gun and a pouch of extra magazines from the ship's arsenal.

"Mohacks stays with the boat," Ran continued. "The rest of us hit them fast and get out fast with the girl. Chances are they don't have weapons that'll penetrate a lifeboat's plating, but we don't know that for sure either. We've all got helmet links, but try to keep your mouth shut unless you've got something that needs to be said. Any last questions?"

"One thing," said Franz Streseman. He didn't look young any more. "You are all brave, and no doubt you have weapons training. *I* am the soldier here, however."

He surveyed his four older companions. "Shoot first, shoot to kill," he said coldly. "Don't threaten and don't hesitate. It may be that Oanh will be mistaken for an opponent. I myself may mistake her for an opponent."

Ran hadn't seen anything as bleak as the young Grantholmer's expression since he faced the Cold Crew in Taskerville.

"I say to you," Franz continued, "it is better that Oanh die than that she remain alive in the hands of these folk. I know them, I *know* their type. She is not human to them. We must not hesitate."

Wanda Holly licked her lips. "And on that cheerful note," she said, "I think it's time to go."

She glanced at the others, then added, "Good luck, fellows. We may all be crazy, but I'm damned glad I know people like you."

"Lift-off," said Mohacks as he engaged the controls.

A fireball belched across the prairie. Grass had ignited in the flux of the magnetic motors thrusting the lifeboat up again at a flat angle.

"Three buildings," Mohacks announced as the terrain came up on his display. This was a lifeboat, not an attack vessel. There weren't any connections to export data from the pilot's console to those braced in the craft's cargo bay. "Looks like a barracks and a big garage across from the boss's house."

The lifeboat rocked and bucked, though 700 kph wasn't as bad in the tubular hull as it would have been in a conventional aircraft whose wingspan would lever turbulence into a hammering. The little vessel had an excellent passenger restraint system, but it wasn't equipped with the quick releases necessary for an assault force. Ran and his three companions wore their weapons slung tight to their chests while they gripped and pressed their boots against stanchions.

"Set us — " Ran began.

"I'm going to set us down in the middle, so the boat's between the barracks and the house," Mohacks continued calmly. "Hang on, I'm going to swing to bring the hatch facing the house."

"Babanguida, watch the barracks," Ran said. "You other two, in the house while I cover you."

Somebody had to do the former job, and Ran knew damned well that neither Wanda nor Franz would accept the order. Wanda was senior to him, and the kid was both a civilian and — as he'd pointed out — the only one of them who'd been trained for this sort of business.

The lifeboat banked hard and braked simultaneously. Ran's feet slipped from the seat stringer where he'd braced them. His legs flailed loose. Babanguida didn't try to grab his superior, knowing that if he did they'd both of them go bouncing around the cabin.

Ran's hands clamped like welds to iron, the way they'd done a dozen times in the past when an unexpected shock threatened to fling him into sponge space for the cold remainder of eternity.

Mohacks slid the hatch open before the lifeboat grounded. The cabin filled with the motor roar that the hull insulation had damped to a rumble. Blue glare reflected like chained lightning, and the windblast pummeled those inside.

Ran used his last momentum to throw himself upright when the vessel grated to a halt beneath him. He unstrapped the long rifle and presented it, bracing his left palm on the side of the hatchway and resting the barrel on that outstretched thumb. Wanda, Franz, and Babanguida bolted past him.

The house was rambling and a single story, with four rooms in one portion and a fifth connected to the others by a covered dogtrot. A man looked out the door of the single room, silhouetted by the lamplight behind him.

Ran fired. The muzzle brake of his weapon spewed red flames back to either side. His body rocked with the familiar recoil. He absorbed the thrust with his back muscles instead of fighting it with the bones of his shoulder.

The man Ran shot threw his arms up. The bullet was explosive, but it was meant to penetrate deep within creatures weighing scores of tonnes. The charge burst in the middle of the room, shattering the windows outward in a violet flash.

The lights in the room across the dogtrot went out. The window was a cool rectangle against the building's warm siding. Ran swung and fired again, aiming at the center of the glass.

This bullet also exploded well within the room. Its flash and the miniature shrapnel of the bullet jacket weren't dangerous, the way a bursting grenade would have been, but they must have distracted the kidnappers inside. Franz kicked through the door an instant after the *crack*! of the 15-mm bullet. His submachine gun lit the interior with ragged yellow flashes. There was no return fire.

Babanguida opened up at the lifeboat's bow, out of Ran's sight. A return bullet clanged off the vessel's sturdy plating, but only one of them, and distant screams proved that the rating wasn't wasting ammo.

The man Ran shot in the single room had slipped to his knees. He gripped the doorjamb with both hands. Wanda Holly pointed her weapon past him, then turned without shooting to follow Franz. The victim slumped further, then rolled supine, his hands clutching the dirt and his boots in the room in which he had died.

Red and yellow flashes quivered within the long end of the building. The local weapons used a propellant that burned deeper in the spectrum than those from the *Empress*'s arsenal. A bullet ricocheted from the building and howled past Ran. It thumped into a cabin bulkhead.

The red flashes reflected from the third room over. Ran aimed at that sidewall, not the window, and blasted the last round in his magazine through what seemed to be some thin cast panelling.

His bolt locked open. Thumbing cartridges from his bandolier loops into the magazine, Ran sprinted toward the far end of the long wing.

An orange flash followed his last shot. He'd hit a munitions store. Ammo detonated in a rattling chain like a tympani riff. A second orange blast knocked Ran down.

That was a good thing because the third explosion, following a heartbeat later, blew off the roof and sidewalls together. The walls were castings, all right: cast concrete. Some of the chunks were big enough to dent the lifeboat's hull.

Ran rolled to his feet and slammed the bolt of his rifle home. He wasn't sure whether he'd loaded two or three rounds.

"We've got her!" squealed a voice too high-pitched to sound like Wanda. Overlaying the words on the same radio channel, Franz Streseman shouted, "Baby baby baby!"

Ran reached the end of the building. A window was open. Someone was running away. Ran dragged his thermal goggles down away from his eyes. The goggles didn't give fine detail, and there was so much light now from the burning building that he didn't need them.

The running man was Gerd von Pohlitz. Firelight twisted the wrinkles of the big Grantholmer's clothing into tiger stripes. He was only a hundred meters away. It was a clout shot for a hunter like Ran Colville, who'd made over seven hundred one-shot kills at that range and longer.

Ran's finger tightened, then released its pressure on the trigger.

Let him go. Oanh was free — and no matter what had happened to the girl while she was a captive, one more corpse wouldn't change the past. It wasn't Ran Colville's business or any one man's business to rid the universe of sadistic sons of bitches. . . .

Von Pohlitz turned. He aimed his weapon, an automatic rifle, back at the building from which he had fled.

Ran didn't feel his trigger sear release — his action was too reflexive for that. His muzzle lifted in a triple flare, red flame from the bore and the side vents. The butt punished him, and for the first time tonight he noticed the enormous WHAM! of his shot.

The 15-mm bullet hit the receiver of the Grantholmer's rifle before punching through to the torso where it exploded. Gerd von Pohlitz's chest expanded. Violet flames flashed from his mouth and nostrils. His left arm fell separately from the body, and his head remained attached only by the neck tendons.

Ran turned. Franz was staggering toward the lifeboat with Oanh's still form in his arms. Wanda backed along behind him, firing short bursts into the house every time popping flames counterfeited motion.

"Come on!" Ran shouted, even though he himself was Tail-Ass Charlie. "Let's get out of here!"

He lumbered toward the open hatch, staggering because fatigue poisons laced all his muscles. But they'd done what they'd come for —

And there would be time later to think about exactly what they *had* done, the five of them.

The sounds of the *Empress*'s loading occasionally rang through the fabric of the hull, but the process was nearly complete. The three-hour whistle had blown, and the passengers dispersed during the layover were dribbling back from hunting or the fleshpots of Calicheman.

"I thought of calling you all together to ask what the hell went on last night," Commander Hiram Kneale said as he paced his cabin. His voice wasn't loud, but it rasped like the coughs of a hunting lion.

Kneale had withdrawn his console into the deck. The decorative holograms on walls and ceiling were muted into a throbbing pearl gray. He was the only person in the room standing. Ran, Wanda, Mohacks, and Babanguida sat in a precise line on the bench extruded from the cabin wall.

Babanguida's left forearm bore a patch of bright pink SpraySeal over a blister. He'd touched it with the glowing barrel of his submachine gun as he cleared a jam. Despite Wanda's goggles, her eyes had been blacked by the same piece of flying debris that raised the livid bruise on her right cheek. Ran moved stiffly because of the punishment the rifle butt had given his shoulder.

Butter wouldn't melt in Mohacks' mouth. He

glanced at his companions as if wondering why he had been summoned with the others.

"But then I decided," Kneale continued, "that I didn't *want* to know what had happened. That would just make me angrier. I think if that happened, I might do something that I would later regret. *Much* later."

He stared at his four subordinates as though he wished he was looking through a gunsight.

Wanda cleared her throat. "Has there been a complaint about our behavior, sir?" she asked.

"*Will* there be a complaint?" Kneale demanded harshly. "Colville. Will there be a complaint?"

Ran licked his lips. "No sir," he said, facing straight ahead rather than swivelling his eyes to meet the commander's.

"You didn't leave any survivors to complain, is that it?" Kneale said.

"Something like that, sir," Ran said. He cleared his throat. "Sir, this was entirely my doing."

"I've listened to your call to the *Empress*, Colville," Kneale said. "I know what you did, and I can bloody well guess what you all did! Look at you, for Chrissakes!"

Only Mohacks glanced around in response to the shouted command. He was still pretending to be innocent, though he knew the commander too well to think that it was going to do a lot of good.

"Sir," Ran said toward the bulkhead in front of which Kneale paced, "what we did, we did for the . . . honor of Trident Starlines."

"What you did," Kneale snarled, "you did because some stupid bastard thumbed his nose at you, and you decided to boot his ass through his shoulder blades to teach him a lesson."

Unexpectedly, the commander smiled. "Which I suppose is as good a definition of honor as we're going to find," he said. "Since we're all human."

Kneale muttered something to the AI. The surfaces of

his cabin flashed back to holograms of the *Empress*'s ports of call. The views weren't precisely restful, but they proved that the commander's mood had changed — or that a level had come off the emotional onion.

"Look," Kneale continued, "you went charging in without any plan, just hoping you'd get away with it. And you did. But it was a lousy idea, and it could have embarrassed the company seriously. Don't do it again."

"Sir," Ran said, meeting Kneale's eyes, "they didn't have time to plan anything either. The snatch had to be set up after von Pohlitz disembarked. He could make a call to a buddy in the area, but this wasn't — "

He smiled.

" — Grantholm's Seventeenth Commando. Except on our side."

"If all Grantholm troops are as good as the Streseman kid," Wanda Holly said to no one in particular, "then Nevasa doesn't have a prayer. I followed him in, and there were six bodies in that first room."

She swallowed. "I think six."

"It's the fact that Streseman was along that permits me to trust your judgment," the commander said. "I'd like to think that you wouldn't have tried something like this if you hadn't had a wire to the top levels of the Grantholm government."

"The girl was our passenger, sir," Ran replied softly. "It's not our war. But she's our passenger."

"So she was," Commander Kneale agreed with a wry smile. He gestured toward the door. "Go on, go on," he said. "Trident Starlines doesn't thank you, because the company isn't going to know a thing about this if we're lucky. But I'm proud of you.

"Only the next time . . ." he went on, "I hope you'll let *me* in on the business."

Kneale's smile had changed into something that an impala might have noticed on the face of the last lion it ever saw.

• SZGRANE

"Ah, sir . . . ?" Ran Colville said as he looked cautiously from the Szgranian guard of honor to Commander Kneale. "I should be going on duty in ten minutes."

Here on their own planet, the Szgranians' accouterments included plasma dischargers, massive tubes that were crew-served weapons in human military forces.

The twenty guards escorted a closed palanquin the size of a boat, the same vehicle which had awaited Lady Scour when the *Empress of Earth* docked. It was carved from ivory which a glance suggested was all one tooth. That didn't seem likely, but the Szgranian ecosystem was in the portion of the hynogogue course which Ran *still* hadn't finished.

"I know what the duty list looks like, Colville," Kneale said with pointed calm. "Trust me to take care of that end, won't you? Our docking here has gone more smoothly than I'd have expected at Sonderburg on Grantholm — in peacetime. That's because of the personal intervention of Lady Scour. I'd say that if the lady wants to show you the town, Trident Starlines should accommodate her. Don't you think so too?"

The city of Betaniche climbed the crags above the combined space- and riverport. Two starships were already on the ground when the *Empress* dropped into the system from sponge space: a small freighter of Grantholm registry, and the private yacht of a merchant stocking his gallery with Szgranian carvings. They had been hastily moved to the edge of the field to give the larger vessel sufficient room.

"Ah," said Ran. "Yes sir."

An earthen levee restrained the river. Flowers covered the inner face of the embankment and the mudflats separating it from the land baked and blasted by magnetic motors. The *Empress* dug craters three meters deep beneath each nacelle when she landed with only four tugs, but the port authorities were too busy greeting Lady Scour to show any concern over the damage.

"Then go, for pity's sake!" Kneale snapped with a brusque gesture.

Ran stepped quickly down the gangplank. He glanced back and saw Wanda Holly entering the Embarkation Hall. They'd planned to get together when his shift ended — Szgrane was a new planet to both of them — but the summons from Lady Scour put paid to that notion. Ran waved to the Second Officer and hoped that Kneale would fill her in.

Szgranian flowers tended to blue and blue-gray petals. Their scent was sharp rather than sweet, and it mingled unpleasantly with the smoke of shanties ignited as the starliner docked.

"Don't do anything I wouldn't do!" Wanda called from the starliner as a female page threw open the door of the palanquin.

The first thing Ran noticed as he got in was that the vehicle had double-wall paneling. The intricate carvings on the outside were complemented by those of the separate sheet some twenty millimeters within. Ran could look out from the shadowed interior of the palanquin, but the offset panels acted the way a one-way mirror does to protect the privacy of those behind it.

The second thing Ran noticed as the door closed behind him was that Lady Scour already reclined on the cushions he was expected to share.

"Good evening, Junior Lieutenant Randall Colville,"

the Szgranian noblewoman said. The palanquin rolled
upward on the shoulders of its eight bearers. "Are you
surprised to see me? I was going to send the palanquin
back... and then I thought I should watch as you got your
first view of my planet."

"I — ah, I'm surprised and pleased to see you again,
Lady Scour," Ran said. His mind clicked through pos-
sibilities, all of which were absurd except for the
obvious male/female connection.

Of course, Lady Scour wasn't human ... though
Ran didn't find her as inhuman as he would have
expected before meeting her.

The Szgranian chuckled, but Ran couldn't be sure
whether the impetus was humor or scorn. They faced
forward in the palanquin. She looked out through the
ivory panels and asked, "What do you think of my
city?"

The vehicle didn't pitch in a front-and-back motion,
as Ran had rather expected, but it rocked side-to-side
as the bearers stepped forward. Eight right legs paced,
then eight left legs, as regular as clockwork. Lady
Scour shifted sinuously so that her hip brushed Ran's
at every stride.

"It's fascinating," Ran said. "I very much appreciate
the opportunity you've offered me."

Starliner crews normally saw only the slums or the
quick-look tourist spots of their ports of call. Even if
they were on the same run for ten years straight, they
had only a day or two at a time unless they were on the
beach — dismissed, deserting, or abandoned. In those
latter cases, the slums provided all the beachcomber
wanted anyway.

None of the human colonies, even the largest and
most powerful, were old enough to have a culture truly
distinct from that of Earth. Szgrane was an alien society.
The portside facilities that catered to starfarers and
deracinated Szgranian watermen were similar in kind

if not in personnel to those of a thousand other ports, but Lady Scour's palanquin left those areas behind in minutes.

Ran was seeing the real Betaniche, the real Szgrane. For all the human aspects of the natives, particularly Lady Scour herself, Ran had the feeling that he'd been shrunk and dropped into an anthill.

The entourage climbed the bluff that bounded the river's floodplain. Instead of a street, the clan mistress's escort proceeded through a tunnel fringed by multi-story houses with walls and roofs of translucent paper. Open walkways crossed between the higher floors. Sunlight trickled through the sides of buildings, creating a shadowless ambiance.

The pavement twisted like a snake's track. It was thronged with pedestrians and shoppers at open-fronted booths.

A guard twenty meters ahead of the palanquin blew a horn made from the coiled shell of some sea creature. The warning note was a deep lowing punctuated with hacking emphasis, like the bellow of a cow desperate to be milked. Commoners struggled to get clear, shouting and waving a desperate profusion of arms.

Lady Scour chuckled again. "Look at Rawsl!" she said. The fingers of her three left hands played over Ran's sleeve like butterfly touches. "Isn't he angry?"

Lady Scour's chief aide followed immediately behind the signaler. He had drawn a pair of long swords, one in each upper arm. Rawsl slashed and thrust at any commoner he could reach, whether or not the target was actually in the palanquin's path. Rawsl's swords were more than a meter long.

"What's the matter?" Ran asked. He tried to keep his voice neutral, despite his distaste. "Didn't he want to make a trip back to the *Empress*?"

Rawsl stabbed through the side of a barrow. Thin wood splintered. The blue-clad woman huddling under a tarpaulin within screamed and thrashed upward, then collapsed.

"Who knows what men think?" Lady Scour said dismissively.

She looked at Ran as her fingers played with his garment again. "He didn't want me to go back," she said. "And more particularly, he didn't want to see *you* again, Ran Colville. But *I* am mistress of Clan Scour."

The palanquin came out into open air. The sun was low on the horizon. The western sky was flame-streaked, sharply changing the balance of light. The paper-walled town filtered out all colors except duns, grays, and yellows so pale that they might as well have been grays.

"This is my home," said Lady Scour. They passed a pair of gateposts, stone but carved as intricately as the panels of the palanquin itself. "All that down there — "

She gestured with the delicacy of a sea anemone clasping prey, one hand/two hands/three.

" — is to serve me."

The palace was a complex of buildings and gardens, encompassed by a high stone wall. An additional score of armed Szgranian males was drawn up in the first courtyard. Beyond them — in the same line, rather than as a separate rank — were officials in court dress, wearing ludicrous but highly symbolic headgear; noblewomen; and so on down through craftsmen to menial servants.

There must have been a thousand people greeting Lady Scour and her entourage. The last in line wore rags and stank obviously of night soil. The palanquin bearers quickened their pace at that point. All of the waiting contingent put their hands behind their heads and warbled tunelessly until their mistress's vehicle swept to the *porte cochere* serving one of the separate buildings.

Ran thought he recognized the maid who opened

the door on his side of the palanquin as one of the pair
who'd attempted to summon him to Lady Scour's suite
on the *Empress*. On the other side of the vehicle, Rawsl
stood stiffly at his mistress's service.

Lady Scour strode by the warrior, ignoring him. She
offered her three left hands to Ran above the
palanquin poles. "Come," she said. "We'll eat first, and
then we'll have entertainment."

She laughed again. "And then," she said, "we'll have
entertainment."

The fine fur on Rawsl's face and bare limbs stood
out like the quills of a porcupine. The muscles of his
arms were as rigid as the blades of the bloody swords
he held.

"Good evening, Abraham," Marie Blavatsky called to
the lone passenger she'd spotted amid the transparent
bulkheads and real fish of the Undersea Grotto. "I'd
have expected you to be out on the town tonight."

Abraham Chekoumian rose from his chair with a
lazy smile. "Szgrane is an exotic place to the other passengers, even the crew, Marie," he said. "Myself, I
import from Szgrane; I travel here ten times a year on
buying trips. Sometimes I come twice a month."

Chekoumian stretched. He held a hologram reader
in one hand and in the other — as Blavatsky
expected — the slick blue spacemail envelope of one of
his fiancee's letters.

"Today," the importer continued, brandishing the
envelope, "I am going home to marry my Marie — not
to do business. I don't need to see Szgrane *this* trip. The
part of their society which they show humans is — "

He shrugged.

" — dirt. And the rest of it, the way the Szgranians
themselves live, that would appeal even less to me if I
had to be here for any length of time."

The section of wall behind the importer was stocked

with benthic species from the depths of Ain al-Mahdi, patterns of slow-moving dots which fluoresced rose and warm yellow. Occasionally two patterns merged in sluggish dance that ended with one partner progressing down the tooth-fringed maw of the other.

Considered merely as a light show, it was a soothing background.

Chekoumian gave Blavatsky a little grin to show that he knew he was being floridly bombastic. "Trust me, little Marie," he said. "Szgrane isn't a place for humans. And it isn't a place for Szgranians either, except for the one who's on top of each community's pyramid."

"Oh, of course I trust you, Abraham," Blavatsky said brightly. "I was just surprised to see you here, is all."

In fact, Blavatsky had been surprised to learn from Bridge that the importer was still aboard when her watch ended — but she'd been ninety percent sure that she'd find him in the Undersea Grotto when she strolled past. Bridge noted that Chekoumian had ordered a drink only ten minutes before.

"Marie's telling me about her sister's wedding," Chekoumian said, waggling the letter again. "That's her sister Irene, the younger one. But please, sit down! You're off duty, are you not? You can have a drink."

He signaled for a steward as he gestured Blavatsky to the contoured chair beside his own.

"Well, maybe a little wine . . ." she agreed shyly. Abraham was aware of her duty hours.

"Irene's the young one," Chekoumian added with a frown. "Marie — my Marie, little Marie — "

He dropped the letter on the circular drinks table to pat the back of Blavatsky's hand.

"Marie's bothered by that, I know, though she doesn't say it," he continued. His broad face brightened like an equatorial sunrise. "But won't she be thrilled when I sweep up to her door in the most expensive limousine I can rent on Bogomil?"

"Sir and madam?" asked the steward who paused at their table.

Chekoumian and Blavatsky looked up. On the wall behind the bar, the brilliant denizens of a coral atoll on Tblisi wheeled in tight patterns. "Could I have something from your homeworld?" Blavatsky asked. "Tblisi has wines, doesn't it?"

"Wonderful!" cried her companion. "Yes, of course. Bring us a carafe of Evran with two glasses — and take this away."

Chekoumian thrust his part-finished screwdriver across the table. "The vintage is from gene-tailored grapes," he explained to Blavatsky. "We're very up to date on Tblisi."

"A carafe of Evran," the steward said to the bartender. Both men were natives of New Sarawak; and both had been aboard the *Empress of Earth* since her maiden voyage.

The bartender glanced toward the only occupied table in the lounge. The passenger had switched on his hologram reader to project plans of the house he intended to build. He was pointing out details of the widow's walk to the Staff Side rating beside him.

The bartender raised an eyebrow.

The steward, out of sight of the couple at the table, hooked the first and middle fingers of his left hand. He jerked them upward, as though they were a gaff landing a prize fish.

Three court ladies sang the 17th-century Terran ballad about Clerk Colville, who'd gone to tell the mermaid who'd been his mistress that he intended to marry a human female. A fourth of Lady Scour's companions provided the lute accompaniment in the dining room paneled in richly-carved woods and ivory. She deliberately used only two hands to achieve the delicate fingering.

"Would you agree that 'My skin is whiter than the milk,' Ran Colville?" Lady Scour asked.

One of Lady Scour's hands flicked her blouse like a bullfighter's cape. The smokey fabric might have been translucent in strong light, but it was effectively opaque beneath the dining room's paper lanterns. The single garment, unless surprise and the mere glimpse had deceived Ran, was the only thing Lady Scour wore over her breasts.

"I would agree with anything your ladyship said," Ran replied. "Because of your rank, and your beauty ... and because of my respect for your mind, all three."

He chose his words carefully so as not to bring up the fact that her words had been from *Clerk Colville*. The line just before the one Lady Scour quoted was, "It's all for you, ye gentle knight. ..."

The clan mistress leaned forward chuckling. She took a shellfish from a dish of pungent sauce and popped it into Ran's mouth. He chewed and swallowed. The tidbit, like most of the meal that had preceded it, was excellent. He'd forced himself to stomach only a few items, and those more for texture than taste.

Lady Scour held out her thumb and forefinger, still red with the sauce. "Go on," she said. "Lick them clean. You wouldn't have the mistress of Clan Scour going about with greasy fingers, would you?"

Ran began to laugh. He was man enough to be flattered by the attention, and Lady Scour was woman enough to be — interesting. Whatever sort of flesh wrapped the package.

The Szgranian's fingertips seemed slightly warmer than a human female's would have been, but Ran couldn't claim perfect objectivity.

Another lady-in-waiting, this one clad like a yellow beachball in swathes of gauze, flounced into the dining room. She whispered in her mistress's ear.

Lady Scour nodded, then rose to her feet with the grace of a willow tree swaying. "Very well," she said in satisfaction. "Now, Randall Colville, for the entertainment. But you'll have to be perfectly quiet. Stay close and let me guide you by touch, because there won't be any light."

She led Ran toward the wall behind her couch. He didn't realize it was a door until Lady Scour touched a band of dark wood. A section of balanced paneling pivoted open on its vertical axis.

The hallway beyond was narrow and almost completely dark. Ran's eyes had adapted enough during dinner to make out a faint glow fifty meters along, but that was all.

The court ladies stared after their mistress and her guest, but they continued to sing. An instant before the door rotated closed again, their voices dissolved into giggles and whispers that Ran couldn't make out.

Lady Scour touched Ran's shoulder and hand and the point of his hip, where her fingertips rode lightly, shifting like valve tappets on a cam lobe.

"Very quietly . . ." Lady Scour whispered, her breath warm on Ran's ear.

The screen at the corridor's end was double-walled like the panels of the palanquin. It looked down into a lantern-lit room in which Szgranians writhed together. For a moment, Ran wasn't sure either of the number or the intentions of the folk he watched. There were too many arms and they could have been locked in murderous violence.

The scene came into mental focus: it was a couple, and they were making love.

"Rawsl," Lady Scour breathed into Ran's ear. "I asked my maid Siris to entice him into this room."

A soft plosion of warmth did duty as a snort. "Rawsl would never wonder why. He thinks he's irresistible."

The couple lurched and staggered around the room. The female was silent, but Rawsl snorted loudly.

He held Siris from behind, clutching her four breasts and spreading her thighs. The maid's feet were off the floor, and her six arms reached back to clasp him.

"Are you that strong, Ran Colville?" Lady Scour whispered as her multiple hands undid the pressure seams of his uniform. "I'm much heavier than Siris. Only someone very strong could support me."

Ran hadn't noticed it happen, but Lady Scour had lost her clothing somewhere. The down on her skin was soft and warm by comparison with the hard fabric of her dress.

"You're not that heavy," Ran said as he turned from the screen to his hostess.

She wasn't human — but neither was Rati, the Hindu goddess of lust.

And nobody could deny that Lady Scour was female.

She had thin lips and a tongue as long and coarse as a cat's. As they kissed, she undressed him. Though the pattern of human clothing must have been at least slightly unfamiliar to her, the Szgranian's six hands and suppleness made an easy job of it.

Ran's eyes had adapted to the current level of light. When he stepped out of his trousers, his elbow nevertheless thumped the wall of the corridor in which they were engaged.

"There's a chamber through that door. . . ." Lady Scour said, nodding vaguely toward what seemed a blank panel, but she didn't stop what she was doing.

Nor did Ran.

At the last moment, it occurred to Ran that the relative size of genitalia can vary widely between species of similar total mass. If that was a problem, though, it was her problem and she was in control. Lady Scour gripped Ran with two pairs of arms and the heels of her feet locked behind his buttocks. Her remaining hands guided him within an orifice that seemed tight but slid smoothly.

All the Szgranian's muscles tightened. She screamed, not in pain but in sheer ecstatic triumph.

Part of Ran's mind wondered what the couple in the room below thought. But he didn't much care.

The Embarkation Hall was lighted at thirty percent of Earth daytime norm — more than adequate to see by, but dim compared to the brilliance of the *Empress*'s exterior floods scattered in through the open hatchway.

"Good evening, Mr. Streseman," Commander Kneale said from the angle of a pilaster as the Grantholm passenger moped past with his eyes lowered.

"Oh!" said Streseman. He was alone. An hour after the *Empress of Earth* landed, stewards had carried his train of static-supported cases across the starport to the Grantholm combination vessel *Thornburg*. He must have paid off the staff at that time, because no little folk from New Sarawak pursued the young Grantholmer now for their tips.

"I regret that you had to be transshipped to reach your destination," the commander said. "I've heard good reports regarding passenger accommodations on the *Thornburg*, though. I don't think you'll find her too uncomfortable for a short hop."

"No, no, of course not," Streseman said. "You couldn't possibly be expected to land on a planet in the middle of war. A ship as valuable as this . . ."

He looked out the hatchway toward the alien city beyond. Betaniche was a dark mass. Occasional lamps glowed through the paper walls like will-o'-the-wisps over the surface of a marsh. Without turning back toward Kneale, the youth asked, "Has there been any word of the *Brasil*, sir?"

"No sir," the commander said. "Nothing at all since she entered sponge space in the Tblisi system. At this point, we can only hope that her passengers and crew are safe somewhere."

Streseman grimaced. "You think she's been hijacked, I suppose," he said. He met Kneale's eyes. "Well, that's the only reasonable possibility, isn't it? First-class starliners don't simply go missing."

"Not often, no," Kneale agreed. "But I don't intend to make unnecessary assumptions without data."

The commander smiled tightly. "Nor," he added, because Franz Streseman ceased to be simply a passenger on Calicheman, "do I intend to let up my guard."

The young man laughed without humor. "I imagine you're glad to get rid of all us Grantholmers here. Well, you've got a right to feel that way — but don't forget that you loaded quite a number of passengers on Nevasa, too. Some of them may just have been getting off a potential bomb target — but you're bound to have taken intelligence personnel aboard too."

The *Empress*'s ventilation system kept up positive pressure, as always on a planet, but the stink of the fires ringing the field still crept into the Embarkation Hall. Streseman's nose wrinkled as he looked out into the night, though the disgust he felt had little to do with the odor.

"I'm not unaware of that, Mr. Streseman," Kneale said quietly. "I hope you don't feel that Trident Starlines has discriminated against one or the other party in the conflict."

"No, of course not," Streseman agreed. "I'm — " He shook his head. "I'm not — in a good mood tonight, sir. I suppose I'd better get over to the *Thornburg* if I'm going."

There was a series of pops and crackles from the night. Commander Kneale visibly stiffened.

The rating stationed on the gangway leaned back within the hatch and called, "It's just fireworks, sir. A bunch of the — "

He looked at Streseman and recognized the youth as a Grantholmer.

" — passengers we disembarked here, they've took over a couple dockside bars and they're having a party. Patriotic songs and as much hell-raising as the locals let 'em get away with."

"Thank you, Rossignol," Kneale replied. When the crewman had returned to his post, Kneale said in a low voice, "You don't have to leave the *Empress*, you know, sir. We have empty berths."

He cleared his throat and added, "Mr. Streseman, I'd find you a berth in my cabin if I had to, after what you did on Calicheman."

Franz Streseman stepped forward and clasped the Trident officer by both hands. "Sir," he said, "I have to go. *You* understand duty. But I thank you from the bottom of my heart."

He turned his head very quickly, but Kneale could hear tears in the youth's voice as he went on, "She doesn't understand, though. I told her that I would come back to her as soon as the war was over, but I *had* to report to my unit. I'm a Streseman. She says if I loved her, I'd stay with her and we'd — we'd build a new life on Tellichery or somewhere.

"But I'm a *Streseman*!"

Kneale squeezed the younger man's hands in sympathy. Streseman forced himself to turn and look Kneale in the face. "What do you think, sir?" he asked. "I'm going to do it anyway. But am I wrong?"

"I think . . ." the commander said very carefully. "That you're eighteen, Mr. Streseman. And yes, I think you're wrong, because you're doing more or less what I did at your age. And *I* was wrong."

He smiled with genuine affection. "But that's what being eighteen is for — making mistakes. Just don't kid yourself about what you're doing."

Streseman squeezed back, released his hands, and wiped his eyes with the sleeve of his jacket. "Sorry about that," he muttered. "I'd best be going. Thank you, sir. I appreciate — everything. You'll give my regards to Lieutenant Colville?"

"I will indeed," Commander Kneale said. "I'm — you might say waiting up for him right now. I think I may have . . . given Mr. Colville an order, more or less, that I wouldn't have done if I'd known quite as much about Szgranian culture as I've found since reviewing the pilotry data in his absence."

Franz Streseman straightened and gave Kneale a stiff-armed Grantholm salute. "Thank you again, sir," he said.

"One thing, Mr. Streseman . . . ?" Kneale said.

"Sir?"

"If you survive what you're getting into just now," the commander said, picking his way with delicacy through his vocabulary. Kneale knew Streseman's rank in Grantholm society; but he *knew* there was no society equal to that of the men and women who held civilization together across the starlanes.

"If you've done what you feel is your duty," he continued, "come and see me, will you? Because Trident Starlines can always use officers who know their duty."

Kneale grinned starkly. "And know how to handle themselves in a tight spot. Which both you do very well."

He returned the salute, not as a Trident officer with palm outward, but with one languid finger to the brow, the way the Parliamentary Guard on Sulimaniya recognized their officers when Hiram Kneale was a boy of eighteen.

The shanties at the edge of the port area were still smoldering when Ran's palanquin swayed to a halt, then grounded. There were no open flames, but the sludgy reek of incomplete combustion hung in a waist-high layer in the pre-dawn air.

The *Empress of Earth* brilliantly illuminated herself. The starliner's glare trickled through hundreds of meters of paper walls, providing a dull beacon for the last stage of Ran's journey back from the palace. A Staff Side rating lounged at the top of the main gangway, the only human in sight at this hour.

Half a dozen of the servants preceding the palanquin carried lanterns. The leading male blew his seashell horn as before, though the streets were empty except for a few figures huddling at the corners of buildings for shelter. Ran wondered if those derelicts had owned the dwellings which the starliner ignited on landing.

He hadn't expected an entourage to accompany him back to the *Empress*. If anything, his escort was larger than had been the force which took him and the clan mistress up the bluff. There must be at least thirty armed and fully-caparisoned warriors surrounding the palanquin.

Rawsl stalked through the streets immediately ahead of the palanquin. Unlike the other warriors, he carried only pairs of swords, daggers, and short-hafted axes — the weapons traditional to his race before Szgrane came in contact with starfaring humans. Several of the escort lumbered along under the heavy tubes of plasma dischargers. The remaining warriors carried either an assault rifle for the lowest pair of hands or a brace of machine pistols with snail magazines.

There were no inside handles on the palanquin doors. While Ran fumbled for a catch which didn't exist, Lady Scour's chief aide twirled the door open and stepped back. The eight bearers had withdrawn to the fringes of the entourage of Szgranians.

"I hope you have enjoyed your trip through Betaniche," Rawsl said, placing his hands behind his neck in the Szgranian gesture of submission.

"Yes, thank you," Ran said as he got out of the vehicle. He ached in unfamiliar places. He was pretty sure that every one of Lady Scour's fingertips had left a bruise on his back as she climaxed the third time.

Rossignol from Commander Kneale's watch was on gangway duty. He straightened with a bored man's interest in any change.

"May we tell our mistress that you are fully satisfied with the way we carried out her instructions to bring you back to your ship, then?" Rawsl asked, still in his formal posture.

"Yes, certainly," Ran said. Rawsl was acting like a concierge prodding his guest for a tip.

"Let no one leave the vessel," the Szgranian aide snarled in his own language.

A dozen of the escorting warriors, including those with plasma weapons, rushed toward the *Empress*. Rossignol bolted backward. Hatches began to shut across all three gangways. A klaxon within the starliner began to honk.

"Since we have satisfied our mistress's instructions," Rawsl said, "now we can satisfy the demands of honor." He drew both his long swords.

Ran bent, grasped a palanquin pole, and jerked. The smoothly finished hardwood was screwed and pinned into its socket. The vehicle skidded a few centimeters when Ran put his back into the effort, but as a weapon it was as useless as the bedrock.

Rawsl gave a high-pitched chirp. He thrust. His swordblades were slightly curved, but if Ran hadn't ducked behind the palanquin, the point would have crunched in and out through the bone and gristle of his rib cage.

"Prod him to me," ordered Rawsl. "This *animal* must not be allowed to hold back in the slaughter chute."

The main hatch had shuddered, then reopened fully again. Szgranians facing the starliner aimed modern weapons up the gangways from which human help might come. The other warriors had drawn their swords. They formed a rough circle with Ran, the palanquin, and Rawsl as the hub. Lower ranking Szgranians, male and female both, squatted beyond the ring of warriors and called encouragement to Rawsl.

Two warriors on Ran's side of the palanquin shuffled toward him, their swords raised like crab pincers. They'd drawn daggers in their central pairs of hands. Ran had as much chance of grabbing a weapon from one of them as he did of surviving a bath in battery acid.

Commander Kneale in his white uniform appeared at the main gangway. A Szgranian fired a machine-pistol in the commander's direction. The burst may have been aimed to miss, but several of the little bullets whanged and howled off the bulkheads of the Embarkation Hall.

This was going to be an international incident — particularly if some of the *Empress*'s crewmen got into a gunfight with the Szgranian escort. Rawsl and his confederates didn't care in the least.

If Ran had thought it would do him any good, *he* might not have cared about an open firefight either. All it would do was get good people killed, though. The *Empress of Earth* wasn't a warship with external weapons. The Szgranian warriors outgunned anything available from the starliner's arsenal. If there was enough ordnance flying around, Ran wouldn't survive long enough for Rawsl to cut him into collops.

How Lady Scour would react to the event was an open question. Ran's bet was that she wouldn't deign to notice it. As mistress of Clan Scour, she had the right to do anything she pleased; but her evening of bestiality was no matter for pride, even to her overmastering will.

Anyway, Rawsl and his confederates wouldn't care if their mistress had them flayed alive. They would have served their honor and their clan's.

A warrior poked his sword a calculated distance

toward Ran's buttocks. The Szgranian didn't want to kill Ran — that was Rawsl's perquisite. But if the human wouldn't go to his death willingly, then he would be thrust to it in a welter of his own blood.

Instead of waiting for the pricking blade, Ran leaped on top of the palanquin. Spectators cackled with delight. Rawsl stepped back and spread his swords wide. If Ran tried to overleap the Szgranian, the blades would come up and cross through his body, cutting the human into three segments while he was still in the air.

Someone switched off the *Empress*'s external lighting. "Down!" cried Wanda Holly as she rose from the edge of a shanty behind the circle of Szgranians. She pointed a broad-mouthed weapon.

Ran jumped off the end of the palanquin, putting himself as far as he could from Rawsl and the warrior who'd approached to prod him forward. Intense light hammered through Ran's closed lids and the flesh of the forearm he'd thrown across his eyes.

Szgranians screamed. Swords clashed together, and a warrior emptied his automatic rifle in a single long burst. It was God's own mercy that one or more of the plasma weapons didn't belch nuclear hell as well.

The throbbing pulses stopped. Ran was flat on the ground, though he didn't remember hitting it. Szgranians sobbed and bellowed.

"C'mon, *c'mon*!" Wanda shouted. Her right hand gripped Ran's arm to guide him as he stumbled to his feet.

She wore the padded, dull-colored overgarment of a Szgranian commoner. She wouldn't pass for a local if anyone looked carefully — but no Szgranian of rank *would* look carefully at a commoner.

The nerve gun and powerpack slung to Wanda's breast weighed forty kilos. Ran didn't see how she could carry it and move so quickly. The weapon projected light pulsing at critical neural frequencies.

These differed for various species — for humans and the great apes, it was just under seven and a half Hertz — but at some frequency, any chemically-based nervous system could be stimulated to dump neurotransmitters wildly.

Hundreds of Szgranians, many of them armed, had gone simultaneously psychotic. Most of them still writhed on the ground, their limbs locked into pretzel shapes that might mean broken bones. One warrior chuckled as he stabbed himself repeatedly in the abdomen. His daggers pumped in sequence like the pistons of a reciprocating engine.

The Szgranians facing the *Empress* hadn't been spared either, because the light had reflected from the starliner's gleaming hull. An arc of servants sprawled where bullets had cut them down, and a warrior was pounding his own feet to pulp with the heavy tube of his plasma discharger.

"You were waiting here?" Ran gasped. He'd scraped the hell out of his right palm and elbow. They felt cool from oozing blood.

Wanda's face was a mirrored ball. She'd polarized her helmet visor to protect her from her own weapon, even though it was calibrated to the slightly higher critical frequency of the Szgranian physiology.

"Don't be a damned fool!" she snapped. "I waited for you at the gate of the palace. You didn't think I'd let you get into something like that without backup, did you?"

Commander Kneale and the two ratings from Ran's own watch grabbed the pair of them and helped them up the gangway. The submachine guns the three men carried clattered against one another and Wanda's nerve gun.

"No," Ran mumbled. "I don't guess you would have."

It was good to have friends.

● TELLICHERY

Carnatica Port was a large, bustling and cosmopolitan city. The last point was underscored by the number of cases of beef, relabeled Calicheman mutton, which had been unloaded from the *Empress*'s holds and trucked past Hindu temples whose courtyards abutted the spaceport. So long as lip service was paid to the planet-wide dietary laws, the business class which controlled Carnatica was willing to wink at foreign tastes — and to share them, it was whispered.

The Trident Starlines offices filled the top three floors of a building just outside the spaceport reservation, overlooking both the port and the town. Commander Hiram Kneale stood on the palm-shaded roof garden. He was checking the *Empress*'s manifest with a hand-held reader linked to the main unit beneath him instead of using a fixed terminal.

A modern office building and a starliner both cut their occupants off from their surroundings. In the case of the starship, enclosure was a necessity. When Kneale was dirtside, however, he preferred to work in a more open environment.

In the street below, electric-powered jitneys crawled through streams of pedestrians without the noise and hostility an observer would note in most cultures. Across the chain-link fence and alarm wires which surrounded the reservation, vans replenished stocks of fungibles aboard the *Empress of Earth* and more jitneys arrived with passengers and their luggage.

The manifest in Kneale's hands quantified the

unusual number of passengers embarking from Carnatica Port on this voyage. Kneale looked down on the foreshortened figures even now sauntering up the gangplank. His face was still, but his mind frowned.

He didn't have to wonder *whether* some of the passengers were potential hijackers. He had to determine which *ones* were the danger.

The door of the hydraulic elevator — chosen by the Trident design team because it could be locally maintained while lift/drop shafts could not — gasped open. Kneale turned, reflexively dimming the holographic manifest to hide it from observation.

The commander expected to see office workers coming up to the garden for a break — though at midday, he hadn't expected to be interrupted. Alternatively, it might have been a Trident officer, bringing Kneale a message that no one trusted to put on a link from the starliner or the data bank below.

The intruders were two passengers from the *Empress of Earth* — Wade and Belgeddes, whom Kneale recognized only because it was his job to recognize all First Class passengers. He assumed they were lost, or —

"Ah, there you are, friend," said the tall one, Wade. "I see you're like me — always out in the open air if I can be."

"They told us we'd find you here," said his plump companion Belgeddes, wiping his bald scalp with a handkerchief. "Mind you, I'd just as soon you stayed indoors where the temperature's at a civilized level. If God had meant us to swelter, he wouldn't have given us climate control."

"Ah, do you gentlemen . . . ?" Kneale began curiously.

"Have business with Commander Hiram Kneale, the First Officer, Staff Side?" Wade continued crisply. "Afraid we do, friend. It's about the passengers, you see. The ones we're taking on here, and no few of those who boarded at the past two or three dockings."

"Dickie's been secret service, you see, laddie," Belgeddes added. He chuckled. "Maybe a dozen secret services, one place and another. To a feller like me, people are just people; but Dickie here spots the wrong 'uns as if he reads their minds."

Kneale began, "Precisely what is it that you're concerned — "

An intra-system freighter lifted off with an increasing roar which overwhelmed the end of the commander's carefully phrased question. Tellichery had a very considerable off-planet trade carried on its own hulls, though most of it was concentrated on asteroid and gas mining in the local system. Tellichery was building interstellar transports, though. One day the planet might rival Grantholm and Nevasa in self-born interstellar trade —

Assuming Grantholm and Nevasa, or either one of them, survived the present conflict as a significant force in the human universe.

"Your starship's a valuable property, Commander," Wade said as the sound of the freighter diminished to a background rumble. "Militarily valuable, I mean. There's some on Nevasa who'd look at her as a war-winning asset."

"You could pack a division aboard her," Belgeddes said. "More than a division. Why, you loaded five thousand troops on a little Ivanhoe Line puddle-jumper on La Prieta, didn't you, Dickie?"

"That was only to orbit and down again," Wade said, dusting his right collar tab with his fingertips. He made a moue of dismissal but caught Kneale's eye as he added, "A Trojan Horse sort of business, you know. Not much to it. The government was scarcely able to organize a fire drill, much less react to a rebel brigade seizing the capital."

"Not a lot of heavy equipment on that little jaunt either," Belgeddes said as though he were making a critical distinction. "Still, Dickie understands this sort of business, don't you see."

The spaceship's hammering motors had disturbed winged creatures from the fringes of the reservation. They rose sluggishly into the air, some of them carrying burdens.

The native winged vertebrates depended on down-insulated skin for lift rather than feathers, but they had toothless beaks and filled the same econiches as the Terran birds which they so closely resembled. These had two-meter wingspans, and they ate carrion.

Tellichery had been settled by a broad cross-section from southern India including Parsees, Zoroastrians of Persian descent. These latter had continued their practice of putting the bodies of their dead on high towers. Tellichery's "birds" were more than willing to complete the disposal of the remains, as vultures had done for the Parsees' ancestors on Earth.

"Gentlemen," Commander Kneale said, "Trident Starlines and the government of Federated Earth will do all they can to ensure the safety of passengers at times of crisis like these. I myself am busy now, doing just that, and —"

Wade spread his hands in prohibition. "Have it your way, friend," he said. "Shouldn't think of poaching on another man's preserve. But I figured it was my duty to say you've got Nevasan troops coming aboard, pretending to be civilians — and that there's some locals from Tellichery here who I wouldn't be a *bit* surprised were paid mercenaries. Near a hundred of the fellers, or I miss my guess. All they need is a few guns and they own your ship."

Kneale said nothing. His eyes flicked between the two self-important passengers, who might simply have chanced across the truth while making up another tall story . . . or who might, just possibly might, be *agents provocateurs* in Nevasan pay, trying to determine what the *Empress of Earth*'s crew knew and what precautions they were taking.

"Like on the *Thomasino*, hey Dickie?" Belgeddes said with a chuckle. "You know, I never did understand why you decided to turn that one around. It was just a family argument, after all. The cousins and their gang would've set us down on Barak, as sure as the first lot."

Wade sniffed. "I don't care to have some chap wave a gun in my face and tell me to stay in my cabin if I know what's good for me," he said. "Besides, we'd paid Captain del Rio for passage. It was him, not his cousins, that I was looking to to complete the contract."

Belgeddes shook his head in amusement. "You just can't resist being a hero, Dickie," he said. "That's your problem."

"Gentlemen," Commander Kneale said sharply, "I appreciate your concern, but I'm afraid I have business of my own to attend to if the *Empress* is to undock on schedule."

"Enough said, enough said," Wade agreed with another lift of his hands. "Sorry to have troubled you, Commander."

The two old men turned together and walked back toward the elevator. "One bribed sailor," Belgeddes said, ostensibly to his companion, "and the hijackers are armed — out in sponge space where Terra can't so much as whistle. Where's the *Brasil*, d'ye suppose?"

"Now, now, Tom," Wade answered in an equally loud voice. "I'm sure that the commander knows a lot more than a couple old buffers like — "

The elevator door closed, amputating the word *us*.

What Commander Hiram Kneale knew was that Bridge had identified 97 passengers as probable agents of Nevasan nationality or in Nevasan employ. That was too close to Wade's "guess" of a hundred for any responsible person to believe it was only a guess.

What Kneale also knew was that so long as there

were hundreds of Grantholm returnees aboard the *Empress of Earth*, the Nevasans could expect a full-scale battle if they attempted to hijack the starliner. And the Grantholmers had disembarked on Szgrane.

The commander stared somberly at his vessel; considering, planning. Something cracked loudly on the pavers behind him.

Kneale spun. One of the birds had dropped its burden onto the roof garden. The object lay between the Trident officer and the elevator.

It was a human thigh bone, with shreds of dry flesh still attached.

" . . . please report at once to your assigned lifeboat," said the silky, synthesized voice as Abraham Chekoumian trotted along the corridor. Very few other passengers were still moving, at least here in the First Class section.

"This is a drill," Bridge repeated through membrane speakers in the wainscotting at three-meter intervals along the corridor and in every cabin. "However, the vessel will not leave orbit until every passenger has taken their position. . . . "

Chekoumian was in the Social Hall when the alarm sounded. Instead of going straight to his lifeboat, he'd detoured to his cabin to pick up his packet of letters from Marie. Just in case.

" . . . in a lifeboat. Please report at once to your assigned lifeboat."

The corridor walls, instead of showing restful land or seascapes, now surged forward in broad arrows overprinted with Bay 32, Bay 34, Bay 40. The fact that some bays weren't mentioned suggested to Chekoumian that while he wasn't the *only* passenger still delaying the exercise, at least some of the lifeboats were already loaded.

A steward with a holographic data link waited at the branch corridor to Bay 32, Chekoumian's lifeboat station. Chekoumian turned toward him, following the arrow. The link zeeped as it compared the passenger's features with those stored within the ship's AI.

"In here quickly," the steward called, though

Chekoumian was already past him. "Quickly quickly, please."

The lifeboat's hatch was broad enough for passengers to board six-abreast in stumbling panic. The interior lighting was dim compared to the bright corridor, but an illuminated yellow arrow slid swiftly down the central aisle to the only empty seat in the 50-place vessel.

Gray faces stared at the newcomer from the occupied places. Many of the passengers carried bundles, quickly gathered from their cabins. Though the announcement had been clear that this was only an exercise, lifeboat drill was unexpected and an unfamiliar event even to experienced travelers.

Chekoumian plumped into the empty place. The companion on his side of the aisle was a heavyset man with a sour expression, holding a disposable hologram reader.

The lifeboats' seat pitch and width were minimal, since the little vessels were designed to accommodate as many people as possible and protect them against the shock of a hard landing. Chekoumian wriggled to settle himself.

He bumped his neighbor. "Sorry," he muttered.

The hatch closed from either end. One of the panels rolled with a singing noise where something rubbed.

"That's all right," his companion answered, speaking Standard but with what Chekoumian took to be a Georgian accent. "If they don't get us out of these sardine cans in another five minutes, though, I'll walk before I lift with Trident again. I thought I was treating myself!"

"You're from Tblisi?" Chekoumian said.

His eyes were adapting to the interior lighting. A sailor seated at the console in the bow carried on a conversation with the starliner proper. Apart from him, the lifeboat was a can containing passengers in four-abreast seating — and five in the last row, where the aisle ended.

"You bet," his companion agreed, switching to Georgian. "Yuri Timurkanov, Gold Star Fisheries. You're from Tblisi too?"

Timurkanov set his reader down on the armrest to shake Chekoumian's offered hand. There wasn't enough room. The reader clacked to the floor.

"Abraham Chekoumian," the importer said. "And yes, from Tblisi, but I haven't been home in five years. I'm going back to be married."

He bent to pick up the hologram reader.

"Please?" a passenger nearer the bow called to the lone crewman. "When will we be able to leave, young man?"

"Oh, don't bother with that thing," Timurkanov said. "It's last week's news-load from Bogomil. It was the only thing I had along when the alarm sounded, but I must have read it a dozen times by now already."

"They tell me that the exercise should only take a few more minutes, madam," replied the crewman. He spoke loudly enough for everyone aboard the lifeboat to hear. "Then we'll be able to return to our business. Believe me, this isn't my idea of a good time either."

"Tblisi news?" Chekoumian said as he poised with the reader in his hand.

"Last week's Tblisi news," his companion said in a tone of mild protest. "Want it? Go ahead." He took the reader and ejected the data chip, which he handed to the importer.

"I had to make a quick run to Tellichery to install a new manager at my outlet here," Timurkanov explained as Chekoumian inserted the news download into his own reader. "Half our exports are to Tellichery, you know. I came over on one of our cargo charters, but I decided to treat myself first class on the hop back."

He looked around in disgust. "At least on *The City of San Juan*, I was only sharing my cabin with one other guy, not fifty."

CLANG

Several passengers screamed.

"What the *hell* is that?" bellowed the well-dressed young man across the aisle from Chekoumian. When the fellow tried to stand up, he found that the restraint system clamped him solidly into his seat no matter how he poked or twisted.

"By the name of the Virgin!" Timurkanov said. "That was a lifeboat launching or I'm a Jew!"

"Please stay calm, ladies and gentlemen," the crewman called. He had to shout to be heard. The timbre of his voice suggested that *he* hadn't been thrilled by the sound either. "There's nothing to be — "

CLANG

More distant, but clearly another launch to those who recognized the sound — and proof that the *Empress of Earth* was breaking up to the passengers who didn't. More people were screaming and tearing in vain at their restraints.

Almost anticlimactically, the hatch slid open — the seats unlocked — and the lighting within the lifeboat brightened dazzlingly to the same level as that of the corridor outside.

"There is no hurry, please, ladies and gentlemen!" cried a steward who was pummeled aside by the first rush of passengers through the hatch.

"I guess we can go now, buddy," said Yuri Timurkanov when he noticed that his aisle-side companion wasn't moving. After a further moment, he tapped Chekoumian on the shoulder. The importer's hologram reader quivered, then slipped from his fingers.

"What?" Chekoumian said, wild-eyed. "Oh — I'm sorry."

He lurched out of his seat and staggered down the aisle without looking back at Timurkanov.

Timurkanov picked up the abandoned reader. "Hey, buddy?" he called. "You dropped this."

The projected news was a report on the wedding the previous day of Marie Djushvili to Ivan Lishke, a timber merchant of Bogomil.

The *whang* of Lifeboat 67's launch echoed metallically through the boat deck.

"One away," said Ran Colville to the six Cold Crewmen with him in the machinery room nestled between Bay 109 and Bay 111.

Swede, a watch chief with twenty-two years in sponge space, grunted. Ran didn't have a clue as to what the fellow meant by the grunt, or if it was even a response to the statement. The remaining Cold Crewmen, all from Swede's watch, were frozen-eyed and silent.

Ran regretted not having Mohacks and Babanguida to back him, but only because he would have liked someone to talk to. Cold Crewmen couldn't talk on duty and didn't talk much when they were off-watch.

Ran didn't have the least concern about the way Swede and his crew would perform if a Nevasan hijack team suddenly rushed up the corridor from Bay 111. Two of the Cold Crewmen had been issued submachine guns. The other four men bore the equipment of their occupation: adjustment tools and, for Swede, an arc shears that weighed sixty kilos and could saw through 70-mm collapsed-steel hull plating at the rate of a centimeter/second.

Theoretically the Cold Crewmen were to back up the Third Officer and his bandolier of stun bombs, which would provide the first line of defense. Realistically — if the Nevasans broke out of Bay 111, there was going to be a bloodbath the like of which hadn't been seen on a starliner since the *Strasbourg* had the incredibly bad luck to collide with an asteroid while inbound toward Earth.

Commander Kneale had looked askance when he heard who Ran wanted for support, given that the

Staff Side ratings on his watch were unavailable. Kneale hadn't objected, though.

Lifeboat 111 fired with a clang and a double shockwave. At a distance, even on the Boat Deck, the suction as the outer doors closed and the inner ones opened to refill the bay was muted. Ran and his men were next to the bay. The hatch to their hiding place was ajar to save time if they were needed. They got the full, ear-popping effect.

They were used to it. The Cold Crewmen were in and out of airlocks at four-hour intervals for as long as the *Empress of Earth* was in transit between the stars, and their berths between watches were just off the engineering control room, where the locks were.

As for Ran — it didn't seem like very long since he'd been in the same business. The intervals between changes had been longer, though, because tramps weren't crewed like luxury liners.

The machinery room had a flat-screen communicator. It was live with a pattern of fluorescent static until the lifeboat fired in the next bay. Hiram Kneale's dark face appeared, wearing a smile that could have been carved in granite. "Congratulations, Mr. Colville," the commander said.

"Wanda's end is all right?" Ran asked. "Ah, Ms. Holly's?"

"Wanda's end is just fine," Kneale said with the smile broadening. "Go ahead and tell our Nevasan friends the score. Bridge will connect you to the talk-between-ships laser."

"Me, sir?" Ran said in surprise. "Shouldn't it be you — or Captain Kanawa?"

The corridors of the Boat Deck began to hiss with the shoes and voices of passengers released from the lifeboats. No one had been assigned to the two bays on either side of 111 and of 67, but some passengers shuffled past the machinery room on their way to lift shafts. Most of them were complaining.

"It was your idea, Ran," Kneale said. "Your *bright* idea, I'm very thankful to say."

Ran shrugged. "All right," he said. "Bridge, TBS to lifeboats six-seven and one-one-one."

The flat screen split vertically to display the backs of Mohacks' and Babanguida's heads on the separate sides. Beyond the two ratings were long ranks of angry men and women, clamped into their lifeboat seats by the restraint system. The passengers were bellowing in fury.

"Mohacks!" Ran shouted to get the crewman's attention. "Babanguida! You're all right?"

The ratings turned with grins that mirrored one another, though there was no direct communication between the two lifeboats.

"You bet, Mr. Colville," Mohacks said. "How's Babanguida doing?"

"You keep your part of the bargain," said Babanguida, "and you don't have to worry about me. Hey, Mohacks hasn't stepped on his dick, has he?"

"You're both fine," Ran said, responding to both expressions of concern. "And your bonuses have been credited to your accounts at the Trident offices on Tellichery. You'll have enough to live on until we pick you up on the next trip."

Mohacks held a compact machine pistol which he should *not* have had, either aboard the *Empress* or on the lifeboat he was conning. It looked like one of the weapons lying around after the firefight on Calicheman.

Babanguida didn't have a gun — well, he probably *did* have a gun, but it wasn't visible to the communicator's pick-up lens. Instead, the tall black rating held an incendiary grenade in his left hand. He'd pulled the safety pin, and he held the spoon down with the tip of one finger.

"You don't know how I plan to live, sir," Mohacks said with a chuckle.

"The hell with the bonus," Babanguida said simultaneously. "*I'm* looking at the amnesty for any little misunderstandings I might've been mixed up in while I've shipped with Trident."

Babanguida was grinning, but Ran Colville had no reason to doubt the sincerity of the statement. Quite the contrary. That was why he'd chosen, and Commander Kneale had approved, the two Third Watch ratings as helmsmen for the lifeboats that would be launched. Mohacks and Babanguida had the balls to do just about anything, and the brains to get away with it. The proof of the latter point was the fact they were both out of jail.

"Let me attend to the rest of this," Ran said. "I don't suppose you can move the screen so more of the passengers can see me?"

The ratings couldn't, but they squeezed themselves against the curve of the hull to keep from blocking the lifeboat displays.

"If I may have your attention?" Ran said, then waited until the angry passengers quieted. On Lifeboat 67, that required a crisp order from a middle-aged Nevasan who was listed on the passenger manifest as a mining engineer. He looked tough enough to *chew* tunnels through solid rock.

"Ladies and gentlemen," Ran continued, "you are in orbit around Tellichery. Your helmsmen will land you at the Carnatica Reservation as soon as the *Empress of Earth* enters sponge space, which we will do momentarily."

He nodded, marking a stage in his discussion. "On behalf of Trident Starlines," he continued, "I apologize to any of you who are genuine passengers. Unfortunately, the bulk of your ninety-six fellows are members of a hijack team employed by a government in contravention of the laws of war and those of Federated Earth, under whose flag this vessel sails."

Lifeboat 111 rumbled with low-voiced threats until

Mohacks waggled the muzzle of his machine pistol toward the faces of those who were being particularly vehement. On 67, the "mining engineer" shouted, "I protest! This is a libel against me and my planet!"

"Colonel Ngo," Ran said, making a guess at the passenger's rank, "Trident Starlines doesn't intend to take action through the government of Federated Earth, even though the crewmen bribed to provide access to the arms crated in the hold say they were contacted directly by officials of the Nevasan Embassy on Calicheman."

That attribution was false, but Ngo — obviously the unit commander — had boarded on Tellichery with the remainder of a team rushed there from Nevasa, packed into a courier vessel. Ngo couldn't be *sure* that there hadn't been a screw-up on Calicheman, somebody operating directly instead of using cut-outs.

Given the way the departments of any government hid mistakes from the outside world, the Nevasa military high command would probably go to its individual graves believing that the Nevasan Ministry of External Affairs had blown the hijack. In fact, the plan had been uncovered by a computer sort of the passenger list, looking for anomalies, backed by the paranoid certainty on the part of all the *Empress*'s officers that there was something to find. The *Brasil*'s disappearance had guaranteed that.

A manual search of hold luggage as it came aboard turned up a capsule marked "DENTAL EQUIPMENT — FRAGILE," which contained weapons for ninety-six troops. In all likelihood, there *was* an innocent man or woman in the two lifeboats that had been launched, but the poor bastard would play hell proving it.

And Ran Colville didn't much care.

"You can't —" Ngo cried.

"Good day, sir," Ran said sharply. "Mohacks and Babanguida, good luck and I'm looking forward to seeing you soon."

Mohacks gave Ran an ironic salute, touching the barrel of his weapon to his brow. Babanguida simply grinned.

"Bridge," Ran ordered, "break contact. Commander, I think that does it."

Kneale nodded from the screen. "I'll inform Captain Kanawa," he said. His face dissolved into fluorescing speckles.

There was silence in the machinery room. By now, the passengers had dispersed from the Boat Deck so the corridor was quiet as well.

"Shit," said one of the Cold Crewmen to Swede. His voice wasn't loud, but there was more hatred in it than Ran had ever heard before in a single syllable. "That's fuckin' it, then?"

Swede nodded. Why he had that nickname — if it was a nickname — couldn't be guessed. He was a squat, dark Kephalonian, as strong as a troll. "Let's get back to quarters. They've wasted an hour, and they'll expect us to make up the schedule for them. As we will."

"I was looking forward," the other crewman said, "t' getting stuck in t' some of them pussies."

He stroked the shaft of his adjustment tool, a three-meter rod with a selection of sharp-edged tools at the head end. The surface of the tool's molecularly-aligned steel was pitted by years of micro-meteor impacts.

"Another time, Lewis," Swede said. He draped one arm over his subordinate's shoulders and walked him out toward their duty quarters on the deck below. The arc shears hung from Swede's other hand without apparent difficulty.

The remainder of the team followed. Ran took the submachine guns as the Cold Crewmen left the machinery room. The first man resisted instinctively, but the second tossed the weapon to Ran before Ran was ready for it. The barrels of the two submachine guns clashed together.

"It's not worth shit anyhow," the crewman said with a sneer. "Next time I bring my tool. See how the pussy screams with my tool sliding through him."

Ran watched Swede's watch disappear down a drop shaft. He felt wrung out. The guns and bandoliers of ammunition were suddenly too much for his arms to bear. He set them on the deck and began unbuckling his own belt of stun grenades.

Wanda Holly appeared at the open hatch. She was beaming. "Nice work, sailor," she said.

"God, Wanda," Ran said. "I feel like I just tended three engines by myself and a double watch besides. And I didn't do *anything*. I just stood here and waited."

Wanda bent and picked up the submachine guns. She frowned. "Let's take the service shaft up to A Deck," she said. "We don't want to startle any passengers in one of the regular lifts."

She leaned over and gave Ran a peck on the cheek. "Not after you and the rest of us did such a job to make sure they *won't* wake up to a nasty surprise," she added.

"Let's hope," Ran said, slipping an arm around his fellow officer's waist for support and companionship. "Let's just hope."

● IN TRANSIT: TELLICHERY TO TBLISI

"That's funny," said Yeoman Etcherly. She spoke loudly enough that Bruns, the Second Officer (Ship Side), would hear across the electronic hum of the bridge though she didn't call to him directly.

Bruns stretched. There were only three of them in the large room at present: Bruns; his helmsman Donaldson; and Etcherly, the navigating technician. That was the normal complement of the starliner's bridge while under way, though Captain Kanawa would inspect at least once during the watch.

While the *Empress of Earth* was between destinations, she dipped at regular intervals from sponge space back into the sidereal universe. The vessel's artificial intelligence compared a blink of a wedge of the visible stars against that synthesized from the data base as existing at that point in space. If the two star charts varied, the AI adjusted the attitude and burn of the fusion engines for the next sponge space insertion. For the human bridge crew, the process was as boring as rereading a telephone directory.

The engines themselves could not be insulated from the series of sponge-space bubbles as the interior of the *Empress* was. Their thrust had to be delivered in sponge space, using the varied constants of those other universes in order to multiply the vessel's movements against the sidereal universe.

The men who serviced the engines could work only in the sidereal universe, but they had to remain on the hull throughout their watch. Sending them

in and out at each extraction would have multiplied
the vessel's transit time. For those men, the Cold
Crews, the navigational extractions provided brief
minutes of normalcy — albeit hard vacuum and
hard work — to punctuate the in-pressing madness
of universes to which mankind and life itself were
alien.

"Oh, all right, Etcherly," Bruns said. Mid-watch
boredom made him lethargic, unwilling to look at anything new even though he had nothing better —
indeed, nothing at all — to do. "What is it that you've
got?"

Etcherly murmured a command. Her console echoed
its data onto Bruns's. She was projecting the chart of the
most recent navigation check. "It's just . . . " she said.
"There's an anomaly. In the upper right quadrant—"

A red carat on the display noted the point of light —
one of literally hundreds of thousands at this degree of
detail.

Before responding, Bruns ran the chart — the real-
time display — against the computed synthesis of what
the chart should have looked like. Red carats lit all across
the display. When the Second Officer corrected for
navigationally significant levels of accuracy — 10^{-17} —
the carats disappeared.

Except for the one Etcherly had noted.

Bruns shrugged. "Right," he said. "It's an anomaly.
One bit of space junk that's too small to be entered in
the data base. It's a big universe, Etcherly, but it's not so
big that we're going to have it completely to ourselves
every time we come out of sponge space."

Donaldson, the helmsman, didn't move while Bruns
and the navigating tech were speaking. His eyes were
open, but Bruns sometimes had the impression that
the helmsman was capable of sending his soul light
years away until recalled by an unexpected require-
ment or the end of his watch.

"Yessir," said Etcherly, "but see —"

The displays, hers and Bruns' together, flickered through the whole run of navigational checks since the watch began three hours previously. The star charts differed wildly from one to the next. Not only were the glimpses separated by great distances, but also the shortest transit through bubbles of sponge space traced a path in no particular order through the sidereal universe. The only constant in the varying stellar panoramas was the anomaly carated in the upper right-hand quadrant.

"Oh," said Bruns. "That's odd."

He rubbed his lips with the knuckles of his right hand. "It's either a problem with the sensors, or a problem with the data base. Frankly, neither one thrills me."

"Bridge says the hardware's okay," Etcherly said. "It says the software's okay, too, but I guess it would. I mean, if there's a problem, it's a problem with Bridge, isn't it?"

Officer and technician stared at one another. The red marks on their displays pulsed softly in unison.

"It's a ship," said Donaldson unexpectedly. He didn't turn his head in the direction of either of the others on the bridge.

"That's impossible!" Bruns snapped. "We've been in and out of sponge space forty times this watch. We couldn't possibly have matched courses so closely with another vessel."

"The lifeboats," Etcherly said, staring at the display in sudden surmise. "Could one of them have been picked up when we jumped from Tellichery?"

"No," Bruns said flatly. He rubbed his mouth again. "We weren't within ten-to-the-twelfth meters when we made the initial insertion. Besides, you don't just 'pick things up' when you insert into sponge space."

He shrugged. "It's a fault in the system and my

money's on the sensors, whatever Bridge has to say about it. We'll get it taken care of on Tblisi, they've got full docking facilities. But it's not a serious problem."

"It's a ship," Donaldson repeated. "It's matching course with us. And it's getting closer."

Bruns glared at Donaldson. The helmsman ignored him. He was staring at his own display, a gentle swirl with the delicacy of a mandala. Donaldson's duties were to maneuver the *Empress of Earth* in the sidereal universe. In sponge space, as now, he *could* not have anything to do.

"That's *nonsense*," the Second Officer said sharply. "Besides, you can't tell relative distances without triangulating. Since the — the anomaly's at the same point, we can't triangulate."

Donaldson wasn't looking at either Bruns's display or that of the navigating tech, except possibly from the corners of his eyes. He couldn't possibly have anything useful to add to the discussion.

"Should we inform Captain Kanawa?" Etcherly asked softly.

"I . . ." the Second Officer mumbled past his clenched fist. He lowered his hand sharply. "No," he said. "That is, we'll inform him when he leaves his quarters. But he wasn't sleeping for the three days before we got rid of the — the hijackers in Tellichery orbit. He didn't say much about it, but he's been worried since we learned about the *Brasil*."

A muted alarm purred, warning that the *Empress of Earth* was about to drop back into the sidereal universe for another navigational check. Bruns blanked his display in preparation.

"Now that he's able to sleep again," he said aloud, "I think we ought to let him."

The new starscape flashed onto the screens. For a moment, it was a rosy blur of highlights. Then, as the artificial intelligence adjusted to navigational parameters, there was only one red carat, high in the right-hand quadrant of either display.

"Pretty hard lines for the fellows they dumped into orbit that way," Da Silva said, staring morosely at the twisted fabric of sponge space beyond the wall of the Starlight Bar. "Damned high-handed. Even if they were right, I mean, and I *don't* think they didn't make some mistakes, artificial intelligences or no."

Dewhurst nodded. "I keep thinking, what if I'd been one of the poor bastards?" he said. "I'd be — well, Trident Starlines would regret it, you can well believe."

"I think . . ." Wade said judiciously. He cocked an eye up at the traveling display which falsely showed the *Brasil* en route from Nevasa to Earth. " . . . that I'd prefer to be in a lifeboat above Tellichery than in whatever holding facility the *Brasil's* passengers are detained. Some desert world, very likely. I doubt they'll be harmed deliberately . . . but they'll be concealed for however long the Grantholm-Nevasa War goes on."

Belgeddes swirled his ice. "And better than what happened on the *Delilah*, hey Dickie?"

Wade grimaced. He stood up and walked closer to the bulkhead, staring out at alien nothingness. "I don't like to talk about the *Delilah*," he said. "You know that, Tom."

"Would another drink help?" Dewhurst asked sardonically. He plugged his chip into the autobar and dialed another round, though Da Silva was still nursing his rum.

To his surprise, Wade didn't take the fresh whiskey.

"He didn't have any choice, you understand," Belgeddes said apologetically. "They were Free-Will Consecrants, with a bomb big enough to blow the whole ship to kingdom come if Dickie hadn't opened the compartment to vacuum."

"Well, do what you have to and don't brood on it,"

Wade said with a stiff chuckle as he turned at last to the drink. "I mean, they had as much chance as I did to get to the lock to the next compartment, didn't they?"

He stood with his foot on a chair seat, a spare old man with a consciously dashing expression. He could have modeled for a whiskey ad. Dewhurst had no doubt that Wade was an actor of *some* sort.

"They didn't have suits, then?" Da Silva said with narrowing eyes.

"None of us had suits," Wade explained. "They'd decided they were going to create their own Eden by hijacking the *Delilah* to some planet back of beyond. Everybody else was going along whether they liked it or not — and I was the only one in Compartment 3 who wasn't a Consecrant."

"The *Delilah* was a trainship," Belgeddes said. "The internal passage to the rest of the ship was blocked during the hijacking, but each segment had its own airlock as well. *I* was playing cards with the Second Officer, I'm happy to say."

He shook his head with an approving smile. "Crawling around the hull of a starship without so much as a suit — that's Dickie's sort of business, not mine."

Da Silva shuddered and turned his head.

"That," Dewhurst said distinctly, "is not only impossible, it's sick."

"Scarcely impossible, friend," Wade replied. "The airlocks were in the same position on each segment, so there wasn't any searching around for me to do."

He shrugged. "I won't quarrel with 'sick.' But there it is."

Da Silva jumped up, overturning his fresh drink when his knee slammed the underside of the table.

"What's wrong?" Dewhurst cried as he slid his own chair back.

"A ship!" Da Silva said. "I swear I saw another ship out there! Just for a moment!"

He turned to look at his companions. To his amazement, Wade and Belgeddes had already left the bar.

The *Empress of Earth* dropped out of sponge space for the forty-seventh navigational check since undocking from Tellichery. Second Officer Bruns and his navigational technician held their breath, while Donaldson blinked at the slowly rotating pattern he ran on his screen until called on to oversee a maneuver.

Bridge completed its check and flashed up the star chart.

"Clean!" Etcherly said. Then, as though Bruns weren't staring at the same display on his own console, she added, "The anomaly's gone!"

"We'll still get it checked in Tblisi," the watch officer said with more emphasis than he'd been able to muster during the period of uncertainty over the starliner's navigational system. "Something like that, even a little transient, might turn out to be serious."

"What might turn out to be serious?" asked Captain Kanawa as he walked onto the bridge. He looked as fit and rested as he had since the *Empress* lifted from Earth, though the pockets of skin around his eyes still looked unusually hollow.

"Ah, sir . . ." said Bruns. Kanawa wasn't one of those captains who expected the crew to come to attention when they entered the bridge, but he *did* expect complete answers to any questions he asked about the watch. "There was a flaw in, I think the sensors, causing an anomaly in the star charts during several observations. Yeoman Etcherly pointed it out, and I've logged it for correction at our next docking."

Kanawa noted it without evident concern. He walked over to his own console and said, "Status."

The starliner's running display came up at once. Changes since the most recent check were highlighted.

Normally the watch officer had the status report on at all times. Bruns hadn't looked at it since Etcherly noted the anomaly before the previous observation, but it all seemed pretty standard —

"Why's the engineering hatch open?" Kanawa demanded. "Has the Cold Crew had an accident?"

"Bridge to Engineering," Bruns said without hesitating an instant. "Why are — "

The Second Officer's demand through the AI automatically switched the upper right corner of his screen to visuals from the target location, in this case the engineering control room. An engineering officer — Crosse on second watch — waited there while the Cold Crewmen under his titular command were out on the hull.

Instead of the bored-looking engineer Bruns expected to see, the visual pickup showed a room full of men in spacesuits. During watch changes, the engineering control room was sealed off from the rest of the starliner. It formed a large airlock so that all eight men of the Cold Crew watch could enter and leave the vessel in a batch, instead of being passed through the hull one at a time through the normal lock.

There were far more than eight men in the large room now. It looked like twenty or thirty, and more suited figures were climbing down the access ladder from the hull.

They all carried guns.

"What's that?" Kanawa cried, looking over the watch officer's shoulder in surprise instead of switching his own display to the scene. "Mister Crosse, what's going on?"

There was no response. Since the engineering control room was airless, the suited men couldn't even hear the blurted question.

"Docking display," the helmsman said to his console. The mandala shrank inward and reformed as a synthesized external view of the *Empress of Earth*. Beside the huge starliner was a much smaller vessel of non-descript appearance.

"A Type Two-Oh-Three hull from the Excelsior Dockyards on Grantholm," Donaldson said, identifying the vessel — a short-haul trader in normal usage — aloud.

As he spoke, the *Empress* concluded its navigational checks and reentered sponge space. The schematic of the starliner itself remained on the helmsman's display, but that of the Type 203 freighter twisted into a complex of lines surrounding the holographic *Empress* in all three dimensions. Data from the sensors that Bridge used to create the schematic were skewed unintelligibly by the alien universe in which they now functioned.

"I've heard about people docking in sponge space," Donaldson said approvingly. "But I never thought I'd see it happen. Of course, if they'd tried to match with us in star space, we'd have had warning and got out of the way."

Bruns wiped the chart. Visuals from the engineering control room expanded to fill his whole display. The external hatch must have closed, because the figures in the room unlatched their helmets.

"Bridge," Captain Kanawa ordered crisply, "notify the passengers and crew of an emergency. The *Empress* has been boarded by a force of armed men who must be assumed to be — "

In the engineering control room, a woman with her scalp shaved and eyes like hatchets aimed a back-pack laser at the engineering console. The last thing the pick-up in the control room showed was the blue-white glare that vaporized its circuitry.

" — hostile," Captain Kanawa finished in a dry voice.

"You know . . ." Ran Colville said.

He paused as he and Wanda Holly passed one of the many alcoves set back from the Enchanted Forest's curving central aisle. The whispers behind the screen of exotic vegetation stopped at the sound of the officers' measured footsteps on the parquet floor.

"I thought when I was assigned to the *Empress*," Ran continued when he was a comfortable distance from the couple hidden in the alcove, "that the duty was going to be cut-and-dried compared to what I was used to on smaller ships. Tense, because of so many people and powerful ones. But dull."

Wanda chuckled. "Well, we've still got half the voyage to go," she said. "Maybe the return leg will be dull. I'd like to think so."

"I'll settle for getting safe to Tblisi," Ran said soberly. "One step at a time."

They were both off duty, so there was nothing technically improper for them to be together; but the Enchanted Forest was the most private of the ship's open spaces, something that had affected Ran's suggestion for a place to walk and perhaps Wanda's agreement. The park-like lounge contained real tropical vegetation from the worlds on which the starliner touched down, blended in with holographic panels of the corresponding animal life. The result was a score of bowers, set off privately from one another and from the aisle.

A three-tonne amphibian eyed Ran and Wanda from a bed of tall Grantholm reeds. The holographic beast worked its jaws forward and back, grinding the coarse fibers into a pulp that bacteria in its gut would convert into energy.

Ran nodded toward the image. "Not a very romantic setting, is it?" he said/asked.

"Speak for yourself," Wanda replied with a careful lack of emphasis.

The officers' communications modules chimed together.

"All passengers must return to their cabins at once,"

the ship's public address system said from several points in the Forest's hidden moldings. The speakers' varied distances from those listening turned simultaneous phrases into a series of sibilant echoes. "Do not use Corridor Four. All passengers —"

Ran whirled around, trying to find a sightline for his commo unit which leaves didn't block. Wanda, more experienced with the layout of the *Empress of Earth*, had already knelt on the parquetry.

"Go ahead," Ran snapped, letting Bridge's voice analyzer identify him without further delay.

A couple lurched through a shield of spike-leafed vegetation from which a Hobilo carnivore leered. The woman was slim and attractive, but at least twenty years older than her teenaged companion. His fly was undone because in haste he had caught his shirttail in the pressure seal.

"This is an emergency," Bridge said needlessly. "Unknown persons have entered the vessel through the engineering hatch. All crew members must act to prevent injury to the vessel's passengers. Await further orders. Out."

The mildly concerned synthesized tones undercut the import of the words. Instead of gently urging the listener, the smooth voice introduced a level of cognitive dissonance which increased the terror of broken routine.

"The hell with that!" said Wanda Holly as Ran looked up from the message he'd heard a moment after she'd received it. "Can't we stop them?"

More couples were drifting out of the foliage. The officers' white uniforms drew their eyes like needles to lodestone.

"It's all right, ladies and gentlemen," Ran said loudly. The tannoys continued to drone their message, increasing nervousness by repetition without any real information. "Some people from Grantholm want to redirect the ship. There's no physical danger whatever, so long as you keep out of their way."

"Go to your cabins at once," Wanda added with calm certainty. "We'll let you know what the situation is as soon as we can, certainly within an hour. But right now, you've got to get out of the way."

"But —" said at least five passengers simultaneously.

"*Move* it!" Ran snapped. He made shooing motions with his hands. "This is as real as lifeboat drill, it's just not as uncomfortable."

Wanda unexpectedly unsealed her tunic. She wore a translucent bodysock beneath it, Ran noted with surprise.

"Sir, madam?" the Second Officer said to a couple surprised from the semblance of a Calicheman riverbank. The screen of dense-trunked trees grew from a common root system. Behind it, beasts the size of hippopotami sported. "Mr. Colville and I need your jackets at once."

She glanced over at Ran. "This isn't any time to stick out like sore thumbs, whatever we want to do."

The two passengers addressed obeyed the sharp command without objecting or even speaking, though the man's mouth opened and closed like that of a carp gulping air. The dozen or so other passengers acted as though a flag had dropped. Their shift toward the door to the corridor became a dead run within three steps.

The man who gave Ran his jacket of pink and puce velour reached for the uniform tunic in exchange. Ran set his hand over the passenger's.

"You don't want this either," Ran said. His voice quivered like the wire of a cheese-cutter.

The passenger jerked away and rushed out of the room, hand in hand with his companion. They didn't look back.

Ran tossed his white tunic into an alcove. Wanda

slipped a small pistol from the sidepocket of her own garment to that of her borrowed one, then hid the uniform with Ran's.

He knelt as the Second Officer had done before. "Colville to Kneale," he said with the transceiver tight against the inlaid wood. "Over."

"How do you know it's Grantholmers?" Wanda demanded, backing into the shelter of the reeds as she looked toward the entrance to the Enchanted Forest. Her right hand was in her pocket.

"Bridge, where the hell is the commander!" Ran shouted.

"Commander Kneale is not aboard the vessel," Bridge said through the disk. "He vanished from his cabin when I sounded the alarm. Over."

"It says he *vanished!*" Ran blurted to his companion. "You can't vanish from a starship!"

What you could *do was die. If a crewman in Grantholm pay had hidden bombs in the officers' quarters to go off in concert with an external attack, for example.*

Ran and Wanda saw understanding in each others' sudden hardening of expression. Neither of them spoke the realization aloud.

"They'll have the arms locker by now," Ran said. "It's on the Engineering Deck, a hundred meters from the Cold Crew hatch they used. I've got my pistol and that cannon we picked up on Calicheman in my cabin, but they'll probably have somebody on Corridor Twelve by now. . . ."

"We'll try," Wanda said in sharp decision. "We need more than one pop-gun, that's for sure."

Her face suddenly fell into a hard smile. "And it's Grantholm rather than Nevasa because the Nevasans were going to hijack the *Empress* from inside. That means if there's a sponge-space commando attacking, it's from Grantholm."

"Excuse us?" a voice called from the direction of the

corridor entrance. The person speaking was hidden by vegetation between him and the officers on the curved aisle. "Lieutenants? We're coming toward you. Your ship's artificial intelligence said you were here."

Wanda drew her pistol. Ran stepped deliberately in front of her, hiding the weapon from sight.

"What is it?" he demanded sharply.

A lanky old man stepped around the stand of Grantholm reeds. It was a passenger Ran had met the day the *Empress* undocked from Earth: Wade, Richard Wade, and his plump cabinmate Belgeddes trailed behind him.

"A Grantholm commando has invaded your ship, Mr. Colville," Wade said. He gave a courtly nod to recognize Wanda as well. "And we thought you might like our help in doing something about it."

"You want to *what*?" Wanda Holly said.

"Thinks we're a couple silly old buffers, Dickie," Belgeddes said, shaking his head sadly. "Well, I suppose we can't blame her."

The plump old man put his index finger to the throat of his tunic and opened it to an undershirt of some bleached natural fiber.

"Gentlemen," said Ran Colville, "please get to your cabin at once. Ms. Holly and I — "

"They'll have somebody in officers' country by now," Wade said, "the Grantholmers will. They won't have had time to search the cabins this quick, though. The two of *you* head that way, they'll come down on you like lizards on a beetle. But if it's you and I sauntering down the hall, Ms. Holly — well, an old fart and his popsy won't ring any alarm bells in whoever's on guard, will we?"

"Best be me with the young lady, Dickie," said Belgeddes as he pulled his undershirt from beneath his waistband. "And it best be me with the little gun, Ms.

Holly, because even if you're better than I think you are, I've got more of this kind of experience."

He tugged the undershirt upward, baring his belly and chest.

"Jesus Christ," Ran Colville said softly.

Much of the scar tissue smeared a bright pink across Belgeddes' pasty torso was of too general a nature to identify its cause, but the line of four dimples from right shoulder to right nipple were obviously bulletholes. It was amazing the man had survived.

Ran glanced back at Wanda. She touched her tongue to her lips but said nothing. Behind her, holographic pachyderms ground away at the Calicheman equivalent of mangrove roots.

"I'm sorry if I've distressed you young people," Begeddes said as he covered his ruined flesh again, "but I had to convince you that we're ... experienced in this sort of thing. Otherwise you'll go off and get yourselves killed without doing a lick of good."

"And don't jump to the wrong conclusion about the scars, young fellow," Wade said to Ran. "Tom's the one who walked away from that one—"

"On Esmeralda, it was," Belgeddes murmured with a wry smile. " 'Ought to be interesting,' Dickie says, and I go along with him because I always do, for my sins."

" — and there were twelve of the others," Wade continued without looking at his plump friend. He shook his head sadly. "Tom's a dab hand with a pistol, no one better. Give him a long gun, though, and the only way he could hit anything is to get close enough to swing it like a club."

Ran looked at the two passengers, and thought how much he wished Commander Kneale were alive—

And how much he wished Mohacks and Babanguida were still on board—

And how much he wished he was anyplace else himself than on the *Empress of Earth* —

And how much he wished he didn't have a sense of duty which would drive him to risks that Trident Starlines would never order, just to save a symbol of peace from the maw of war.

And realized that he didn't wish that last thing. He didn't wish not to be Ran Colville.

"All right," Wanda said decisively. "If you gentlemen are in, I'm glad to have you. What about you, Ran? The company can't order — "

Ran put his hand on Wanda's velvet-clad elbow. "The company doesn't have to order this," he said. "I'm doing it for — it doesn't matter. I'm in."

I'm doing it for my Dad.

"Right," said Wanda. "First to the officers' section off Corridor Twelve. Ran's got a pistol and a rifle in his room; we'll get them. After that — well, we'll see how the Grantholmers deploy."

Wanda linked arms with Belgeddes, hugging close to the plump old man in a way that suddenly struck Ran as obscene — though he'd seen a score of similar couples on every passenger vessel he'd crewed. The women with boys half their age were equally common, but the women who cared about youth in that fashion also cared about their own physique.

The four of them walked briskly out into the main corridor. The pistol was in Wanda's pocket, not Belgeddes', though his left hand was near it also.

Wanda had the rank, which put her in charge so long as everybody agreed she was in charge. That was one of the problems with a scratch force of volunteers. They weren't doing this officially, none of them, and they sure as *hell* weren't an army.

Suddenly, as clear as Bifrost's sun on a glacial valley, Ran knew where *he* was going to look for reinforcements.

"Wanda," he said aloud, "I'd just attract attention in Corridor Twelve. I'm going down to Engineering

Deck. The Grantholmers're probably holding our Cold Crew under guard until they get things organized. I'm going to do something about those guards.

"And then we'll see who organizes what . . ." Ran added. His voice trailed off as the eyes of his mind stared into sponge space.

Corridor 12 served two of the *Empress*'s imperial suites as well as a score of ordinary First Class cabins. The end which abutted officers' country was buffered by the Prairie Lounge, a group of alcoves decorated in what an architect imagined was Calicheman fashion.

The segments of the Prairie Lounge held tables and chairs of hair-out cowhide and rough wood — sealed and stabilized with synthetic resins — with walls of porous concrete and the raw ends of rusticated stonework. Sprouting from pots were a mix of grasses and the broad-leafed plants which grew among them on the prairies.

The lounge missed the reality of Calicheman by not being filthy, the way settlements in that world of self-ruled egoists usually were; but it was still one of the lesser-used of the starliner's public spaces.

Holly, Belgeddes, and — at a slight distance — Wade walked into the lounge. All three of them talked loudly though not directly in response to what the others said. They carried drink tumblers from the autobar just outside the Enchanted Forest.

Farther back in Corridor 12, a male passenger holding a toddler by either hand shouted at a cabin door, "Barbara! Barbara! Open the door, for God's sake!"

At the other end of the lounge, three men worked in loose uniforms which blurred like chameleon skin to take on neighboring colors. Instead of boots, they wore soft shoes which fit within the spacesuits they'd worn to board the starliner. Two of the men carried submachine guns. The third had a doorknocker, a stocked launcher for rocket-driven 15-cm impact grenades.

The soldiers' uniforms bore no national or unit markings, but the weapons were Grantholm issue.

"Halt!" ordered the soldier watching the backs of his fellows as they struggled with the locked door into officers' country. He pointed his submachine gun at the trio straggling into the lounge.

Holly giggled and threw herself into a chair. "C'mere, sweetie," she said, tugging at Belgeddes's arm. "Come to mama, cute l'il baby."

"Can I help you, gentlemen?" Wade said, walking forward with a deliberation more suggestive of drink than a stagger would have been. "I have great experience in construction methods and problems. I am the largest contractor, I say with no exaggeration, within a hundred kilometers of Point Easy."

"Get the hell *out* of here!" the guard snarled.

The other two Grantholmers held an electronic pick against the lockplate of the hatch to the continuation of Corridor 12. The pick was designed to duplicate the combination of simple locks like this one by sheer number-crunching. The coarse concrete surface of the panel caused alignment problems.

"If *you* can't get this fucking thing to work," snarled the soldier with the slung doorknocker, "*I've* got a trick that will!"

"My wife left me," Wade said, continuing to walk toward the trio of soldiers. "Me, the largest contractor within a hundred — "

"Get *back*, you stupid bastard!" the guard shouted. He stepped forward and brought his weapon around in an arc that slammed the side of the wire stock into Wade's head. The thin old man hurtled over a chair with a streak of blood bright against the white hair of his temple.

The pistol shots were so sharp and swift that the

three of them together could have been the first whipcrack of a nearby thunderbolt.

One of the soldiers lurched against the closed door, hard enough to bloody his nose on the rough gray finish. His partner simply slumped, releasing the electronic pick as he fell. The bullet wound beneath either man's left ear, under the lip of the soldiers' tight-fitting helmets, looked like a blood blister rather than a hole.

The guard continued to rotate with the inertia of the force with which he'd struck Wade. He had a surprised expression and no right eye because of the bullet that had killed him an instant before his fellows died.

Wade got up from his flailing sprawl. He patted his left temple gingerly, looked at the blood on his finger-tips, and grimaced.

"Told you Tom here was a dab hand with a pistol," he murmured to Holly as he bent to pick up the sub-machine gun with which he'd been clubbed.

The passenger fifty meters down the corridor screamed uncontrollably. He let go of his children's hands to find his room key, then dropped the key when he tried to touch it to the lockplate. The toddlers gripped their father's trouser legs and added their high-pitched voices to his shrieks.

Holly opened the corridor hatch with her key. She grabbed one of the soldiers to drag him through. "We don't want them found any sooner than we can help it," she muttered in a voice pitched more for herself than for informing her companions.

Belgeddes dropped the pistol into his tunic pocket. "A nice little weapon," he said conversationally as he took another soldier by the collar with both hands. "I'll keep it, if you don't mind."

The corpse Wanda Holly was dragging suddenly began to thrash like a pithed frog. She pulled it another half-meter forward to get the feet out of the hatchway.

Then, unexpectedly to herself though not to the old

men, she knelt and vomited out the whole contents of her stomach.

Passengers pranced nervously up and down the corridors of the *Empress of Earth*, their eyes as wide as those of does separated from their herd. None of them really looked at Ran Colville, incongruous in white trousers and a jacket of pink and puce streaks.

There was a three-man team from the Grantholm commando in the Embarkation Hall. Ran scuttled past the soldiers to a drop shaft. Four passengers, caught on the wrong deck as Ran had been, lurched from their stasis at the edge of the hall and followed him into the shaft. All of them hunched as if to draw their heads within their shoulders, turtle-like.

A Grantholm submachine gun followed the movements, but the soldiers didn't deign to speak. They were in the Embarkation Hall and other key points as an earnest of intent. The fifty or so troops in the commando couldn't control thousands of people directly. So long as the passengers were trying to get to their rooms, the Grantholmers had no need to act.

In the shaft, as in the corridors and other spaces, the cloying machine voice repeated, "All passengers must return to their cabins at once." Bridge had dropped the request to avoid Corridor 4, because by now the Grantholmers had penetrated the *Empress of Earth* like snake venom in a victim's bloodstream.

"Oh my god, my god," a woman in the drop shaft gasped into her hands. "I'm going to be raped, I'm going to be raped!"

"For god's sake, Frances, shut up!" snarled the man beside her. "They'll have better things to do than poke you, whoever they are."

Ran's lips tightened. It would be easy to forget that the husband was under as much strain as his wife, so that he wasn't responsible for his words either.

The passengers got off in couples on Decks B and A, scuttling quickly toward their cabins. Ran hadn't seen any of the bombast and disbelief he'd have expected among people whose wealth was implied by the fact they were traveling First Class on the *Empress*. The Grantholm troops looked like exactly what they were: merciless killers. So long as passengers realized that, the loss of life in the operation could be very low.

Not that the government of Grantholm really cared how many neutral civilians died, so long as they got their war-winning prize.

The Stewards' Pantry and quarters were on Deck 1, beneath the passenger spaces but above the holds and the Engineering Deck, 4. Ran got off the drop shaft nervously, aware that if he'd been planning the assault, there would be at least one Grantholm team here before him.

Instead, a dozen stewards waited in the receiving area around the lift and drop shafts, chatting tensely and listening to their transceivers. They jumped to attention when Ran appeared, recognizing him despite his civilian jacket. There were no soldiers present.

The Grantholm planners hadn't served as officers on passenger liners. They didn't know that the stewards were the people most likely to face a passenger emergency, and that they therefore had to be equipped for one.

"What are your orders from the bridge?" Ran demanded sharply. Every time he focused on a steward, the steward's eyes clicked off in the direction of Ran's ear or a corner of the moldings.

"*Get* moving," Ran ordered. "Check all the corridors, all the public spaces. When you find passengers, guide them to their cabins. Carry them if you've got to!"

He paused, glaring around the foyer. More faces peered out of the pantry beyond. Some ducked back, but a few joined those Ran was lecturing.

"Nobody needs to be hurt at all if we just get the

passengers out of the way till things settle down," Ran continued more gently. "That's our job, the safety of the passengers. Let's do it."

He nodded toward the lift shafts. After a moment's hesitation, one steward and then the whole mass of her fellows moved to the shafts. They disappeared upward toward their duties.

Ran walked into the pantry. A few more brown-uniformed stewards pressed themselves against the freestanding consoles and smooth equipment lockers. All told, the shirkers on Deck 1 amounted to less than ten percent of the three hundred-plus stewards aboard the *Empress of Earth*.

"Go on," Ran said tiredly. He poked his thumb back over his shoulder toward the lift shafts. "You heard me. Get the passengers to cover and then we can sit on our hands."

The Chief Steward was a thin, puritanical-looking man named Medchen. The voyage to date had taught Ran that Medchen was a greater crook than Mohacks and Babanguida together, and that he lacked the ratings' genuine willingness to do their duty — or a long ways beyond it if someone had the guts to lead them in the right direction.

The Chief Steward stood in front of his alcove at the far end of the long room. "My duty post is *here*, Mr. Colville," he said, "and you have no authority over me anyway. Besides, you're out of uniform."

"And going to be more so," Ran agreed in a mild voice. "Get me a steward's uniform. One of yours ought to do — "

He smiled at Medchen. It wasn't a nice expression.

" — though I guess I'll rip the back out if it comes down to cases."

Ran tossed his borrowed civilian tunic onto the narrow shelf of a console. It slipped to the deck as a spill of pink and puce.

Medchen stepped into his alcove and lifted out the fresh uniform hanging behind the open door. He waited till Ran had stripped off his white trousers, then handed it to him.

"What do you hear from the bridge?" Ran asked conversationally as he changed clothes.

"Two minutes ago," Medchen said, "Captain Kanawa announced that a group of armed men had entered the bridge and ordered him to stop speaking. There hasn't been anything since then, except the AI yammering."

"I'll need a food cart — " Ran said as he straightened.

Medchen nodded toward a rack near the pantry entrance. The carts were stored vertically in collapsed form. Ran jerked one down and extended it. A web of cross-braced wires joined the tray to the static repulsion plate that floated just above the decking.

"I have my own unopened dinner in my office," the Chief Steward volunteered unexpectedly, nodding toward his alcove. "Do you want that too?"

"Yes," Ran said, "I do."

He'd thought he'd have to get that from the Galley off Corridor 3, on the opposite side of the deck. Also, he'd thought Medchen was going to be a problem . . . though it appeared he was wrong in that expectation.

The Chief Steward stepped into his alcove and came out again with covered plates and a setting of flatware, still wrapped in its napkin. The Grantholm attack must have occurred just as he sat down to dinner.

"Right," Ran said. He kept his voice unnaturally calm. "Now, some stun-gas projectors. I want about six."

Medchen pointed. "Locker Four," he said, "beside you. There's a gross of them."

Ran opened the locker. Boxes of nerve-numbing gas, each projector about the size of a knife hilt, were stacked on the bottom of the cubicle. Medical supplies filled the shelves on top.

The gas — actually an aerosol — was skin absorbed.

It numbed motor nerves without affecting the autonomic nervous system. The humans it struck went instantly catatonic, whether they were drunk, furious, or mad as hatters at the moment they received the dose, but it had no long-term side effects.

That last point was desirable when the target was a cook with a cleaver. It was absolutely necessary when the problem involved, say, a passenger trying to strangle his wife.

Ran took the six projectors he'd decided on when he made his plan. It was tempting to grab more now that he saw the dozen full boxes, but he restrained himself. Quantities of equipment weren't going to turn this hijacking around. Luck and guile would have to do.

He looked back at the Chief Steward. "One thing, Medchen," he said. "I hope you're not thinking of reporting this to our friends from Grantholm?"

Medchen shook his head slightly. "No, Mr. Colville," he said. "I'm not going to say anything about it to anybody."

"That's good," said Ran softly. "Because if you did — you can't be sure that they'd kill me, Medchen. And you can be very sure that I'd come back and kill *you* if I was still alive."

The Chief Steward nodded. "Yes, Mr. Colville," he said. "I'm well aware of that."

His smile was as hard and tight as a wrinkle on a walnut's shell. "But I hope they *do* kill you, Mr. Colville," he added.

As Ran slid his cart out of the pantry, it occurred to him that while Medchen was certainly a bastard, he wasn't at all a stupid bastard. . . .

Rural landscapes from central North America shimmered silently from the walls as Wade dragged the third corpse into Ran Colville's cabin. He was panting slightly. Belgeddes sphinctered the panel closed

behind him. Wanda Holly took Ran's pistol from the
drawer which she'd opened with the same master chip
that had unlocked the cabin.

Wade unclipped the sling of the dead soldier's submachine gun. "Now, little lady," he said as he examined
the weapon, "this is going to get — "

"Call her 'lieutenant,' Dickie," Belgeddes said as he
took the pistol from Wanda's hand. "Not 'little lady,'
you know."

"You can have the other submachine gun if you
want it," Wanda said to Belgeddes. As she spoke, she
switched on Ran's console. "You — you're a better shot
than I am."

"Now, Lieutenant," Wade resumed, "this is going to
get very unpleasant, I'm afraid. Perhaps — "

"Not for me, good lady," Belgeddes said as he compared the two identical pistols with a broad grin.
"These suit me very well."

The grin slipped into something feral. "As you've
seen, I should have thought."

"*Do* let me finish, Tom," Wade said sharply.
"Lieutenant Holly, there isn't any clean way of
proceeding from here. If you care to wait — "

"Mr. Wade," Wanda said, "*I* am in charge here. We
will proceed as follows. We'll have to ki — eliminate —
the isolated soldiers before we attempt the bridge controls. We'll — we'll trust Ran to take care of
engineering control."

"See, Dickie?" Belgeddes said as he reopened the
drawer the pistol came from. He rummaged around
until he found a box of cartridges among the hard
copy. "All under control."

"How do you propose to locate the hostiles,
Lieutenant?" Wade asked formally. "And if I may suggest . . . ? They appear to be deployed in threes, not as
individuals."

"Yes, that's correct," Wanda said with a sharp dip of

her jaw that passed for a nod. "And we'll locate them like this."

She unclipped the communicator from the front harness strap of the body she'd dragged into the cabin. It worked on the same principals as Trident's intra-ship communications rigs, but it was somewhat larger and extended a rigid wand to a structural feature instead of using a transceiver chip and a length of flex.

She touched the wand to the console's face. "Bridge," she ordered, "on a schematic, locate the points within the *Empress* that a communicator of this — " she broke squelch " — modulation has been used in the past ten minutes. Over."

Six labeled decks appeared in blue outline, shrunk to fit on a single console display. The nine red dots were at expected locations — the bridge, engineering control, and public areas including the main lift and drop shaft foyers on four decks. The commando looked surprisingly sparse against the starliner's enormous volume. They must have lost half their strength in their blind ship-to-ship crossing through sponge space.

Survivably sparse, it might be.

Wade looked over the 15-mm rifle from Calicheman that leaned against a corner of the cabin. "Interesting," he murmured.

He turned to Wanda Holly. "Very good, Lieutenant," he said. "Now, as for the method of procedure — may I suggest a course?"

"Go ahead," Wanda said curtly. Every time her mind tried to grapple with what came next, it mired itself in bodies thrashing as she tried to slide them along the deck.

"Right," Wade said. "First, we'll need a scout. That's you, Tom. Signals intelligence is all very well, but we don't want to stumble into a team that didn't bother to report in."

He looked at Belgeddes.

The plump man clicked home the reloaded magazine of Wanda's pistol. "You know me, Dickie," he replied without concern. "You lead, I follow. In this case, follow from in front."

"Right," Wade repeated. He slung the submachine gun and raised the bomb thrower by the handle on top of its receiver. "Then with your agreement, Lieutenant, we will proceed as follows. . . ."

"And the more fool me," Belgeddes added with a chuckle.

"I *heard* shots," said Trooper II Weik, waggling the muzzle of her submachine gun down the corridor toward the bow.

Corridor 7 widened into a foyer and mini-lounge toward the stern of Deck A, where the shafts opened. The ambiance was from the Moghul Empire, with columns decorated in tilework helixes and florid carpeting on the deck. A band of knobbed brass bannisters ran around the top the walls as though there was an upper-floor balcony, and the holographic murals were of minareted palaces with reflecting pools and lush vegetation.

"That's fine," said Trooper III Buecher, the team leader. He watched the lift and drop shaft openings from over the sights of his submachine gun. "We all heard shots. The people who got nervous and fired them will report to Colonel Steinwagen, who will *not* be pleased. My team will not be nervous."

The trouble was, they weren't a team. The planners had allowed for fifty percent casualties as the commando crossed from Attack Transport *Vice-Admiral Adler* to their target vessel, the *Empress of Earth*. The planners couldn't determine which soldiers would be lost, however; which would disappear as twists of light into a universe of twisting light, with no boundaries and no hope.

Rather than the team he had trained with for this operation, Buecher commanded troopers whose teammates, like his own, were running out of air in an alien spacetime. Teammates closer than lovers, closer than blood kin. Teammates who no longer existed when Buecher's magnetic boots suddenly clanged and bit on the hull of a starliner which had been a warp of infolded shadow until the moment Buecher touched it.

Buecher understood how Weik could be unhinged by the experience. She was a woman, without the strength of will that stiffened Buecher. The will that prevented Buecher from killing these sniveling rabbits, Weik and Magnin, who reached the starliner while Buecher's proper teammates did not. . . .

"I didn't hear shots," said Magnin. "It's a big ship. Noise is funny. The Colonel will tell us if there's anything we ought to know."

Magnin faced the stern with his doorknocker. The planners had allowed for the possibility that the commando would have to fight its way through a series of firedoors lowered across the corridors. The squash-head bombs of the 15-cm assault weapons had shown in tests on Grantholm that they would wreck the locking mechanisms of the firedoors and spall a sleet of fragments into defenders on the opposite side.

The reasoning was good, but the crew of the *Empress of Earth* were cowards who used the presence of civilians as an excuse not to oppose the commando. The doorknocker was of limited use in a normal firefight, because the thin-cased missiles had no direct fragmentation effect: only concussion and, perhaps, bits of fittings and furniture flying about as secondary projectiles.

If opponents attacked from the stern end of the corridor, Magnin's weapon could not give as satisfactory a response as a submachine gun would; but the concern that roiled Buecher's mind was a false one, he realized, because the cowards who would not defend themselves weren't going to attack either.

They weren't going to give Buecher an opportunity to avenge his teammates.

There were no civilians in wartime, and no neutrals either. The only immoral act in wartime was to fail, and Grantholm would not fail.

" . . . *Sweet Betsy from Pike*," warbled a thin, cracked voice from a cross-corridor joining 7 twenty meters astern of the shaft foyer. "*She went to Wyoming with —*"

"Magnin, watch the shafts!" Buecher ordered —

— though the bombs had a five-meter arming range and wouldn't go off if somebody did pop from a shaft opening while the singer distracted his team —

— and spun to cover the corridor sternward with his submachine gun.

" *— her husband Ike,*" the singer caroled as he staggered around the corner, a fat old man with drink stains down the front of his plush jacket.

He stared owlishly at the muzzle of Buecher's submachine gun.

"I'm so very sorry," the passenger said. He attempted a bow and had to catch himself on the bulkhead to keep from falling. "I mus' be in the wrong room."

As he spoke, he *did* topple back around the corner.

"Bomb!" Weik shouted.

Buecher flattened, sweeping both ends of the corridor with his peripheral vision. His weapon pointed sternward, because there would be a rush from that side, but a 15-cm projectile sailed on its spluttering rocket motor in a flat arc from the cross-corridor toward the bow.

The projectile was almost as slow as a lobbed grenade. Because the shooter had been afraid to expose himself, the bomb would hit the wall opposite the shaft openings. The concussion would be heavy

but survivable, and when the attackers rushed in behind their bomb —

Buecher hugged himself to the deck, his trigger
finger poised to begin shooting at the instant the bomb
went off.

The fat passenger stepped into Corridor 7. He aimed
a pistol in either hand, though only one was firing.

The muzzle flash of the first shot was all that
Buecher's disbelieving eyes saw. The bullet punched
through the bridge of his nose. Belgeddes had learned
to correct for the pistol's slight tendency to throw left.

An instant later, the rocket projectile smacked the
wall and ricocheted, a dud because Wade had removed
the base fuze. The wet slap of plastic explosive deform-
ing was lost in the snap of Belgeddes's next two shots
and the roar of Holly's submachine gun as she entered
Corridor 7 from the bow side.

The bomb skittered a further moment until its
motor burned out. The case had burst open. Volatiles
from the explosive added their sharpness to the
residues of rocket fuel, gunpowder, and the blood
mingled with feces that was the smell of violent death.

"No time to lose," Wade warned crisply as he
stepped out behind Holly. He had reloaded his projector with a live bomb, just in case. A submachine gun
was slung across his back.

"Right," Wanda said in a cold, dry voice. "We'll take
the Embarkation Hall next."

"There's always time to reload, Dickie," Belgeddes
said with arch disapproval. He thumbed loose rounds
into the magazine to replace the three he'd fired.

*The bridge of the nose, the left earhole, and the point where
the spine of the flattened woman entered the back of her skull.*

The bitter gases poisoning the air made Wanda
cough as she swapped magazines. That could have
been responsible for the way her eyes were watering
also.

*   *   *

Ran Colville hummed *"Won't you come home, Bill Bailey?"* as he got out of the drop shaft, pushing the food cart before him. He moved at a deliberate pace, like a steward who wanted to avoid a rocket from his superiors but wasn't trying to set any speed records.

Moving, basically, at the pace of a steward who doesn't expect much of a tip at the end of his journey no matter how quickly he reaches it.

The Engineering Deck was laid out for cargo operations, besides being narrower than all but one of those above it. The single corridor, 15, kinked around bays intended for passengers' hold luggage. There was no point, as there was on the passenger decks, where a three-man team could dominate four hundred meters of straight corridor with their weapons.

Ran couldn't be sure where he was going to meet Grantholm troops, or even whether he would meet them. It was unlikely that there was no one guarding engineering control, however; and the *Empress*'s Cold Crew would be a special problem for the hijackers.

"I'll do the cooking, honey," Ran whistled. *"I'll pay the rent...."*

The Grantholm team, all three of them male, stood in front of the open corridor hatch giving onto the engineering control room. When Ran appeared a moment behind his off-key whistle, the soldiers tensed as cats do when starting their stalk.

One man faced sternward, though so far as Ran knew there was nothing but long-term cargo stowage in that direction, and no way to enter those bays except through the hull while docked. Maybe the Grantholmers thought somebody was going to come out of a bulkhead to get them.

"Halt!" the team leader ordered over the sights of his submachine gun. "What are you doing here?"

Ran stopped where he was, twenty meters from the

soldiers. "It's dinner for a Mr. Schmidt," he called. "Look, don't point that thing at me. This is just a job, okay? I'm just doing my job."

"I didn't order dinner!" objected the soldier aiming at the blank wall. He twisted to look over his shoulder. Then, when his leader didn't shout at him, he pivoted to face in the same direction as his fellows.

"Tubby Schmidt?" the third soldier asked. "Only he's with the bridge crew, isn't he?"

"He would be if he'd made it aboard," the leader said briefly. Then he added, "Cover me," and walked toward Ran and his cart.

"Look," said Ran. "They told me Schmidt at engineering control and look lively. That's all they said, Schmidt."

"It can't be *Lieutenant* Schmidt," the third man mused aloud. "He's out on the hull, and they can't come inside so long as we're in sponge space. We *are* in sponge space, aren't we?"

"How the hell would I know?" snarled his team leader. He peered at the dishes on the cart. They were sealed with optically-clear covers which were opaque in the infra-red spectrum, so that their contents could be viewed but stayed hot.

"Honeydew melon, Green Turtle soup," Ran said in a bored voice. "Roast gosling with aubergine in tomato." He pointed as he went along. "And asparagus in Hollandaise sauce."

Viewed dispassionately, it must have looked delicious. Ran couldn't be dispassionate, because he was trying to imagine how he could handle the situation if two of the Grantholmers stayed that far away from him. He couldn't. He'd have to go back and find *somewhere* a weapon that wasn't only point-blank like the gas projectors —

The team leader turned and stared at his men. "One of you wise guys used the ship's commo to order a meal, didn't you?" he demanded.

"Not me!" Schmidt — Smitt, Shmidt, Smid, or whatever variation of "metalworker"*this* Grantholm soldier bore — insisted.

"I'd be in my rights to keep it all for myself," the team leader said. "But I guess there's enough for three."

He looked appraisingly at the multi-course meal. "They don't half do themself good, do they?"

Then he added harshly to Ran, "C'mon, you." He jerked his thumb toward engineering control and his two subordinates. "Bring it over."

The leader stayed behind Ran. The Grantholmer faced down the corridor, toward the shafts, as the Trident officer sauntered obediently forward.

Ran grounded the cart in front of the two soldiers. "Gentlemen . . ." he said as he whisked the lids off the first pair of dishes, then knelt to stow them on top of the cart's repulsion tray.

"What's that?" muttered Schmidt.

"Aubergine," replied the team leader. "Whatever aubergine is when it's at home."

"And there ought to be extra flatware down — " Ran murmured. "Yes!"

He straightened with a napkin-wrapped tube in either hand. He smiled obsequiously and fired the gas projectors into the faces of the Grantholm soldiers.

Ran had been worried about getting the double, but the cones of droplets sprayed perfectly across the faces of the two subordinates. They lurched backward with blank expressions. Their eyeballs rolled upward so that only the whites showed.

The team leader caught the dose in the throat, which should have been fine. Either he was resistant to the tranquilizer or his reflexes operated at a more basic level than those of his crew. His finger clamped his submachine gun's trigger and held it back as he toppled onto his face.

The stream of bullets shattered the cart, the dishes

on it, and one of the Grantholm soldiers from waist to ankles. Blood and the pale gray stars of bullet cores splattered the bulkhead behind the pair of men.

Ran thought the other soldier, Schmidt, had escaped until he noticed an ooze of blood and brains spreading beneath the Grantholmer's head. A ricochet had bounced through the back of his skull.

Echoing muzzle blasts and the *whiz* of ricocheting bullets went on for what seemed to be minutes.

Ran swore softly. He unfastened the sling of Schmidt's weapon. With the submachine gun in his right hand, he grabbed the team leader by the collar with his left.

He dragged the staring-eyed man to the cargo bay directly across from engineering control. The practical way to deal with the fellow was to kill him, using a bullet or the fighting knife hanging from the Grantholmer's harness.

Ran hoped he never returned to being that practical.

He used his ID chip to unlock the bay's personnel access hatch. This bay was the garage, holding passengers' private vehicles. There was no way to open it from within, so it would serve to hold the Grantholm soldier until this business was over. Ran's next task was to find the Cold Crew and —

The hatch withdrew into its jamb. Swede lunged out with his hands open for a choke hold. The rest of the Cold Crew, all three watches, was behind him.

"Hold it!" the watch chief bellowed. "It's Mr. Colville! What are you doing in that shit suit, sir?"

Cold Crewmen shoved out past Swede. As they did so, Ran noticed one of the engineering officers, Crosse, huddled well to the rear of the compartment. It can't have been a lot of fun to find yourself locked up with angry Cold Crewmen.

"I'm pretending to be a steward to get the *Empress*

away from these Grantholm hijackers," Ran said. He spoke loudly to be heard over the scrape of boots. "It's dangerous, and it's likely to mean killing. Are you in?"

"Hell, yes," said Swede. "What do you want us to do?"

Lewis looked critically at the Grantholm team leader on the deck beside him. "Did a piss poor job on this one, Mr. Colville," he said.

He stamped his boot down on the back of the Grantholmer's neck, hard enough to snap the spine. Then he stamped again.

"We're going out on the hull to take the engines back," Ran said, speaking dispassionately. "After that, we'll worry about the troops inside."

He didn't look down at the fresh corpse at his feet. He'd worked the hull long enough to know it was Cold Crew etiquette always to kick a man when he was down. That's when it was easiest to do, after all. . . .

Ran felt the *Empress of Earth* thud slightly — once, again, and onward repeatedly in a set rhythm.

"Whazzat?" a Cold Crewman demanded, spinning on his toes to find a source of the noise. The sound was unfamiliar, and the Cold Crew worked too close to the edge of survival to like changes.

"They're shutting the firedoors," Ran explained. "Our new masters, I suppose, since the bridge crew didn't during the attack. I wouldn't be surprised to learn that our Grantholm friends've got fewer troops now than they did when they boarded."

"No friends of mine," Swede said. "No masters, neither."

The Grantholm commander must have noticed that some of his teams weren't reporting in. Dropping the firedoors wouldn't prevent Wanda and her companions from moving between sections since the Second Officer's ID chip gave her local control of the barriers.

Grantholmers on the bridge might think they could

follow their opponents' progress by seeing which firedoors opened. Wanda knew the *Empress*'s complex layout perfectly. All the Grantholm commander would get from this ploy was a series of false scents that drew his teams into killing grounds.

Swede picked up his suit, dumped on the floor of the engineering control room with the others when the commando herded the duty watch into the starliner's interior.

"They shot three of my people out there on the hull when we dropped into star space," Swede added in a tone of reflective calm. "Not a lot we could do about it — in star space."

He very deliberately spat toward the airlock. "In the Cold, those guns of theirs, they won't be worth shit."

Swede's men were donning the suits sprawled on the deck. The starboard watch, off duty at the time of the attack, took their own gear out of the locker covering one wall of the room.

As Lewis worked his limbs into the semi-rigid suit, he said, "I dreamed every day for a year about the time I'd get Reesler alone outside and put him *right* off the hull."

"Got a suit for me?" Ran asked Swede.

"Try Locker Nineteen," the watch leader said. "Albrecht's in the sick bay, laying on his butt as usual. *Ear* ache, if you can believe that."

Lewis continued emotionlessly, "I'm really going to stick it to them bastards that shot Reesler before I got him."

The engineering officer on duty during the attack stood at-ease, his hands crossed behind him, at the console ruined by a laser. His spacesuit, necessary because engineering control was often open to vacuum, lay on the deck beside him.

"You don't want a piece of this, Crosse?" Ran asked as he closed the plastron of the borrowed suit. It wasn't a great fit, but it was better than the one he'd had to use aboard the *Prester John* ten years before.

The engineering officer swallowed. "We're under strict company orders to do nothing that would endanger the lives and safety of the passengers, Mr. Colville," he said.

"You bet," Ran said.

He turned to the crewman who was handing equipment out of the locker. "I'll take an adjustment tool," Ran called.

"Mr. Colville, I've never been able to stand sponge space!" Crosse said. "I — whenever I have to go out, I — I can't move! I ought to be in the bridge crew."

"Best get out of engineering control, then," Ran said without great interest. "We're going to void the room as soon as we drop into star space the next time."

He took the telescoped rod the Cold Crewman handed him. It would lengthen to three meters when he slipped the joints as soon as he passed through the airlock.

With the adjustment tool in his hands again, Ran no longer thought of the sidereal universe. Star space and the Cold. Star space and Hell. . . .

Crosse bolted from the room. Swede spat idly after him and closed the airlock hatch to the corridor.

"How many d'ye figure they've got on the hull?" Swede asked Ran.

Ran shrugged, then realized the crewmen watching him intently couldn't see the gesture beneath the hard torso of his suit. "Maybe eight," he guessed aloud. "One for each engine. I don't guess they could have more than that."

He grinned, staring into the past with wide, blank eyes. "They must've been trained specially for this hijack. I never saw a Grantholmer on a Cold Crew, did you guys?"

"There'll be eight less to see in a little bit," Lewis said. He giggled.

"Listen up!" Ran said. He wanted to rub his hands

together, but he couldn't do that through the gauntlets and it wouldn't look right anyway. He was in charge....

The Cold Crewmen stared at him. Some looked angry; one or two might be friendly. Most of the faces held no more expression than the swirling cold of sponge space did.

"We're going out there in about —" Ran continued. He glanced toward the console for a time check. The clock had been destroyed by the laser blast.

Ran pulled off a gauntlet. " — a minute and a half," he said, using the bio-energized watch tattooed into the dermis of his left hand.

He'd been *very* drunk when that happened, but he'd left it there as a reminder not to let something similar happen again. The watch kept Earth time, and Ran felt vaguely proud of himself for converting to ship's time without dropping a beat. "*Nobody* moves from the air-lock area until we're back in the Cold. They've got guns, they'll kill us. Simple as that. In sponge space, they're our meat."

He'd caught a glimpse of his own visage in the polished bulkhead. His face was indistinguishable from those of his men: empty eyes and a mouth as cruel as the seam the laser had cut through the console.

"We don't know just where they're stationed on the hull," Ran said, "so everybody heads for his normal duty station. When we drop back into star space, move fast. Anybody who isn't wearing the right suit, he goes."

He looked around. "Any questions?"

Nobody spoke. Cold Crewmen weren't talkative, and there wasn't much to say anyhow.

"Then close your helmets," Ran said, "and follow me."

He felt a shiver as the *Empress of Earth* reentered the sidereal universe, bringing the interior of the starliner back into the same spacetime as the outer skin. You had to be experienced to notice it *here*, but out on the hull it was a difference as great as that between death and life.

Ran locked his faceshield down and reached for the switch controlling the hull airlock.

"Let's get stuck into them bastards," said Swede on the suit-to-suit radio. His voice was a growl like that of an avalanche headed for the valley despite anything in its path.

When the hullside lock opened, air banged out and the light within engineering control grew flat because there was no longer an atmosphere to scatter it. Ran waited reflexively for the buffeting to stop when the last of the air voided.

He'd known people to start for the hull too fast and be carried on out before they got their safety lines hooked. If there was a bright side to the stories, it was that the victims died in star space instead of in the Cold. . . .

The old skills were still with him. He moved fast as the windrush ended, so that Swede's hand on his shoulder was a companionable pressure rather than the shove it would become if the man at the head of the line balked.

People did balk during crew changes. Usually not on their first watch, but at the start of their second or third, when they knew the Cold and knew exactly what was waiting for them when their vessel left the sidereal universe again.

This wasn't a formal watch change, just a navigation check programmed before the hijacking. The outbound element was of twenty-one men rather than the normal eight of a Cold Crew on the *Empress of Earth*: the survivors of all three watches, and Ran Colville in the lead. There wasn't any time to lose if they were all to get onto the hull before the starliner inserted into sponge space again —

And anyway, Cold Crews didn't waste a lot of time on people who couldn't do their jobs. If Ran — if *anybody* — blocked the hatch during a watch change, he went out anyway — and maybe too fast to hook his line at the high end.

The Cold was an inhuman, dehumanizing experience. The men of the Cold Crews not only knew that, they bragged about it.

Ran took the ladder in two steps against artificial gravity, felt that fade in a familiar queasiness in the pit of his stomach as his torso lifted above the skin of the ship. He latched his line, one-handed because the adjustment rod was in his left gauntlet, and planted the magnetic sole of his right boot on the hull with a slap he could feel all through the stiff fabric of his suit.

Ran Colville was going home again to Hell.

The tracks to the *Empress*'s eight engine modules were inlaid into grooves on the hull, rather than being paint which would be worn away by the scrape of men shuffling flat-footed toward their duty stations. Ran followed Track 3, because that had been his first station on the *Prester John*. Home again. . . .

The Grantholmers had no reason to put a guard at the hull side of the hatch. It was still possible that one of the soldiers-turned-engine tender had found the strain of the Cold too much and was coming in — dispirited but still armed.

Ran stepped forward, pivoting his body to make up for his inability to turn his helmeted head to see sideways. As he moved, his hands worked the adjustment tool, locking both of the tube's joints into their extended position. There were no Grantholmers in sight.

He'd told his men to stay bunched at the hatch until sponge space hid them from sight. Despite that, he stepped forward himself, *just to the next staple* —

The Cold was coming. No one who had felt it could remain static and await its return.

The stars of this portion of the sidereal universe

formed a hazy blur banding the blackness at an angle skewed to the *Empress*'s present attitude. The starliner was in the intergalactic vacuum which made up most of the real universe. Only Bridge and the vessel's data banks could turn this location into a waypost on the journey to Tblisi — or to wherever the hijackers planned to divert her.

The *Empress of Earth* herself was a gleam little brighter than the distant galaxy, the reflection of light from millions, even billions, of parsecs away. The converted freighter which carried the hijacking party was a darker hint in the black sky. It must be very close, but distances in the void were uncertain without absolute knowledge of the other object's size.

From the hatch, four of the *Empress*'s engine modules were bulges above the starliner's smooth curve. Ran's objective, Engine 3, was on the "underside" of the hull, not visible from where he stood. The inlaid track, a centimeter higher than the surrounding skin, would take him there.

He reached the next staple, twenty meters closer to his destination. He planted his boots, but he didn't bother to unreel his second line and set it before he hit the release stud. A command pulsing down the line opened the hook attached to the staple at the hatch opening.

Ran caught the hook as it sailed toward him, a wink in darkness. He set it to the new attachment point and shuffled on. Men had been known to smash their own faceshields when they snatched the safety line toward themselves too quickly and didn't catch the heavy hook in the end of it.

Two of the engine modules stood out above the hull to which they were joined by basket-woven wire. They were distanced from the skin to protect the vessel in the unlikely event a fusion bottle failed. The elevation also gave the engines wider directability than they would have had if mounted lower. At the moment, the two

visible pods pointed thirty degrees to starboard of the
starliner's nominal axial plane.

Ran turned and looked behind him. The rest of the
Cold Crew — *his* crew — had spilled out of the hatch
and was moving along the hull. Some of the men were
hidden beneath the massive curve.

Ran walked onward. He reached the third staple.
From that point, he could see all of Engine 7, the pod
and strutwork almost down to the hull. A Grantholm
soldier was locking in a fresh fuel connector with his
adjustment tool. He was a tracery of highlights rather
than a figure. The submachine gun slung across his
back distorted the image still further.

It was time. The *Empress of Earth* slid again into
sponge space.

On the one hand, everything was light; on the other,
Ran was blind, stone blind, because the impulses trip-
ping his rods and cones had no connection with the
code which those impulses would have represented in
the sidereal universe. He could see nothing, no *thing*.
Not the hull beneath his feet, not the gauntlet which
held his safety line.

But he could feel the track against the side of his
boot, and his hook snapped in a familiar way into the
upstanding staple. Ran slid onward, with the three
meters of his adjustment rod out before him.

He had a long way to go to reach Engine 3, but he
might meet a Grantholm soldier at any point in the
track. Ran's first warning would be the shock of his
tool's contact. If that happened, he would withdraw the
rod to his arm's length, then ram it forward again.

Ran knew from one past experience that he could
strike hard enough to put the tip of an adjustment tool
through a suit and half the body within that suit.

Ran was very well aware that the Cold Crewman following him was likely to do the same, even though the
fellow knew there was a friendly on the track ahead. In

the Cold, a mistake was something that got you killed. By extension, an action that didn't get *you* killed wasn't a mistake, or at any rate not a serious one.

Another twenty meters, another staple. Ran unhooked and brought his line forward hand-over-hand instead of with a clean jerk as before when he could see the hook coming. When he was *on* with the Cold, he could sense motion within its flaring emptiness, but he'd been away too long to trust his instincts now.

The chilling light flooded through his flesh and marrow. Even if he closed his eyes, he would see the swirls that were almost patterns. When he was in the Cold, Ran thought that the bubbles of sponge space might be alive, might be Life itself in the abstract.

Might be God; but if they were, God was Siva the Destroyer.

He had felt the Cold every night for ten years in his dreams, and now he was home again within its desolation.

Another staple. Another. At the fifth point, Ran didn't bother to reconnect his line. It slowed him down and bound him to the universe of which his soul was no longer a part.

At the fifteenth staple, Ran Colville reached down and it was there, the hook of another safety line, and he'd seen it in the glaring night before his gauntleted fingers fondled the curve, the catch.

He released the Grantholmer's line manually. A part of Ran's mind knew that he should have set his own hook, but his soul was one with a spacetime which hated the universe to which Mankind had been born.

With the cunning of a hyena poised to tear the face off a sleeping woman, Ran took up the slack in the unseen Grantholmer's line. When he felt resistance, he gave a fierce left-handed tug.

Through blind light as penetrating as a sun's heart, Ran saw the startled soldier lurching toward him, spinning; his limbs flailing, his tool flying off on a trajectory of its own as the man tried to grasp his slung weapon in a soldier's reflex.

Ran's right arm cocked his adjustment tool like a javelin for throwing. In the event, he didn't bother to bring the tool forward in the smashing blow his intellect had intended. Instead, Ran pirouetted aside like a bullfighter.

The Grantholm soldier slid past invisibly on a vector that took him clear of the starliner's curved hull, off into an alien eternity. The victim must be screaming, but radio waves propagated as oddly as light did outside the sidereal universe. If the man was heard at all, it would be as a ghost whispering in the ears of Cold Crewmen unimaginably distant in time and space.

Ran Colville walked away from the track so that he would no longer be in the path of the crewman who followed him. There was nothing to do but wait, now, until the *Empress* dropped into star space and the Trident crew could return without danger from its own members.

Nothing to do but wait; and to feel the Cold drink him in; and to listen to the unheard screams of a Grantholm soldier whose death was a living sacrifice for Ran Colville.

"Ran," the Cold said. He felt the word tremble through him. "Ran, come with me. Lift your right foot."

His eyes opened. He stood in star space. The realization so shocked him that he flushed, and for a moment his skin burned as though he had been dropped into hot oil.

"Ran," repeated the figure who held him. Their helmets were in contact, so Ran heard the words directly instead of through the radio link. "We're going in now."

"How l-long do we have before the next insertion?" Ran asked.

His voice cracked in the middle of the second syllable because his throat was dry. He must have been standing with his mouth open, hearing and seeing nothing, for — he couldn't guess for how long.

Standing in the Cold, even though the *Empress of Earth* had returned to the sidereal universe at least once during the period.

The suited figure holding Ran jerked away. "You're all right?" the voice said in amazement, through the helmet radio now. The voice was Wanda's. She must have been calling to him as she trekked across the hull, unheard until their helmets made physical contact.

How long had he been mired in Hell?

"I'm fine," he said, hoping that was the truth. "When do we reinsert?"

Ran began a swift, skidding pace in the direction Wanda urged him. He didn't know where he was on the hull, didn't know the hull of the *Empress* at all because each ship is different. He was fully aware that his safety line dangled loose, and that Wanda had loosed hers to fetch him from where he stood far from the tracks and staples.

"Not until Bridge recalibrates," Wanda said. Their gauntleted hands, his left and her right, gripped, though the greater safety in the contact was spiritual, not physical. "And not until I bring you in. Commander Kneale promised that."

"He's alive?" Ran said. His mind fought its way to the surface through layers of icy, flaring slush. Memory of what had sent him onto the hull was slowly reasserting itself through the smothering Cold.

"He's alive," Wanda said. Her voice was detached. "We're all alive, mostly. They killed a steward, nobody knows why. We found him in Corridor Six. And there was a passenger with her children, two little boys. They were hiding behind the counter of the Paris Bistro on Deck A and the soldiers thought they were us. . . . "

In the near distance, a Cold Crewman reset the nozzles of an engine pod manually. Delicate electronics failed quickly in sponge space, but men continued to do their jobs.

A figure shuffled across the hull toward Ran and Wanda. It carried something long and thin, but even in dim starlight the object didn't appear to be an adjustment tool.

"So they killed them, the soldiers did," Wanda continued in a voice as pale as the light of the distant galaxies. "And we killed the soldiers while they were looking the wrong way, Wade and Belgeddes killed them, and I did. And then we killed more soldiers."

The third figure joined them. "Hold on to me," an unfamiliar voice directed over the helmet radio. "I've hooked six safety lines together. No point in having a problem when we've gotten this far."

"Wade?" Wanda said.

"The same," the radio agreed. Wade slung the object he carried, the huge rifle from Calicheman, and held out his hands to the pair of officers. "I'm afraid I've shot off all your ammunition, Mr. Colville. Seems to have done the trick, though. The Grantholm freighter is gone, eh what?"

Ran looked up. He couldn't see the other vessel, but it could have been subtended by the *Empress*'s greater bulk.

"It pulled off because you shot at it?" he asked in amazement. He supposed the 15-mm bullets could do some damage to the thin plating of a colonial-built freighter — but not enough, he was sure, to cause a picked Grantholm assault force to abandon its mission.

"Not here," Wade said with a chuckle. Ran and Wanda moved much faster now that they were tethered to the starliner's massive reality. "In sponge space. I thought I might puncture a compartment, you see, and they wouldn't be able to calculate the change in mass precisely enough to continue matching us. The mass of their own vented atmosphere, you see."

Ran looked at the other man, anonymous in a suit borrowed from the Cold Crew. "That's impossible!" he said. "You can't hit anything in sponge space."

They were nearing silvery inlaid tracks, spreading like the braces of a spider's web from the engineering hatch. The outer airlock was open.

" 'Impossible' is one of those words used more often than wisely, my boy," Wade said. "I've always found that I *could* see in sponge space, after my — well, my mind, I suppose, not my eyes — had a chance to acclimate."

"Don't say that," Ran whispered through the sudden blazing fog he remembered swelling across his marrow and soul.

They were within twenty meters of the hatch. Wade's linked lines bellied out behind them in a great loop. Ran felt the *Empress of Earth* shudder through his bootsoles.

"What's that?" he demanded. He pivoted on one foot to look all around him. There was no plume of plasma glowing behind the four engine pods he could see, so the starliner wasn't accelerating.

"A lifeboat," Wanda said. "The enemy commander and his bridge crew, five of them. They agreed to evacuate the ship if they were given a lifeboat."

"The Grantholm commander failed," Wade said conversationally. "Chap named Steinwagen, knew him when he was a pup. Not bad at what he did, but too narrow for an operation like this, I would have said."

"We couldn't storm the bridge," Wanda said, "but he'd lost control of the engines and his outlying teams were — gone."

She edged Ran in the direction of the hatch. He

remained with his feet planted, watching the lifeboat swell from its bay in the *Empress*'s side like a whale broaching in a limitless ocean.

"They're abandoning ship *here*?" Ran said. The nearest galaxy was a milky blur. "Do they know that you . . . ?"

Wade read Ran's concealed expression in the younger man's tone. "Now, lad," he said. "Steinwagen wasn't going home a failure. Nothing I did —"

The lifeboat exploded in a flash, soundless until a chunk of plating struck the starliner and made the hull ring through Ran's boots. The ball of expanding gas had a rosy glow that disappeared as it cooled. The solid debris was invisible in the night of stars.

"Colonel Steinwagen didn't dare be identified," Wade explained. "He'd have liked to have died fighting, he was that type, but he couldn't subject his government to the embarrassment of having his body identified. That saved us a nice little problem about how to deal with him and his chaps on the bridge. Though we *could* have, Ms. Holly."

Ran was moving again. They reached the hatchway. Wanda and the civilian both urged him down the ladder ahead of them. He was too drained to argue.

"I knew your father, lad," Wade's radio-thinned voice continued. "He served under me on Hobilo. A good man, Chick Colville. Stopped at nothing to accomplish a mission."

Ran was trembling so hard in his suit that he was barely able to thrust his gauntlet against the switch controlling the outer airlock door.

"His only problem was," the unseen civilian continued, "he brooded too much about things afterwards."

The lock was swinging shut like a clamshell. The *Empress*'s hull plating would block radio signals completely. . . .

"No point in that, young fellow," Wade's cool voice

continued as the massive door closed. "You do what you do and go on from there. Mustn't brood on things, eh?"

Light flooded the airlock when the inner door opened. Ran lunged convulsively from the lock's narrow confines. He heard voices shouting congratulations as other people helped him out of the spacesuit.

The only thing Ran saw was the memory in his mind's eye, a Grantholm soldier sailing past Ran Colville and into blazing eternity.

• TBLISI

"Good morning, Ms. van de Meer," Ran said, sliding in front of the expensively-dressed woman who seemed determined to use luggage of Hobilo lizardhide as a battering ram through the crowd before her. "What an extremely attractive coat."

The mood of passengers in the Embarkation Hall ranged from funereal to that of a carnival crowd. What was particularly notable was the number of them. Instead of the usual departure staggered by individual fuss and delay, virtually every passenger aboard the *Empress of Earth* was ready to leave as soon as the gangways fell.

Some of them, like van de Meer, seemed ready to jump and damn the gangways.

"Oh!" the woman said. "I —"

She grounded her twin bags on the deck and lifted out the lapel of the garment, gleaming felt from the fur of a giant Calicheman water rat. The steward drawing the rest of van de Meer's luggage was far back in the mass. "Do you really think so, Mr. Colville? It was just something I got for knocking about."

Van de Meer wasn't young, which didn't matter; and she had the heft of a rhino, which wasn't an absolute bar to Ran finding her . . . interesting. Unfortunately, she had the personality of a rhino also. The only possible interest Ran could have in her was a professional one — at the moment, to keep the self-centered hog from injuring somebody or starting a riot.

"It goes well with your hair, besides," Ran said. He

had no idea of whether or not that was true or even what the statement really meant, but it was the sort of thing women liked to hear. "Why don't you just sit tight here, though, ma'am? The hatch will open in less than a minute."

The mix of people in the tall room was that of tapioca pudding, nodules of frightened silence embedded throughout a matrix of artificially bright chatter. The stewards had been carefully briefed to stand in front of passengers instead of following them in normal fashion; but that wasn't always possible. All the Staff Side personnel were on hand in the Embarkation Hall, prepared to be as direct as the circumstances required.

Ran turned sideways to survey the hall, looking for hot spots. He saw Wanda, but he couldn't catch her eye. She was planted like a bollard in front of a couple from Calicheman, dressed in fringed layers of suede leather. The ensemble looked rough, but Ran had seen similar outfits in starport boutiques for three thousand credits and up.

The couple *was* rough, however, and they appeared willing to knock Wanda down and stamp her flat if that would speed their exit from the starliner. The Trident officer wasn't giving a millimeter. Her face was bleakly forbidding in a fashion that Ran hadn't seen until recently.

Until the Grantholm commando had died, some of them beyond the muzzle of Wanda Holly's gun.

The *Empress* bore very little sign of the fighting. A corner of the Social Hall was a gray bulkhead instead of the facade of the Temple of the Divine Julius, because the blast of a Grantholm door-knocker had damaged the hologram projector for that segment. Stewards whisked away the damaged furniture and rearranged the rest as if nothing had happened, though. The bullet holes scattered here and there across the vessel were mostly hidden by the shimmering holograms themselves.

The same was true of the stains, though stewards scrubbed each of the battle sites thoroughly. Patterns of coherent light wouldn't hide the smell of rotting blood.

"*Here* we go!" called a rating from the Second Watch, in a perhaps unintentionally loud voice. The main hatch split horizontally, the halves rising and lowering simultaneously onto the mobile shelter extension from Bogomil Terminal.

"Welcome to Tblisi, ladies and gentlemen!" Commander Kneale called from the opposite side of the Embarkation Hall. Though he shouted, his voice was barely audible over the tramp of feet surging forward on the resilient flooring.

The attempted hijacking had done even less physical damage to the passengers than it had to the structure of the ship. The psychic injuries were something else again.

Ran edged aside to let the rush of passengers pass. There would be no trouble, now that they had the freedom to leave what they thought of as a cage.

He pressed his back against a pilaster, looking at the suddenly jubilant crowd but thinking of — other times, and other places; and of the Cold.

"Do you think any of them will ever get back on a starliner, Ran?" Wanda asked from beside him.

He looked down at her and smiled, glad to return to the present. "Sure," he said. "Most of them have somewhere to return to, anyway. And they'll forget. It'll be an adventure, once they've been away for it for a couple days . . . and until it happens again."

Passengers poured past them in a joyous torrent, humans and the leavening of alien faces. Wakambria, Rialvans — an individual Szgranian who must have been a courier, female and dressed in drab colors instead of glitter and weaponry. What did the aliens think of the human squabble which had almost cost them their schedule if not their very lives?

"You think it's going to happen again?" Wanda asked softly.

Ran didn't look at her. His eyes stared past the sea of heads and luggage bobbing down the ramp to solid ground. "Until the war ends," he said. "Or something happens to the *Empress*. The company's going to have to take her out of service. She's too valuable a prize."

The crush in the Embarkation Hall had passed, leaving only a few passengers fussing in the great room with unfastened bags or concern for something forgotten in their cabins. The scattered figures quivered like puddles in a spillway after the impoundment has emptied. Commander Kneale made his way toward Ran and Wanda, tossing affable greetings to the passengers whom he passed.

"I hope they take her out of service," Wanda said softly. She too was staring toward the gangway but seeing memories. "Because . . . if I had to do what I did. Again. I don't think that I could."

Ran reached to his side without looking and took the Second Officer's hand. They were on duty, and in public; and when that occurred to him, he still didn't give a damn.

"You can do anything you have to, Wanda," he said. "*Anything*. But that's not a reason to do it."

"Why don't you two take the next forty-eight as leave?" Commander Kneale offered from a meter away. "I'm not disembarking myself because the repair crews are coming aboard, and — I think you've earned it."

Ran looked at Wanda, then met his superior's eyes. "Sir," he said. "We need to talk, you and I."

Kneale nodded calmly. "All right," he said. "Do you want to do it now?"

Ran looked out toward the gangway and thought about the domed skyline of Bogomil beyond. "No sir," he said. "Right now I want to get off the *Empress*. Almost as bad as the passengers did."

Kneale nodded and smiled. His square, powerful hand swept smoothly toward the gangway. "Then go," he said. "We'll talk another time. You've earned that too, Mr. Colville."

The sky was so clear and vast that Dewhurst's wife didn't even comment on the slight orange tint to the sunlight that would in normal circumstances have been her first public reaction to Tblisi. She spread her arms and cried, "Oh, what a *terrible* experience! I was sure that we were all going to be killed."

"Now, now, Ms. Dewhurst," Wade said. "It didn't cost us anything but perhaps eight hours off our scheduled arrival, and surely the chance of a good story was worth that to all of us. Eh, Dewhurst?"

Dewhurst shook his head more in wonder than disagreement. "Adventures are things that happen to other people, Wade," he said. "Personally, I think I like it that way. Anyway, I can't claim that hiding in my cabin for several hours was much of an adventure, though I suppose —"

He looked hard at Wade.

" — it might be possible to embellish the facts a little."

Belgeddes chuckled. "Adventure's where you find it. Isn't that so, Dickie?"

"What I'd like to know . . ." said Da Silva as his eyes slid back to his companions from the buildings across the boulevard from the terminal. Ten- and twelve-story brick facades, with swags and carved transoms, lined the thoroughfare. " . . . is just how many of the Grantholmers there were. It can't have been more than a handful, and there were *thousands* of us aboard."

"You think we should have — what, attacked men with guns?" Dewhurst said. "Refused to cooperate?"

"Nothing of the sort!" Wade said forcefully. "Leave

that to the professionals, to the ship's officers and crew. That's no business for passengers, after all."

Ms. Dewhurst elbowed her husband and nodded toward the fleet of buses and taxis jogging forward to carry away disembarked passengers. "Shouldn't we . . . ?" she said.

"Yes, I suppose we should," Dewhurst agreed.

He looked at his companions for the voyage. "I don't suppose you chaps are booked for the return sailing?" he said, a trifle wistfully.

Da Silva shook his head. "We're not all vacationers," he said. "I'll be here a month at least. Longer if my firm decides to set up a permanent office."

"Nor us, friend," Wade agreed, "though we'd considered it. The difference between vacationing and retirement is that nobody expects us to be anywhere. We'll take another ship from here. Maybe a freighter, for a change."

"There's always something popping around Dickie," Belgeddes said, shaking his head with a wry expression. "Been saying that for fifty years, so I suppose it's the way I like things to be."

"Well . . ." Dewhurst said. His eyes narrowed. "What on earth is that in your luggage, Wade?" he demanded. "A cannon?"

"Something like that," Wade agreed, looking at the 15-mm rifle strapped onto his well-worn trunk. Even taken down into two pieces, the weapon looked long and clumsy. "It was given me as a souvenir, I suppose you'd call it."

"Dear," said Ms. Dewhurst, tugging her husband's sleeve.

Dewhurst twisted his arm away. "In a damned minute!" he snapped.

"From Calicheman?" Da Silva asked.

"I believe so, originally," Wade agreed.

Belgeddes chuckled.

"Shouldn't doubt there'll be a story in it the next time somebody comments on the thing," Dewhurst said — half gibing, but half sorry to know that he wouldn't be present when the story was told.

"Shouldn't doubt that you were right," Belgeddes agreed.

A limousine pulled into the cab rank. When a taxi hooted its horn angrily at the interloper, a uniformed traffic warden rapped the cab's windshield firmly enough with her baton to threaten the glass.

"There he is," said Belgeddes.

"*Your* ride?" Da Silva said in amazement.

"Not exactly," said Wade. "Tom and I have business, well, elsewhere for the while. But we took the liberty of arranging three days for you in the penthouse of the Circassia Palas. Manager's a friend of ours, you see. He's sent his personal car for you."

"The *penthouse*?" Ms. Dewhurst gasped. "We could never afford that, Mr. Wade!"

"It's on me, good lady," Wade explained with a courtly bow. "The least I could do after all the drinks your husband and Mr. Da Silva here bought me during the past weeks."

Belgeddes nodded. "Never remembers to carry small change," he murmured. "You'd think Dickie'd have learned in fifty years, but he never has."

"Perhaps we'll meet again," said Wade as he straightened. "It's not so big a universe as some people think."

"Until then," Belgeddes added. He gave Da Silva and the Dewhursts a languid salute, then followed his taller companion back toward a door in the terminal marked OFFICIAL PERSONNEL ONLY.

Even Ms. Dewhurst gaped after them. The limousine's chauffeur waited stolidly, continuing to hold the vehicle's door open.

* * *

"It's a triumph of people over architects," Wanda Holly said to Ran as they sauntered through a trottoria with tables of extruded plastic and exquisite, hand-carved chairs.

Bogomil Old Town was an area of slab-built concrete buildings set in a rectangular grid of broad streets, a district as functional as a prison. Though preserved as a monument to the early days of the colony, Old Town was a living museum whose current-day residents added humanizing touches.

Apartment facades were individually painted, and no two suites had identical sets of shutters. The entranceway of a seven-story box was framed with pillars of hammered copper extending to roof level and supporting balcony railings at each floor. On all the buildings fronting the Mirza, an arm of the sea too shallow for commercial navigation, the ground-floor shops were open in front so that they could spill out onto the boulevard.

"Happy-looking place," Ran commented.

"Peaceful" wouldn't be the right word, however. Locals sipping clear liquor not infrequently shouted and made the flimsy tables jounce with their fists. There was passion as well in the haggling of brightly-dressed shoppers; and though the knives most men wore were for show, a culture whose ornamentation includes weaponry is not wholly peaceful.

But then, no organism that survives to pass on its genes will be *wholly* peaceful.

"A place you'd like to live?" Wanda asked.

Ran looked out over the Mirza. Couples were rowing there. It must be possible to rent boats somewhere.

"No," he said softly. "I wouldn't belong here."

He faced Wanda. She was watching him, and he couldn't read her expression. "I don't belong anywhere, Wanda," he said. "Not even on Bifrost, not after I went through the library Dad brought back from — from Hobilo."

Ran smiled, and though he had to force it, the impulse was real enough. He was better off than most people. It was just that he knew where he was, while not many other folks seemed to. Maybe they were happier not to know, but ignorance hadn't been something Chick Colville held forth as a virtue to his son.

"I'm . . ." Ran continued. "Everybody's — out of place, you know, on a starliner. I'm happy there, I'm where I ought to be."

They skirted a shop selling hologram projectors and other electronics, much of it locally made. Tblisi had considerable industry, though grain and fisheries were its main exports, and out-system trade traveled on foreign bottoms. The *Empress of Earth* docked in a three-meter news projection, while a newsreader's voice gave a garbled account of the attempted hijacking.

"I've got my job," Ran continued, "and I'm good at it. And most of my duties . . . "

He glanced back at the hologram of the starliner. He imagined the sullen splendor of sponge space wrapping the vessel and those on her hull, dissolving their souls and filling the psychic cavities with Cold.

Wanda squeezed his hand.

"Most of my duties," Ran said, "I like a lot."

At the cafe ahead of them, waiters were beginning to serve plates of fish and pasta as well as drinks. It was late morning in Bogomil, several hours behind ship's time.

"I wouldn't mind some lun — " Wanda began. The rest of her sentence was drowned by excited shouts from those watching the news in the electronics store.

The Trident officers turned, their faces pale and sickly in Tblisi's orange-touched sunlight. They strode back toward the holograms.

For a moment, Ran thought the *Empress* was the starliner filling half the huge projection while the newsreader spoke from the other side of the display. The vessel was deep in an atmosphere, but her landing outriggers were not deployed.

"No, it's the *Brasil*," Wanda said, correcting her own similar misapprehension aloud.

"What's happening?" Ran demanded of an old man wearing a horizontally-striped shirt and a straw hat squeezed shapeless by long use. The fellow had been watching the news when Ran and Wanda passed the first time.

"The Grantholm-Nevasa war's over!" the local said. "It was going to be terrible for trade, just terrible. I'm in shipping, and I know that."

The old man's eyes were bright with memories of the time when he had a life that required more than watching the news in a public place. That must have been years past.

"Lin Van Thiet, formerly the Minister of Culture and now Interim President of Nevasa," the newsreader said, "urges all Nevasan citizens to cease hostilities and actions which might be seen as hostile by the government of Grantholm. The situation on Nevasa is difficult. Attempts to prolong the conflict can only lead to untold suffering for the survivors."

"The Minister of *Culture* is running the planet?" Wanda murmured. "What on earth . . . ?"

The image of the *Brasil* was blurred. That had the effect of making the picture more real to those watching. This was real data from a vessel accompanying the starliner, not a computer simulation.

"Tblisi received a communications torpedo with the news," Ran said. "From Nevasa, it must be. Lin must be really serious about ending the war if he's sent direct messages to colonies this distant."

"It's Nevasa, that's for sure," Wanda said. "Look at the sky."

The Nevasan atmosphere fluoresced in dazzling

sheets to swaddle the plunging starliner. The lenses recording the scene couldn't penetrate the fog of light, except to record the yellow-white glow of the *Brasil's* dense hull.

"Casualty figures are still being assembled," the newsreader said in the tones of someone who can't really believe what he's seeing, "but it appears that damage to Nevasa City and the region around it has been extensive."

"*Christ!*" said Ran Colville. "If she hit Nevasa City at orbital velocity, there *isn't* any fucking Nevasa City any more!"

"Grantholm hijacked the *Brasil* and used her as a missile," Wanda said. She gripped her companion's left hand and squeezed till blood started from where her fingernails cut into the skin. "Ran, they killed — tens of thousands of people. Hundreds of thousands of people!"

"No," Ran whispered. "Grantholm didn't do that."

The newsreader vanished. The image from Nevasa expanded to fill the display. The starliner's track was a cone of roiling pastels reaching toward the ground until it merged with the distance-softened sprawl of Nevasa City.

"If Grantholm had taken the *Brasil*," Ran continued, "the Nevasans would never have let her get into planetary orbit. She had to be in Nevasan hands when she — dropped."

The hologram image shuddered from atmospheric distortion. The display flashed indigo verging on ultraviolet, then white, and finally all colors as a lightning-shot bubble swelled across the surface of the planet. The impact of hundreds of thousands of tonnes hitting Nevasa at astronomical speed converted the contact surfaces to plasma and a huge additional volume to gas.

"They were bringing the *Brasil* to Nevasa to be converted into a troopship," Ran said. He lifted Wanda's hand to his lips and kissed it gently to remind her of her grip on him. "As they would have done the *Empress*, if we hadn't dumped the hijack team — the Nevasan team — on Tellichery."

"They lost control?" Wanda said. The bubble continued to swell on the display. Its rim was picked out by black specks, fragments weighing hundreds of tonnes splashing out of the impact zone. Many of them would reach escape velocity.

"Yes," said Ran. "And I think I know how." He swallowed. "I want to get back to the *Empress*," he added.

Wanda kissed the back of Ran's hand. Her tongue tasted his blood. "I'm sorry," she whispered. "Yes, let's go."

"The war's over!" the local man beside them repeated gleefully.

The walls of Commander Kneale's suite were set to show holographic scenes of Nevasa. The ceiling was a view (downward, disconcertingly) of the *Empress of Earth* descending onto Con Ron Landing, haloed by her squadron of tugs and the fluorescing atmosphere.

The city nestled into the hills about the spaceport. Large swatches of green interspersed the built-up areas.

"Sit down, Ran," the commander offered from behind his big desk. He looked weary but composed.

"No, I don't think I'll do that," Ran said harshly. "I heard what happened on Nevasa. *To* Nevasa."

"Yes," Kneale said, "so did I."

He stretched. "Do you have any suggestions about who could fill a rating's slot on my watch? One of my people — Blavatsky — she's leaving the company here to marry a passenger."

He grimaced and shook his head.

"Do you know how many people died down there,

Commander?" Ran shouted, pointing up toward the image of Nevasa City. "How *many* died?"

"Fewer than would have died if the war had gone on another ten years," Kneale said calmly, "as it might have done. But that's none of my business."

Ran twisted his eyes away from the commander's face. On the right-hand bulkhead, images of Nevasan children gamboled on the floor of a narrow gorge while their parents watched indulgently. The whip-trunked native trees grew up both walls of the gorge and wove together at the top, filtering the sunlight to soft green without glare or shadows.

The scene was a famous park, near Nevasa City. Probably too near Nevasa City.

"Commander," Ran said as he sat/collapsed into the cushioned armchair on his side of the desk. "They were innocent people. Most of them were innocent."

"If you want innocent, Colville," Commander Kneale snarled, "then think about the five passengers killed when those bastards tried to hijack the *Empress*! D'ye think it was any different aboard the *Brasil*?"

Kneale stood up, clenching his hands together as though he was trying to crush something between his palms. His face distorted with anger and self-loathing. "Those five passengers were our business, yours and mine. And we failed them, Ran Colville."

Ran gestured toward the bulkhead where he'd seen the crew of strangers installing equipment before the *Empress* undocked from Earth. "What's back there, Hiram?" he asked quietly. "Behind the kids playing and the false panel."

"An autopilot," Kneale said. He sat down, looking surprised at having found himself standing. "With an override that takes precedence over the ordinary systems on the bridge. As you already guessed."

Ran nodded. "And you would have done the same thing," he said. "Hidden behind the false wall of your suite and programmed the *Empress of Earth* to crash into Sonderburg on Grantholm. Or Nevasa City, whichever."

"Not exactly," Kneale said emotionlessly. "I was told that when the ship had a full load of the troops from the hijacking planet, it would enter sponge space and never return. If that's really what the autopilot was programmed to achieve, then something went wrong."

He licked his tight lips. "It's possible," he added bleakly, "that government officials lied to me."

He raised his eyes to the vision of the *Empress* lowering herself onto Nevasa in all her unique splendor. "There were provisions for the — officer in charge of operation to escape by lifeboat. I doubt Commander Cunha left the *Brasil*. I certainly would have ridden the *Empress* down if a similar — error — had occurred. If it hadn't been for you, Ran, and Ms. Holly; and some few others."

"Sir," Ran whispered, "it could be a million people died. There were better ways. Earth could have sent a fleet to Nevasa. This was a government problem, not the company's."

"Who do you think installed this equipment?" the commander snarled, thrusting an angry thumb toward the bulkhead's false innocence. "You *know* Federated Earth can't play galactic cop openly. The voters would never stand on it, and every ex-colony from here to the Rim would be up in arms at the idea."

"They hijacked —" Ran offered.

"Prove it!" Kneale retorted. "The *Brasil* is gone, the *Empress of Earth* would have been gone — *prove* which of the warring parties hijacked her. Or either of them!"

"It'd have come out," Ran said. He rose and turned so that he didn't face the commander's fierceness. "They couldn't hide her — either ship — once they used her to ferry troops for an invasion."

Holographic farmers worked terraced fields in the

area of Bu Dop, across the planet from the steaming
crater that was now Nevasa City. The embassy official
he'd met . . . Susan. She was going to Bu Dop, she'd said.

"*And* the guilty party would pay an indemnity to Trident or Consolidated, whichever," the commander
rejoined. "*And* they'd release the passengers, probably,
from some detention camp on a planet nobody ever
heard of, where they'd have enough food and most of
them would have survived. For years! And Federated
Earth *wouldn't* take military action, because the villains
had apologized, hadn't they? And it was all the former
government anyhow. And —"

Ran turned to face him. Kneale too was standing.

" — they'd do the same goddamned thing again, and
other people would, and star travel would never be
safe for any peaceful purpose ever! Isn't that true, Ran
Colville?"

Ran licked his dry lips. "Yes," he said. "I suppose it
is."

He drew in a deep breath. "Who knew about this?"
he asked.

"I did," said the commander. "And you've guessed.
One or two members of the Company's board of direc-
tors. A few people — very few — in the bureaucracy of
Federated Earth. None of the elected officials."

Kneale looked up at his ceiling image again. His tone
softened. "The installers wouldn't have known what
they were doing, though it's possible that some of them
have guessed by now also. What I'm quite sure of . . . "

He locked his eyes with Ran's again, and his voice
rasped like the tongue of a lion. "What I'm sure of is.
That as a result of Nevasa. Everybody in the galaxy
knows or will know. That if you hijack a Terran ship,
your planet will be gutted. And the government of
Federated Earth will smile and go its wholly deniable
way."

"Oh, God, Hiram," Ran said softly as he kneaded his

brows with his fingertips. "And Grantholm goes on, and . . . ?"

"Nobody picked Nevasa City," Kneale said. "The Nevasans picked it, and — if the crash wasn't an autopilot error — it *would* have been Sonderburg except for what you managed to do. But there won't be a next time. That's what makes it worthwhile."

Ran shivered. "I . . ." he said. His lips quirked in a smile. "There isn't really anything to say, is there? It's done. I guess I'll go now."

"Sometimes quick ruthlessness is the gentlest course in the long run," Kneale said. His voice fell into a whisper. "Governments have to think about the long run."

Ran reached for the latch plate. As he did so, his eyes strayed to the left, toward the image of children playing on the outskirts of Nevasa City.

"Want a drink?" Ran asked.

Wanda was drawing figure-8 patterns with her index finger across the face of the autobar at their table. "Not here," she said.

They were alone in the starliner's Darwin Lounge. On the walls, cartoon figures capered through skits illustrating evolution: the evolution of drinks, from rancid grape juice to the incredibly-complex cocktails in which the lounge's autobar specialized; the evolution of transport, from log float to the *Empress of Earth* herself; the evolution of living spaces, from cave to the Darwin Lounge. . . .

The scenes were so funny, and so obviously non-serious, that "nobody could take offense at them"; though of course people did, several on every voyage, for reasons as diverse as they were uniformly absurd. For that matter, passengers had been known to complain about the rest rooms off the Social Hall, because the crossing patterns of the plaid decorative scheme "suggested Christian motives."

A pair of stewards entered the lounge, noticed the two officers, and lowered their voices as they walked on through to the Carthage Salon beyond.

"What I'd like to do," Wanda resumed, looking across at Ran and smiling fixedly, "seeing that we'll be laid over on Tblisi for an extra forty-eight hours so the home office can decide how to modify our schedule. . . ."

She took a deep breath. "Is for us to rent one of the fishing cottages out at the head of Bluewater Bay. And spend the next while getting to know each other better."

Wanda forced her smile broader. The tip of her index finger was white from the force with which she pressed at the autobar. "Is that clear enough for you, Ran?" she said.

He spread his right hand flat on the table and pushed. "Didn't you hear what I said?" he demanded. "They deliberately crashed —"

"Listen to me!" Wanda said as she covered his hand with her own. "I was there when they were installing the autopilot in the commander's cabin, remember? When we watched the *Brasil* — you didn't have to tell me what was going on, Ran."

Ran shuddered. He wouldn't meet her eyes, but he turned his hand palm-up to clasp Wanda's. "And it doesn't matter?" he asked.

"It's done," she said. "Whether it was a good idea or a bad one . . . and yeah, I think it probably *was* a good idea, the same as the commander does and you do. I'm just glad that it wasn't me who had to — do what was done."

She clasped Ran's hand between both of hers. "Look at me, Ran," she whispered.

He obeyed, giving her a wan smile. "I dunno, Ms. Lieutenant Holly," he said. "I'm not sure I'm tough enough for this business."

Wanda laughed. "You're tough enough for anything you have to do," she said. "I'm paraphrasing somebody I trust on that. But our job is to get the *Empress* in on schedule, with happy passengers. Not to worry about — other people's jobs, that they've already done and we can't undo if we wanted to."

She cleared her throat. "And because we've done our jobs to the satisfaction of our superiors, we've got some time for ourselves. Which I want to spend with you."

Ran lifted their knotted hands and kissed the woman's knuckles. "Wanda," he murmured, "look, it wouldn't . . ."

"*Look* at me, Ran," she insisted.

He met her eyes. "I've known my share of women — " he said.

"Yes, I've noticed that," Wanda said drily.

" — but they didn't mean anything, any more than I did to them. I — "

"Are you really that naive?" Wanda asked. "That they were just having a bit of fun, because you were?"

Ran shrugged angrily. "Look, that's my business. What's your business is that you — for pity's sake, Wanda, you're a friend of mine. And I don't fuck my friends."

"Then who does that leave, Ran?" she responded softly.

He straightened as though he'd been slapped. "Wanda," he said. "I don't want anybody to get hurt."

She shook her head. "You can't control that," she said. "You're hurting people now with what you do. And you're smart, so you know that, whether you admit it or not. And you're right, it's none of my business, except — "

She squeezed fiercely at his hand. "Except that it doesn't have to be like that. You care about people or you wouldn't be so upset about what happened on, t-to Nevasa City. You can care about *a* person too, Ran."

He chuckled. "I wouldn't bet on that," he said.

"I *am* betting on it, Ran," she replied. She got to her feet and drew him with her. "Come on," she added. "It's an hour by ferry to Bluewater Bay, and that's longer than I want to wait."

Ran slipped his hand around her waist as they walked out of the lounge. "I'm not much of a hand for fishing," he said in a neutral voice.

Wanda laughed. "To be really honest," she said, "I wasn't planning to rent fishing tackle."

The stewards, completing the post-landing check of the Carthage Salon, could hear the officers' laughter carol all the way down the corridor to the Embarkation Hall.

THE END

DAVID DRAKE
HAMMER'S
Slammers

The meanest bunch
of mercs who ever
killed a world for pay—
only from Baen Books!

Hammer's Slammers—The original! Plus—an all-new short novel, "The Tank Lords."
69867-2 • 288 pages • $4.50 ☐

At Any Price—The 23rd-century armored division faces its deadliest enemies ever: aliens who *teleport* into combat.
55978-8 • 288 pages • $4.50 ☐

Counting the Cost—The toughest mission in their history: can the Slammers do it? Not if they abide by the rules of civilized warfare . . . but nobody ever said the Slammers were *nice*.
63955-5 • 288 pages • $4.50 ☐

Rolling Hot—They've got 300 miles of hostile territory to cover, fighting all the way. Their chances are not good—but those who oppose them have no chance at all, because war-worn and battle-crazed as they may be, they *are* Slammers, and they are *Rolling Hot*.
69837-0 • 329 pages • $3.95 ☐

The Warrior—They were the best. Colonel Alois Hammer welded five thousand individual killers into a weapon more deadly than any other in the human universe. But different styles of being "the best" meant a bloodbath, even by the grim standards of *Hammer's Slammers*.
72058-9 • 288 pages • $4.95 ☐

Available at your local bookstore, or send this coupon, your name, your address, and the cover price(s) to Baen Books, Dept. BA, P.O. Box 1403, Riverdale, NY 10471.

BAEN
BOOKS